MOONBLOOD

Moonblood

Philip G. Williamson

LEGEND

First published by Legend Books in 1994

1 3 5 7 9 10 8 6 4 2

Copyright © Philip G. Williamson 1994

The right of Philip G. Willamson to be identified as the author
of this work has been asserted by him in accordance
with the Copyright, Designs and Patents Act, 1988

First published in United Kingdom by
Legend Books Limited
20 Vauxhall Bridge Road, London SW1V 2SA

Random House Australia (Pty) Limited
20 Alfred Street, Milsons Point, Sydney,
New South Wales 2061, Australia

Random House New Zealand Limited
18 Poland Road, Glenfield
Auckland 10, New Zealand

Random House South Africa (Pty) Limited
PO Box 337, Bergvlei, South Africa

Random House UK Limited Reg. No. 954009

A CIP catalogue record for this book
is available from the British Library

ISBN 0 09 931461 4

Printed and bound in Great Britain by
Cox & Wyman Ltd, Reading, Berkshire

For
my daughter,
Elizabeth,
who daily renews my sense of wonder.

MOONBLOOD

(Being the adventures as a young man of the wily Khimmurian merchant-adventurer, Zan-Chassin sorcerer, spy and philanthropist, Ronbas Dinbig.)

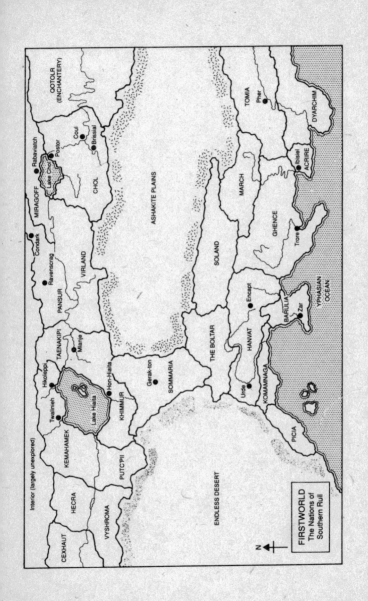

FIRSTWORLD
The Nations of
Southern Rull

N

Interior (largely unexplored)

OOTOLR
(ENCHANTERY)

CEXHAUT

HECRA

KEMAHAMEK

VYSHROMA

PUTCPII

KHIMMUR

Twalinieh

Hikoleppi

Mlanje

Lake Hiata

Hon-Hiata

Gerak-ton

SOMMARIA

TAENAKIPI

PANSUR

Ravenscrag

VIRLAND

Condark

MIRAGOFF

Rabaviatch

Lake Chol

Postor

CHOL

Coul

Brissial

ASHAKITE PLAINS

THE BOLTAR

SOLAND

MARCH

Encapt

HANVAT

Urde

KOMAMNAGA

Zar

BARULA

GHENCE

Trore

PICIA

ENDLESS DESERT

YPHASIAN
OCEAN

ACRIRE

Ibisiel

DYARCHIM

TOMIA

Pher

Initiation

We perceive but an aspect of this world, if we only knew it. Beyond what we know are other domains, other shades of the real, unrealised realms within the greater Realm. Vague intimations reach us, perhaps. Things inexplicable; presentiments, stirrings, intuitions, a half-sense of something preternatural, something *other*. But ordinarily for most, the greater reality remains forever undisclosed.

To a few it may be revealed. Its revelation can be a way to knowledge, to power and understanding. But it is an uncharted way, filled with perils. Many have been lost along its course. Others have discovered more than they would ever have wished.

So it was that I approached my initiation with a mixture of anticipation and deep disquiet. Across the rough-hewn walls of the central chamber strange light manifested in dancing colours, cast by flickering torchflames. Shadows played upon the mystic runes and symbols etched onto the polished marble floor. The air was thick, a reeking pall of smouldering herbs and incense. From a concealed sidechamber issued the muted pulse of a drum.

Garbed in full ceremonial attire the veiled figure of the Chariness waited beside the High Altar where the Fire of the

Sacred Spirit burned. The nine Witnesses seated in ritual postures chanted sonorously, encircling me. As I knelt the Chariness stepped slowly forward, a glazed clay bowl in her hands.

'All is as it should be. All is complete. Seeker, are you ready now for your trial?'

I swallowed, my sweat cold. 'I am.'

She offered the bowl. 'Drink, then. The Water of the Realms will purge your flesh and free your spirit for its journey.'

I accepted the vessel, brought it to my lips and drank the chill, bright water. The Chariness's solemn grey eyes above her veil watched my face. She took back the bowl and retreated to the edge of the circle of Witnesses.

'Your time has come. You will leave this plane for the Realms beyond, to find and if necessary do battle with, in order to bind to your service, your First Entity. With success the Entity will become your Custodian, Guardian of your Flesh, freeing you to journey at will beyond this realm. Fail and you may be lost to our world and doomed to an uncertain fate beyond. Do you understand and accept this?'

'I do.'

'While your spirit is absent we of the Hierarchy will guard and protect your flesh. But the trial is yours alone. We cannot aid you in your wanderings. Do you know and accept this also?'

'I do.'

'Seeker, knowing the dangers as well as the rewards of the path you have chosen to follow, custom decrees that you be offered one final chance to reconsider. You may leave this chamber now, without shame or penalty, never to return, if that is your wish.'

'I will face my trial.'

'Then by the grace of the Great Moving Spirit, Moban, leave us now!'

The nine Witnesses shifted into defensive postures, to protect my flesh from any assailant as I journeyed elsewhere. I entered trance, taking note feature by feature of the physical world around me. I centred myself, as I had been taught in years and months of practice, focusing on my physical being. By degrees I dissolved the corporeal world.

I rose, to rest a little way above my body. The torchlight played below me, cloaking the nine ritual figures in wavering shadows around my still form. The Chariness raised her eyes as if perceiving me. Her voice seemed cast from a great distance. '*Go.*'

I ascended, through the rock ceiling, leaving the central ceremonial chamber of the *Zan-Chassin*, up through the secret warren of chambers and passages that were the *Zan-Chassin* catacombs. I passed through the solid granite that lay beneath the Royal Palace of Hon-Hiaita, up above the Palace itself and the town of Hon-Hiaita. I rose into the skies over Khimmur, high above the forests and hills and the glittering waters of the inland sea, Lake Hiaita. I soared further and further above the physical world, and then, pausing only briefly, rent the fabric of reality and passed through into First Realm.

I had been here before, though never alone. And I had only rested on the edge. I had been taught the means to pass from the corporeal into the First Realm of Non-Being, the sphere of existence which lies immediately beyond our normal experience. I had glimpsed what waited there, and then I had returned. I had never journeyed. The Realms are vast and unpredictable, their nature varying, their denizens capricious and diverse. One does not venture there without long and proper training.

The spirit-entities which dwell within the Realms possess unknown powers. Those of First Realm tend to lesser strength; the more potent denizens generally keep to the deeper Realms beyond. Yet, by their very nature, even the lesser spirits can prove to be fearsome and resourceful opponents.

I passed through into a mindscape of strange perspectives which altered as I gazed. I stood upon a wide, flat plain which stretched away in all directions. Shifting mountains, dark purplish blue, occupied the horizon. They rippled and swayed slowly, like massive fronds touched by a watery breeze. Shapeless clouds of coloured substance rolled across the plain, dispersing even as they appeared to be assuming form.

No particular feature took my eye, and I set off in a direction chosen at random. I scoured my surroundings as I went, eyes peeled for signs of an entity. As far as I could make out I was not observed – this region of First Realm seemed deserted – but I knew that here my perception might be far from reliable.

I had walked for some time when I descried, seeming to form out of the landscape ahead, an outcrop of rock. It rose in weird formations, inert blue-grey slabs, pillars and shards exploding out of a lumpy core. I changed direction so as to approach it, more alert now, sensing the imminence of my first encounter.

Closer to the outcrop I saw that it was not, in fact, inert. There was a sense of its growing and diminishing, almost imperceptible. It altered substance, altered its nature, organic, perhaps even sentient. And as I stepped into its shadow I saw something else.

I acted unaware – indeed, what had caught my attention may have been imagined. But I stood and gazed casually beyond the rock, and within a few heartbeats glimpsed it again at the edge of my vision. A movement, so slight. Something lurked within the cover of the rock. Something hid there, and watched me.

I lowered myself cross-legged to the ground beneath the rock's overhang, taking some solace in the fact that I had not been attacked outright. A hostile entity may strike without warning, seizing any advantage, either to injure and then flee, or to kill, or, if sufficiently powerful, to capture. Alternatively the entity may be frightened, mischievous, curious, deceitful, even friendly, but certainly suspicious. I, who was a stranger in their land, had to be prepared for anything.

Maintaining the pretence of ignorance of the entity's presence, I held it within the broad scope of my vision. Plainly I was under appraisal and might yet be attacked.

Now I glimpsed the flicker of two eyes, watching intently. A small, cautious movement followed as the creature slipped forward along a limb of rock to gain a fuller vantage. It was a slight, wispy thing, difficult to make out – and I knew that the image I saw might bear little resemblance to the thing itself. Perception in the otherworld is in large part a matter of judgement and guesswork. As with our domain, one can never be wholly certain that impressions reveal actuality. But in our domain we have at least the reassurance of familiarity; in Otherworld everything is strange.

Satisfied that I was being scrutinized with great interest, I reached into my robe and withdrew a small cloth-bound package. This I set upon the ground before me. On the limb of rock overhead I perceived the blink of two huge sallow eyes and sensed the inquisitive craning forward of a short brownish snout.

I rested my hands above the cloth and commenced chanting in a low, rhythmic voice. After some moments I saw, out of the corner of my eye, that the entity was edging closer. Curiosity overcoming caution, it leaned towards me from the branches of rock until it was almost wholly unconcealed. I let my voice fade; I unwound the cloth to expose its contents.

'What are you doing?'

I glanced up, pretending surprise. 'Why, I am conducting a small ritual.'

The entity leaned down low, wrinkling its snout, intrigued by both myself and my accoutrements. 'I have never seen anything like you.'

I nodded. 'I would imagine that is so.'

'What are you?'

'I am a man.'

'Man? What is that?'

'Is it what I am, this thing that you see before you.'

'It's an odd thing.'

The entity hopped down from its rock and hovered warily, keeping a distance. Its eyes darted from the items on the cloth to me and back again. 'Where do you come from, Man.'

'From a place beyond this, a realm you do not know.'

'There are strange things in the deeper realms, and it's true that I know little of those regions, yet you are wholly beyond imagining. An accentricity; an aberration. Utterly bizarre.'

'You are most kind. But you are mistaken. I do not come from the deeper realms. My domain is a place of which no Realm entity has knowledge.'

This further intrigued the creature. 'Where is this place?'

'Beyond. . . . To try to explain would take too long.'

The entity cocked its head quizzically. 'Are you called by any name, other than Man?'

'My name is Dinbig.'

'That's a funny name.'

'Some think so.'

'Dinbig, Dinbig. Man, man.'

'And you?'

'I am Yo.'

'I am very pleased to make your acquaintance, Yo. Will you sit with me for a while?'

He was a touch uncertain at that, but his curiosity kept him from leaving. He pointed at the oddments on the cloth before me.

'What are these things?'

'Treasures, from my domain.'

'They are pretty. I have never seen anything like them.'

'There are many treasures like these where I come from.' I held one up.

'What is it called?'

'It's a flower: a rose. And this is a feather; and this a small lump of salt.'

'Can I have them?'

'I'm afraid not. I require them to conduct my ritual in order to return to my home.'

With a sudden darting movement the entity leapt forward, snatched up the three items and was gone, speeding away across the plain.

I had expected something of the kind and was on his tail in seconds, yet his speed was startling and I found myself hard put to keep up. We sped towards the distant frond-like mountains. Yo darted and dived ahead of me, striving to throw me off his tail. As the mountains loomed large I grew worried. They would provide cover where Yo might conceal himself and evade me. Other entities – more powerful than Yo – might lurk there in ambush. And the further I was drawn, the closer I came to passing beyond this Realm, into deeper levels where the perils would be greater.

Yo swooped, weaving towards a narrow pass now visible between the weird heights. His path took him obliquely across mine, offering me an opportunity to gain on and perhaps even intercept him. I shot towards the mouth of the pass which I perceived as being his destination.

He saw my manoeuvre and modified his path. At the same time he performed his first truly aggressive act against me. Something materialized in the space between us and shot towards me. It was a shapeless mass of rapturized stuff, plainly intended to do me harm.

I darted to the side, invoking a chant of negation. I struck lucky; the stuff vanished. Now a pressure, like an invisible membrane, slowed my motion and began to push me away. Again I invoked a dispellation. The pressure eased, and I broke through.

Yo, dismayed by my ability to nullify his magic, faltered and I was able to move closer to him.

'Yo, don't be frightened. I intend you no harm.'

'What do you want with me? Why have you come here? Go back to where you belong.'

'You have taken something that is not yours.'

'I want them. They are so pretty. Can't I keep them?'

'Yo, they do not exist. They are conjurations, mental constructs, images held within my mind. I brought them here as projections from my domain. Look, what do you hold now in your hands?'

The entity opened his paws. 'They have gone! What have you done with them?'

'I have told you, they do not exist. As soon as you snatched them I dissolved their images. They were but representations.'

'That was an unfair thing to do.'

'Was it fair that you should try to steal things that you knew were mine?'

'I only wanted to look. Can you show them to me again?'

'Not here. But in my domain there are more, many more. And other wondrous things, the likes of which you have never seen. I can show you all of these if you will accompany me there, just for a short time.'

'Do you think I am so guileless? You will take me there and abduct me.'

'No, Yo, I will offer you a compact.'

'A compact?'

'Between you and I. I wish to show you my domain, and I will then offer you complete freedom of access to it. You will have an opportunity rarely given to your kind. I will provide you with the body of a creature of my world which will enable you to inhabit that domain, to familiarize yourself with it and partake freely of its wonders.'

'And be severed from my own world?'

'No. You will be able to return at any time to this Realm.'

The entity eyed me shrewdly. 'And in return?'

'You pledge yourself to me, as servant and companion. And in itself, this bestows a further benefit. I will require you to occupy my body, become its custodian during the periods when I journey

7

here in your Realm. You will gain the first understanding of what it is to be human.'

'And if I refuse?'

'I shall trouble you no further. I will go now, and return alone to the corporeal domain. At a later time I shall come here again to find another entity who will become my servant and partake of the bounties of two worlds.'

'Show me,' said Yo.

He was mine; I knew it, as, I had no doubt, did he. I took him back across that ethereal plain, parted the fabric between realities, and led him from First Realm into the world of the corporeal. We hovered above the hills and forests of Khimmur. I showed him the trees, the rivers, herds of grazing animals, wild creatures roaming the woods. We went lower. I showed him flowers, feathers and salt. I showed him bees and butterflies, fishes, lizards and birds. I showed him towns and villages, and the people, my own kind, who passed their lives there.

He was agog; he had never known such wonders could exist.

'All this can be yours, Yo. You have only to pledge your service to me.'

To my surprise he shook his head. 'Get hence, Dinbig Man. I want none of your temptations.'

'Ah, well.' I called his bluff. I shrugged and departed.

I did not go far.

'I will do it,' said Yo, suddenly at my shoulder. 'I will serve you.'

I smiled. 'Then tell me now your true and secret name.'

Now he looked fearful. 'That I cannot do.'

'You must. It is your sacred and binding oath, the means by which I measure your sincerity. I will hold it secret, and never reveal it to another unless you betray me or in some way purposefully attempt to break your oath or do me harm.'

'But it will give you power over me.'

'As I am giving you power over me. Remember, you will be Custodian of my flesh. I must know, without a spectre of doubt, that I cannot be brought to harm by your doing. Your true and secret name is the covenant between us. Tell it me, or be gone.'

He glanced about him, just briefly, taking in again the wonders and diversities of the corporeal world. Then he spoke the word that bonded him to me. I felt a surge of elation: *I had bound my First Entity!*

Quickly I taught Yo the ritual that would permit him to pass instantly between his realm and mine. 'Now, Yo, I go. I shall commence preparations to acquire you an animal body, that you may roam freely in this world. In the meantime, be alert at all times for my summons, for I will call upon you from time to time, to instruct you, or to have you occupy my flesh while I am absent.'

'I am your servant, Master.'

Yo turned, with a last wide-eyed look at the physical wonders of Firstworld, then departed, back into his own realm. I too sped away, down towards Hon-Hiaita and the secret catacombs where the Hierarchy members held watch over my still form and anxiously awaited my return.

A sense of certainty filled me – a knowledge of the future opening before me. I had succeeded in my quest; I had passed my First Realm Initiation.

I was *Zan-Chassin*!

Chapter One

It was not entirely coincidence that brought me to Ravenscrag at the time of its troubles. Of course, I had no inkling of what was about to ensue, but I was well aware of the imminent birth of a second child to Ravenscrag's ailing lord, Flarefist, and his spouse, Lady Sheerquine. And I knew, too, that major celebrations were planned to mark the occasion.

Taking into account my interest in foreign affairs, the significance of this birth could hardly have escaped me. Elmag the farseer had been summoned to Ravenscrag castle the moment Lady Sheerquine's pregnancy had been discovered. In a fug of smouldering incense and herbs she shook mistletoe and juniper sprigs over Sheerquine's belly, cast runes, rattled beads, uttered chants and invocations, examined Sheerquine's spittle, and declared that the babe would be a boy – the longed-for heir to the Ravenscrag fortune.

Irnbold, Ravenscrag's astrologer, applied himself with diligence to his charts and records, arranging his complex instruments just so – eventually to announce the date and hour of the birth. Great joy! proclaimed Irnbold: the stars, moon and planets smiled most beneficently upon the unborn babe. The child would be born strong and healthy and would live a long and illustrious life; Ravenscrag would at last be rescued from the failing fortunes that had dogged it over recent decades, and would see the restoration of its former ancient glory.

Over weeks and months Irnbold, encouraged by his initial reception, augmented his claims with further insights into the forthcoming life. All boded so well! Irnbold charted the passage of the celestial bodies over a period of years. Their alignments spoke of unprecedented harmony. Irnbold began to predict wondrous events that would befall Ravenscrag's heir.

Few gave more than passing note to the specifics. Irnbold was known to be of an imaginative bent, fuelled by the fine Pansurian spirits which, with the passing of the years, he turned to in greater quantities as palliative against inflamed joints and a debilitating melancholy. But the broad tenor of his words held the message that all wished to hear, none more so than Flarefist and his family. Ravenscrag had suffered decline for too long, through irresponsibility, lack of insight, and simple misfortune. Now there was widespread hope, even belief, that those days must soon come to an end. Thus Irnbold found himself courted at Ravenscrag, in a manner he had not known for many years.

I had scheduled my itinerary to include Ravenscrag in anticipation of the forthcoming celebrations. The town is isolated deep in Pansur's remote heart, and ordinarily is visited by few foreign merchants. But its market at that time was adequate, and such an important event would attract a lot of interest and ensure that business was brisk.

Accordingly in Twalinieh in Kemahamek I had stocked three of my seven wagons with a variety of exotic items from far climes. I knew from experience that such goods would be well received by the insular folk of Ravenscrag. And Pansurian spirits, cloth, pottery and perhaps a few of their famed harps, would fetch a good price in Miragoff, Kemahamek, or back home in Khimmur.

I rode into Ravenscrag late one afternoon in summer, in the middle of a freak storm, only a day, as it happened, before Flarefist's son was born. My spirits were undampened by the weather. I foresaw days and nights of merriment, of eating and drinking, dancing and lovemaking in prodigious quantities, and a handsome profit at the end of it.

Rarely have I been so mistaken.

Bris, my most trusted henchman, rode up beside me as we first came in sight of Ravenscrag. His back was bent against the driving rain, hunched in a strong waxed cape.

'It may be better to halt a while, Master Dinbig. If the descent is steep the wagons could slip from the trail or get bogged in mud.'

I looked up at the sky, the rain lashing my face. The cloud was uniform, dark and lowering, but to the west was a hint of brightness.

'The way twists and loops, but the gradient is not particularly demanding, Bris,' I called. The wagon shuddered under a powerful gust of wind, the rattle of its tarpaulin cover almost drowning my words. 'The storm won't last. Send two men ahead to check that the trail has not been washed away. I deem it safe to proceed.'

Before us, squeezed into a narrow valley between dramatic upthrusts of tree-covered limestone, Ravenscrag was visible through the rain: a chaotic huddle of distant rooftops behind a rotting stone wall. It was a typical Pansurian town, badly maintained, proximal to nowhere, largely unaware or indifferent to events in the outside world. True, rumours from abroad would filter in from time to time, usually hoary and wildly exaggerated or distorted. And folk would prick up their ears in passing excitement, briefly debate the import of the news, and then it would be forgotten, pushed out of mind by more immediate concerns. Pansur is a wild and secretive land. Its scattered communities live in intimacy only with the forests and mountains that surround them, small universes unto themselves.

Behind the town Ravenscrag castle loomed, an ancient hulk clinging to a windy crag, all mouldering turrets and bowed walls. In fairer weather, true to its name, ravens could usually be seen circling overhead. The crag and castle precincts had been their home since ages past.

The road, which was barely more than a track, had been transformed from hard, sun-baked earth to mud in minutes by the deluge. Tired, I scanned the wet, grey landscape as we advanced gingerly towards the town. I was relieved to have come so far without major incident. My men had been troubled when they'd learned that we would be leaving the main trading routes to travel into the heart of Pansur. Giants once roamed this land – and may have done still, though I had never seen one; the forests were said to be the haunt of dire creatures such as gaunts, ogres, vhazz, witches and other unnameable things. I had found it necessary to augment the men's salaries in order to retain their services for this venture.

The way had not been easy. Two days beyond Khimmur's border, in the mellow grasslands of Putc'pii, we had been attacked by brigands riding up out of the Hills of the Moon. My men put up stalwart resistance, but we were outnumbered. Two were killed and I feared we were about to be overrun and murdered to the last man, but by chance a Putc'pii patrol came to our aid and drove off our assailants. The Putc'pii escorted us north to the White River and the main trade route into Kemahamek. On the way I learned that they were in the pay of the Kemahamek authorities, who were concerned at a recent surge of banditry along the southern trade road which was affecting traffic into Kemahamek. Unemployed mercenary bands was the explanation. They had recently fled Cexhaut in the west, where they'd pledged themselves to the wrong side in a fierce and prolonged civil war. Rootless and prevented from returning west, they had fallen back upon brigandry, finding relatively easy pickings along the Putc'pii trade routes of Wetlan's Way and the Great Northern Caravan Road.

In Kemahamek itself, as we travelled northeast towards Twalinieh, the capital, we were delayed by foul weather, ever Kemahamek's bane. Trade stops in Kemahamek took up more time than I had anticipated. We passed on through Taenakipi and eventually entered Pansur more than six weeks after setting off from Hon-Hiaita in Khimmur.

The trade road wound eastwards towards Miragoff, keeping close to the north shore of the great White River. Four days into Pansur's wilds we abandoned the road and struck north along a little-used track that would eventually bring us to Ravenscrag. Much work was required. The track was overgrown. We were obliged to halt several times a day to clear fallen boughs, boulders and dense undergrowth, and on occasion toppled trees in order

14

that the wagons might pass. And all the time my men muttered among themselves, and peered nervously into the trees, more troubled here by the unseen and half-suspected than by all the bandits in Putc'pii.

The greater irony then, to come so far and lose a wagon here, in sight of Ravenscrag's walls. So it seemed at the time. I would later have cause to wonder whether a power more oracular and unfathomable than mere irony had played a part.

Three of the wagons had already passed safely when a section of the edge of the track gave way. The road, criss-crossed by torrents of rainwater, had doubtless been weakened by the storm. It had not been prevented from falling into a state of general disrepair, and an influx of unaccustomed traffic in recent days had probably served to undermine it further, for Lord Flarefist and Lady Sheerquine had demonstrated unwavering confidence in their advisors, broadcasting news of their forthcoming happy event far and wide. Invitations to the celebration had been dispatched some weeks earlier, establishing a rare contact between Ravenscrag and other Pansurian communities, and resulting in an unusual number of visitors now arriving in the town. Even so, there was little to indicate the danger.

The driver of the fourth wagon was a boy named Moles, thirteen or fourteen years of age. Lacking great experience, he had allowed the wagon to run a touch close to the outer edge of the road, although any driver might easily have done the same. Just a couple of feet from the wheel-rims a rock-strewn slope led down to a small, fast-flowing river fifty feet below.

A section of track gave way without warning. Mud, brush and clumps of grass slid away and left a gaping hole beneath the rear outer wheel of the wagon. Even then the wagon might have been saved, for it did not tip immediately. But amid warning shouts the boy-driver became confused.

At first he did the right thing, urging his two draught-horses forward. Then he seemed to change his mind. With frantic movements he began jerking the reins. The animals became alarmed. They snorted and stamped. Their movement pushed the wagon backwards.

I saw what was coming and cried out, but it was too late. The boy had lost control. The wagon began to list.

Bris leapt from his mount and reached for the harness of the

15

nearer of the two now terrified draught-horses, striving to bring them under control. The rear of the wagon sagged into the space beneath its axle. A front wheel lifted off the ground. Beneath the undercarriage more earth and rock slid away. The wagon groaned and slewed. The other front wheel lifted and the wagon started to slip from the road, dragging the two horses with it.

Moles leapt for his life as the wagon tipped right over. The horses, eyes rolling in terror, pawed helplessly at the crumbling road. But though the slope was not particularly steep, the heavy rain made it slippery and gave them no purchase. The full weight of the falling, laden wagon was too much for them to bear. Attached by their harness to the wagon's wooden shafts the poor beasts were hoisted high and flipped spectacularly onto their backs. Their squeals cut through the drum of the rain as they were thrown over and over with the wagon as it crashed towards the foot of the slope, spewing goods as it went.

I leapt from the road to the stricken boy. He had fallen against rocks, smashing his hip and shoulder. A dark stain of bright red blood soaked his trousers, and more blood poured from his nose and cheek. I guessed the nose was broken, probably the cheek-bone too. His face was white and contorted with pain. I gave him into the charge of two of my men, and ran on with Bris and three others, skidding and sliding towards the river.

The wagon had come to rest on its side in shallow water. The horses were beside it still trapped in their harness. The nearest lay still, breathing hard, its head upon the pebbles at the water's edge. The eyes were open and bloody foam bubbled at its mouth. Its body was horribly twisted, the spine plainly broken.

Its companion was in the water thrashing against its harness in a vain struggle to regain its feet. Around it the water clouded deep red.

Bris waded into the river. He swiftly examined the second horse then looked back, shaking his head, the rain streaming down his face. 'She's opened her belly on rocks or something. And one leg at least is broken.'

I stared regretfully at the two beasts. 'Do what must be done.'

As Bris drew his sword I went to inspect the wagon's contents. Much was strewn over the slope. More lay in the water. I waded around to the back – nervously, for I was never happy in the company of water of any quantity – and there found fine

Kemahamek silks and chiffons ruined in the muddy swirl. Expensive ceramics were in pieces at my feet.

I instructed my men. 'Salvage what you can.'

A few feet away a wooden chest lay up-ended in the mud. Rivulets of rainwater tumbling down the slope divided around it. The lid hung open, iron hasp and brackets buckled. Its contents had spilled around it in the mud.

A sodden mass of ruined material lay at my feet, half in and half out of the chest. I stooped and gathered it up. It was an elaborate ball-gown of dark crimson satin and cream lace, set with gold braid and tiny glass beads. The gown had been made in Twalinieh in Kemahamek, whose masques and grand balls were legend. I had intended to present it as a birth-gift to the proud Lady Sheerquine.

Close by was the gift I had brought for her husband: a terracotta figurine, about fifteen inches tall, of a huntsman slaying a boar. It had been crafted by Corthren of Sigath, one of Khimmur's finest sculptors. The figurine was wrapped in cloth and I lifted it carefully, with hope, and began to unwrap it. My hope was not to be rewarded: an arm was broken and the huntsman's head had been dislodged. I let it fall back into the mud.

One other gift had been carried on this wagon: that which I had brought for the unborn child. It was some yards away up the slope, wrapped in good strong sackcloth. It was the model of a Ghentine war-galleass, a magnificent example of Pician workmanship, constructed in a variety of woods. The ship was perfect in every detail, right down to unfurling sails, tiny figures on rigging and deck, and working catapults and ballistae in prow and stern. As I picked it up I knew that it too had failed to survive the fall. Two of its three masts were broken and the wood had splintered on one side of its hull.

I straightened and stared at the upturned wagon. Out of seven it had to be this one that was lost. I had no inkling then of how portentous this accident would turn out to be.

Something beyond the wrecked wagon drew my eyes. For a moment I thought I'd glimpsed a figure, dressed in green, observing us from the shade of distant trees. I blinked and raised a hand to shield my eyes from the rain. When I looked again there was nothing to be seen.

I discarded the smashed ship and went back to join my men as they struggled to salvage those goods that were not ruined.

Chapter Two

Thankfully the way was not so badly damaged as to prevent the remaining wagons from passing, with due care. We rolled on towards Ravenscrag, all of us anxious to change into dry clothes. The storm began to abate as we approached the town gate. The rain thinned then ceased, and wide beams of misty golden sunlight fell upon the landscape.

Townsfolk came from the shops and homes to watch as the wagons rumbled down the main thoroughfare to Ravenscrag's market-place. Even with the relative influx of visitors we were enough of a spectacle to command attention. Children scampered beside the horses, calling up and holding out their hands. A few mangy hounds trotted with us, hopeful of scraps.

At the market-place I made enquiries for a physician for the injured boy. I had done what I could for Moles, but my *Zan-Chassin* healing abilities were limited. A physician lived in a nearby street and Moles was taken to him on a stretcher. Next I made arrangements for storing my goods in a warehouse, then left my men to the task of unloading. With Bris and one other good fellow, Cloverron, as bodyguards, I went about my business in Ravenscrag town.

I chose an inn called the Blue Raven for lodgings. It was set at the edge of the market-square. The Blue Raven made claims for being Ravenscrag's finest hostelry, which was a boast that carried no great cachet. The inns and boarding-houses of Ravenscrag generally left much to be desired. A traveller was fortunate if he found himself an establishment – like the Blue Raven – which could offer serviceable, dry, rat-free chambers and provide clean linen and a bathtub of hot water. And he could count himself doubly lucky if the food he was served did not keep him up all night with gripes and runs or worse.

Such basic amenities did not come cheap, but I was and am a wealthy fellow, and found no advantage in frugality. I took the chamber I had occupied on my last visit to Ravenscrag some eighteen months earlier. Its balcony overlooked the market square with its rows of sun-faded coloured awnings. I bathed and changed into a long, blue, wide-sleeved tunic with scarlet trimming and slashed hems, then stood for some moments at the window and observed the comings and goings in the market-place.

The sun eased its way towards the horizon, leaving all but one side of the square in shadow. The moss-grown roofs were already almost dry, though large puddles still lay in the streets. The stalls and booths appeared to be enjoying better than average trade. Many of the customers and browsers were well dressed, in the manner of visitors of some distinction. Once or twice I caught accents from Miragoff, and noted the pale faces and distinctive garb of a couple of Kemahamek nationals.

A few faces were familiar to me; I recognized several merchants from outside Pansur. Bunting and streamers added to an air of general good-humour bordering on frivolity in the square. The impending birth of Flarefist and Sheerquine's offspring had been deemed worthy of note by more folk than I had anticipated.

I donned a nonchalant hat of crimson velvet topped with a plume of bright blue feathers, and left my chamber.

My first task was to let it be known that I had arrived.

Contacts and acquaintanceships were to be renewed, to which end I would make a tour of the main centres of communal life in Ravenscrag town – the taverns and bars near and around the market square. A seedbed of political intrigue Ravenscrag was not, but opportunity may be found anywhere if one takes the time to look.

Before departing the Blue Raven, however, I went to the common-room.

I had written a number of letters in my chamber – to Lord Flarefist and Lady Sheerquine, and to one or two other persons in Ravenscrag whom for differing reasons I held in almost equal high regard. Taking time for an aquavit with Cloverron and Bris, I called messenger boys and had the letters delivered.

Two hours later the first boy found me in a seething marketside inn, one of a number where merchants, whores and tricksters complimented one another's trades, and cutpurses bedevilled the unwary. The boy carried my first reply, from the castle: Lord Flarefist would receive me that very evening.

I bade my associates good night and made my way through the winding, hilly streets to the castle. Two assistants accompanied me, pushing a cart which bore new gifts I had chosen from my wagons.

At Ravenscrag castle a slouching footman led the way through dim passages to a west-facing arcade of decaying stone arches which overlooked a sunlit gravel courtyard. Pots and urns held neglected shrubs, a trickle of water seeped from a cracked, algaed fountain in the centre of the courtyard; a liver and white hound twitched fitfully in sleep on a warm step.

Lord Flarefist sat at a table in the shade of the arcade, drinking wine with two others. He looked up as the footman announced me, and gestured me forward.

'Ah, Dibdin! You are the magician, are you not? From . . . from. . . ?'

'Khimmur, Lord Flarefist. And it's Dinbig. Ronbas Dinbig.'

'Dinbig? Yes, that's what I said, isn't it?' Flarefist was a tall man, once robust but now wasted with age and ill-health. His skin was loose, sallow and mottled, his cheeks sunken – more so than when I'd last set eyes on him. His hair was wispy and grey, bound with a circlet of yellowing silver. He looked up at me, squinting through deep grey, watery eyes. His expression and manner conveyed the disconcerting certainty of the addle-minded, but I was aware that he was not without vigour or decisiveness. He was in his seventh decade and had been a renowned huntsman and capable soldier. His temper was legend, as was his love of good living. Virtual king in Ravenscrag, as Pansur lacked a central power, he was considered just, if a little lax. I had heard that more recently he was not always lucid and was subject to sudden, sometimes alarming swings of mood. He seemed cheerful enough at the moment. 'But you are a magician, are you not?'

'I have the honour of being a Realm Initiate of the *Zan-Chassin*.'

'Excellent! You must entertain us with some of your tricks. We know so little of magic here. As I recall, you are a masterful juggler.'

'Not I, Lord Flarefist.'

'Oh?'

'Perhaps you are confusing me with another of your guests.'

'Is that so?' He turned to one of his companions, whom I recognized as Irnbold the astrologer. 'Irnbold, what was the name of that marvellous juggler who entertained us earlier in the spring? Do you recall?'

'I think you are referring to Linvon the Light,' replied Irnbold, a scrawny old fellow with a face that was curiously both old and young. 'If you recall, after his departure we were unable to locate several pieces of the Ravenscrag silver.'

'Yes, that's the bastard, damn his soul! A scoundrel if ever one was born. Did we ever find him?'

'No, sir.'

Lord Flarefist looked back at me. 'You're not he?'

'Most assuredly not.'

'Hmph! Well, don't doubt that I'll have his hands chopped off when we find him. He'll toss no more balls, I can promise you that. A pity, though. He was a first-rate entertainer. Played the fife, too. Are you a musician, Disbin?'

'Dinbig, sir. No, I regret that I have minimal talent in that direction.'

'Ah. Pity. And you don't juggle?'

'I do not.'

'Well, no matter. Please, be seated. Join us in a goblet of wine. This is a joyous occasion, and your arrival could not be more opportunely timed. You will join us as we raise our cups once more in honour of my new son.'

I threw him a questioning glance. Was the child born already,

21

without my knowledge? Irnbold put me right. 'I have predicted that Lord Flarefist's son will be born tomorrow, in the evening.'

'Are you confident in your precision?'

'Oh yes.' Irnbold nodded, but did not eludicate. We drank the child's health. The wine, I noted, was excellent.

'The preparations have all been made!' announced Lord Flarefist heartily. His hands rested upon the pommel of a stout stick, which he raised and banged several times upon the flags. The sound reverberated off the stone walls, disturbing the sleeping hound, which lifted its head, then, identifying the source of the disturbance, let it settle back onto the step again. 'Yes, it's an auspicious time. An auspicious time indeed.'

I wondered at his confidence. It was not my affair, but such a complete absence of doubt in regard to the success of the forthcoming birth was surprising. I said, I hoped not tactlessly, 'You obviously foresee no complications.'

'Complications? No, Binsdig. Absolutely not.' Flarefist's watery gaze rested upon me, his smile stiffening slightly. His head swayed a touch drunkenly on his shoulders. 'I am advised by experts, you see. The excellent Irnbold, here; our dear lady of the Clear Sight, Elmag; and others.'

I glanced at Irnbold beside me. As was his wont he was garbed in a flamboyant costume which he no doubt considered distinguishing. It fitted snugly upon his frame, accentuating his thinness. It was coloured in a pattern of conjoining yellow and red stars. Each of these held planet symbols and/or zodiacal signs. From the sleeves hung loose braids of the same material. A flared, split red cloak was draped carefully over one shoulder. Irnbold's head was covered in a wimple-like affair, which encircled his face and sat low on his forehead. A panache of red and yellow braids sprouted from the crown and hung beside his face. I was not persuaded as to his infallibility.

Irnbold returned my look with a self-satisfied smile, raising a thick dark eyebrow. His long nose was purple, as were his narrow cheeks, which were traced with a network of broken veins.

'But forgive me, I am remiss!' barked Flarefist. 'You have not been introduced to my other guest. Good Bimbid, I do not think you have met my esteemed second cousin, Ulen Condark, Lord of Condark and all its dominions.'

22

The man on my other side inclined his head politely. He was fiftyish, a tall, broad-shouldered man with high cheekbones and resolute blue eyes. His fair, greying hair was trimmed in a short fringe across his forehead. I regarded him with interest.

'Lord Condark, I am honoured.'

Relations had not always been level between Ravenscrag and House Condark. Present circumstances, I suspected, were not set to make them any easier, at least not as far as Ulen Condark was concerned. Condark and its lands and estates lay some distance to the northeast. It was a powerful house, ruled by a powerful family. By collateral lineage Ulen Condark was currently set to inherit Ravenscrag upon the death of Lord Flarefist, but with the birth of Flarefist's son his claim would be negated. I wondered how well that sat with him.

Lord Condark returned my greeting in a quiet, level voice, his smile showing even white teeth. This was a man with whom it would be advantageous to cultivate good relations.

'And how is your august King Perminias, Dimdig?' enquired Lord Flarefist.

'Dinbig, sir. Perminias is king of Sommaria. I am Khimmurian. Gastlan Fireheart is my liege, and king of Khimmur.'*

'Good. Well, how is he?'

'He is in splendid health, and requests that I convey to you his most cordial regards and congratulations upon the birth of your child.' Unwittingly I had fallen into the mood of the place, offering congratulations for an event which had yet to occur.

'Ah, how kind. And your journey here? How was it? Any encounters?'

I believed there was a slight edge to his voice. 'Encounters? Not exactly, though I suffered an unfortunate accident only this afternoon, within sight of your town gate.'

'Accident?' Flarefist leaned towards me. 'What manner of accident?'

I told him of the loss of my wagon, and the gifts it contained. He settled back, thoughtful, and expressed his regret. 'But other than that your journey was uneventful?'

---

* The events in *Moonblood* take place some years prior to those described in *The Firstworld Chronicles Vols I–IV*, and precede King Gastlan Fireheart's bloody relinquishment of the Khimmurian throne to his eldest son, Oshalan.

'Largely. To what kind of encounters do you refer?'

Lord Flarefist pulled a scornful face and gestured dismissively with one hand. 'Witchery.'

'Witchery?'

'There have been one or two isolated incidents in recent weeks,' Irnbold explained. 'We are not really concerned, but my lord was anxious lest rumours of it discourage guests from attending this event.'

'In what manner has it manifested itself?' I began, but Flarefist interrupted.

'There is to be a Grand Banquet here at the castle tomorrow, following my son's birth. You will attend, will you not, Bin . . . Bin . . .'

'Dinbig, sir. I would be honoured to attend. Might I enquire as to the health of the gracious Lady Sheerquine?'

'Sheerquine is blooming! She is in marvellous health! Currently she rests, her physician in attendance.'

'I would convey to her my good wishes. As she is indisposed, perhaps you might. . . ?'

Lord Flarefist nodded. I continued: 'If it is your wish, Lord Flarefist, I will present my gifts to you forthwith.'

'Let it be so!' The old aristocrat swivelled upon his seat and gestured to a footman in the passage. 'Have the gifts brought here.'

'Your own gift, Lord Flarefist, is a little cumbersome to be carried to you directly. I would advise that it be taken straight to your cellars. It is a hogshead of good red wine, soft and full-bodied, harvested at my own estate in Khimmur. Also, preserved fish, and a sack of cacao beans. I trust you will find these palatable.'

'Most definitely, sir! You are of a generous spirit, a man after my own heart. In such trying circumstances your gesture is doubly appreciated.'

He was right, I had been generous. The wine would have put a weight of silver in my pocket; even more so the fish and cacao beans, which were rare delicacies in Pansur. The visit was costing me dear, but I had an eye on the future. I just hoped that in coming months or years Flarefist, or at least his wife, would be capable of remembering who I was.

My assistants brought the remaining gifts.

'For Lady Sheerquine,' I said. 'I regret that it is not the offering I had intended. I hope she will consider it an acceptable substitute.'

I held up a lined velvet cloak, deep blue, trimmed with lace. Again, it would have fetched a fine price from one of the wealthier ladies of Ravenscrag.

'Excellent.' Flarefist nodded his approval.

'For your new son I have ordered a wardrobe of nursery clothing, fashioned from cottons and silks which I brought with me. Ravenscrag's best seamstresses are at work at this moment to complete the order. I hope the garments will be ready for presentation to you tomorrow.'

'My thanks to you, Dimsdig. I say again, you are a rare and generous man.'

'And finally, sir, my gift for your daughter, Moonblood.'

As I spoke I caught from the corner of my eye a movement in the dim passage from which I had emerged into the arcade. A figure approached, half shadow, slight and silent, with tentative steps. A moment late I recognized the maiden in question, Moonblood, framed in the arched portal.

Had she been standing there in the passage eavesdropping on our conversation, or was it coincidence that brought her here at this moment? I watched her as she came forward to stand beside her father's chair. She curtsied, at once self-conscious and inquisitive.

I smiled. I had met Moonblood briefly on an earlier visit, though we had exchanged no more than a few words. I found her an intriguing child. She was now aged about fourteen. She was slender, almost waiflike, and carried with her an air of wistful solemnity. By all accounts she was intelligent, if a touch wilful, and showed a love of learning. By many she was considered remote and somewhat aloof.

She could not be called beautiful, but her large, clear, sea-green eyes, almost translucent pallor, and expressive lips attracted and fascinated the eye. When Moonblood was present it was difficult not to watch her.

She had altered since I last set eyes on her. The lines of her body were softer, had begun to fill out. She wore a slightly rumpled pale green frock, against which nubbin-like breasts pressed. Still a child, she was yet on the threshold of womanhood, and was aware of and somewhat disconcerted by it.

Around her neck she wore a crescent moon pendant cast in silver on a silver chain. At her breast was pinned a brooch of unusual configuration, set with glittering gems. Her hair was unbound, long and fair, quite unlike her father's which had formerly been deep brown, or Sheerquine's mass of magnificent copper red. On her feet were simple green slippers.

'Moonblood,' said her father with a slanting grin. 'You have arrived at a propitious moment, perhaps not entirely by chance.'

Twin points of colour blossomed on Moonblood's pale cheeks. She compressed her lips and cast her eyes down.

'Good day, Lady Moonblood,' I said. 'It is a pleasure to see you again.'

'Thank you, sir.' She looked towards me but could not meet my eyes. She put her hands behind her back and stood awkwardly. Plainly she did not recall me.

'And are you happy at the thought of the baby brother you are soon to have for company?'

Intent, wistful. Then a dimpled smile and her green eyes met mine, shining, her expression both sweet and grave. 'I am.'

I took a bundle bound in cloth from my assistant and carefully unwrapped it. 'This is for you, with my compliments.'

I observed Moonblood's face as I peeled away the last layer of the cloth. The present was a doll, brought from Twalinieh in Kemahamek. It was carved in painted wood and dressed in traditional Kemahamek costume, with moveable joints on arms, legs and neck. It was the one original gift to have survived the accident that afternoon. It had been carried in another wagon, there being no space in the chest which had contained the other gifts.

A puzzled frown had crept onto Moonblood's brow as she watched. It vanished as she set eyes on the doll. Her eyes widened and a delighted smile leapt spontaneously on to her face. Animated, she reached forward to take the doll. 'Oh, sir, it is beautiful! Thank you. Thank you.'

'What will you call it?'

Moonblood's eyes lifted to the ceiling and she held her inner lip with her teeth in a moment of concentration, clutching the doll to her breast. 'Kestanna.'

'A lovely name. Is there a reason?'

'I know a story about a young maiden called Kestanna, who goes alone into the forest one night and is taken prisoner by an evil ogre.'

'What a sorry fate! Does Kestanna escape?'

'She runs away, and meets a bold young vagabond knight called Sir Esler who slays the ogre. They have many adventures together, and eventually Kestanna returns to her home where she discovers she is a princess. She marries Sir Esler, and becomes queen.

'A charming tale, and a fitting name for your new doll.'

Then a distant, almost disconsolate look clouded Moonblood's expression. After a moment's reflection she said, 'But no, I will not call her Kestanna. She shall be Misha, after my little sister who died when she was a tiny baby. *Oh, Rogue!*' Moonblood cried out playfully, addressing the old hound which had woken up and ambled across to greet her, his tail swaying, snuffling at her waist. She crouched down to ruffle his head. 'Rogue, look. Say hello to Misha.'

The dog mootly sniffed the doll, then turned back to his mistress and licked her face. She giggled.

'Father, may I take Misha to my chamber now?'

Flarefist nodded with an indulgent smile. Moonblood curtsied, flashed another shy smile at me, and turned. I watched her as she skipped away, the old dog trotting at her heels.

A steward brought lanterns, for the sun had now settled behind the crags. This was the first night of darkmoon, and the darkness gathered quickly.

Chapter Three

The evening was mellow and still young. As I left Ravenscrag castle I had it in mind to return to the taverns. Crossing the market square I was approached by one of the messenger boys I had sent out earlier.

He handed me a sealed note. As I opened it a waft of perfume of lily-of-the-valley reached my nostrils, apprising me instantly of the sender's identity. I allowed my eyes to close for a moment, savouring memories and anticipations.

By lanternlight I read the single sentence handwritten there:

I will come to your chamber this evening.
                                                        C.

I altered my plans and returned straightaway to the Blue Raven.

Two hours later, when I had bathed, changed, eaten and rested, I heard a soft rap upon my chamber door. I rose and opened it. A woman stood there, hooded and veiled, swathed in a long black velvet cloak.

Cametta!

She swept quickly into the room and threw back her hood and

pulled aside the veil as I closed the door. Her arms encircled my neck and she pressed her lips to mine. I held her. Her kiss, the scent of her, and the pressure of her lithe, warm body against mine were deeply stimulating.

'So long!' Cametta said, breathless, drawing back. She gazed into my face. 'I thought you would never come again.'

'It has been difficult. I made every effort, but . . .'

'I came as soon as I could after your note arrived. I can't stay long.'

'Where is your husband?'

'On duty. He may be home at midnight.'

'He believes you to be there?'

'The household think I am out organizing for tomorrow.'

Cametta's husband was Darean Lonsord, captain of Ravenscrag's guard. She and I had met upon my first visit to Ravenscrag, when she had purchased fineries from me. That was four years ago when, following years of struggle, I was becoming known as a successful merchant beyond the borders of Khimmur. Cametta and I had become lovers then and our passions had been rekindled on my subsequent visits.

Cametta unfastened the clasp of her cloak and shrugged the garment from her shoulders. She took my hands and moved backwards towards the bed, smiling. 'Come, my love. There is much lost time to make up.'

Releasing my hands she undid the fastenings of her blouse, smiling as she watched the expression on my face. The candlelight reflected off her long auburn hair. She was exceedingly beautiful, young, fresh-skinned and slim. Her hair fell loosely around her shoulders. She slipped the blouse off; she wore nothing beneath.

'Dinbig, my magician. Work your spells and come to me!'

I needed no further bidding. Quickly conjuring erotic raptures, subtle enhancements to pleasure, I strode to her and took her again in my arms.

When the candles had burned low Cametta lay drowsy, half asleep, her head on my chest. I gently stroked her hair. She murmured, 'We know nothing of magic like yours in Ravenscrag. Ah, my love, were you to stay you would find no lack of employment here.'

I lifted an eyebrow. 'Among the ladies of Ravenscrag?'

She pinched my flank. 'You know I didn't mean that. *That* magic you will share with me and no other!'

'Ah.'

'But others would pay handsomely to learn the rudiments of magic. With that and your knowledge of trade you would quickly grow rich. You would become a prominent citizen here. Will you not consider staying?'

'It is not so simple.'

Cametta had married for love, or what she had genuinely taken for love at the time. But the marriage had also not been disadvantageous. It had elevated her to prestigious status in the community. She was very young when she fell for the dashing Darean Lonsord, and only later did she discover him somewhat coarse. She learned too of his appetite for ale and his reputation for brawling and, far worse, wenching. I had happened along at the right moment, bringing unusual wares from far locales, attracting both her desire for novelty and change, and her roving eye. But now she was of a mind to make me stay, or perhaps take her away with me, neither of which fitted my plans.

'Lord Flarefist is of a mind to learn,' persisted she.

I chuckled. 'He may be of a mind but he is not of an ilk. Lord Flarefist has no flair for magic.'

'Irnbold, then.'

'A more likely candidate, though he is no longer young and his brain I suspect is irreparably fogged by spirits of the wrong kind.'

'But there are many others.'

'I don't doubt it.'

'Then won't you consider staying?'

'Very well, I will discuss the arrangement with your husband. I'm sure he will be most accommodating.'

Cametta sighed. 'Then take me away with you.'

'Alas, that I cannot do. It would be unfair to uproot you from your home and family. What of your sweet son, Alfair?'

'Alfair could come. He is young but he longs for adventure, as do I.'

'Where I go there are oft times more than adventures. The dangers lie large and unannounced. I would not jeopardize either his life or yours by subjecting you to the vicissitudes of a life such as mine.'

She sighed again, and would have said something more, but I shifted the topic of interest. 'I have brought you something.'

'For me? What is it? Can I see?'

'It is not here. Shall I bring it to your home? When can I call?'

'Darean is on duty from midday.'

'Excellent! Then the reputable and dashing Khimmurian merchant, Ronbas Dinbig, will stop by your house early in the afternoon, with wares to display for your delight. I trust you will be able to arrange some privacy whilst you peruse my goods?'

'It can be arranged.' She raised herself onto her elbows, kissing me. 'I must go, my love.'

'So soon?'

'I told you, Darean may be home soon after midnight.'

With lingering kisses she left the bed and began to dress. I watched her, becoming aroused again at the sight of her nakedness as it was stolen from my eyes.

'Cametta, stay just a few moments more.'

'Would that I could, magician mine!' Fully clothed she returned to me, touched her fingers to her lips, then mine. 'Until tomorrow.'

She replaced her veil, then pulled the hood up over her head.

'Tomorrow,' I said.

Chapter Four

Tomorrow came, in the habit of all tomorrows, shedding its skin in the dark hours, transforming itself unseen to emerge with the dawn as a new today. In this instance, a bright, cloudless, breezeless today, hot even at first light, almost torrid.

I took a light breakfast in my chamber, seated at the window so that I might observe the activities in the market-place. Shop-keepers, or their lackeys, were sweeping clean the cobbles before their premises as the first merchants arrived to set up their booths. One or two street entertainers entered the square, hopeful of early pickings. The heat rising from the rooftops already addled the air; ravens hung lazily in the shining blue overhead. Gradually the market began to fill with folk from Ravenscrag and beyond.

Most of that morning I spent in the pursuit of business. It had taken many years to build up the reputation and success I now enjoyed. As a child I had grown up at Castle Drome, seat of one of Khimmur's most powerful warlords, the Orl of Selaor. My father had been head steward there. But I had quarrelled with the Orl's son, Kilroth, a boy of my own age. Later Kilroth took offence when, seeking initiation into the *Zan-Chassin*, he was twice rejected, while I succeeded without great effort.

Kilroth exercised his resentment by making life at the castle as difficult as he could for myself and my family. Upon the death of his father he assumed the hereditary title of Orl, and dismissed my father from service on a fabricated charge of petty misdemeanour. With my family facing starvation I made my way to Khimmur's capital – Hon-Hiaita. There, living on my wits, I rapidly developed the requisite talents for successful business, and began to prosper. Now my name and reputation were known far and wide.

In the Ravenscrag taverns the previous evening I had extended invitations to a number of merchants and persons of means to call today at the warehouse where my goods were stored. I put them at their ease with a good chilled wine and gossip while displaying the wares I had brought, to agree prices and arrange transactions. Subsequently I visited the warehouses of local merchants, and the market itself, to peruse goods and make note of possible purchases, and in one or two instances to place firm orders.

I lunched well in a local tavern and, with the sun blazing past its zenith, made my way through the baking streets to the house of Cametta and Darean Lonsord. A boy accompanied me, puffing and sweating even more than I as he laboured with the handcart containing the gifts I had chosen for Cametta, plus a few other fineries I thought might tempt her.

True to her word Cametta received me in a spacious drawing-room, then dismissed her servant so that we might be alone and undisturbed while she inspected the goods I had brought. We made love throughout the afternoon, on divan, floor and console, in a haze of erotic magics, and I left as evening approached, sated, wholly depleted of energies, and suffused with a warm, drowsy afterglow and a sense of all having been set to rights in the world.

I went next to the castle. One of my wagons carried a weight of tasty delicacies brought from Sommaria, Kemahamek and elsewhere, which I hoped might at some point tempt the palates and grace the dining-tables of Ravenscrag high society. But my arrival was ill-timed; the castle, to the last man and woman, was in frantic preparation for the evening's celebration. Lord Flarefist and his spouse were indisposed, as was the chief steward and chamberlain. The chefs sweltering in the great kitchens could likewise spare no time to speak to me, but bade me return on the morrow.

33

All this activity only served to rekindle my apprehensions over the imminent confinement. I knew that Sheerquine had previously given birth to stillborn infants on more than one occasion. Neither she nor her husband could be said to be in the first bloom of youth. Yet the extraordinary optimism and certainty over the arrival of Ravenscrag's heir – now apparently only hours away – still prevailed.

Surely among the castle staff, if not Ravenscrag's family and its close advisors, there were doubts unexpressed, I told myself, for this was not normal. Yet I saw no evidence of such. The contagion of euphoria had spread even to some of the foreign guests whom I had spoken to earlier in the day. They were perhaps less inclined to give premature vent to hopes as yet unrealized, but none seemed to consider the mood unreasonable.

The molten orb of the sun settled towards the heights, rendering the sky in merging shades of rose-pink, peach and crimson. I kept to the castle precincts for a while longer, observing the preparations, then ascended to the battlements to gaze out across the town and beyond, into the immense Pansurian wilds. Illuminated with red-gold and shadows of deepening blue, the surrounding peaks rose in full and splendid majesty, dwarfing that upon which Ravenscrag crouched.

Visible towards the rear of the castle some distance away, beyond walled gardens and orchards, was the glimmer of water, a little river, reflecting red between trees. A small figure passed through a portal in one wall, casting a long shadow. A second, shorter figure moved rapidly up alongside it. As I watched they made their way towards the rear of the castle's main wing via a grassy avenue of neglected topiary.

Their direction brought them close upon my position. I descended, passed along a corridor into an arcade, and spied the two again across a shadowed sward. I stepped out so that our paths might intersect.

'Lady Moonblood!'

Moonblood, seeming in a reverie, hesitated in her step and looked around. Recognizing me she gave a shy smile. Her companion, the old hound Rogue, wandered off a little way, his pink tongue lolling, and slumped down in the shade.

I approached the maiden. At her back the sunset had become a bloody stain across the sky. I shifted my position a little to avoid the dazzle of the low sun.

I appraised Moonblood's waiflike figure, clothed in a light cotton summer dress and sandals. Her strange, expressive little face conveyed intelligence and reservation; she was inquisitive, eager, and yet unsure and a little awkward. Her incipient womanhood, though still barely expressed, nevertheless exerted its effect upon my senses. Soon, I thought, a year, perhaps more . . . I stopped the thought before it could run its full course.

'Good evening, sir,' said Moonblood. Tiny beads of perspiration gilded her slim nose and forehead. The light cast a ruddy glow upon her normally pale features, but her cheeks seemed flushed apart from this. She was slightly out of breath.

'Good evening. It is an enchanting evening, is it not?'

'Yes, but too hot.'

'You look as though you've been exerting yourself.' On Moonblood's dress, and caught in the tiny hairs of her damp skin, was a covering of what I at first took to be dust, but upon closer inspection saw was mainly pollen and minute seed husks. She wore a circlet of wild flowers on her fair head, and chains of daisies around her neck and wrists. I was intrigued to know where she had been, but it would have been a gross impertinence to ask directly, and she gave no explanation.

'I hope you do not mind my speaking to you. I was taking a stroll, my business for the day being concluded, when I saw you approaching.'

'Of course not, though as you can see I am hardly presentable. I must repair to my chamber to wash and dress for the banquet.'

'Perhaps I might walk with you the short distance back into the castle?'

She nodded graciously and I took my place beside her. 'You must feel great excitement at the prospect of this birth, now so close upon us.'

'Excuse me? Oh, yes. Yes, I do.' Moonblood seemed distracted. I sensed a slight edginess about her. I wondered at first whether she might be displeased at having encountered me, yet I felt that her smile was quite genuine, and that in fact I was in favour – I had made the right move in my presentation of the doll, Misha. So I put her unease down to other factors, as yet unknown.

'A brother, I understand, if all the signs are true.'

'Yes, a little brother. My father's heir.'

Was there a catch in her voice? Could it be that Moonblood was aggrieved by the prospect of a sibling heir to Ravenscrag? Surely not, for even in the absence of male offspring power would never have fallen to Moonblood upon the death of her father. I risked probing a little deeper. 'Does the prospect not entirely please you, Lady Moonblood?'

'Oh, it pleases me. Of course it does. And it will be so marvellous for my father and mother. But I – Oh, it's foolish really. I'm just a bit anxious. When the baby is born and is seen to be safe and well, then I'll relax, I'm sure.'

Now here was something! For the first time I was hearing doubts expressed about the forthcoming birth, and coming from a member of the Ravenscrag family.

'But I thought all was secure and without doubt. The predictions . . . The tone I have so far encountered has been one of supreme optimism.'

Moonblood gave a nervous little laugh. 'Yes. I'm being silly. It's just that sometimes – I don't know – it's unnatural. I can't help feeling afraid.'

She glanced up at me with a charming, vulnerable expression, half-smiling, half-beseeching.

'In what form do these fears manifest?' I asked.

She glanced away. 'I cannot say. They are just feelings. Sometimes I have nightmares. Oh, you must think me foolish.'

'No, there is nothing foolish in being aware of your senses. Dreams and nightmares can provide an invaluable fund of reference to things we are incapable of recognizing or comprehending in waking consciousness – and I would never dismiss presentiments out of hand.'

Moonblood seemed at first encouraged by this. 'Do you really think so?'

'I know so. Yet we must exercise extreme caution in our interpretations of their apparent messages, for we are liable, often unwittingly, to mislead ourselves rather than acknowledge the truth of what we may be led to discover. It is a complex process, and we are capable of tremendous self-deceit. Have you expressed anything of your fears to anyone else?'

'No. I mean . . . No. Nobody here would take any notice of me. I'm just a silly, fanciful girl.'

'I doubt that.'

We had arrived close to the end of a major corridor intersecting the castle. Moonblood halted near the foot of a flight of stone stairs, deep in thought. I observed the animated play of expressions across her round young face. She raised her head to look at me with a troubled gaze. Her expression changed. She stepped back, uttering a little gasp, as though with fear.

'Lady Moonblood, is something the matter?'

She quickly collected herself. 'No, I am sorry. I thought I saw something, but it was nothing.'

'What was it that you thought you saw?'

She shook her head. 'No, it was nothing. I am tired, and a little overwrought. I must go now.'

I would have given much to have spoken with her some more, but I could not detain her further. 'I hope I will see you then at the banquet.'

She gave a quick smile. 'Yes, and my brother will have been born and all will be well.'

'And might I request in advance that you permit me the honour of a dance?'

She smiled again, dimpling. 'Of course. Now I must go. Thank you, sir. Thank you for your company.'

She turned and made off quickly up the stairs. I watched until she was lost from sight around the angle of the wall, then went pensively on my way. Within me was a growing feeling that there might be more, much more, to this fey girl-child than met the eye.

Chapter Five

Over Ravenscrag the bells were ringing, into the nightclad forest and rocky heights all around, announcing the birth of Flarefist and Sheerquine's child. Guests assembled at the castle, eager to partake of the celebratory banquet. When the bells ceased their jubilant tolling the cheers of the townsfolk could be heard rising from below to the castle walls.

The child was born not long after the sun had set on this, the second night of darkmoon. It was a boy, brought immediately to the banqueting hall to be proudly displayed. His birthtime corresponded exactly with the predictions of the astrologer, Irnbold.

He was tiny and pink, with puckered skin and a fine growth of bright red hair. His wet-nurse, a large-boned peasant girl named Blonna, who until recently had lived on the outskirts of the town, cradled him to her ample bosom. She cooed gently, hot-cheeked with embarrassment as the guests crowded around, giving good voice to their feelings.

Lady Sheerquine was not yet in evidence. Lord Flarefist, ebullient and proud, raised his hands and called for silence that he might speak.

'My friends, lords, ladies, honoured guests, be in no doubt that this is a great occasion. My son has been born, in accordance with the predictions of my most expert advisors. Here he is, at long last, the heir to Ravenscrag!'

Another rousing cheer from the hall. Lord Flarefist took the babe from his wet-nurse. Irnbold stood beside him garbed in another preposterous costume, this time in flowing purples, blues and reds, a customary matching wimple framing his face. His small chest was thrust forward, his face abrim with pride. Close by was Elmag, the far-sighted: bearded, snaggle-toothed and smiling. Other family members surrounded them, including Hectal, Lady Sheerquine's feeble-minded twin brother. Discreetly to one side stood Moonblood. She wore a gown of cornflower blue, sashed in silver at her slender waist. Her white hands hung before her, fingers loosely linked. She gazed upon her tiny brother, her pale young face quite radiant, yet with an unreadable expression in her eyes.

Lord Flarefist cast aside the linen blanket that was wrapped around his son. Clasping the infant in one hand and a golden goblet of wine in the other he endeavoured to climb up onto a table. The wet-nurse stood wide-eyed in horror, her hands at her mouth. Two servants rushed forward to help the old lord. Wine spilled over the table and floor. One of the servants relieved him of the goblet.

Eventually Flarefist was aloft, though he looked none too sure on his feet. He lifted the baby high with both hands, peering around at the upturned faces.

'My son, Lord-designate of Ravenscrag.' The child had woken. He kicked his tiny legs and waved his arms. His thin wail cut through the dense smoky atmosphere. Flarefist chuckled delightedly. 'His name, fittingly, is Redlock. As you can see, he has inherited his mother's fine head of hair. My friends, I call upon you to fill your goblets if they are not already full. Raise them in a toast to my son, Redlock, Lord-designate of Ravenscrag.'

The toast was duly made, with more raucous cheers and clapping from the guests. Lady Sheerquine appeared at a portal at the foot of a stairway which led up the the private family apartments. A tall woman, stately and proud, almost heavy, she was pale and drawn after her labour. Her mouth was pursed and she seemed hardly at her ease. Her long hair, lustrous red turning to grey, was unbound. It fell around her shoulders and the jade-green robe she wore. A maid accompanied her, holding her arm.

Lady Sheerquine's eyes fell upon her husband. She froze for a moment, aghast, then strode forward, tiredness forgotten. 'Flarefist, get down off there at once! What do you think you're doing, you foolish old goat! Give me the child before you drop him! Do you want him to dash his brains out on the floor?'

Flarefist turned obediently and bent to hand over the precious bundle. Taking her son, Sheerquine summoned the wet-nurse. 'Take the baby to his nursery.'

'There are guests yet to arrive who will wish to see him,' Flarefist protested tamely.

'Blonna will bring him down again later on. But you will not handle the child, Flarefist. I'll have no more of your antics. After all this time, that you should act so irresponsibly! Have you lost all sense?'

Flarefist was no longer listening. He hailed his guests. 'My wife, the brave and beautiful Sheerquine, who has brought me all I have wished for. A toast, friends! A toast to Lady Sheerquine!'

As goblets were lofted once more Flarefist called out again. 'And now, make merry, eat and drink your fill, and make this day one to be remembered for all time!'

Helped down from the table, he disappeared into the gathering, throwing arms around shoulders, slapping backs, kissing cheeks. With regal dignity Sheerquine took herself to a carved oak chair and sat down, stony-faced yet strained and distant, as though her thoughts dwelt on imminences unknown.

Servants began filing into the hall, bringing trays and platters bearing roasted haunches of venison, a spitted pig, roasted quails, pigeons, pheasants and geese. More platters came with a host of accompaniments. The guests took their places at the long tables set around the hall, and the feasting began.

Later there was music and I took the opportunity to request a dance with Cametta. She accepted with grace, leaving her husband Darean Lonsord drinking ale with a number of cronies. Her eyes sparkled as together we paced out the steps of a courtly pavane; the memory of that afternoon spent at her home lingered like honey held upon the tongue.

'When can we meet again?' I asked as the dance drew towards its close. I noticed Moonblood upon the floor, dancing expressionlessly with a brown-haired youth.

'I'm leaving the banquet within an hour or so,' replied Cametta. 'Darean will be here until long past midnight. Come to my home again.'

'Concerns of business keep me here. I don't know when I'll be able to leave.'

'Tomorrow, then. Darean is on duty at noon.'

'Good.' I escorted her from the floor. 'I shall come in the morning, with more goods for your perusal.'

'And bring your magic, Dinbig.'

'As if I would forget!'

Moonblood now stood alone at the side of the hall. Her eyes were cast down. Some distance away I saw the youth with whom she had danced. He stood with Lord Ulen Condark and his wife, Lady Magleine, and cast frequent glances in Moonblood's direction.

I crossed the hall as the musicians struck up a galliard, and approached the young girl. 'May I remind you of your earlier promise?'

She looked up, reddening slightly, then smiled and placed her hand upon mine.

'Why so downcast?' I enquired as we followed the sprightly dance.

'Am I downcast, sir? I thought the opposite.'

'Dinbig, please. You display some animation now, but moments ago you stood solitary and solemn, despite the happy birth of your brother. Prior to that I observed you dancing with a not unhandsome young gallant. Yet you appeared to lack enthusiasm.'

Her eyes flickered with a hint of smouldering resentment across the hall. 'Ilden Condark. He has a wart upon his nose and his teeth are yellow.'

'We are none of us perfect.' Ilden was Ulen Condark's third and youngest son.

'I don't really dislike him, though we have scarcely met,' Moonblood said upon reflection. 'But I don't want to marry him, nor any other that my father chooses.'

'Marry him?' I nodded to myself. I could see how Lord Flarefist's mind worked. Marrying his only daughter off to a scion of House Condark would have many advantages. 'Then what of other young notables? There are plenty here tonight.'

'They are clodpolls and donkeys.'

'All of them?'

Moonblood pulled a pettish face. 'I don't wish to be married. I'm too young.'

'Quite so. But simply as companions – do you find them all unsuitable?'

'I don't lack companions. I have Rogue, and Misha and my other dolls. I have my books, and . . .' Her look became distant, then her face brightened suddenly. 'How did you know, Dinbig, to bring me Misha? She is a perfect present.'

'I simply recalled that when we last met eighteen months ago I was impressed by your fine collection of dolls.'

'And you remembered all this time?'

I smiled. 'I remember clearly that you had them ranged before you upon a step. You were reading them a story. My only concern was that you might have grown up so much as to have left them behind.'

'Oh no. I love them all; and Misha will be princess among them.'

'When I saw her I thought she would make a fine addition to your collection.'

'Oh, she does. She does.'

'And what, then, of your newborn brother, Redlock? He is a beautiful babe is he not?'

Moonblood smiled, but it was half-hearted and almost rueful. 'Yes, he is. But I would not be in his place for the world.'

'Why so?'

'He inherits only troubles and debt. There is much resentment among my distant relatives.'

'House Condark?'

'My father says they think Ravenscrag should be theirs. I don't understand these things.' Abruptly she changed the subject. 'Dinbig, is it true that you are very rich?'

'Only modestly so.'

'And famous?'

42

'Again, I am known in certain quarters.'

'And you have travelled everywhere, have you not?'

'I have seen much of the world, it's true.'

'How did you come to make your fortune?'

'I worked hard, seized opportunity where it presented itself, and created it where it did not. I concede that a modicum of luck may also have played a part.'

'And is it also true that you know magic?'

'I know something of it.'

Moonblood was all eagerness now. 'What can you do? Can you change things? Can you turn a mouse into a shining white charger, or make winged slippers that fly? Can you teach me how to talk to fairies? I would like to change things. I would like to make things better.'

I laughed. 'I know of none of who can do these things, save perhaps Enchanters in faraway Qotolr. The magic I know is of a different kind.'

'But will you teach me? Is it easy to learn? I would so love to learn magic!'

'Fortunately it is not so easily taught, nor grasped. Few gain so much as the fundamentals, even after years of dedicated study. And none gain mastery, for magic is a mystery, a force far greater than we, and one that we do not wholly understand. That said, I sense that you may have a natural affinity for the art. Regrettably, though, I am not the one to teach you.'

She frowned. 'Why not?'

'*Zan-Chassin* magic can be taught only by highly trained practitioners in secret schools in Khimmur.'

Moonblood formed her lips into a thoughtful pout. 'Khimmur is a long way away, is it not?'

'It is.'

'Then surely no one would know were you to teach me just one small spell.'

'As I said, Lady Moonblood, it is not so simple.'

'But I would tell no one, Dinbig! I promise!'

'One day perhaps you might come to Khimmur and enter one of our schools. You would learn from adepts far more knowledgeable than I.'

I could not explain the dangers of *Zan-Chassin* magic. Its power comes almost exclusively from the realms beyond the corporeal world. Extant there are strange spirit-denizens which, once subdued, can bestow privilege and rare abilities upon the aspiring adept. But many have died, been lost or driven insane pursuing these goals, and for this reason initiation into the *Zan-Chassin* is a long and graduated process.

Trifling raptures have at times been taught to the unqualified by unscrupulous initiates in return for coin or some other favour – often with disastrous consequences. The *Zan-Chassin* Hierarchy frowns upon such practices, and the perpetrators, when discovered, are generally stripped of rank and ability, and expelled.

'Can I?' queried Moonblood, then her face fell. 'My parents would never allow it.'

'I would not be so certain of that.'

'I have tried so hard to learn.'

'You have? With what result?'

Moonblood hesitated, looking away. 'None. It is too hard.'

I smiled. She mused for a moment, then, beseechingly: 'Will you not perform a single trick for me?'

'Perhaps later. Now is not an appropriate moment.'

I changed the subject, and enquired about the brooch she was wearing, the same she had worn when we had met the previous evening. I thought if I could acquire others like it at reasonable cost, they would fetch a good price elsewhere. 'I have never seen its like. It looks particularly delicate. Finely made, but a most unusual design.'

'Yes, it is unusual.'

'Might I ask where it came from?'

Moonblood glanced away. 'It was a present . . . from a friend.'

She did not seem to wish to enlarge on the subject. The dance ended. I bowed and escorted Moonblood from the floor.

Lord Flarefist's voice cut through the hubbub. He had climbed onto a table again. His hands were raised for quiet, his cheeks florid. His knees were slightly bent and servants stood by the table, one on either side, ready to grab him should he inadvertently step off the edge.

'Friends,' called the old lord of Ravenscrag. 'Many of you have only quite recently arrived, and missed the presentation of my son and heir, Redlock. Be not disappointed! I have commanded this minute that he be brought back down for you all to see.'

He slewed around to face the open portal which led upstairs, alongside which I happened to be standing with Moonblood. At that moment I caught a strange sound from somewhere overhead. It was a distant, muffled shriek.

Seconds later it came again, closer this time, on the stairs. A high-pitched cry, then loud, hysterical sobs. A woman, wailing in distress.

I turned to the door. There were footsteps on the stone stairs, rushing to descend. A moment later the wet-nurse, Blonna, rushed into the hall. Her face was streaked with tears, her hands at her head, hair all wild.

She threw herself onto the flags before Lady Sheerquine and Lord Flarefist, who was being helped from the table.

'What is this, maid?' demanded Flarefist. 'Whatever is the matter with you?'

'He's gone! He's gone!' wailed Blonna.

'Who's gone? What?'

'Your son, sir! My lady! Redlock! He's gone from his crib!'

'Well, he can't have gone far, he's a baby!' Lord Flarefist clambered down from the table and began to advance towards the stairway.

Lady Sheerquine sat glued to her seat, her body rigid. The blood drained from her face as she stared at the prostrate nurse. Blonna, raising herself onto one elbow, stretched out an arm towards Flarefist's retreating back.

'There's something else, sir! In the crib! It's not him! Not Redlock.'

Flarefist turned back in irritation. Then suddenly his face changed as the full import of Blonna's words struck him. He swayed, then lunged again for the stairs.

There was a surge towards the portal. Moonblood slipped through behind her father, Irnbold the astrologer close on her heels. In the confusion I managed to follow. We climbed the stairs, passed along a short corridor, entered another. Past doors on right and left, then into the chamber which was the baby's nursery.

To one side of the nursery stood a wooden crib. Flarefist halted beside it, staring down at the striped blanket which had covered his child. The blanket moved, and from underneath it came a snuffling, gurgling sound.

I peered over Irnbold's shoulder as Lord Flarefist leaned over the crib and reached inside, hesitant now. His hand shook as he took hold of a corner of the blanket and drew it back.

Lord Flarefist stiffened. He gave a strange, strangled gasp.

Upon the little mattress a baby lay, stretching its tiny limbs into the air.

But it was not Redlock, heir of Ravenscrag and all its properties.

Nor was it human.

Chapter Six

It was Cametta who alerted me to my wisest course, which was to get out of Ravenscrag immediately.

She did so inadvertently. I had escorted her back to her home while her husband Darean Lonsord remained at the castle, endeavouring to restore order. Cametta was fraught from the sudden dreadful turn the evening had taken, and we did not make love. I simply acted as gracious chaperon, quite publicly, so that none would have cause for suspicion.

Cametta talked almost ceaselessly on the short journey from the castle. She talked about this and about that, circumnavigating the awful scene we had witnessed, then leaping suddenly to address it, disbelieving, distraught. I felt I should not leave her immediately, and so accompanied her indoors and sat with her in her parlour.

Cametta's maid, Lani, her face puffy with sleep, brought aquavit. The heat of the day had passed and the night had grown a touch chill with a breeze springing up from the north. Lani brought a shawl for her mistress.

Cametta sat hunched in her chair, clutching a handkerchief in one hand, the fingers of the other clasping her goblet. She was pale and trembled, her eyes red with tears. I had deliberately left the parlour door open so that we would be visible to those few members of the household staff who were not in bed, so I could offer her nothing more than words as comfort. Her teeth chattered and the muscles of her jaw and throat were visibly taut as she tried to still them.

'Sip your drink. It will help you relax,' I urged her gently.

Cametta raised her goblet and took a large gulp. She gasped at the sudden fire in her mouth and throat.

'Dinbig, what *was* it?' she implored me for the dozenth time.

I had no answer. I stared into the empty hearth before me. 'I have never seen its like.'

Cametta closed her eyes and shook her head, trying to shake off the image that filled her mind. She gave a small cry; her hand went to her mouth and she gagged.

I called Lani. She came immediately and knelt beside her mistress, taking her hand. 'There, there now. Calm yourself, ma'am. Here, have another sip. That's it. That's the way.'

She turned her eyes to me, diffident but questioning and concerned. 'Perhaps I should send for the physician, sir.'

'I don't think that will be necessary, Lani. Mistress Cametta has witnessed a rather distressing event – as have we all. But I think she will be all right in due course. Perhaps a little warm milk might help.'

'Yes, sir.' Lani rose and left the room.

The milk was an afterthought on my part, but it served to give Cametta and I a few moments alone – more than enough time to conjure a calming rapture. I don't know why I'd not thought of it earlier. I suppose I had not understood how affected Cametta was.

The effect was near-instantaneous. Cametta let out a long sigh, and her body visibly slackened as the muscles released their spasm. She slumped back in her chair, and briefly closed her eyes. I watched with some relief. I had been a little concerned that the rapture might have proved too powerful; I had only ever used it on one other occasion, and that was to calm a spooked mare.

Opening her eyes after a few moments Cametta lifted her goblet to her lips. 'That's better. I'm sorry, you must think me feeble.'

'Not at all. It's quite understandable.'

She frowned. 'I'm still . . .'

'I know. It's hard to take in.'

Lani returned with a small jug of warm milk and a mug. She poured the milk and passed the mug to Cametta.

'It's all right, Lani. I'm better now. You needn't stay.'

Lani withdrew. Cametta looked at me and through me. Her expression grew troubled and tears started at her eyes. 'The baby. Poor Redlock. What has happened to him?'

I tugged at my whiskers. 'It is a mystery. For all we know that may be he.'

She fixed me with a look of horror. 'That monstrosity? Oh, by the spirits, how?'

'I don't know. But it would appear that the child has either been abducted by persons or forces unknown, and that thing substituted in his place, or he has been magically transformed into . . . into whatever it is that lies there in his crib.'

'But why? What is behind it?'

I gave an impotent shrug. We had been through this already, many times, on the way here, and there were no answers.

Cametta stared blankly. 'We know almost nothing of magic here, Dinbig. I think when Lord Flarefist regains his senses he may want to ask your advice. Do you think you can be of service?'

These were the words that brought home to me my position. I had not considered it before. I experienced a sudden quiver of unease in the pit of my gut.

Yes, Lord Flarefist and Lady Sheerquine were all too aware of my unique status here. They might well choose to employ my services in the unravelling of this mystery. I wanted no part of it. This was not my affair. Who knew how long I might be held up in its investigation? What perils might I be exposing myself to should I become involved? And if I failed to solve the mystery, what then? Emotions were running very high. I had seen less than an hour ago what Flarefist was capable of when his temper got the better of him. No, this was no place for me.

And another thought came. If Flarefist suspected magic – and in the circumstances, not to think that way would be obtuse – then might he not also suspect me?

The danger to myself was perhaps more immediate than I had first thought.

I drained my goblet and rose from my chair, taking Cametta's hand. 'I do not know if I can be of help. We shall see what transpires. Now I should leave.'

She glanced behind to check that we were alone, then whispered, 'When will I see you again?'

'Soon. For now, try to sleep. There's nothing you can do at present.'

I signalled to Lani, who hovered in the hall outside.

I bowed, touching my lips to Cametta's cold fingers, and took my leave.

I went straightaway back to the warehouse where my goods were stored. The night was close, utterly black. Far away overhead the galaxies hung in infinity, clouds of milk-white stars cast across the unseeable, moonless sky. On Ravenscrag's streets small lamps were isolated spheres of brightness, casting scarcely any light. I carried a lantern and my footsteps echoed eerily in the silent streets.

I took some satisfaction in finding that the two men I had assigned as guards at the warehouse were awake. 'Rouse the others,' I commanded them. 'Pack everything into the wagons. We are leaving at first light.'

I would have left immediately but the town gates were barred until morning. I went back to my chamber at the Blue Raven.

I lay in bed, my mind turning over the events at Castle Ravenscrag.

Upon setting eyes on the creature that occupied his son's crib, Lord Flarefist had frozen, then staggered back as though struck by a physical blow. Recovering, he'd stared in shock for some moments more, then looked up. His eyes passed around the chamber, but he seemed dazed, hardly seeing us. Then, as if with sudden purpose, he strode from the nursery.

Gasps of shock, exclamations of horror and disgust as people looked in at the thing that lay exposed in the crib. A lady fell in a faint to the floor. Another had to be helped from the chamber. Then I became aware that something had changed.

I looked up from the crib. All eyes had moved to the threshold where Lady Sheerquine now stood. She was ashen-faced, her eyes fixed rigidly on the cradle at the side of the room. She gripped the jamb of the door with both hands.

Silence descended. Lady Sheerquine started forward into the crowded chamber. Her movements were stiff, as though her limbs were made of wood. A maid offered support. Lady Sheerquine disdained her with a queer, harsh sound from somewhere deep in her throat, and a twitch of her arm, her eyes never leaving the crib.

Lady Sheerquine approached the cradle and stood over it. One hand upon her chest she reached in and lifted aside the blanket that had again partially obscured the occupant. She stared transfixed, her mouth falling open, then drew back, uttering in a sibilant rasp a single word: '*Abomination!*'

Lady Sheerquine's fingers gripped the corner of a nearby table, the knuckles turned white. The arm wavered. Her face was ghastly, wholly drained of blood. Her knees buckled and gave way. Lord Condark, who stood beside her, moved quickly, as did her maid. They caught Sheerquine before she hit the floor.

At that moment the air was split by a deafening roar.

I spun around, startled. Lord Flarefist had reappeared in the doorway, his face apoplectic. In his hands he wielded a bright sword. He threw himself across the room, hefting the weapon, bellowing with rage, and swung at old Irnbold the astrologer.

'*Deceiver!*' he roared.

Irnbold attempted to throw himself backwards, but he was not quick. He would have died, his blood spattering the nursery walls, had not Lord Flarefist collided with a guest. The blade missed the astrologer by a hair. It clanged into the wall, chipping stone and drawing sparks.

Irnbold knew better than to stay and plead. He fled. Lord Flarefist wheeled and made off in bellowing pursuit.

Pandemonium, then! None was sure how to respond. I cast my eyes around for the farseer, Elmag. I thought she might be the next focus of Lord Flarefist's wrath. But Elmag had had the foresight to make herself scarce.

I moved to Cametta who was leaning against a wall, her hand to her brow. I took her arm. Darean Lonsord appeared with two men-at-arms.

'Clear the room!'

A momentary disquiet as he approached us, but he merely glanced at us and would have brushed by. I stopped him. 'Your wife is distressed. She should be taken home.'

51

He quickly appraised Cametta, and nodded. 'I cannot leave. Would you take her? I apologise, it is inconvenient, but in the circumstances . . .'

'It is no inconvenience. Think nothing of it.'

I helped Cametta from the nursery. Lady Sheerquine lay upon the floor, her head supported by a pillow. She was reviving under the ministrations of her maid, who passed spirits of salts beneath her nose. Darean Lonsord knelt at her shoulder.

'My lady, we should search the castle for your son.'

'Yes, search.' Sheerquine's reply was vague. Blonna the wet-nurse sat alone in a corner, weeping.

And the child . . .

As I lay there in my chamber in the Blue Raven, I saw again the monstrous thing that had occupied Redlock's cot. It *was* a babe, I would say that much. But beyond that simple fact my familiarity with it ended. I was mystified. A babe of what kind of creature? Its skin was putty grey over most of its surface, with darker mottling here and there. It was covered with glistening droplets of moisture. Sparse hairs sprouted over lank grey limbs and back. A raised mass of loose flaps of leathery flesh ran from its crown down the length of its short spine to the tip of its tail. Yes, it had a tail, long and naked, which writhed with a peculiar, mindless zest.

Its hands and feet were long, each with four clawed fingers or toes. Its belly was large and bulbous, paler-skinned than the rest of it. A shrivelled red umbilical cord extended from the navel.

It had a squashed goblinesque head, almost as large as the body, which was squat and froglike. It had a short, broad, blunt snout, vaguely like that of a cat. When its mouth opened I saw glistening bright pink gums, a small purplish tongue, and two rows of sharp yellow fangs. It dribbled a whitish fluid into the crib. Its ears were large and floppy, its brow and most of its face puckered into countless folds and wrinkles of damp skin. Two little dark bumps protruded above the ears, like the nubs of horns.

The mattress upon which the baby lay was stained with brownish slime, and a sour, noxious odour rose from the creature. I thought at first that it might be blind, for its eyes were closed. But as I stared one eye blinked suddenly open. The iris was yellow, the pupil a dark oval slit, reflecting red. It was perhaps then that I had my greatest shock, for undoubtedly the creature was helpless, but when that yellow eye opened it focused with deliberation on me, and its gaze was disquieting. It seemed to appraise me, intelligently but with calculating malevolence, and its tiny hands reached up and clawed the air as though striving to rip the flesh from my face. The creature was alien, but it was not some mindless beast.

I don't believe I slept that night. Gradually, after what seemed like many hours, I became aware of a dim greyness dispelling the darkness in my room, and knew that dawn approached. Haggard, I rose and bathed. Downstairs I settled my account with a bleary-eyed landlord and made for the warehouse.

My wagons were assembled, laden mostly with the very goods they had brought here. I'd had time to complete only a very few transactions the previous day, and though I'd gained assurances of others, neither goods nor money had yet changed hands. Nor had I had an opportunity to purchase Pansurian goods for sale abroad.

Aboard the front wagon I growled an order to Bris, and we set off.

Ravenscrag was almost lifeless at this time. The sun had yet to haul itself above the peaks, its light a pearly wash tinged with citron low in the east, partially illuminating a near cloudless sky. I glanced up at the beetling walls of the old castle as we passed beneath.

Minutes later we arrived at the town wall; the gate was closed.

I hailed the sentry. 'At what hour is the gate unbarred?'

'Normally at sunrise.'

'The sun is all but risen now. Are we to be kept waiting while it ambles into full view?'

'Special circumstances today, sir.'

I'd feared it. 'What circumstances?'

'My orders are that the gate is to be kept barred all day. No one is to leave the town.'

He spoke with a certain pleasure, indicative of his willingness to partake of this departure from dull routine. There were other soldiers on the ramparts, more than was usual. They were watchful, observing our exchange.

The gatehouse door opened and Darean Lonsord stepped outside. Two guards came at his back. He walked to my wagon with an easy swagger and stood with his feet firmly apart and hands upon his hips.

'Master Dinbig, good morrow, sir. I had expected to find you at the Blue Raven but the landlord told me you had already left.'

He affected politeness but there was insolence in his smile, and his eyes drilled. He was unshaven and his skin was drawn; I assumed he'd been up all night.

'Captain Lonsord, I'm on the point of departure, yet your sentry informs me that the gate is to be kept barred.'

'Such a hurry to be away? I had no idea you planned to leave so soon. Surely you've not yet made a healthy profit of us?'

I stared back at him. 'Is this true, that I cannot leave?'

'It's so, until further notice. The rule applies to all. You will understand, I'm sure, being acquainted with the circumstances.'

'It is highly inconvenient.'

Darean Lonsord merely spread his hand with a fulsome expression of sympathy. 'My orders are to escort you to the castle, sir.'

'To what end?'

'Lord Flarefist wishes to speak with you. Your wagons may return to the market-place.'

There was plainly nothing to be gained from further argument. I spoke to Bris. 'You and Cloverron accompany me. Tell the others to return, but not to unload the wagons.'

'Your men may accompany you,' said Darean Lonsord. 'But I must insist they first surrender their weapons to me. And yours too, if you would.'

'Am I under arrest then, Captain?'

'Not at all. You are Lord Flarefist's guest.'

I was effectively trapped. I nodded to Bris and Cloverron to hand over their weapons, then unbuckled my light sword and knives. I carried a concealed dagger strapped above my ankle, which I considered keeping, then thought better of it. To be searched and found carrying it would not help my situation. However, a short length of garrotting wire, sewn into my belt where none but the most meticulous searcher would discover it, I felt I might safely hang on to. I did not favour its use, but on more than one occasion in the past it had saved me in difficult circumstances. As a last resort it should not be dismissed, and I felt happier knowing it was there.

I climbed down from the wagon.

Chapter Seven

Darean Lonsord took me to a chamber in the private apartments
of Castle Ravenscrag, on the second storey of the ancient central
keep. Lead-latticed windows, lavender with age, filtered a modicum of early morning light into the chamber. Through a gauze of
smoky cobwebs, insect husks and general grime one could look
out over the cluttered rooftops of the town.

In the middle of the room stood a long table set with three silver
candlesticks, each of which held a pair of fat bayberrywax candles.
Lord Flarefist and Lady Sheerquine sat at this table, one at each
end.

Lord Flarefist was hunched in his seat, his hair all dishevelled,
his gaze inward and bereft. He did not look up at my entrance. His
wife, by contrast, sat stiff and upright, spine perfectly erect. Her
face was a marble mask, revealing no emotion. Her hands rested
upon her thighs beneath the table. Her copper hair was swept back
from her face and bound severely into a tight bun at the rear of her
crown.

It was Sheerquine who spoke first, dismissing Darean Lonsord.
Then she addressed me, though like her husband she seemed
unable or unwilling to look in my direction.

'Please come forward, Master Merchant. Be seated. Our conversation is to be informal.'

I took the only other chair present, positioned halfway along the table. Lady Sheerquine said, 'Do not make the mistake of taking us for fools.'

'My lady, I – '

'You consider Pansur a backward nation populated by churls and bumpkins.'

'Not at all. I – '

'It is a general view, we are aware. You are not on trial for calumny. But I would caution you. We perhaps lack some of the sophistications and advances of Kemahamek, or certain nations in the south. But to my knowledge your own country, Khimmur, can hardly be said to be on the same cultural level as these. We know it to be a nation of semi-barbarians, torn by internal strife. I do not think it can justifiably consider itself so superior.'

'Lady Sheerquine, I would not say – '

'Good, then that's settled.' She turned her pale green eyes to me for the first time. 'Now I would address another matter. During the course of this interview do not think to influence myself or Lord Flarefist with magic. We lack your knowledge and skills of application, it is true. But there are those among us who are quite familiar with the aura of magic, even in its most subtle forms. Make no mistake, should you attempt to alter our minds with spells you will be found out, and it will not be to your advantage.'

Her expression was magisterial, her body still motionless and erect. I wondered at the tumult of emotion she contained behind that impassable exterior. She was in her forties and would bear no more children. She had been married to Flarefist for many years, and in her efforts to produce an heir had given birth to three stillborn infants since Moonblood. A fourth had survived birth, but lived only a few days, so I understood. I doubted that old Flarefist, even in the unlikely event that he should choose to take another spouse, would ever sire another son. Our shared knowledge of the gravity of their situation hung between us, weighting the air.

As for magic, she might have been bluffing. I sensed a testing of wills here. It is true, there are those who are sensitive to the presence of magic. Most are practitioners in their own right. Here

57

in Pansur it was possible that magical ability was latent in a small minority of folk. Such persons might well be able to detect the presence or use of magic, even though unable to use it themselves.

Was Lady Sheerquine one of these? The implication was definite; it would be unwise to discount the possibility. Or might others be concealed in some secret spyhole in the chamber, watching, listening? I resisted the urge to cast my eyes around.

I wondered to what extent my abilities were overestimated in Ravenscrag. I was a First Realm Initiate of the *Zan-Chassin*, which does not in itself confer awesome powers. My first ally, my Custodian, Yo, had not yet been given physical form.

Zan-Chassin magic is greatly misunderstood, and many are wary of us for abilities they only imagine us to possess. Our greatest strengths lie in our ability to take leave of our body and fly free of the corporeal world, to interact with the spirit denizens of the realms beyond corporeality, and to commune with the spirits of our dead ancestors. Physically speaking, our highest adepts, though formidable and frighteningly talented in comparison to the average person, do not have the powers that many believe. Such misapprehensions are not without value, of course, and we make no attempt to discourage them.

My own environment-altering abilities were not particularly impressive. No one need have worried that I might bring the walls of Ravenscrag crashing down upon their heads. The rivers would not flood – at least, not by my doing – the mountains would not spout fire. No plague of boils or cankers would be visited upon the people of Ravenscrag as a result of any mistreatment I might suffer here. They could lie safe in their beds at night, more or less free from intrusions by vengeful demons, if they but knew it. And I hoped they didn't.

As for influencing minds, it was probable that I could do that. I sensed that I might walk free from this chamber, leaving Lord Flarefist and Lady Sheerquine giggling like loons. But what if outside Darean Lonsord waited with a dozen guards? I could hardly overpower them all, and any effects I might create would be shortlasting. The casting of raptures, though it becomes second-nature, none the less requires unusual concentration. It is taxing, and quickly depletes mental energies. I would at some point find myself unable to cast more.

Conceivably I might even walk out of the castle and town gate, but my wagons, goods and men would be left behind. And I would be alone in the woods, hunted and probably caught eventually, or destined for the belly of some dire monster.

It seemed wiser to remain here, at least until I'd learned the lie of the land.

'Have no fear on that score,' I assured Lady Sheerquine. 'I am not here with ill-intent; nor would I abuse your hospitality.'

She raised a sceptical eyebrow, but nodded infinitesimally.

'However, I should point out that I have been brought here – if not precisely against my will, then at least it is fair to say with little choice in the matter.'

'We merely requested your presence, Master Merchant. If Captain Lonsord was a trifle heavy-handed in the prosecution of his orders, we apologise. He lacks a certain subtlety in his manner, I know. But he is after all a soldier, not a diplomat.'

'Quite so. It was, however, made plain to me that I was not to be allowed to leave the town.'

'And surely no explanation is required? You know the circumstances!'

'I do. But what is my part here?'

'You cannot guess?'

Lord Flarefist spoke now, before I could reply. His voice was distant, tremulous, tragic. 'My son has gone, Bigdin.'

I looked at him. He had turned tearful eyes to mine. In his face there was no trace of the impulsive fury of last night. He looked feeble and drained. In a single night he had aged a decade. I faced a broken old man.

'You have my deepest sympathies, my lord. I know how much your son meant to you.'

'He's gone.'

His tears streamed freely, without shame. I could hardly bear to look at him, such a forlorn figure he made. Lady Sheerquine sat as before, her eyes fixed upon a spot above her husband's head. Again I sensed the colossal denial, the terrible struggle within her. She was, in her own way, magnificent.

'We called you here to ask for your help, Master Dinbig.' Sheerquine's voice wavered slightly, betraying her. Lord Flarefist had pulled a handkerchief from his sleeve and was blowing his nose.

'My help? In what manner can I help you?'

'I think you know the answer to that already. You possess unique abilities, at least in comparison to us of Pansur. I have made an academic study of your *Zan-Chassin* craft. I know that you excel in information-gathering skills. We would ask you to employ those skills to aid us in finding out what has happened to Redlock, our son.'

'Lady Sheerquine, my talents are – '

'The choice is yours, Master Dinbig.' There was a sudden harsh emphasis in her tone. 'You will be rewarded, should you accept. We are not wealthy, but we can guarantee you favourable trade concessions here in Ravenscrag and elsewhere in Pansur. Perhaps some gold might be added as a further incentive.'

'I see.' In normal circumstances I would have demanded a high price for my services, but I suspected that there existed little scope for negotiation in this instance. Moreover, I was conscious of old Flarefist hanging on my words. I knew already that I could not walk from this chamber and leave him without hope. I was disconcerted and deeply moved by his sudden decline. But before I said anything more I wanted to discover precisely what my position was. 'And if I refuse?'

Sheerquine's pale green eyes returned to hold me in their gaze. She said, quietly, 'Your wagons and goods will be impounded. We have not quite decided further than that.'

'That is unlawful. I have committed no crime.'

'What about kidnapping, or conspiracy to kidnap?'

'What? You know that is not true.'

'We know nothing, Master Dinbig. That is precisely our dilemma.'

'I should, then, remind you that I am an emissary of my country. My king would not look kindly upon such an act.'

'Khimmur is far away, Master Dinbig.' Sheerquine stared at me in silence for some moments, then added, 'However, we have considered the position, and it is true, we would prefer to avoid possible repercussions. An alternative, then, is that you be permitted to escape. Your subsequent death in the forest would be an unfortunate accident.'

'In the circumstances it would look suspicious.'

'Yes, but does King Gastlan value you so highly that he would dispatch an army here merely out of suspicion? Can he even do so without placing himself at risk from his own intransigent warlords? Would his forces be granted passage through foreign lands? And what of the colossal expense? Are you truly worth so much to your country, Master Merchant?'

I said nothing.

'There is another alternative,' continued Lady Sheerquine. 'It is possibly the most reasonable.'

'I am intrigued to hear of it.'

'It is simply this: some knowing person might decide to have a quiet word in the ear of Captain Lonsord. He would undoubtedly react with customary fire when he learns what there is to be learned.'

They knew! Cametta and I . . . *our secret was no secret!*

Sheerquine allowed a trace of a smile to lighten her features as faint she watched my face. 'Regrettably we would be unable to prevent him responding as any cuckold might be expected to do. Your body would be returned to Khimmur, with a letter of explanation and deepest regret. I think King Gastlan will understand, when he learns of the full circumstances. He would surely acknowledge the inappropriateness of retaliatory action. The greater tragedy, of course, is that Captain Lonsord, once informed, would almost certainly turn his wrath upon his wife as well as yourself. It would be a pity. I like Cametta. But . . . ' She gave a small shrug.

I don't know whether Lord Flarefist had been listening to all this, but he chose this moment to raise himself shakily from his seat and lean fully along the table. He extended his thin arms and grasped my hand with both of his. He looked beseechingly into my eyes. 'Will you help me, Dinsbin? Will you bring back my son?'

'Lord Flarefist, I can offer no guarantees.'

'But you will try?'

'Your incentives are persuasive. I will do whatever I can.'

'Good man! Good man!' He settled back into his seat, dabbing at his eyes, but smiling. 'I said to Sheerquine that you are a good and honest fellow. I told her we could rely upon you. I know a good man when I meet one.'

'There are conditions,' I said.

'We will hear them,' replied Sheerquine imperiously.

'I know nothing, at present, of what has happened.'

'You know as much as we.'

'Perhaps. But I must insist upon the freedom to interview whomsoever I wish, whenever I wish, yourselves included. This may prove to be a most difficult task and I confess I do not know where to begin.'

'Granted.'

'Is Irnbold still living?'

'He managed to secure himself in his apartments, and so saved himself from Lord Flarefist's initial wrath. He has not yet emerged, but he will be available whenever you wish to speak to him.'

'And Lord Flarefist slew no others?'

'None, though one or two he injured, and others he clapped in irons.'

'They must be allowed to live.'

'Of course.'

'Are any of the injuries serious?'

'No. They have all been attended to by Markin, the physician.'

I thought I detected something evasive in her manner. I asked, 'Who are these injured persons?'

Lady Sheerquine made a dismissive movement of her head. 'The names escape me.'

I regarded her for a moment, unhappy with her reply. I would have left it, though, but she seemed to relent, saying, 'Lord Condark did receive a glancing blow.'

'Lord Condark?' I looked from her to Flarefist and back again.

'It was nothing.'

'I am most relieved to hear it. Yet, even though his injury may be slight, can the same be said for the consequences that may follow?'

Lady Sheerquine made no reply. Her husband showed no interest in the topic, seeming to be absorbed in his dejection. I let the subject drop, saying, 'I must be permitted to go wheresoever I wish.'

'You will have the freedom of Ravenscrag, though your movements will be monitored. Don't think to run – we will know and we will catch you. As I said earlier, you should not underestimate us.'

'If I doubted it earlier I do so no more, Lady Sheerquine. And if I wish to leave Ravenscrag?'

'You will apply to us directly. And you have been allocated rooms here. Your belongings are being brought from your wagons.'

'Then, if you will allow me, I will go and apply myself immediately to the task. Ah, one other question.'

'Speak.'

I spoke in a low voice, in deference to Lord Flarefist. 'In all honesty, I am not entirely optimistic of success in this venture. What, then, if I fail?'

Lady Sheerquine allowed herself a moment's contemplation. 'Let us deal with each contingency as we meet it, shall we?'

I rose from my seat. Sheerquine spoke again, and this time her tone was softer. 'Master Dinbig, please understand what this has done to us. We act only out of desperation. We want our son.'

She almost smiled, and I found myself at a loss to reply.

'A servant will show you to your chambers.'

'And you can keep the silver,' said Lord Flarefist, beaming through tears.

'What silver, sir?'

'You know, the silver you took last time you were here.'

'No, no, Flarefist, this isn't the fellow,' interposed Lady Sheerquine quickly.

'It isn't?'

'No. That was Linvon, or some such name. *He* took the silver.'

'And this is not he?'

'No. This is the Khimmurian sorcerer and merchant, Master Dinbig. He's the fellow we discussed during the night.'

Flarefist frowned. 'But he's going to find Redlock?'

'Yes. That has just been settled.'

'Oh, good.' He looked at me again. 'But you are a juggler, aren't you?'

'No, sir. That I believe was Linvon also.'

'And it was he who took the silver, not you?'

'So I understand.'

Flarefist nodded and pursed his lips. 'The bastard!'

I bowed and withdrew.

In the corridor outside I was approached by Hectal, Lady Sheerquine's twin brother. He came from a side door, and sidled up beside me.

'Fooled you, then?'

'Who?'

'My sister, and the remnant.'

'Fooled me in what way?'

'They've got you working for them. Pretending they don't know.'

'Don't know what?'

Hectal gawked up at me. He was a small, ugly, lumpy man; a halfwit. His face was contorted into an enigmatic expression of pained mockery. It resembled his sister's, but in an unsettling, caricaturistic way. He grinned inanely, shifting along beside me with a listing gait, his body twisted and bow-legged, giving the impression of a hunched back. He raised a bony finger to one cheekbone and drew down the lower eyelid. 'Don't know what's happened. To the little one.'

'Redlock? Do they know?'

Hectal cackled gleefully.

'How do you know I'm working for them?' I asked.

'You have to.'

'I see.'

'You don't know anything, do you?'

That at least was true.

'Well, I'll tell you a something. You will not understand her fate, nor know the blood.'

'Whose fate? What blood?'

Hectal cackled again, loud and staccato.

'Now I'll tell you some somethings that are true and some somethings that are not true.'

'And how will I know which are which?'

This delighted him. 'You won't. You won't. Listen, this is true if you believe me: Condark knows.'

'Ulen Condark? He knows what?'

'Hee-hee-hee!' giggled Hectal. 'Nothing! Ha-ha-ha! Nothing! He's a fool! Like me! Now, here's a something else. Condark's troops will come here.'

'Why so?'

'Because of what's happened. Flarefist, see. Gone too far.'

Hectal scratched vigorously beneath his armpit, ducking his balding head into his shirt, searching for the culprit that caused his itch.

64

'Tell me,' I said. 'Do you know anything that might actually be useful to me – that is, useful to your sister in her desperation?'

Hectal withdrew something too small to see from his armpit. He held it close to his eyes between finger and thumb, inspecting it with simian intensity. He put it in his mouth and chewed rapidly. 'Oh yes, I do, I do. Here's another something for you: the baby isn't dead. And here's another something: the baby is going to smell good when it's cooked.'

'I see. Well, thank you, Hectal. You've been a great help.'

'I have another something. This is a good one.'

'What is it?'

'I see things,' said Hectal, touching his eye again. 'I hear. I watch. I know.'

'Hmm. And is that all?'

He touched my arm. 'A something for you: tonight is the last of darkmoon.'

'I know that.'

'Hmm. But there will be another before you know it. Shadownight comes.'

I halted. 'Shadownight?' I queried, but he gave a queer laugh and was gone, darting away down a passage which led I knew not where.

Chapter Eight

My new chambers were adequate if a touch austere. They were set high in a round tower in Castle Ravenscrag's west wing. Through small windows I was able to look out over walls and between towers, onto the forests and heights. The chambers were accessed via a single, narrow set of winding stairs.

I was assigned a servant, named Radyerd, whose duties I naturally assumed included reporting on me. At my request Radyerd brought me a breakfast of bacon and bread, honey cakes, dried apricots and ale.

The sun had risen and a shaft of bright light penetrated my room. I stood at the window, deep in thought. In the distance the trees rippled under a strong, warm breeze. The *rap* of marching feet came from below. By craning my neck I was able to look down onto the parade-ground one hundred feet beneath me. There a squad of soldiers paced half-heartedly through drill. A couple of labourers piled wood-faggots and brush in the middle of a nearby courtyard set away from the main thoroughfares of the castle. I decided I would begin my investigation by speaking to Blonna, the wet-nurse.

Blonna, as far as I was aware, had been the last person to see

Redlock. His abduction – or transformation – had taken place while he was in her charge. Informing Radyerd of my intention, I descended from my tower.

Brief enquiries revealed that Blonna had not been clapped in irons. She was however confined to her room, which was adjacent to Redlock's nursery. As I made my way there I remarked upon the mood of the castle. The expectation of the preceding days was gone, as was the gaiety of the previous evening. Servants passed by with eyes downcast, hurrying tensely about their duties. Guards were apparent in some number. I saw no sign of Ravenscrag's guests.

Outside Blonna's door an elderly sentry propped up the wall. He barely glanced up as I approached. Apparently word of my new station had been passed, for when I announced myself and my purpose he produced an iron key-ring from his belt and dutifully unlocked Blonna's door.

Blonna's chamber was a tiny cell, barely large enough to contain its sparse furnishings of pallet, small table and wooden bench. Still, she had probably counted herself fortunate to have her own room at all. The majority of the castle menials bedded where they worked, on floor, bench or table, in kitchens, sculleries or stables.

Blonna was seated on the bench beneath the window. At her feet was a small wooden tray containing a bowl of porridge and a mug of water, both untouched. She looked up as I entered, her eyes red, face pale and streaked with dry tearmarks. She was obviously distraught, and fearful at the sight of me.

'Blonna,' I said softly, 'I am Ronbas Dinbig. I have been asked by Lord Flarefist and Lady Sheerquine to make enquiries into the dreadful circumstances of last night. I would like to ask you a few questions.'

Blonna fell to her knees, weeping. 'Oh, sir, what's going to happen to me? I didn't do nothing! It wasn't my fault.'

'Calm yourself, Blonna.' I bent and put my hands to her arms, helped her back onto the bench.

'Don't let his lordship kill me, sir. Please.'

'He won't kill you, Blonna. Your master is inclined to emotion, as you are aware. In such grave and distressing circumstances it is not difficult to understand his mood last night. But he is in a more rational frame of mind now, and simply wants to get to the bottom of this mystery.'

'But I can't help you, sir. I don't know what happened. I just went out of the nursery for a minute, and when I came back poor Redlock was gone and that thing was in his place.'

'Ah! Already you *have* helped me, Blonna. You have just provided me with my first clue. You went out of the chamber, you say, and left Redlock alone.'

'Oh, sir, I didn't mean to. I didn't!'

'Of course you didn't. I am not faulting your conduct. But why did you go out of the nursery?'

The sound of hammering came from some short distance away outside. Blonna flinched. 'I had to get some water. The bowl was empty and little Redlock was dirty. I needed to clean him up before he could go downstairs again.'

'So you went out to fetch water. And are you sure Redlock was in the nursery at the moment prior to your leaving?'

'Oh yes, sir. I'd been holding him. Then I put him in his crib. He was fast asleep. I tried to tell Lord Flarefist last night but he wouldn't listen. He was mad, sir! I thought he was going to kill me!'

The hammering stopped. Beyond the wall, somewhere below us outside, a faint, gruff voice called something incoherent. Blonna stared at me with round, terrified eyes. 'Don't let them burn me, sir. Please don't!'

'Burn you, Blonna? No one's going to burn you.'

'But they're making a fire, sir. When Lymilla, one of the servants, brought my breakfast she said they're going to burn the little creature. Don't let them do it to me, sir! Please!'

'Burn it?'

The poor girl began to weep hysterically. 'I don't want to die! I was doing my best!'

'Excuse me, Blonna.' I stepped quickly up onto the bench so that I might look out through the window. What I saw made me stiffen with alarm.

I was on the first level, some thirty feet above the ground. Off to my left some distance away was the small courtyard in which I had earlier observed servants stacking faggots. Now the purpose of their exercise was plain.

The wood formed a neat bonfire, ready to be touched with a flame. On its crest was the nursery crib which had been Redlock's, and which latterly had contained the creature that had taken his place. The crib was empty. A ladder rested against the piled wood.

Figures stood around the unlit fire. Most of them had their backs to me. Some were Ravenscrag guards, three or four of whom held blazing firebrands. The majority of the others were the guests who had been at the banquet last night.

Alongside the bonfire a makeshift wooden platform had been constructed – hence the hammering I'd heard. As I watched Lord Flarefist emerged from somewhere inside the castle, Lady Sheerquine close behind him. They slowly approached the platform and mounted it via four wooden steps at its rear. Flarefist held something in his right hand.

He stood for some moments mute before the bonfire, his head hung low, back bowed. Then he lifted his head and spoke, though I could not hear what he said. He raised his right arm, and I saw quite clearly what it was he held.

Dangling there, struggling, gripped by its ankles, was the little grey-skinned monster that had occupied Redlock's crib the night before. Flarefist gave a signal to the soldiers with the firebrands. There could be no question of his intention.

'*Moban!*'*

I cried out, but the group was a good distance away and the wind blew directly into my face, so that none heard me, or if they did they gave no sign. As Lord Flarefist intoned words I could not hear two soldiers moved to the foot of the ladder, while three others stood close with the firebrands. One man held the ladder steady while the other ascended and removed the crib. He passed it down and his companion took it and held it up directly beneath the monstrous baby helplessly suspended in Flarefist's grip.

Into my mind came Hectal's words: *The baby is going to smell good when it's cooked*!

'This must be stopped!' I leapt down from the bench and dashed out of Blonna's cell. The old sentry outside was too startled to respond. I ran down the passage, down the stairs, into the great banqueting hall where servants were clearing the debris of last night.

*Used in this instance expletively. Moban is the Great Moving Spirit which created all. Moban is considered an omnipotent but indifferent deity. Some cosmogonies hold that, having created Firstworld, Moban then forgot all about it.

'Which way to the courtyard?'

'Which courtyard?'

'Where they're burning the child.'

I was met with blank faces. I raced across the hall and out through the main door. An intersection of passages faced me. I mentally calculated my position in relation to Blonna's cell, and ran to the left. A door loomed before me; I lifted the latch and hurled myself through. I was in a scullery. A startled maid looked up from her work.

'How do I get outside?'

The maid pointed the way I had come. I rushed back into the passage, found another door beneath which pale light filtered. I wrenched it open and ran through, and found myself outside on a patch of walled-in wasteland at the base of a round tower. Two ravens pecked at the ripped carcass of some small creature. To each side, set into the crumbling wall, was an ancient wooden door. But which one would take me in the direction I needed to go?

I hesitated there, struggling to get my bearings. A thin voice came from somewhere overhead. I glanced back, scanned the castle walls. There! Above me, off to the right, Blonna leaned from her little window, pointing frantically.

I ran in the direction she indicated, to the portal in the wall to my left. The hinges had rusted, the door sagged. Its ancient timbers had sunk into the ground. I heaved, dragged. The door groaned and drew back, but not far enough. Desperate, I dropped to my knees, tore away earth and grass, pulled at the door. The rotten timber at its base splintered. I lifted, pulled, managed to open it a little more, and was able to squeeze through.

I stood at the edge of the parade-ground. On the far side was a doorway in the wall which would take me through to the little courtyard where the child was about to be roasted. I sprinted across the parade-ground. Soldiers looked up as I passed, but none pursued me. A trio of ravens lifted off in alarm. I reached the door, breathless, wrenched it open and hurled myself through.

The awful scene met my eyes: thirty or so figures staring at the fire, or at Lord Flarefist who stood on the platform. One hand was raised, fist clenched. In outraged tones he declaimed, '. . . this abomination cast into flames. Let no one think they can destroy

70

Ravenscrag so easily. Your evil plot is ended before it has beg
Behold, the monster burns!'

The crib had been placed back on top of the fire. The tin}
creature lay within, kicking at the air, lashing its tail, emitting a
thin, gargled wail. The ladder had been taken away. Flames had
just been touched to the base.

The tinder and brush caught quickly. The crib was obscured as
thick grey smoke poured skywards. The brushwood crackled.
Flames licked upwards to the stouter wood.

'Stop!' I screamed. A few heads turned. I dashed forward.
'Lord Flarefist, this is madness!'

Flarefist heard me, and now he turned, flushed-faced, glaring as
I rushed towards him.

It was plain he had no intention of heeding me. I ran straight
past the platform. Heedless of the flames I leapt onto the fire. I
threw myself upwards, scrambling over the crackling, burning
wood, reaching for the crib. Wood shifted beneath my feet, came
away in my hands. Blinding smoke choked me, scorching my
lungs. I touched the crib, slipped back, aware of a fearsome heat.

The baby cried out. I hurled myself higher up the mound,
caught the rim of the crib again, yanked hard. The crib tipped. Out
tumbled the squawking infant, and disappeared into the smoke
before I could grab it.

I tore frantically at the wood. A sudden rush of flame and sparks
flared with terrible heat almost directly into my face. A terrible,
agonized scream. The wood above me parted, the whole structure
began to collapse upon itself.

I glimpsed the child, balanced precariously just in front of me.
A branch shifted, the baby sliding, falling into the red flames. I
reached, further than I knew I could reach, and grabbed a tiny
limb, rolled away, slipping, tumbling into murderous heat.

I found myself on my knees on the court stones, hugging the
horrible creature to my breast. My lungs burned, I coughed,
gasping for breath, my eyes streaming. Somebody grabbed me
under the arms and heaved me erect and away from the roaring
heat at my back.

Chapter Nine

'What is the meaning of this outrage?'

Lord Flarefist glared down incensed from his platform. His wife stood behind him, showing no emotion.

'It is not I who have committed outrage,' I rasped.

Flarefist's eyes bulged as the smoke whispered about him. 'Explain yourself, sir!'

I lifted a limp hand. 'A moment.' I could barely speak. I felt numb and disorientated. I was not yet sure whether I'd suffered serious burns. I was dripping wet. Someone had thrown a bucket of water over me. The weird-cub strained against my breast. 'Lord Flarefist, less than an hour ago you assigned me to investigate the mystery of your son's disappearance. Yet now I find you sabotaging the very first efforts I have made.'

'It's no sabotage. We must be rid of this demon's spawn!'

'Then I reject the commission. I cannot help you solve this mystery.'

Lady Sheerquine intervened. 'Are you not a man of honour?'

'I am,' I replied, though I wasn't.

'Then how can you go back upon your word?'

'Lady Sheerquine, earlier you acknowledged that I am a man of

72

certain unusual talents. My talents may be the key to unlocking this mystery – that is, if it can be unlocked. But even I cannot advance when my endeavours are simultaneously undone or undermined by yourselves.'

'Of what possible value is this devil's by-blow?' Lord Flarefist blustered.

'Lord Flarefist, can you not see? This "devil's by-blow", this "demon's spawn" may yet be your son.'

Flarefist's head jerked back. His eyes blazed. 'Disding, you insult me!'

'I intend no insult.' I coughed to clear my burning throat. The smoke blew in twisting wreaths, up and across the platform. 'Lord Flarefist, Lady Sheerquine, you are taking it as proven that Redlock has been abducted, and this creature put in his place. But we do not know this. It may well be that he has been transformed, and that this is he. If that is so, then you have cast your only son and heir into the flames. Had I not intervened you would have lost all hope of ever reversing the spell that has changed him, and he would have died a slow and agonizing death.'

I looked down at the horrid little thing in my arms. It drew back its leathery grey lips and bared its teeth and hissed. Its flesh was surprisingly cold to the touch, and it seemed unharmed by its ordeal.

Lord Flarefist's facial muscles worked convulsively as he struggled with the unpalatable concept.

'But let us consider the other prospect, which is that this creature is not Redlock,' I said. 'Even then, can you not see that it is in your best interests to keep this infant safe? Think! This baby may have parents who, like you, must be grieving for the loss of their precious child. Somewhere beyond these castle walls those terrible progenitors roam, searching. Perhaps even an entire community of the creatures! They may even have Redlock! Do you want them to come here, to find that their beloved child has been cast living into a fire?'

'Grotesque and preposterous!' stammered Flarefist.

'Grotesque indeed. And preposterous, on the face of it. But the facts are what they are.' I addressed Lady Sheerquine. 'My lady, why did you allow this to happen?'

She elevated her chin, allowing her gaze to encompass

something distant and vague beyond the courtyard wall. 'It was his lordship's decision. He is lord and master here.'

I knew from earlier experience that this was not entirely true. Flarefist was lord and master in name, but I had seen that the greater power was wielded by his wife. To Flarefist I said, 'If I am to conduct this enquiry in a proper manner I must insist that you make no more such decisions. The safekeeping of this child is vital to all our interests. If you cannot accommodate this, then I can be of no assistance to you.'

'Captain Lonsord, flog him!' commanded Lord Flarefist. 'A dozen lashes.'

Lonsord stepped forward and put his hand to my upper arm, gripping it tightly to steer me away. I made to protest. Lady Sheerquine spoke quietly into her husband's ear. Lord Flarefist clenched his teeth, then spoke again. 'Not yet, Captain. I have chosen to exercise lenience. He shall be given another chance. But be aware, sir, I will tolerate no further delinquency.'

'Lord Flarefist, I am merely endeavouring to exercise my commission in accordance with your own instructions.'

'You're a scoundrel. I know it and you know it. You will be making a mistake if you attempt to fool with me.'

'Might this child be examined, and if found to be unhurt, taken to some place of safekeeping?' I asked. As I spoke the hideous infant stretched itself in my arms and emitted a strange mewling sound. I glanced down. It opened wide its jaws as if to yawn, and promptly disgorged a jet of thick, warm, foul-smelling yellowish liquid into my face.

I wiped myself with my charred sleeve. Lady Sheerquine gestured to a servant who came forward and gingerly relieved me of the writhing burden and dropped it into a jute sack.

'Are you harmed yourself, Master Dinbig?' Sheerquine enquired.

'I think I have suffered only minor burns.'

'You have lost your hair and eyebrows.'

'If that is my only loss I count myself fortunate.'

'I will send my physician to your rooms.' She turned to leave the platform.

Flarefist, apparently in two minds, made to follow her. He aimed a parting shot at me: 'Remember, I can have you clapped in irons at any time. You will all rot together in my dungeons.'

All?

For the first time I became aware of our audience: Ravenscrag's guests. Pansurians predominated, and the majority of these I assumed to hail from Ravenscrag town or its environs. There were also the notables I had recognized in the market-place, from Kemahamek and Miragoff, plus a few unfamiliar faces. Many of these folk were fettered and manacled; others stood unchained, yet it was plain from the attitude of the castle guards that they were prisoners. I gaped in disbelief. Lord Ulen Condark returned my stare with bland dignity; one arm was bound in bloodied linen. His wife beside him was stiff with impotent anger; their son Ilden sullen and hot-eyed.

I turned back to the old lord of Ravenscrag. 'Lord Flarefist, do you know what you have done?'

Flarefist paused upon the top step of the platform, enveloped for a moment in smoke. The breeze lifted his wispy grey hair. He regarded me as though I were an imbecile. 'I've arrested 'em!' he said.

'On what charge?'

'Charge? What charge do you think, man? One or more of them is behind it! They've taken my son!'

'Do you have evidence of that? Many of these people are foreigners of important status.'

'When I have the identity of the perpetrator the innocent will be free to leave.'

'Lord Flarefist, this action will bring the wrath of nations down upon your head. And what of House Condark? Do you expect its members to sit idly by, knowing that their head and his family are incarcerated in your dungeons?'

Flarefist pointed an angry, trembling finger at Ulen Condark. 'It is House Condark that has engineered this subversion! *He* thought to inherit Ravenscrag, and when he learned that my son was to be born, he took him from me!' His voice had risen in pitch to a near shriek. He fought back tears. 'They will pay! The guilty will swing! Captain, take them away from my sight!'

Madness! Madness! I looked to Lady Sheerquine for a rational response, but she was on the other side of the courtyard, disappearing into the castle. Flarefist stomped down the steps, hammering his stick and muttering incoherently, and crossed the yard in her wake.

The 'guests' were led away. As I made to leave I caught a queer chuckle close by my shoulder. There stood Hectal, the lunatic. He looked up at me, cocking his head like a knowing bird, innocent cunning in his seamed face.

'Hee-hee!' he cackled and touched his finger to his right cheek, drawing down the eyelid. The wind shifted; the smoke gathered around the two of us, then blew away. Hectal grinned. He pointed at the sky, then turned and scampered off into the castle.

Chapter Ten

Markin, the castle physician, came directly to my chambers in the tower. He examined me and pronounced me not seriously burned. He applied cooling salves and compresses to injured parts, bandaged a knee and advised me to expect blistering and delayed shock.

Markin had been the family physician for more than two decades. I marked him down for later questioning. In the meantime I had dispatched my servant, Radyerd, to Lord Flarefist and Lady Sheerquine requesting an immediate, urgent audience. Radyerd returned while Markin was still attending to me, with the news that Flarefist and Sheerquine expected me forthwith. I regarded myself in the mirror on the wall. Gone were most of my long brown locks; in their place were short, crisp, frizzy tufts and shapeless, startled strands. My brows and finely trimmed beard and moustache were likewise reduced to spiky patches. The skin was red and black and in places blistering. I scarcely recognized myself. The young, elegant, self-assured fellow of an hour ago had been replaced by an unsightly, part-cooked ruin.

Leaving my room I found I was in some pain, which I minimized with a healing rapture. I reflected on my action in the courtyard and wondered at my daring. After all, I had no desire to remain here. I had risked my life when it might well have been preferable to allow the weird-cub to die. I could have then justifiably renounced all involvement, on the grounds already expressed to Flarefist and Sheerquine, that they had destroyed any hope of ever resolving the mystery. Instead I'd been a witless hero, and gained no thanks. I was fortunate to have escaped both a terminal roasting and a painful flogging.

Flarefist and Sheerquine received me in the same chamber in which we had spoken earlier. They sat as before, one at each end of the long table, the candles burning between them as if they had never moved. The only difference was the acrid smell of wood-smoke upon their persons, and Lord Flarefist's mood, which was one of stubborn defiance.

'I must implore you to reconsider,' I urged them. 'I cannot emphasize this enough. You have placed yourselves and the entire community of Ravenscrag in jeopardy.'

'Explain,' demanded Flarefist curtly.

'Isn't it obvious? As soon as it is learned what has happened here you are going to find the troops of House Condark, and quite probably Miragoff and Kemahamek, camped outside your walls.'

'They will not know. I have prevented anyone from leaving the town.'

'Your men cannot watch every gap in the wall.'

'I have men patrolling the road. They will catch and bring back anyone they find, or kill them if they resist. Anyone trying to avoid the road and make their way through the forest will become lost, and almost certainly devoured or worse. There are things in that forest you would never wish to meet.'

'There are other methods.'

'Such as?'

'Pigeons.'

Flarefist had not thought of this. He stared at me, his mouth opening slightly, his defiance dented. Testily he said, 'It is no matter. Let them send soldiers. Let them send entire armies. They will not attack while I hold their precious people here.'

He would not be budged, and turned a deaf ear to my further attempts at reason. I appealed to Lady Sheerquine. She was oddly silent, and seemed reluctant to involve herself.

'Bring back our son, Master Dinbig,' she said, 'then all will be settled peacefully. If you can't, what does it matter what happens here?'

I could not breach such a united wall of resistance. I said, 'Then at least give me your assurance that your prisoners will come to no harm.'

'They are guests, Master Dinbig. They are still our guests.'

'But they're in chains.'

'It is only our own people and a few foreign ruffians of no significance who are fettered. The others are simply confined to their quarters. I have told you before, we are not fools.'

'Will you guarantee that they will not be tortured or mistreated?'

Her eyes narrowed shrewdly. 'They will suffer no mistreatment – for as long as your investigation continues satisfactorily.'

'And if it should fail to do so?'

She shrugged and looked away.

'May I speak with them, freely and without restraint?'

'You may.'

'Extract a confession, Disding,' said Lord Flarefist fiercely. 'By whatever means. Give us the guilty, so that this foul business can be ended.'

'And what if they are all innocent?'

'That is not possible.'

I came away angry and filled with misgiving. Suddenly the welfare of Ravenscrag's guests had become my responsibility. I could not divorce myself from this affair, nor could I fail to solve it. Either course would result in the torture and possible deaths of more than thirty men, women and children, most if not all of whom were innocent of any crime against Ravenscrag.

My apprehension grew when I interviewed Lord Ulen Condark and his family minutes later in their chambers. Lord Condark confirmed that pigeons had been set free by aides immediately after his arrest the previous night.

'One does not willingly step into the den of a demented bear, even if that bear is feeble in mind and body, unless one knows that one has the means to step out again.'

'Quite so. Yet when the pigeons arrive it will take time for your

79

brothers to mobilize their forces, assuming that to be the course they take. How long do you estimate it will take for Condark troops to arrive here?'

'Light cavalry can be here within two or three days. Siege troops will take longer, as much as two weeks.'

'I would that it were sooner.'

'I too, considering that our lives are at stake.'

'Do you have soldiers here?'

He shook his head. 'It would have been impolitic to bring more than a basic bodyguard. It is a long time since any of us have had direct contact with Flarefist. We were not aware how serious his mental decline has become. We could not have anticipated this.'

'Can you predict in any way how he is likely to react now?'

Ulen Condark glanced aside, checking that his wife and son were out of earshot. He spoke in a low voice. 'He is demented. I believe him capable of anything.'

'Including having you executed?'

'You saw him last night.'

I glanced at his left bicep which was bound in linen to staunch the wound he had received when Lord Flarefist ran amok with his sword. 'I did not witness his attack upon you. I learned of it from Lady Sheerquine only this morning.'

'Well, be assured, he would have killed me then had he been able.'

I nodded. 'Have you suffered mistreatment?'

'Apart from this, only inconvenience – so far. Master Dinbig, as you know Flarefist holds an obsessive belief in regard to my designs over Ravenscrag. In this he is deluded. I would have been pleased to inherit Ravenscrag, certainly, had Flarefist died without an heir. But with that not being the case, I would not trouble to force the issue. I would favour a marriage between our houses, for the sake of tradition, mutual interest and the interests of Pansurian unity. Conflict between us would serve neither of us to our advantage.

'But now Cousin Flarefist has overstepped himself. This outrage will bring my brothers running, and should Flarefist survive – and he cannot survive long anyway – he will be forcibly but justifiably removed from office on the grounds of diminished responsibility. I – or a deputy appointed with my approval – will take his place.'

'Unless Redlock is returned.'

'Even then, Redlock is but a babe. Someone must rule in his stead until he is of an age.'

'Do you know anything of the circumstances behind his abduction, Lord Condark?'

'I have explained. I have no interest in such methods. Nor do I have the means to achieve them. Do you?'

'I do not.'

'Yet you know magic.'

'Not of this kind.'

'Master Dinbig, how is it that every guest bar yourself is confined? Particularly when you are a practitioner of the very craft that has been employed in bringing about this dire mystery.'

'I have asked myself the same question. As yet I do not know the answer.' I made ready to leave. 'I have gained assurances from Lady Sheerquine and Lord Flarefist that neither you or your family, nor any others of the guests, will be molested or mistreated in any way while my investigation proceeds.'

Condark nodded. 'It is regrettable; Flarefist's decline has turned an admirable if eccentric man into an unpredictable and dangerous fool.'

'The birth of his son was all he lived for.'

Condark studied me intently. 'You like him, don't you?'

I chose my words carefully, for I was anxious to gain the favour of this man in the future – if he had a future. 'Fate has dealt Lord Flarefist a cruel blow, at a time in his life when he is least able to recover from it. To Flarefist it must seem that he, or his house, is cursed; that the gods themselves mock him. For all his faults, he does not deserve this.'

Ulen Condark nodded pensively. 'Let us hope then, for all our sakes, that you are quickly successful in your efforts to resolve this mystery.'

Ravenscrag's foreign guests who, like myself, had originally taken lodgings in the town, were now installed in chambers in the dilapidated east wing of the castle. They had been deprived of weapons, and a guard was posted on every door. They were not permitted to leave their rooms, and hence had had no opportunity to speak with one another, other than briefly in the courtyard earlier. Apart from this they had received no ill-treatment.

To a man they were, understandably, sorely aggrieved. There were three Kemahamek, all well known and respected merchants, plus family members and retinue. One was a count, with high-ranking connections in government. There were two merchants from Miragoff, and one of these served as a minor government minister. A Chol and a Sommarian made up the foreign complement. All of them were known to me, some more so than others. They, like Ulen Condark, had made every effort to get word abroad of their predicament.

Briefly visiting each in turn, I did what I could to ease their minds, and assured them of my unstinting efforts on their behalf. I was, however, circumspect. I doubted their complicity, but I could not be wholly certain that they were all innocent of any involvement in Redlock's abduction.

The Pansurian guests had fared less well. Flarefist, indifferent to their fate, had incarcerated them in chains in Ravenscrag's gaol. In darkness and dread they waited, locked in dank cells, each separated from his fellows, with only basic food and water for comfort. If torture or execution was to be meted out, it would almost certainly be to these men first, and they knew it. I spoke to each of them and gave them what meagre assurances I could.

Midday was approaching by the time I emerged from the gaol. I was grateful for the warm daylight. The sight of the bright sun overhead, its warmth on my skin, and the azure sky streaked with small, high white clouds helped lift the oppression that had invaded my spirit. I made my way to Blonna's chamber to resume the conversation that had earlier been curtailed.

On approaching Blonna's door I had to pass the nursery. Its door was closed, but I lifted the latch and found it unlocked. Under the wary gaze of the old sentry I entered.

The nursery was not a large room. I recalled how, the previous evening, it had been crowded with little more than a dozen persons inside.

It was sparsely furnished. A little way in was a table, a chair half under it, somewhat askew. A large earthenware bowl and a metal candlestick stood on the tabletop. Beyond the table Redlock's crib had stood. There was a bench affixed to one wall, a small cabinet and a chest in adjacent corners. Dominating the room was a massive armoire of lacquered black wood which jutted slightly from a recess in the wall.

I looked inside the chest, which was unlocked. It contained linens, bedding, and baby's clothing. Among the tiny garments were the sets I had had made up for Redlock two days earlier. The cabinet held candlesticks, a blue porcelain vase and a few sundry items.

I opened the double doors of the armoire, which was almost eight feet high and large enough to contain three or four persons. It looked empty but for a hanging tabard quartered with the Ravenscrag colours and arms, and an old, frayed ceremonial costume. I moved these aside to peer further into its dark depth. As I did so I dislodged a heavy ceremonial polearm from a rack at one end. The weapon toppled and fell against the rear of the armoire with a hollow thud, bringing a shower of dust particles onto my head.

I withdrew and closed the doors. I went to the nursery window and looked out. The exterior wall dropped sheer to the inner ward below. It would have taken near-superhuman skill to have scaled that wall. Persons capable of such a feat existed, I knew, far away in the Endless Desert. But it was inconceivable that Aphesuk warriors would be here.

A tall ladder might have been used, but I felt it unlikely. A ladder would have had to have been brought from some distance away, and then returned. The risk of detection would have been immense. Furthermore, the sill and the wall beneath it bore no scuffs or scrapes which the ends of a load-bearing ladder would surely have left.

I craned my neck and looked upward. The roof was a long way overhead. There were other windows, but not directly above the nursery. Again, somebody might have abseiled down, but I was not happy with this explanation. A better one was beginning to suggest itself.

I went next door to see Blonna.

She was on her bench, her arms wrapped about her middle. The front of her brown dress showed the dark wet stains of unused breastmilk. I crouched down in front of her.

'You were very brave, sir. Are you burned badly?'

'Not badly, Blonna, thank you. Now, I want you to stop worrying. You are not going to be burned or harmed in any way. I hope quite soon that you will be free again. To that end I would like to continue the conversation which was interrupted earlier.'

Blonna nodded.

'You told me something very interesting, Blonna. You said that you left Redlock alone for a brief period.'

'It wasn't my fault, sir. I had to get more water.'

'I understand that, Blonna. You are not being blamed. Now, from where did you fetch the water?'

'From the kitchen well, sir.'

'There is a well-shaft on this level, isn't there? Why didn't you simply draw it up?'

'I had to go down to get another pitcher, sir.'

'You didn't have a pitcher?'

'That's the funny thing, sir. I did, but it disappeared.' She had begun rocking her upper torso back and forth.

'Disappeared? How, by magic?'

'Sir, I don't know. I had it earlier, I know I did. I'd filled it myself. But when I came to look for it, it had gone.' She clasped herself tightly, biting her lower lip.

'You're saying somebody took it?'

'I don't know, sir. There was nobody in the nursery. But it was there earlier, I know it was. It's the truth, sir. I swear to you, it's the truth.'

'Don't fret, Blonna. I only want to get to the bottom of this. Let's go back a little. We must be very precise. Now, after Lord Flarefist had shown Redlock to his guests, you brought the child up here. Is that so?'

She nodded.

'And you were alone with Redlock until the moment came when you found the water gone and you had to go out to fetch more.'

Again she nodded.

'That was a period of approximately two hours. Did anybody enter the room during that time?'

'No, sir.'

'You are absolutely sure of that?'

'Yes, sir. But . . .'

'But what, Blonna?'

She shook her head, sobbing. 'I dozed, sir. Only for a moment, I'm sure of it.'

I straightened, and spoke gently. 'Good. We are getting somewhere. Thank you for your honesty. Tell me, do you think it is possible that somebody might have entered the nursery while you dozed, and taken the pitcher of water without your knowing?'

'I don't know, sir. Why would they?'

'Why? They wanted the baby, but they could not risk picking him up for fear of his crying out and waking you. So instead they removed the water, knowing that at some point you would have to fetch more. They watched from along the corridor, and when they saw you go out they sneaked in again and committed the foul deed.'

'They must have been very patient, sir.'

I massaged the back of my neck. 'But is it possible that it happened that way?'

'It might be. I was so tired. Redlock had fallen asleep, and I just sat down for a moment, and my eyes closed . . . but it was only for a moment, I'm sure of it.'

'Come with me, Blonna.'

I took her hand and led her out of her cell. In the passage outside the old sentry came erect with a look of alarm. He gripped his pikestaff uneasily.

'I am taking Mistress Blonna into the nursery for a moment,' I said. 'You may accompany us if you wish.'

In the nursery I addressed Blonna. 'Where was the pitcher?'

'On the table, sir. Standing in the bowl.'

'You're certain?'

'Yes, sir.'

'And where did you sit when you dozed off?'

'Just here, sir.'

I pulled the chair across. 'It was here? You're sure?'

'Yes, sir.'

'Please sit there again.' She sat down. 'You're absolutely certain that this is the spot where you sat last night?'

'Yes. I had my feet against the hearth, here. I know it was warm and there was no fire, but it's a habit.'

I ushered aside the old sentry, who stood bemusedly chewing his moustaches in the doorway. Grasping the door-handle I pulled open the door. It came a short distance then halted, blocked by Blonna's chair.

'Blonna, this is most important. Are you absolutely sure that all the details you have given me are correct? That is, the position of the pitcher, and that of your chair?'

Blonna nodded. I shook my head. To get to the pitcher on the table our intruder would have had to pass Blonna. But Blonna was blocking the door, preventing it being opened more than a few inches. No one could have entered.

Blonna had seen it too. She grew distressed again. 'I'm not lying, sir. Honestly I'm not.'

'When you went out to fetch the water, did you pass anyone in the corridor, or on the stairs?'

'Not that I noticed, sir. I had to pass the door to the banqueting hall, so I saw all of you there. And there were servants in the kitchen.'

'But nobody up here.'

'No, sir.'

'How did you come to get the position of wet-nurse to Lord Redlock?'

'My own baby was born dead, sir. Just five days ago. I've been a scullery-maid here for the past three years, so her ladyship made me wet-nurse.'

'Do you know who else is lodged on this level?'

'His lordship and her ladyship have their apartments here, sir. At the far end, just around the corner. And Mistress Moonblood –her chambers are along the passage.'

'Anybody else?'

'Master Hectal, sir. He has rooms further along, in the tower.'

'Thank you. I will probably want to talk to you again later. For now, this good fellow will escort you back to your room. Thank you for helping me, Blonna, and don't be afraid. You will not be harmed.'

The poor girl threw me a stricken look as she followed the sentry outside. I stood alone, gazing around the nursery. I hoped I was right. I hoped I could guarantee her safety.

Chapter Eleven

It came to me then, quite suddenly, as I stood puzzling over the enigma of Redlock's abduction. It was actually staring me in the face: nobody had entered the nursery while Blonna slept. They hadn't needed to. *Because someone, or something, was already there!*

The culprit had entered the nursery much earlier, had remained there awaiting an opportunity to abduct or magically transform the child. He, she, or it could only have entered in Blonna's absence. Blonna had been absent only at the beginning of the banquet, when Flarefist was presenting his newborn son to his guests.

I stared at the great black monolith that towered against one wall. The only other explanation was that Blonna was lying – and that I did not believe.

No! One further possibility: the fireplace. I made a cursory inspection, and rejected it. Certainly someone of unusually slender build might have entered via the flue. But they could never have done so without displacing a large amount of soot, which would have fallen into the area in and around the fireplace. The fireplace was clean but for a few particles of lint and wood splinters.

I advanced to the armoire and opened its heavy doors. This time, as I poked my head inside, I looked for something specific. I was not disappointed. The layer of dust on the floor of the armoire showed signs of having been disturbed, as if somebody had recently been within.

I climbed inside. I drew closed the doors and sat down. A slim dart of light pierced the dark through a small crack where one door did not meet flush with the central pillar of its frame. With an eye to this crack I was able to view much of the room, just as our faceless intruder would have done. I could see quite clearly the table and the door, and the area where Redlock's crib had stood.

This intruder, then, had waited until Blonna slept. I wondered, had her tiredness been induced? A drug in her drink or food? I would ask her what she had eaten or drunk that evening, though it was now hardly more than an academic point.

So, the felon had removed the water, knowing that Blonna would have to fetch more. And when she did, obliging soul, the door of the armoire had opened. An unknown had crept out, had abducted or performed perverse magic upon Redlock, and had then left via the nursery door.

Abducted, or transformed?

If Redlock had been abducted, the kidnapper must have brought with him the monstrous little creature that was put in Redlock's place. But could the creature have been kept silent during the entire time it was held there in the armoire? This was a period of as much as two hours. From my brief acquaintance with the creature I deemed it highly unlikely.

I was looking, then, at magic. Very powerful magic. That scrabbling monster which Flarefist had thrown into the flames was in fact his newborn son and heir, Redlock.

A chill ran down my spine. With *what* were we dealing here?

I decided to talk to the astrologer, Irnbold. He was quartered in an area of the castle towards the east wing. There was no guard upon his door; Flarefist had assumed correctly that the old astrologer would be too terrified to emerge from his apartment.

Irnbold did not immediately answer my knock. When I knocked again I heard, after some delay, a movement inside, then a low voice. 'Who is it?'

I announced myself and my purpose. There was a sliding of bolts and a lifting of latches. The door opened a little way. Irnbold peeped nervously out. His eyes, wide beneath startlingly thick, dark eyebrows, darted over me then into the passage beyond, fearful of any company I might have brought.

Inside I came straight to the point. 'I am most curious as to your manner, your utter, apparently unshakeable confidence regarding your predictions concerning Redlock's birth.'

That confidence was notably absent now. Irnbold quailed before me, quite drunk, but unfortified. He wrung his thin hands. His old-young face, with its long purple nose and purple cheeks threaded with broken veins, was etched with anxiety. He wore no flamboyant costume today, just a simple green robe. His head was uncovered, which to my knowledge was unusual. For the first time I saw his pate. It was completely hairless, the skin shrivelled and mottled red and white and curiously criss-crossed with pale bluish scars and markings which extended over the back of his neck and his ears.

'It was in the heavens,' declared Irnbold, swaying. 'It was written there, plain to see.'

I glanced about me. We were in Irnbold's work-area, which occupied a large part of the chamber in which we stood. On tables and shelves were tomes large and small, ancient and modern, plus the various arcane instruments, aids and bric-à-brac which an astrologer utilizes in plying his trade.

I shook my head. 'Too precise. The entire castle was of a mind. You seemed infected, unnaturally so. Normal astrological predictions cannot account for that extraordinary certitude.'

'But I was correct! Don't you see?' He swung his arms in an exaggerated gesture which caused his balance to falter. He gathered himself. 'The child was born on the day and the hour that I predicted. He was a boy, as I said he would be.'

'You did not say he would be abducted, or transformed by magic into an unrecognizable monster. Why could you not predict that?'

Irnbold stared at me fretfully. His hands pecked one at the other in agitation. 'That was a random event. It was not in the stars.'

'Just so. Your craft is not infallible, your predictions may at any time be rendered invalid by the unforeseen. Yet you treated

Redlock's birth as if it had already occurred, as if there was no possible question as to its successful outcome. And somehow you managed to persuade Flarefist and others to your point of view, to an extent beyond all reason.'

'It was not only I.'

'I'm aware of that. But I suspect yours was the most persuasive voice.'

With an anguished groan Irnbold slumped onto a chair. He groped for a mug and a flask of spirits which rested on a table beside him. 'Can you protect me?'

'As to that, I cannot say positively. If I am successful in solving this mystery I think your life will be spared.'

He filled his mug, slopping the amber liquid over himself as he did so. 'I'm finished here.'

'That may well be so. But if I am able to say to Lord Flarefist and Lady Sheerquine that you gave me your utmost cooperation, you may yet leave here with all your bodily parts intact.'

'There's little else to tell you. I made my charts, they showed that all would be well. Elmag, with her gift of farsight, arrived at the same conclusion quite independently. When we met and compared our findings we were amazed. Amazed! The concurrence was absolute. And everything accorded with the Legend.'

'Legend? What legend?'

Irnbold belched. 'The Legend of Ravenscrag.'

'I am unacquainted with it.'

Irnbold's dark eyebrows lifted, then fell back again. The mug slewed in his hand. He began to recite, haltingly, slurring his words:

'*O you who have witnessed Ravenscrag's sad decline,*
see ye now assembled 'neath the hidden moon,
before the solstice nigh.
On the second eve, make merry!
For four must perish since the blood of the moon was spilled,
but that done, one at last will come.

A boy! You will know him by his head of flames.
He shall step from the fiery hand.
He shall render Ravenscrag anew.

See the skies!
Darkness and decay have ended.
Regard the light on Ravenscrag!

Rejoice! Lift up your hearts and sing!
You will know him, the saviour of Ravenscrag.
Your sad days are gone.'

I sat perfectly still. Irnbold's long fingers scratched at his scrawny thigh. His knee bobbed rapidly up and down, his hands incessantly mobile. His head lolled upon his shoulders, then tipped forward as though the weight was too great for his neck to bear. I stared at the strange markings on his scalp.

'From where does this legend come?'

'It's ancient.' He spoke into his breastbone. 'It's the Legend of Ravenscrag, inscribed upon an ancient scroll kept in the castle archives. There is more to it, but that is the relevant part.' He lifted his head and with an effort pushed his upper torso forwards. 'But d'you see? Everything's there. Redlock's coming; the circumstances surrounding it. It all fits. That's why we were so sure.'

My thoughts seemed to revolve slowly as they found their way around his words. This was extraordinary. Everything apparently did fit.

The second eve of the hidden moon, before the solstice nigh. Redlock had been born on the second eve of darkmoon, and the summer solstice was due later in the month.

Four must perish since the blood of the moon was spilled. Sheerquine had lost four infants since giving birth to her only daughter, Moonblood.

You will know him by his head of flames. He shall step from the fiery hand. I recalled my one and only sight of the newborn child; how striking was his bright red hair.

And the fiery hand? Surely Flarefist, his father?

'I would see this legend in its written form,' I said.

'Then apply to Flarefist or Sheerquine.'

I peered at his shrivelled old dome. The strange markings were aged and no longer clear, but I could see now what they were. I said, 'What was your crime in Komamnaga?'

Irnbold started. His free hand flew to his unprotected scalp; his drink spilled from his mug. His face registered dismay as he realized his omission: that in drunkenness and terrified distraction he had forgotten to cover his head. He glared at me with hostility, then his eyes seemed to brim with tears. Miserably he slumped back in his chair. 'I loved someone.'

'In itself that is no crime, there or anywhere.'

Komamnaga is a nation in the south, on the shores of the great Yphasian Ocean. It had once been a member-state of the mighty Ghence-Hanvat Confederation.

'I loved a boy, younger than I.'

I nodded. Irnbold hid his brow with one hand. 'He was beautiful, so beautiful, strong, brave, very intelligent. He was the son of a man of influence. It was many years ago. I was twenty-four.'

'How old was the boy?'

Irnbold spoke softly. 'Fourteen.'

'Is Komamnaga your birthplace?'

'Yes.'

'But you have never been back.'

'I cannot. I was mutilated; they burned off my hair and scored the marks of deviancy upon me. I am under sentence of death should I return.'

'And since then?'

'I wandered, far and wide. Eventually Ravenscrag became my home.'

'Do Flarefist and Sheerquine know anything of this?'

He shook his head. 'I have always kept my head covered. Even had I not, I doubt that any Pansurian would know the significance of these marks, but it was better that they asked no questions.' He dropped his hand and looked at me, his features gaunt with pain. 'Did I deserve this, a lifetime of misery, simply for loving someone? I have never forgotten him, you know.'

I was unwilling to speak. I knew that his punishment had not stopped at a scouring of the head. Mutilation for crimes was commonplace in Komamnaga. Irnbold would never have loved another since that day, at least not in the physical sense.

And now he faced banishment again. He had been arrogant; he had perhaps deliberately misrepresented what he knew in order to gain favour for himself. But did he deserve such punishment?

What was just? What was deserved? I could not say. I wondered where he would go.

'Will you tell them?' Irnbold said.

'I see no reason, unless it is somehow relevant to this investigation.'

Perhaps encouraged he leaned towards me again, imploring. 'Impress upon Flarefist that I was right. I correctly predicted Redlock's birth, and that was all I was asked to do. Tell him that. Make him see.'

Chapter Twelve

There was a commotion in the inner ward as I made my way back from Irnbold's apartment to the main wing of the castle. A couple of soldiers were manhandling a woman in the direction of the gaol. She was struggling and protesting loudly. I changed direction to intercept them. As I drew close I recognized the prisoner as old Elmag, the farseer.

Her wizened, wispy-grey-bearded face was bloody, as was the front of the blue peasant's smock she wore. I halted angrily in front of them. 'What's happening here?'

'We've brought her in. She tried to escape.' The soldier who spoke was young and plump, with small piggy eyes and hot cheeks. From the corner of my eye I saw Darean Lonsord approaching us from the gatehouse.

'They beat me!' yelled the old woman. 'Me! I'm frail and can't defend myself, yet they beat me. Poltroons! Gutless curs!'

She threw back her head and spat into pig-eyes' face. His lip curled; he raised his fist to strike her. I stepped in and grasped his wrist. 'What precisely were your orders?'

It was Darean Lonsord who replied. 'To find the hag, wherever she might be hiding, and bring her back to the castle.'

'Captain Lonsord, did your instructions include inflicting violence upon the woman?'

'My instructions, Master Dinbig, included curtailing her life if I judged it requisite under the circumstances. As it happens she tried to run off into the woods when we found her, and I might well have ordered my men to put a few arrows into her ragged old hide, but I refrained. But when we caught her and she struggled like a demented nanny-goat it became necessary to subdue her with a punch or two. Does that answer your question?'

I admit I was uncertain of myself. I knew that a word could put me under Lonsord's brutal charge. Facing him, I had no delusions. He would be proficient in the application of torture. Knowing what he would know, he would make my agony endure, and relish every moment of it. I said, 'Captain, I would cordially remind you that I am appointed by your liege-lord to conduct an investigation into the disappearance of his son and heir. This woman is a vital witness who can perhaps provide invaluable evidence. She may be innocent of any crime. Please bear this in mind.'

'If she comes to the gaol without a struggle she'll suffer no further discomfort,' said Lonsord tonelessly.

I turned to Elmag. 'I would advise that you do as he asks. I will speak to Lord Flarefist and insist that you be kept safe. I will speak to you in due course.'

'All I did was what I was asked,' bleated the old woman, unwittingly echoing Irnbold's parting sentiment to me of just moments before. 'I know nothing about last night.'

'Then why did you flee?' demanded Lonsord, prising something from between his teeth with the nail of his forefinger.

'I knew what would happen. And I was right, wasn't I?'

'If you are innocent you will not be harmed,' I told her. 'It's better to go with them quietly.'

I exchanged a loaded glance with Lonsord. He nodded to his men, and the old woman was led away.

I came upon Lady Sheerquine in the banqueting hall. She was supervising the last of the clearing-up operation from the night before. I watched her for a moment before announcing my presence. She was remarkable, robust, vigorous; it was hard to believe that she had given birth less than twenty-four hours earlier.

'Your ladyship, Elmag the farseer has been brought in. I understand your men were given orders that she might be killed.'

'Only if the situation warranted, Master Dinbig.' She did not look at me.

'Such a condition offers wide scope for interpretation. I wish to interview her later on. I would be grateful if you could ensure that she is well cared for.'

'I will send word.' She gestured irritably at a lackey polishing an escutcheon upon the wall. 'You have moved it, you fool! Place it back as it was!'

'Lady Sheerquine, why did you not mention the Legend of Ravenscrag?'

Sheerquine elevated her chin with an abrupt movement, arching her elegant neck. She surveyed me coolly down the length of her fine nose. 'Is it important?'

'By the account I have, you have adjudged it of prime importance.'

'You have been talking to whom? Irnbold?'

I nodded. 'As regards my investigation, I consider this legend may be of incalculable relevance. May I see it in its original written form?'

Lady Sheerquine sighed. 'This is tiresome. It was in the care of Sardus, Master of Ledgers, but he died two months ago and we have not found a replacement.'

'Is there no one else who can show me?'

She twitched. 'Oh, very well, I shall take you myself. Follow me.'

Walking straight and erect she led me along passages deep into the castle, to areas I had never been. At one point she paused to light a candle at a sconce. We moved on, through lightless places, through air that was heavy with must and age. At length Lady Sheerquine halted before a small arched portal. She produced an iron key from somewhere and unlocked the door, which opened with a doleful groan of hinges.

We stepped into a dark chamber. Lady Sheerquine quickly lit tapers from her candle. Their light showed a chamber of moderate size, long but of no great width. Dusty racks and shelves lined its walls. Upon these rested ancient tomes, scrolls, manuscripts. A small work-desk occupied one corner.

As Sheerquine searched for the manuscript I had requested, I cast my eyes over some of the covers. There were ledgers and registers, records and charters from Ravenscrag dating back over many generations. There were also works of learning, ancient and modern, many from far abroad. Texts on history, myth, science; religious and philosophical treatises; mystical, magical and astrological tracts; works on art and literature; sagas, poems, and more. Ravenscrag was not quite as detached from the outside world as I had supposed.

Sheerquine extracted a hardened leather cylinder from a shelf. 'Here is the Legend. It may not be the original manuscript, but it is old. At least two hundred years old. I know of no other surviving version that predates it.'

'Has it been in your family's possession all this time?'

'It has. Before that the Legend was handed down by oral tradition. It is a timeless work, integral to Ravenscrag's heritage. None can say from where it originated, or when.'

'But you have chosen to keep it private.'

She made no comment. I took from the cylinder an ancient scrolled parchment. It crackled as I unfurled it, and gave off a faint odour of time. I took it to the desk and laid it upon its top. Seating myself, I scanned by candlelight the faded words etched there in ornamental script. As Irnbold had said, there was more than he had recited, but from what I could make out the initial verses were preamble, merely setting scene and historical and social context. I found nothing in them to arouse my interest. But the last section, which Irnbold had quoted quite accurately, grabbed my attention:

O you who have witnessed Ravenscrag's sad decline,
see ye now assembled 'neath the hidden moon,
before the solstice nigh.
On the second eve, make merry!
For four must perish since the blood of the moon was spilled,
but that done, one at last will come.

A boy! You will know him by his head of flames.
He shall step from the fiery hand.
He shall render Ravenscrag anew.
See the skies!

Darkness and decay have ended.
Regard the light on Ravenscrag!

Rejoice! Lift up your hearts and sing!
You will know him, the saviour of Ravenscrag.
Your sad days are gone.

I studied it for some moments, deep in thought. 'It appears to be incomplete.'

Lady Sheerquine leaned forward stiffly and peered down at the parchment. In the hovering light her face looked gaunt and strained. I caught her perfume of winter geranium. With my finger, I showed her. 'See, there is an intricate border design here, at top and sides. It is missing from the bottom. And look, the bottom edge is uneven, as though it has been inexpertly cut away. Was there more written here?'

Sheerquine straightened. 'It was done two generations ago. The parchment was found to have deteriorated quite badly over time. There was no one at Ravenscrag with the expertise to restore it. Flarefist's grandfather ordered that the lower border be cut away that the deterioration might not progress. There was no more script.'

'May I take this with me.'

'It is not to be removed from this vault. You may commit it to memory.' She began snuffing out candles. 'Now, I have duties elsewhere. If you have done, Master Dinbig . . .'

I made my way back to my chambers, thinking to take a repast there while mulling over what I had so far learned. It was almost midday and I had not eaten since breakfast.

As I mounted the foot of the stairs leading up to my apartment I heard a mad chuckle at my back. I turned, to see Hectal squatting upon a window-ledge, knees to chin, arms hugging his shins.

He grinned. He leered. He scratched the top of his head and pushed his tongue out of one corner of his mouth. 'I have a something.'

'I would be pleased to hear it.'

'It is nothing!' He cackled delightedly. 'That is the something: nothing there!'

'I see.'

'I am a foooool!' laughed Hectal. He screwed up his face with mock seriousness. 'Empty.'

'So it is said.'

'Nothing there. That is the something.' He lifted his hand and pointed at his temple. 'Empty. See!' He balled a fist and knuckled himself quite hard on the forehead. '*Thonk!* Ouch! Nothing behind. Oh me oh my!'

He giggled. He winked. His features formed again into a strange, living caricature of his twin sister.

'Thank you, Hectal,' I said.

'*Thonk!*'

I turned away again.

'Make use of the something!' Hectal called. His laughter accompanied me to the top of the stairs.

Chapter Thirteen

The servant, Radyerd, brought me a luncheon of cold meats, potatoes, fresh salad greens, fruit and good red wine. Excellent red wine, I should say, for I recognized its flavour. It was from my own estate in Khimmur, the wine I had given to Lord Flarefist two days earlier.

As I ate I tried to sort through the information I had gleaned during the past few hours, but something hovered distractingly at the edge of my consciousness. I found my thoughts kept returning to the halfwit, Hectal.

Thonk!

Empty-headed? Or was there more to Hectal than met the eye? His 'somethings', ostensibly babble, were turning out to be quite relevant to my investigation.

The baby is going to smell good when it's cooked. Hectal had known that Flarefist intended to burn the child.

Thonk!

He had also predicted that Ulen Condark's troops would come to Ravenscrag.

Thonk!

Neither of these facts was indicative of special knowledge.

100

Hectal had simply imparted them to me in cryptic form before I had a chance to become aware of them myself. Nevertheless, they revealed that he had an understanding of what was going on, which was more than most persons would have given him credit for.

Thonk!

What else had he said? *Tonight is the last of darkmoon, but there will be another before you know it. Shadownight comes.*

Was this pertinent? Did it even make sense? Or should I dismiss it as the ravings of an imbecile? What did he mean by 'Shadownight'? I wondered whether Hectal played a game with me, the rules of which were known only to himself.

I could not get him out of my mind.

Thonk! Empty.

This latest encounter: was there a message there?

Empty. Nothing behind.

I sipped my wine. I was becoming irritable. Hectal was preventing me from concentrating upon the truly important aspects of the case. For instance, the Legend: an extraordinary item, passed down over centuries and filled with symbolic meaning. I considered Lady Sheerquine's explanation that the lower border of the manuscript had been cut away to prevent deterioration. It may have been true; perhaps it *was* true as far as she knew. But it was also rather convenient. I wanted something more substantial – positive proof that the Legend as it was written had not itself been tampered with. The Legend was surely of extreme relevance. Indeed, it was pivotal to Redlock's birth and misfortune, and consequently the future fortunes of Ravenscrag. But had I viewed it in its entirety? Was there more to it than I had seen?

Nothing there. That is the something.

I damned Hectal. His mad jabberings intruded upon my mind and I lost my train of thought. I thrust aside my plate, which collided with a heavy bronze figurine standing near the edge of the tabletop. The figurine toppled and fell from the table, landing with a hollow thud on top of an empty wooden chest which stood alongside.

Thonk! Nothing behind!

I stared. I blinked. I reached across and picked up the figurine.

It was a small sculpture of a female figure holding a child. I lifted it and let it fall again onto the lid of the chest.

Thonk!

'*Moban!*'

I sprang to my feet and ran for the door, colliding with Radyerd who was bringing in a tray of cheeses, fruit and sweetmeats. To the crash of scattering dishes I ran down the spiral stairs.

Hectal was gone from his perch. There was no sign of him in the corridor. I strode on as fast as I could, restricted by bandages and stiffness of burned limbs, along passages and galleries to the main wing. I ascended to the first level, passed the family apartments, entered the corridor which led to Redlock's nursery. I strode past the old sentry, who was half asleep. I thrust open the nursery door and entered. The sentry jerked himself into a semblance of alertness and followed me in, wobbling and dazed.

I went without hesitation to the armoire and yanked open its heavy doors. I stepped inside pushing aside the costumes. Lifting the polearm that I had earlier dislodged, I let it fall against the back panel of the armoire.

Thonk!

A hollow thud. Not the dense, solid sound of something heavy falling against wood backed by ungiving stone.

Nothing there! Nothing behind!

'An axe!' I yelled at the sentry. 'Get me an axe!'

Then: 'No! Wait!'

I stared at the panel. *There had to be a mechanism!*

Inside the armoire I could see little. I climbed out, bringing the ceremonial costumes with me. 'Get me a candle.'

The sentry unhesitatingly took the candlestick from the table and went out into the corridor to light it from a sconce. In his absence I examined the exterior of the armoire.

It was set into a recess in the stone wall. I had assumed it to be free-standing, yet its side-panels were flush to the stone. It rose eight-feet high, almost to the ceiling. By clambering onto the table I was able to see across its top. There was a foot or so of stone wall above it. But what was beneath that?

The sentry returned with the lighted candle. I jumped down, took the candle, and stepped into the armoire. With the light I was able to see that the rear panel was actually three vertical pieces. I knocked each with my knuckle. Only one, the leftmost, which had been obscured by the hanging garments, proved to be hollow.

I pushed on this panel; it did not give. I passed the candlelight over it and found nothing. But on the side-panel adjoining it, a little way above my head, I came across an unevenness in the wood. The light showed a knot in the stained timber, and when I passed my fingertips over it I discovered that the centre of the knot was very slightly loose.

I pressed, and was rewarded with a satisfying muted metallic click beside my ear. The rear panel had shifted infinitesimally inwards, and when I pushed it swung silently in.

I stared into absolute dark.

A light, warm draught bent my candleflame towards the nursery behind me, carrying with it a musty odour. Tentatively I leaned forward into the opening, extending my hand with the candle. The light showed a narrow area, a passage, between the stones of the wall. I could not see how far it extended, but I knew what it meant.

Our intruder had not after all entered the nursery when Blonna was downstairs with Redlock prior to the banquet. He, she or it had not waited patiently in the armoire all that time. He had come in his own time, had chosen the moment when Blonna slept to steal the pitcher of water, and when Blonna went to fetch more had crept out and done the foul deed.

And the intruder had not exited the nursery via the door, as I had earlier assumed. He had gone back into the secret passage.

Where did it lead?

I turned back to the sentry. 'Give me a weapon.'

He clamped shut his open jowl. 'Can't do that.'

'I must explore.'

'I'll fetch his lordship.'

He went. I was anxious to explore this secret way before Lord Flarefist or anyone else arrived, for I suspected I might be forbidden from entering, at least until Flarefist had inspected it to his own satisfaction. I mentally prepared a couple of raptures, though I was not confident they would be effective. If I were taken by surprise in the darkness of the passage I would have no time to cast them. And what might I meet? Would it be susceptible to my weak magic?

I reached for my belt, and the garrotting wire, only to recall that

I had left it in my chamber when I had changed my garments after the fire. I swore. The polearm that was in the armoire was far too long and cumbersome. Weaponless, my heart pounding, I stepped into the dark.

The passage extended to the left. I could see only a couple of feet in front of me. It was narrow so that I had to advance with my shoulders held slightly obliquely. The floor beneath my feet was solid stone and rubbly earth. The dank musty odour was stronger, and there was much dust and cobwebs. But only a couple of times did I find webs actually stretched across my way, and they were newly spun.

After a few feet the passage turned sharply to the left. I judged that I was passing now within the outside wall. Three stone steps took me down – beneath the sill of the nursery window – then up again. Something scraped the stone beside me. I moved the candle, heart in my mouth, to reveal the gleaming eyes of a large black rat in a niche in the stone. Another rat ran across my foot.

I moved on, edging forward for another minute or so. I stumbled once or twice, almost dropping my candle. The darkness seemed to close in around me so that I lost my sense of bearing. The air was stale; the bright candlelight in front of my eyes dazzled me, became a hindrance rather than a help. A sense of panic closed in. I could hear my loud breathing and nothing else.

Then at last, quite suddenly, the passage ended. My hands pressed against solid stone.

I moved the candle around and found what I sought. The wall to my left was of wood, not stone. A further brief search revealed a heavy iron catch, which when lifted enabled me to draw back the panel. As I pulled, carefully, a door slid back into a housing inside the stone of the wall.

Before me was a heavy blue drape. I waited, listening, and heard nothing. With caution I drew the edge of the material aside.

I found myself looking into a spacious, well-appointed bed-chamber. A half-canopied bed occupied one corner, with a small table beside it. Elsewhere there was a dressing-table with mirror, a cabinet, chairs. There was nobody in the chamber. I stepped inside.

I knew immediately where I was, though I'd never been there before. There were books on shelves and on a small work-desk.

There were brooches on top of the dressing-table, a pair of fine silver chains, and other small pieces of jewellery. There were items of needlework and embroidery, a lap-harp, and various dresses and robes strewn carelessly about. The bed was rumpled. Several dolls sat on it in disorderly array; others were arranged in a semicircle on the floor. Among them was Misha, the doll I had brought from Twalinieh in Kemahamek. This was Moonblood's room.

And on the floor, next to the bedside table, stood a solitary earthenware pitcher. It matched the bowl that rested on the table in the nursery.

As I stood pondering my next move the door opened and a woman walked in. She stopped dead at the sight of me. Her hands flew to her mouth and she uttered a sudden gasp of shock.

I recognized her as Marshilane, Moonblood's maidservant. Behind her came Lord Flarefist. He too came to a halt and fixed me with an angry, questioning stare, one hand going to the hilt of his sword. 'What are you doing here?'

'Proceeding with my investigation, my lord.'

'In my daughter's bedchamber?'

'I am as surprised at finding myself here as you are at finding me.'

'How did you know?'

'Know what?'

Flarefist addressed Marshilane. 'Have you spoken to this fellow?'

'No, my lord. I came straight to find you. I haven't told anyone.'

'Has something happened?' I enquired.

Lord Flarefist eyed me scowlingly, his lips moving in apparent indecision. Then he mumbled, 'My daughter's disappeared.'

'Moonblood? When?'

He seemed to have entered a trance, his look suddenly inward, and made no reply. I looked at Marshilane. She was tearful and in a state of nerves. 'I don't think Mistress Moonblood's been seen since last night.'

Lord Flarefist spoke again, his voice loud and trembling. 'Show me, Marshilane.'

Marshilane moved fearfully to the bed and drew back the

rumpled covers. There was a garment lying there, a pale linen night-robe. It was torn at the shoulder, and spattered further down with blood. Marshilane reached out and picked it up. I saw that beneath it the bedsheet also bore the bright stain of blood.

'This is Moonblood's night-robe, I take it,' I said quietly, after a silence.

Flarefist's jaw moved in agitation, making a wet sound as he stared transfixed at the bed. Gone was the brash demeanour of moments ago. His tall lean frame had sagged, his face was bereft, the old eyes filled again with anguish. One hand had begun to shake convulsively and he leaned heavily upon his stick.

I was again filled with an overwhelming sense of sympathy. I was facing the same shocked, broken old man I had sat with early in the morning, who had beseeched me to help restore some meaning to his shattered life. The proud old warrior had been pummelled into submission by mysteries he could not comprehend. He could not even bring himself to speak.

Marshilane wept quietly by his side. I caught her eye and she nodded in affirmation of my question.

'You say she was last seen last night?'

'After the banquet, sir.'

'Did not you or someone else wake her or attend her this morning?'

'No, sir.'

'Is that usual?'

'It's not unusual, sir. Mistress Moonblood often prefers to be left alone. Sometimes she gets up early and goes off, or she stays here studying or playing if she has no lessons or other duties. Generally, if she needs me before breakfast she rings for me.'

'But it's halfway through the day. Were you not concerned earlier?'

'No, sir. Often a goodly part of the day will go by without my setting eyes on Mistress Moonblood. I wouldn't have thought it odd today had it not been that when I came to make her bed I found this.' Marshilane's chin trembled and she gave way to a flood of tears. 'Oh the devils, what has become of her?'

I stepped across the room and drew aside the heavy drape, revealing the secret entrance by which I had come. 'Do you know about this?'

Her face told me that she did not.

'Lord Flarefist?'

The old fellow looked around blearily. 'What?'

'Are you aware of the existence of this secret passageway?'

He closed his eyes, frowning, perplexed. 'Secret?'

'This passage leads directly to the nursery.'

Flarefist stirred himself as though with a vast effort, and shuffled towards me. He peered into the blackness of the passage for a long time, then at me questioningly. 'What's happening here, Bisding? I don't understand. Why all this?'

At that moment there was a sharp knock at the door. Flarefist turned slowly.

'Come,' he said in a soulless voice.

The old sentry from the nursery entered, puffing and red-faced. Evidently he had been all around the wing in search of Lord Flarefist, only to find the old man just along the corridor.

'My lord – ' he began, then was lost for words as his eyes fell on me.

'He has come to relay a request from myself that I be permitted a weapon in order to safely explore this passage,' I said.

'You wish to explore it?' asked Flarefist.

'Not now, Lord Flarefist. I have already done so.'

Lord Flarefist scrutinized me as if trying to remember who I was. His brow furrowed. 'What has happened to your face?'

'I burned it, Lord Flarefist. In your fire.'

A fierce anger came momentarily to Flarefist's eyes. 'Deceivers!' he growled, straightening.

'Who?'

'All of them! Why? What do they hope to gain? They'll get nothing from me!'

Then the brief fire was gone. His body sagged again. He took a shuddering breath, heaved his old shoulders and sighed, shaking his grey head disconsolately from side to side.

'I don't understand,' he slurred. His stick scraped upon the floor. He turned and made his way slowly from the room.

Chapter Fourteen

Irnbold had still not found the courage to venture out of his apartment, but he had covered his head. His chosen headpiece was unelaborate, a length of yellow and white cloth, wound so as to cover scalp, ears and nape, its end hanging down his back.

I told him about Moonblood; he gave a cry of despair and covered his face with his hands.

'Again, it is something your predictions failed to give warning of.'

'Yes, that is how Flarefist will see it! Oh woe! I'm destroyed! He will kill me!'

'I'm not sure – '

'Did you tell him? Did you make him see that I was accurate and correct in regard to Redlock's birth?'

'An opportunity has not yet arisen.'

'Nor will it now. Oh, he will blame me for Mistress Moonblood. He will have me hanged or burned. But I was not called upon to cast Moonblood's birthchart. How can I be blamed?'

'Had you cast it, would you have foreseen this?'

'Who can say what would have been revealed?'

'What if you cast it now? Might it give a clue?'

Irnbold hesitated. 'It may indicate possible negative influences on this day. It cannot be precise about the way in which those influences manifest.'

'In Redlock's case you were less reticent.'

'Because of the Legend! Redlock's was a birth foretold.'

'Do you know of any more of the Legend than that which you recited to me?'

Irnbold looked blank. 'That is all that I am aware of. Did you not read it yourself?'

'I did. I simply wondered whether there might be more.'

He thought for a moment, scratching his cheek with one hand. I noted the swelling around his joints, presumably aggravated by his current mental state. 'I did once hear passing mention of a bane of some kind, though it has never been repeated in my hearing before or since. It was Sardus who spoke of it.'

'Sardus? The Master of Ledgers?'

'That's he.'

'He died recently, so I understand.'

'That's so.'

'What was the cause of his death?'

Irnbold shrugged. 'He was hoary with age. He simply passed on.'

'And there was no one trained to take over his role?'

'It was hardly necessary. Sardus was all but redundant. He appeared from time to time to oversee certain rituals. Apart from that he merely kept records and accounts, a task which was given to a clerk when Sardus's eyes grew weak and his hand too unsteady to write.'

'Tell me about the bane.'

'Truly, Master Dinbig, I have said all that I know. It was merely something I overheard Sardus say to Lord Flarefist. "The bane is unproven," said he, "but I would ensure that all conditions are met." I took little note at the time. I had no reason to, for I did not know to what it referred. But on reflection it was obvious that they were discomfited at the thought that I might have overheard.'

' "Ensure that all conditions are met." That would seem to refer to the conditions contained in the Legend.'

'I would think so.'

'And Flarefist, presumably, was happy that all conditions were met.'

'As were we all. You have seen the Legend yourself; everything was in accord.'

'Yet disaster has befallen Ravenscrag.' I gingerly kneaded my tender jaw between finger and thumb. 'What can you tell me about Moonblood? You have been her teacher, have you not?'

Irnbold nodded. 'She has long expressed interest in my craft. With her parents' permission I began teaching her the rudiments. She is quick to learn, and eager. She asked me to show her magic, believing me to be secretly adept.'

'Are you?'

Irnbold managed a troubled smile. 'If I were, would I be here now?'

'I know magic, and I am here.' I watched his face. 'Do you like Moonblood?'

'She is an intelligent, engaging child. I enjoyed the periods we spent together. Others have found her flighty and headstrong, and when the fancy takes her, so I understand, capable of wilful disobedience. But that has not been my experience. She seems often preoccupied, though; sometimes impatient, as though her thoughts dwell on matters and goals elsewhere. What can have become of her? Oh, this is a tragedy!'

'Do you know of the secret way which connects Moonblood's chamber with the nursery?'

Irnbold's anxious eyes widened. 'No. Is this true?'

I nodded.

'Then that means . . .'

'We do not yet know what it means. Nor can we afford to jump to conclusions. To your knowledge, when not engaged with her lessons, how does Moonblood occupy her hours?'

'I cannot say with any certainty. Other than when she comes to me for lessons our meetings are infrequent and largely haphazard. We are present occasionally at the same table, or will meet incidentally somewhere within the castle. She has a liking for solitude, sometimes taking herself off for hours at a time.'

'Where does she go?'

'I do not know. Sometimes into the forest, I have heard.'

I recalled my chance meeting with Moonblood the previous evening. 'Is that not dangerous?'

'Evidently it has not been adjudged so.'

'Has she no close companions?'

'Not to my knowledge. But truly I am not the person to ask. You would be better enquiring of Lady Sheerquine, or Moonblood's maid, Marshilane.'

'What of suitors? Moonblood is of an age, and is not uncomely.'

'There have been a number. Flarefist guards her jealously; he would marry her into House Condark, or elsewhere into a position of influence and advantage. But Mistress Moonblood wants none of it. To Flarefist's chagrin she spurned all her admirers bar one.'

'And who is the one?'

'The vagabond, Linvon.'

'Linvon the Light? The juggler?'

'She seemed enchanted by him. And he was by no means unheeding of her. But when Flarefist became aware that there existed a reciprocal interest between them he had Linvon ejected from the castle.'

'But not before Linvon had lifted some of the Ravenscrag silver.'

Irnbold nodded.

'Describe him, this Linvon.'

'He is young, perhaps twenty years of age. Clever, witty, charming in a roguish sort of way. Not at all of the usual run as far as Ravenscrag is concerned. It is easy to see how Mistress Moonblood could be captivated by his charms.'

'Handsome?'

'Oh, *very* handsome.' Irnbold's eye held a distant look, a wistful smile touching his purple lips. He grew aware of himself and looked away unhappily.

'Where is he from?'

'No one knows. He came, he went. That, I imagine, is the pattern of his life.'

'And he was here . . . when?'

'About two months ago, in the spring.'

'And he has not been seen or heard of since.'

'No.'

I gave myself to thought. Was Linvon the culprit I sought? Had he taken far more than mere silver – had he taken Ravenscrag's daughter? Worse, I saw again the bloody garment on Moonblood's bed – was Linvon her murderer? Was it Linvon who had taken Redlock and replaced him with that drooling monster?

I stopped myself. I was in danger of committing the error which just seconds ago I had warned Irnbold against, leaping to conclusions, impelled by wild speculation, hurling myself without reason into the churning dark.

I said, 'It's curious. Lord Flarefist vividly recalled Linvon's theft of the silver, yet he made no mention of his "friendship" with his daughter, which in his eyes was surely the greater crime.'

'Lord Flarefist's memory is at times, how can I put it . . . "selective",' Irnbold explained. 'He remembers what he wishes to remember, or perhaps what his mind will permit him to remember. I suspect worms in his brain. He is a very sick man.'

I nodded. 'Tell me now about the witchery. It was mentioned when I first arrived.'

'A couple of isolated incidents, nothing more. A report came in from a nearby village. Local women were suspicious of a neighbour whose cheeses had ripened too soon. A month later a woman from another village was reported to have taken a were-lover who visited her in the night. They were said to have conducted rituals by moonlight. Two children died suddenly, seized by violent fluctions, fever and vomiting.'

'What action was taken?'

'Lord Flarefist sent men to investigate. The women were arrested and examined. In both cases they were found to be marked with the supernumerary nipple. They suffered the mandatory punishment. They were immersed alive in boiling oil. Witchery is greatly feared in these parts.'

I held back my emotions. 'Were they given a trial?'

'The evidence was deemed sufficient in itself to leave no question as to their guilt.'

'Are you, of all people, satisfied with that explanation?'

Irnbold cast his eyes down. 'I am not a law-maker.'

'And they were executed by Flarefist's command?'

Irnbold nodded. I closed my eyes. Flarefist – a man I had felt pity for.

But he had never been considered cruel, I reminded myself.

Prone to excess, yes. Somewhat cantankerous, and given to bursts of temper. But on the whole just, even benevolent. Until recently. His mental and physical decline had turned him into a tyrant, a monster, a man beyond reason, a law unto himself.

'Who was it who examined these women and discovered the "evidence"?' I asked.

'Captain Lonsord, I believe.'

'Did he apply to Lord Flarefist before carrying out sentence?'

'I believe not. His orders were sufficient in themselves to permit him a degree of autonomy.'

'No doubt.' I expelled a long breath between my teeth, and shook my head. The deed was done; I could not undo it. I endeavoured to put it out of my mind. 'Flarefist was concerned about this "spate" of witchery, wasn't he? Did he fear that something might impend – something of the nature of what we have witnessed here?'

'If he did he did not confide as much to me.'

'I wonder . . .' I mused out loud. Then: 'Irnbold, this creature, the weird-cub that has taken Redlock's place, have you ever seen its like?'

Irnbold shook his head. 'Never.'

I rose, baffled. 'Nor I.'

Irnbold reached out and grasped the sleeve of my tunic, his face twisted with anxiety. 'Master Dinbig, I have done all I can to help you. Now help me if you can. Please. Moonblood's disappearance . . . Flarefist will be convinced I know something. Perhaps my fate is already sealed, but speak for me. Tell him I am blameless.'

'I will do what I can,' I said. There were tears in Irnbold's eyes. I squeezed his hand, and he winced with pain. I apologised. Obviously his joints were extremely tender. 'You will not be harmed. Flarefist and Sheerquine are anxious to have this mystery ended. They know that I rely upon you for information. And when I have the information I require, they will see that you are innocent. That is, of course, if everything you have told me is true.'

Leaving Irnbold I returned to my apartment, had Radyerd bring me quill and ink, and wrote and sealed a brief message. I summoned my guard, Bris. He and Cloverron had been kicking their heels around the castle all day. They were disarmed and quartered in a stable-loft, and from what I gathered had spent the latter hours playing dice and winning good money from off-duty Ravenscrag guards.

'Have you learned anything useful, Bris?'

He shook his head. 'The guards are zestless and wary, in their manner and their game. They will not be drawn into conversation. What's more, they accuse us of cheating when we win!'

I passed him the letter. 'Take this to Mistress Cametta at her home, and bring back her reply.'

The message was a request to visit Cametta, ostensibly to discuss her purchase of certain fineries from the selection I had brought with me to Ravenscrag. When Bris had departed I went out to speak to Moonblood's maid, Marshilane.

I found her in the company of two other members of the castle staff. She was still in a state of some distress and they were endeavouring to comfort her. At my request she agreed to a walk around the castle precincts where we might speak together candidly and in relative privacy. I asked her how long she had been Moonblood's maid.

'Since she was an infant.'

'And presumably you have come to know great affection for her.'

'Oh yes, sir. Very much so.'

'And would you say that she feels a similar affection for you?'

'Oh, I can't say as to that, sir. Mistress Moonblood thinks me an old fuddy-duddy and a fusspot. She is always telling me I am too strict, or old-fashioned, or over-protective. Then sometimes she comes running to me for comfort, or we sit together and she tells me stories, or I tell her, or we read poetry to one another. Sometimes she plays tricks on me, just to make me angry. Then she laughs when I do. And sometimes . . .'

Her voice trailed off.

'Yes, Marshilane? Please hold nothing back. It is important for Mistress Moonblood's sake that I build up as detailed a picture of her personality as I can.'

'Well, sometimes – when she's peeved, or I've had to scold her for some misdemeanour or caprice – she says unkind things.' Marshilane dabbed at her reddened eyes with a white linen handkerchief. The end of her nose, too, was red from weeping. 'She calls me uneducated, or stupid, or timid.'

I looked aside at Marshilane. She was a dumpy woman of average height, in her mid-thirties. Her hair was dark brown, gathered beneath her maid's cap. There was a reserved kindly, stolid air about her. I believed her unmarried, and imagined that would probably be unlikely to change. She smiled to herself. 'Then later she'll come back and tell me how she's made herself sad for saying such things, and beg me to forgive her. As if she need ever beg!'

'It sounds to me as though Moonblood is as fond of you as you are of her,' I said. 'You say she is also a solitary child.'

'A dreamer. Oh, she's bright and inquisitive. Always asking questions, about things I can't answer. Always talking about fairies and giants and magic and things. A head full of stuff and nonsense. She even told me she'd met a giant. I don't know where she gets it all from. I'm sure.'

'Are there giants hereabouts?'

'I've never seen one, sir. Nor has anyone else that I know of. I remember my grandfather telling me when I was little that he'd seen giants when he was a young man hunting away in the north. He said there weren't many left; they were dying out.'

We stopped in a sunny arcade where yellow roses twisted around the old stone columns. A raven eyed us from atop a low, crumbling wall. At the base of the wall the old liver and white hound, Rogue, was stretched in the sun. I looked out towards the forest and crags shimmering in the afternoon heat. 'Irnbold tells me that Moonblood goes alone into the woods sometimes.'

'I was worried at first. I didn't know where she was getting herself off to, and when I asked her she didn't want to tell me. I told her that I would have to tell her mother, in that case, and that Lady Sheerquine might well confine her as a result. So Moonblood told me. She has a secret place she goes to. It's not in the forest proper, it's down over there, by the stream, just beyond the old castle wall. Even so I didn't like her going there on her own. But she said it was a magic place and that she was quite safe. She said Gorodur made sure no harm came to her.'

'Gorodur?'

'That's the name of her giant, so she told me. I took no notice;

115

there are no giants here. Mistress Moonblood gets carried away. Sits there dreaming all day long and comes back with a head full of stories. Still, I had her show me this secret place, giant or no giant. I told Lady Sheerquine about it, though of course I made no mention of magic or giants.'

'And Sheerquine allowed Moonblood to continue going there?'

'As I say, it's right close to the castle, and it's quite safe. Lady Sheerquine saw no harm in Mistress Moonblood's going there. She said if she forbade her, Moonblood might well prove rebellious and get herself into real trouble somewhere else.'

'I would like to see this secret place.'

'I'll take you if you like, sir.'

Chapter Fifteen

Marshilane led me from the castle buildings, beneath a long pergola over which green vines twisted in the sunlight. We emerged from its shade onto a pathway, and passed between tall hedges into an ornamental garden, poorly tended but bright with flowers and shrubs. Another path took us left through a vegetable garden, then we made our way along the edge of an orchard, through a rotting portal in the wall, and were beside a small river. Beyond was dense scrub, and then the forest and crags loomed, high pinnacles of tree-covered rock rearing in the near distance. I was convinced that I was about to discover where Moonblood had been when I saw her the previous evening prior to the banquet.

It was hot and I had begun to sweat. The heat made me more aware of the burns upon my skin. Marshilane paused to mop her brow. 'Not far now, sir.'

She pushed gamely on through thick bushes and tall grass. The way descended abruptly and became very steep. Marshilane scrambled down, heaving herself inelegantly over boulders, clinging to roots and branches, while I followed close behind. We stood at length in a secluded dappled dell.

It was quiet but for the sounds of nature: birdsong, the

intermittent buzz of insects, the rustle of the wind in the trees and the sound of a waterfall which tumbled from above, splashing off ledges of rock to form a small, sunlit lagoon. Foxgloves, columbine, monk's hood and a profusion of other wild flowers grew around the edges of the dell; bright red poppies and lady's slipper on the higher banks. Butterflies and bees flew among them. Around the clearing alders and green willows offered shade from the sun. It was a tranquil spot – touched by magic, one might have said.

With this in mind I attuned my senses to the ambience of the dell. I detected nothing unnatural, no sense of forces untoward. Rather, it was nature I sensed, a feeling of unsullied harmony, of peacefulness.

But I was no fool, and did not consider myself infallible. I recognized that magic far stronger than anything I might muster could yet have held sway in this place.

Marshilane rested with her buttocks against a mossy boulder, her plump cheeks flushed and perspiring as she regained her breath. She gestured widely with a pudgy arm. 'You see, sir, there isn't really anywhere she could go from here, apart from back the way she came.'

It appeared to be true. The dell seemed entirely cut off from the rest of the world. The bluff on the far side of the lagoon, down which the waterfall cascaded, was sheer and sometimes overhanging, quite impossible to climb. The slope down which we had come was steep and rocky and dense with scrub. It presented a discouraging prospect, other than via the way we had descended.

'It is perhaps possible to clamber up this side, into the trees there.'

'And go where, sir? Into the forest? Mistress Moonblood wouldn't go there on her own. She knows the dangers. And besides, you can see that the cliffs up there are impassable.'

I nodded. The crags rose abruptly like an immense protective rampart. 'But if she met Gorodur here – '

'Oh, you don't believe that about the giant, do you, sir? I mentioned that only as an illustration.'

'You're convinced she imagined it?'

'I think so. Don't you?'

'Perhaps.'

I scrambled up some rocks at the water's edge in order that I might peer behind the waterfall. The cool spray was welcome on my skin, but I clung hard to my perch for fear of slipping and tumbling into the lagoon below. Behind the fall the cliff was solid and unbroken; no concealed cave entrance. I took a long look around. It was not entirely inconceivable for Moonblood to have scaled the rocks on one side and gone further than this spot. But again it was plain that she could not have gone far. Furthermore, I could see that it was the dell which would have held the real attraction for her.

I jumped back down onto the grass. Marshilane had taken off her sandals and was bathing her feet in the cool water. I sat on a slab of limestone beside her, a little further back from the edge. 'Are you aware of the Ravenscrag Legend, Marshilane?'

'Yes, sir. Everyone here is.'

'It's very old, is it not?'

'Oh, it goes far, far back, so I'm told. Nobody knows where it came from, but it's been sacred to Ravenscrag for longer than anyone can say.'

'And its prophecy was all but fulfilled, and then . . .'

'It's a bitter shame. The lord and lady, they don't deserve this, not after waiting so long.'

I wondered whether Marshilane knew about the boiling of so-called 'witches'; whether there were other excesses of which I had yet to learn.

'Do you know anything of a bane or curse associated with the Legend?'

She looked at me with apprehension in her eyes. 'I've heard nothing of that, sir. Why do you ask?'

'Just speculation, Marshilane. I'm trying to find an explanation for this dark mystery. Think no more of it. Come, let's go back to the castle.'

I helped her back up the slope. As we made our way through the orchard and gardens I asked her to tell me about Linvon the Light.

'That no-good rascal.' Marshilane shook her head, though I noted she was smiling to herself and her voice was without rancour. In fact she spoke almost with affection.

'He was taken with Moonblood, so I understand.'

'And she was not indifferent to him!'

119

'What was he like?'

'Oh, charming, handsome, debonair. He captivated us all.'

'Except Flarefist,' I corrected her.

'Oh, Lord Flarefist was taken with him at first, sir. So was Lady Sheerquine. Until they discovered he'd taken a shine to Mistress Moonblood. Then it was a different story. Linvon's just a young vagabond, sir. Not fit company for a lady.'

'Did Moonblood see a lot of him?'

'Can't have been a great deal, I don't think. But she was entranced, I'd have to say. She talked about him a lot until she realized her parents disapproved. She'd told me he was teaching her magic.'

'Linvon is a magician?'

'He knew some conjuring tricks. He'd entertained us all with them. But I don't see that it was real magic. More sleight of hand, that sort of thing.'

'How long was he at Ravenscrag?'

'A matter of three weeks in all, I'd say. He'd been entertaining in the town before someone brought him to the castle.'

'Who brought him to the castle?'

'I don't rightly know, sir.'

'How did Moonblood react when Lord Flarefist had him ejected?'

'She was miserable. Wouldn't speak to anyone for some time.'

'And after he'd gone, do you think they continued to meet in private?'

'It occurred to me, sir.' Marshilane gripped her lower lip with her teeth. She gave a little anguished sound. 'Oh, I should've kept a better look out for her. Oh my, what can have become of her now?'

We had reached the castle. 'Marshilane, have you touched Moonblood's room since we were there earlier?'

'No, sir.'

'Then please do not. I will want to look at it again more closely. If you can, ensure that no one else enters. Thank you for your help. Try not to dwell on what you fear may have happened. Nothing is certain, and we may yet find that your mistress is safe and well.'

Returning to my chambers I found Bris awaiting me with a reply from Cametta, inviting me to call upon her. Before going I had hoped to speak to Hectal but I found no trace of him in the immediate castle precincts, nor was there any answer at his door when I knocked. No one I asked could enlighten me as to his whereabouts.

Brief enquiries of servants led me to Lord Flarefist and Lady Sheerquine in the arcade where I had first spoken with Flarefist two days before. I approached them without formality. 'I have reason to believe there exists a bane which may have been placed upon Ravenscrag. It is in some way pertinent to the Legend.'

Lady Sheerquine looked around sharply. 'All conditions of the Legend have been met. You saw that for yourself.'

'That is something I hope we may discuss at greater length in due course. For now I can only reiterate my misgivings over the Legend as written. I am not convinced that it is intact. I implore you both, if you know anything of a bane or curse, or anything that in any way relates directly or indirectly, favourably or adversely, to the Legend as you have shown it to me, tell me now. If I do not have your complete honesty and cooperation I cannot continue with my investigations.'

Lady Sheerquine's haughty look served to remind me that I had little choice; but Lord Flarefist growled moodily, 'You've been listening to that duplicitous star-gawker.'

'Irnbold is anxious to prove to you his innocence of any involvement in this sad affair. To that end he has been most helpful.'

'He's anxious to save his damned deceiving hide, you mean!'

'I would not deny – and nor would he – that that is also true. Lord Flarefist, how can I impress this upon you? Your son has gone, now apparently your daughter too. You have offended your kinsmen and foreign nationals of high status. Troops from House Condark and probably elsewhere are on their way – '

'Bah!' Flarefist rapped his stick upon the floor. 'You're wrong, Bigbin. It is *they* who have offended *me*! And what do I care about their troops? I have already told you, they can do me no harm that has not already been done.'

I took a deep breath. 'Ravenscrag seems set for sure disaster. You have appointed me to try to solve this mystery, against my own better judgement. I have done everything I can. I find myself following numerous tangled leads with no true sense of moving towards a satisfactory resolution. Now I believe the Legend may hold a vital key. Again I implore you, both of you, if there is anything, anything at all that you have not revealed to me, then speak now. Your own lives, the lives of your children and the future of Ravenscrag may depend on it.'

Flarefist shuffled his feet in agitation; his wife tautly raised her chin, her lips puckered, her nostrils flaring. She stared at her husband until she caught his eye. I noted the look that passed between them. Flarefist, gaunt, his jaw trembling, seemed embarrassed and torn. Eventually he closed his moist grey eyes, sighed, and gave a nod. Lady Sheerquine looked down for a moment, one hand upon her breast. Then she said, 'Come.'

We left the old man to the torment of his raging psyche. Lady Sheerquine took me into the castle, to a small chamber in their private apartments. 'Lord Flarefist is becoming overwrought. His mind will not stand more stress.' She closed the door. 'We can speak here without fear of being overheard.'

Considering the secret passage I'd found little more than an hour before, I wondered whether this were so, but for now I said nothing.

'There is supposedly a bane,' said Sheerquine shrilly. She stood sidelong to me, facing into the room. 'But it cannot apply in this case. It refers to what might happen should the conditions of the Legend not be fully met. But as we know, all conditions have been met, thus rendering it invalid.'

'Nevertheless, I would see it.'

'You cannot. I do not have it. I can tell you what it says.'

'Where is it?'

'It was stolen.'

'When?'

'I don't know . . . exactly.'

'You have no idea?'

'I kept it in my chamber. One day I discovered it was gone. I had not looked at it for many months. It could have been taken at any time.'

'And you have no suspicions as to who might have purloined it?'

She hesitated just a moment. 'None.'

'What form does the bane take?'

'It is an inscription, on parchment.'

'The same parchment as that which holds the Legend?'

A flicker of discomfiture upon her marble face. 'It is.'

'So the parchment was not separated to prevent deterioration. What was your reason for cutting it?'

'There you are wrong, Master Dinbig. What I told you earlier was true. The bottom half of the manuscript had deteriorated, and was kept separately. I simply took it from its shelf in the archives.'

'Why?'

She glanced down at her hands. 'That Flarefist might not see it.'

'Lord Flarefist doesn't know about it?'

'He knows about it, of course. But his condition of mind has been such in recent months that he has forgotten it. I'm concerned for him. It is better that he is not reminded of the content of the bane. If he reads it there is no telling how it might affect him.'

The thought came that we might all sleep easier in our beds if the shock of it struck him dead, but again I held my silence. 'But he just gave his assent for you to talk to me.'

'He thinks we are discussing the Legend. Perhaps he has an inkling that there is something else, but his concentration span is limited. I think his mind will not allow him to recall that which he so desperately wants to hold at bay.'

'Did you know of the secret passage between Moonblood's chamber and the nursery?'

'Of course not. I learned of it and of our daughter's disappearance only minutes ago.' Sheerquine stepped towards the window, gathering her thoughts. She spoke haltingly, her back to me. 'I am going to tell you things that are not generally known, which have never been written. You are to learn Ravenscrag's secret, and you will disclose it to no one. Is that understood?'

'Of course.' I watched her, fascinated. She had not lost her composure. Her face was hidden but she remained statuesque, stoical, her emotion only evident by the slight tremor in her voice and a barely perceptible twitching of the head.

'Tradition states that the Bane was cast by Molgane, wife of Draremont, one of the first lords of Ravenscrag,' Sheerquine said. 'Molgane was convicted of dire witchery. At that time no law banned the practice, for the magic of witches was found to be, on the whole, benign. But Molgane had apparently been drawn to the dark side. She became powerful and malign. Her deeds brought misery and conflict to the land and its people. She was therefore executed by order of her husband.' Sheerquine paused, her head high. Then she turned to face me, her fingers linked in front of her. 'In her death agonies Molgane is said to have screamed words of vengeance upon House Ravenscrag. No written records exist, and so her precise words cannot be known. But it's said that she damned Ravenscrag for all time, stating that her spirit would haunt the place and that her kind would be ever present to ensure Ravenscrag's eventual ruin.'

'Did these events occur before or after the origin of the Legend?' I enquired.

'Listen without interruption, Master Dinbig, and you will learn.' Lady Sheerquine arched her neck and lifted her shoulders. 'Draremont passed a decree outlawing witchery. He fell to grieving, for he had greatly loved his wife. He became withdrawn, suffered anguish day and night, and by degrees lost his mind. One morning he was discovered dead in his bed. It was said that his final expression was a mask of horror, as though at some unspeakable vision.

'History is blurred, and we do not know precisely the turn of events. But Molgane's Bane has become interwoven with the Legend of Ravenscrag. The Bane is not spoken of, but to the few who know it is always a dark shadow lurking in the back of the mind. Yet it is plain that the Legend, being met in all its conditions, cannot be corrupted by the Bane. Sardus, the Master of Ledgers, spent a lifetime researching both Legend and Bane. He was convinced that it was so.'

'Of what did Sardus die?' I asked.

Lady Sheerquine replied with a disdainful smile. 'He was old, Master Dinbig. Very old. That is all. He caught a chill which turned to fever which he lacked the strength to fight. There are no suspicious circumstances.'

'Then tell me what is the content of Molgane's Bane, as it is understood.'

'That qualification is an important one, for the Bane as it relates to the Legend is cryptic and not easily interpreted. It speaks of Ravenscrag's long decline, then, as I said, appears to state a caveat in regard to the circumstances pertaining to the birth of the child who is destined to restore Ravenscrag's fortunes.' She closed her eyes:

> *'Waver so much as once from that which is said to be,*
> *and your hopes and your longings will fly . . . and you shall see*
> *that Ravenscrag will give birth not to its saviour*
> *but to its Iniquity.'*

'Iniquity?' I said.

Lady Sheerquine opened her eyes and gave a small shrug. 'That is what is written.'

'But there is more, surely?'

She stared at me fixedly for some seconds, breathing deeply, her breasts rising and falling beneath her grey robe. Her green eyes held a look almost challenging. 'There is a further reference, Master Dinbig, which implies that Molgane's Bane can yet be nullified even after its effects have become apparent. It can be done only by a specific person. That person is described as *the one who comes from afar, bringing strange knowledge and shattered gifts.'*

It took a moment to sink in. Then I returned her stare, dumbfounded. Here, apparently, was the answer to Ulen Condark's question as to why I alone had not been imprisoned with all the others of Ravenscrag's guests; and why I, who by dint of my magic might be most suspected to being involved in Redlock's abduction, had instead been appointed to investigate it.

It was written in the Legend! *Somehow, at least by Sheerquine and Flarefist's reckoning, I was a part of Ravenscrag's destiny!*

'And there is one other thing,' said Lady Sheerquine, her gaze unwavering. 'It states only that that person may find the means to lift the Bane, but that the price of his success may be his own life.'

Chapter Sixteen

'Mystery upon mystery upon mystery, and now a sentence of death into the bargain!' I flopped back in my seat, suddenly exhausted.

Cametta gazed at me, with concern. She wore a loose, pale red dress which left her slim arms bare and was gathered low over her breasts. She looked ravishing.

She had received me, somewhat to my disappointment, in her parlour. Unrealistically I had entertained hopes of something more. An hour or two of rapture-enhanced erotic play would have provided the distraction and solace I needed just now, notwithstanding my burns. Over the past fifteen hours my mind had become a tumult of unrest, the puzzles and insanities of the day clamouring and babbling there relentlessly. Oh, for some diversion!

Darean Lonsord was still at the castle. His duties weighed heavily upon him just now, and Cametta had seen nothing of him since last night. Nor did she know when to expect him back.

The temptation was great, but we both knew that to make love in Cametta's home at present would be inviting trouble. Now, of all times, we could not afford to arouse the slightest suspicion.

Upon my arrival Cametta's first utterance had been one of shock, though her reaction was tempered by the constraints of our situation. 'What has happened to your face; and your arms?'

I related to her much of what had happened since we'd last spoken. Lani brought dark ale, fruit cordial and biscuits. I drank the ale gratefully, and as I finished my account Cametta said, 'You must escape,' then added in a near-whisper, leaning towards me and glancing towards the door: 'Take me with you.'

'I can do neither. Sheerquine made it plain at our initial interview this morning that she had me under surveillance. Now, with her latest revelation, she has assigned a pair of lurching guards to me, that I might be under no illusions as to my standing. Their orders appear to be to stomp beside me wherever I go, clattering and clanging to the highest degree of their capabilities. They were with me as I came here from the castle; they await me outside now and will stomp back with me when I leave. They will no doubt sleep outside my door, and will be stomping at my back throughout my every waking moment, whether it be in the pursuance of my investigations or the voiding of my bowels!'

'Can you not elude or disable them with magic?'

'I could, yes, but it would gain me no advantage.' In a few words I endeavoured to explain to her something of the nature and limitations of *Zan-Chassin* magic. 'And moreover, Sheerquine and Flarefist have me in a trap. For the sake of those poor folk held now in Ravenscrag's dungeons, and those foreign dignitaries who are confined to their chambers, I'm compelled to strive to resolve this murky business. If Flarefist has free rein, any or all of them may die. War looms and dark forces seem to gather to create mayhem; doom hangs over Ravenscrag, and I unhappily have a part to play. Would that I could shrug my shoulders and walk away, but I can't.'

'I will speak to Sheerquine,' Cametta volunteered. 'We are friends. I've given her counsel in the past and she has heeded me. I think she will do so now. And Darean, if I tell him what is amiss, will add his words to mine and give them more weight.'

I shook my head ruefully. 'My love, you cannot. Sheerquine knows about you and me. This is the greatest threat she holds before me. You are yet another pawn in her desperate game.'

Cametta gave a gasp of horror. 'Oh the gods! Darean! He will kill me!'

'Darean knows nothing,' I hissed, glancing to the door. 'That is Sheerquine's threat; if I fail to do her bidding he will be told.'

Cametta was white with shock. 'Then we *must* escape. Together. And with my son, Alfair.'

I would have taken her hand to comfort her, but household staff passed to and fro beyond the open door. So I shook my head and said only, 'That is not the way.'

'Then how can we save ourselves?'

'I must do as I am bid, to the best of my ability. That way you at least will be safe.'

'But therein lies your death sentence.'

'I have heard Sheerquine's malediction, it's true, but I've yet to see the written word. Nothing is sure, of that I am convinced. Moreover, I count myself fortunate that I am not a man of exceptional courage. I will not rush heroically, blades flashing, into any affray, but rather will take every precaution to preserve my well-being. I like life and its bounties; I am still young. I've no yen yet to experience the bitter taste of death. So, I will proceed guardedly, with senses pared and nerves atwitch. If, as Sheerquine has stated, my death is implied in this mystery's unravelling, then at least I am forewarned, and thus forearmed. And my first task must be to unearth Molgane's Bane, for therein, it is plain, there are surely keys to the unlocking of this dire business.'

Cametta furrowed her beautiful brow. 'Molgane's Bane?'

I had forgotten, she knew nothing of the Bane. In my explanation I had made only oblique reference to it as a missing section of the Legend. My reservation was not out of consideration of my promise of silence to Lady Sheerquine; I had no qualms, ethical or moral, on that score. But I did not want Cametta to become alarmed, nor to speak of the Bane to others. 'It is just a name given to the missing part of the Legend,' I said with feigned nonchalance. 'But understand that I have taken you into my confidence. I need both your comfort and your counsel, but say nothing of what has passed between us here to any other. It is our secret.'

'My love, of course.'

'Tell me what you know of the misfortunes that have befallen Ravenscrag in your lifetime. How did they come about?'

Cametta narrowed her eyes and pouted her lips momentarily in concentration. She gave a small shrug of her elegant shoulders. I quivered as I fought with my desire for her. 'I don't know a lot. For many years, going back to before my birth, there have been political differences with House Condark. It is widely held that Condark wishes to add Ravenscrag to its dominion. But there has never been open conflict on that score, only coolness in relations, as far as I'm aware. The greater misfortune has come about through the long-term squandering of funds.'

'By Flarefist?'

'Lord Flarefist is responsible in part, certainly. He has frittered away untold amounts of the Ravenscrag fortune on lavish galas, fêtes, pageants . . . He has always been given to extravagance, bestowing generous gifts upon those who please him. This very house was given to Darean in return for his service. And at the same time Flarefist has failed to properly maintain his properties and estates. He has done nothing to encourage development or economic growth. He is remiss in collecting dues, and has allowed taxes to remain unrealistically low rather than incur the resentment of the people. But he is not solely responsible. His forebears acted in a similar manner; he merely carried on in the way of generations.'

'Yet it must have been evident for many years, perhaps decades, that the coffers could not support such extravagances,' I mused, and thought to myself: *Almost as if the successive lords of Ravenscrag were induced, or indeed possessed, to behave in such a manner.*

I stopped myself. Was it not demonstrably in our basic nature to partake short-sightedly of the pleasures of the moment at the possible expense of long-term interests? Indulgence was the norm wherever the harshness of life gave space to admit it. It was a vast leap of imagination to associate it with supernatural possession.

Yet the thought lingered, and I cursed again that I was unable to view the written words of Molgane's Bane.

'Tell me, what was the feeling when it was learned that Lady Sheerquine was pregnant with Redlock?'

'Oh, immense joy!'

'Mingled, surely, with apprehension? For since Moonblood had she not lost four infants at or near birth?'

129

'Yes. But when the pregnancy was announced it was with a feeling of euphoria, of being at one with destiny. Most especially when Irnbold and Elmag gave their forecasts. For the Legend has for so long been on everyone's lips, and now, suddenly, here it was, a time foretold. You cannot imagine how we all felt. Such hope, Dinbig. Yes, in our hearts we questioned whether it could possibly be true. But all the signs were there. Even the most cynical among us were drawn to believe.'

And I thought: *And quite possibly you were not mistaken, for the Legend appears to have come true, but in its fullness, in the parts known only to a few.*

'Did not one of those four babies, the one most recently born, survive its birth?'

Cametta nodded sadly. 'By a few days. She was a little girl, born two weeks early. Yet for all that she was a good size. She might have survived had not the weather been so bitterly cold and damp. Her nurse found her dead in her crib one morning.'

'Am I right in thinking that Moonblood was fond of her?'

'She doted on her. She was very distressed when the baby died. Moonblood is a lonely child.'

'Was the baby named?'

Cametta nodded. 'Misha.'

'How long ago did this occur?'

'About three years.'

I sipped my ale and wondered how things might have turned out had that unfortunate infant lived. After some moments of reflection I said, 'It has struck me as odd that while witchery is outlawed here, and is met with summary punishment, old Elmag is permitted to practise her craft – at least, she has been till now. And Irnbold too, for that matter.'

'Elmag is a farseer, not a witch. She has never cast spells, nor brewed potions, nor taken a familiar. She gives neither blessing nor curses; she simply divines. Her gift has been validated on a number of occasions over many years. Long ago she won Flarefist's confidence by predicting perfidy on the part of a local baron, Vesmund by name. Acting on Elmag's advice Flarefist secretly visited one of Vesmund's confidantes and learned, through threats and cajolements, that Vesmund planned his, Flarefist's, murder. It would be passed off as a hunting accident.

Thus, as Vesmund and his assassin rode to join the hunt, they were attacked and killed by persons unknown.'

'Hardly an unequivocal demonstration of Elmag's powers of clairvoyance; but point taken. What of Irnbold?'

'Astrology is a science, a method of interpretation. We all desire a glimpse of what the future may hold. Irnbold has provided advice, comfort and insights into the life-problems of many of us, without recourse to witchery.'

I smiled. 'You sound like an expert astrologer.'

'Irnbold has taught me something of the rudiments of his craft.'

'As he did Moonblood. Do you know anything of giants?'

Cametta shook her head. 'There are none.'

'You are sure?'

'Perhaps far to the north, towards the mountains of the Interior, a few still exist. But they have not been seen near human settlements, not in a hundred years.'

'But there are other things in the forest.'

Cametta gave a small shudder. 'So it is said. Even our woodsmen do not venture further than they need into the forest.'

I sat back, one elbow upon the arm of my chair, forefinger crooked beneath my nose, thoughtful. Cametta's face was set in questioning concentration, but she smiled when she saw that I was gazing at her. A strand of long dark brown hair had fallen in front of her face. My gaze travelled over her body. She put her cup down upon the table, her breasts beneath her dress quivering slightly with the movement. Her slim thighs and knees were held loosely together, her pale, shapely calves and ankles were bare. There was an urgent pressing in my trousers. I leaned towards her. 'Cametta, I ache to take you in my arms and make love to you. Is there no way that we could contrive to spend an hour or so alone together?'

'Oh, my love, would that we could, for I too want nothing more. But it is impossible, you know it is. For all I know Darean may be on his way home even now, and I cannot come to you at the castle. The only way is that we leave this place somehow, together, with my son. Then I will be with you for all time.'

Its impracticality aside, this was not what I'd had in mind. But she was right, and I'd known it: to give way to our passions now might prove to be a fatal error.

'I must return then, alas, and apply myself further to this increasingly strange and complex business.'

We both stood, and Cametta gazed at me anxiously. 'I am afraid. For you, for me, for all of us.'

I took her hand and bent to kiss it, inhaling her perfume, allowing my lips to linger just a second or two upon the mounds of her knuckles. 'Calm your fears. I will not allow you to be harmed. Say nothing.'

She gave a sharp little gasp. Her eyes were wide, focused on something behind me. I released her hand and turned. In the doorway stood her husband, Darean Lonsord.

'Master Dinbig,' he said without warmth, advancing with a swagger into the room. 'I am surprised to find you here. Surely your time is taken up entirely at the castle?'

'Not entirely, Captain. I am first and foremost a merchant, remember.'

'A merchant who lacks access to his goods, I believe.' He lifted the jug of ale and, there being no third mug, brought it directly to his lips and drank.

'Master Dinbig came here to apologise, Darean,' put in Cametta, with an admirable tone of indignation. 'Yesterday I gave him an order for a number of gowns and some outfits for Alfair. Now he brings me the news that he is unable to deliver due to restrictions placed upon him by Lord Flarefist and Lady Sheerquine. He says he is denied access to his stock. Is this so?'

Jug in hand her husband moved to her and threw a muscular arm about her shoulders. 'It is.'

'Then it's too much! I was so looking forward to receiving those garments today. I have nothing to wear now.'

'Which is just the way I like it,' leered Lonsord. He pushed his face in front of hers. 'Now, does a husband get a welcome-home kiss?'

I suppressed my anger: he *was* her husband after all.

'It isn't good enough, Darean. They are such beautiful clothes. I am so disappointed.'

Cametta tried to move away but her husband's arm kept her to him. She used her feigned disappointment to justify denying him the kiss, though. He frowned. 'Ah, so that's how it is. Very well, I'll speak to Sheerquine when I return to the castle. Is that good enough?' He looked back at me with an inimical smile. 'Nothing but the best for my wife, eh, Master Merchant?'

'Quite so. Madam Cametta is deserving of only the very best.'

'And she has it, in me!' He laughed like a boor and swigged again from the jug of ale. 'And now, I believe you were leaving, weren't you? My beautiful wife and I wish to be alone.'

He winked, his tongue sliding along his lips. I fought down my feelings, wished them both good day, and departed.

I returned to the castle, my two lummocking guards stomping at my shoulders. I was making for Moonblood's chamber, to look again in the hope of finding some clue. Passing through the main wing I came upon Lady Sheerquine who was instructing a maid upon some household duty in a side passage off one of the main corridors. I stopped and addressed her.

'My lady, I would have a brief word with you, if it is not inconvenient.'

Her green eyes flickered over me unwelcomingly, but she sent the maid on her way, then addressed the guards. 'You two, wait along the corridor.' She turned back to me. 'What is it? Please be brief, I am very busy.'

'Firstly, this latest move on your part is intolerable. How can I be expected to conduct investigations in a full, proper and discreet manner with a pair of coarse, clanking troopers forever at my side? I cannot possibly proceed under these conditions.'

'What would you have me do?'

'Remove them.'

'So that you may remove yourself? Come now, Master Dinbig. I have already cautioned you not to take me for a fool.'

'I am a man of honour. I have given you my word – '

'No, you are not. You are a sly opportunist who considers his own skin before all others. What do you care about us? Nothing! And I'll wager that when you know your own life is at risk you care nothing for your men – or Cametta either.'

'Lady Sheerquine, even were I to attempt to escape, the odds are heavily against me, as you must acknowledge. The fact is that, regardless of Molgane's Bane, my best hope is to continue here to try to bring about a satisfactory end to this mystery. But I cannot do that – it is impossible – with two lumbering jobbernowls endlessly clonking at my side.'

Sheerquine surveyed me down the length of her nose. 'I will give the matter due consideration. Is that all?'

'One other thing. Tell me, how did you come to name your daughter Moonblood?'

Her chin rose and a wariness crept into her gaze. 'It was a decision made between my husband and myself. The name appealed. Why?'

'It is an unusual name. Unique in my experience. Is it common in Pansur?'

'No, not at all.'

'It has a certain poetry to it.'

'Perhaps, if a single word can be described as a poem.'

'Two words, in effect. Perhaps you are familiar with stories of the Mabbuchai cult of orator-poets of south-western Dyarchim, who strive to reduce their art to its simplest and most essential form. Several have achieved poems of only two or three words. It is the manner in which they recite them that is all-important, of course. A few have reputedly created single-word poems, though admittedly none of these has been officially acknowledged by the Dyarch Academy of Music and Verse. But there is one, Or-Hurun the Melancholic, who has attained the ultimate. He has originated poems which contain no words at all; the poetry of pure silence. Folk, rich and poor, flock from far and wide to witness Or-Hurun saying nothing.'

Sheerquine snorted. 'Then they are credulous gulls; and he is a charlatan, or a fool.'

'Perhaps, but he gives them what they desire and none complain. And he has achieved wealth and fame as a result.'

She fluttered her hand in a gesture of irritation. 'Where is this leading, Master Dinbig? I have no time for idle chat.'

'Leading nowhere, my lady. It is a mere aside. Though it is undeniable that very often that which we do not say may be of greatest importance in our lives, wouldn't you agree?'

She stared at me balefully.

'My interest is in your daughter, and her name,' I said. 'You see, I cannot help but wonder whether the name was chosen purely and simply to fit the Legend.'

Her mouth opened, then she became suddenly still. Her body seemed almost to swell, and her look would have withered a lesser man. Plainly I had succeeded in touching a raw nerve.

Sheerquine collected herself with a shuddering breath. But the signs of her discomposure could not pass so quickly. I had never seen her so lose her iron control. 'Not at all,' she said.

I nodded. 'Ah.'

Sheerquine made to move away. 'Is that all now?'

'For now, yes, indeed. Thank you, my lady. You have been most helpful. You won't forget my escort, will you?'

She was gone, with a rustling of her robe and a waft of winter-geranium, pacing straight-backed along the corridor, her head held high.

Chapter Seventeen

Through a narrow arched window, as I continued on towards Moonblood's chamber, I caught a glimpse of a solitary figure standing by a stone wall in a sunlit quadrangle below. I paused thoughtfully, then hastily retraced my steps and descended by the stairs, the two bearded oafs cantering thumpishly in my wake.

I emerged onto the sunbeaten earth and flagstones of the quadrangle. On the other side Hectal still stood, his crooked back to me, apparently intent upon something on the wall before him. I began to approach, then turned back to my guards. 'You two remain here. I will be in full view and can go nowhere, but I cannot have Master Hectal being distracted by your presence.'

They exchanged shifty glances and muttered uncertainly, but were plainly unfamiliar with the concept of making decisions for themselves, and so obeyed me.

I approached Hectal somewhat sidelong. I saw that he was picking small clumps of green moss from the wall. He scrutinized each fragment fastidiously, turned it around in his fingers, examined the dark, dry earth on its underside, sniffed it, first with one nostril then with the other. Then he flicked it away, testily shaking his bald head and tut-tutting to himself, and gave his attention to the next piece.

As I drew close Hectal came upon a scrap of moss that seemed to meet with his approval. He grinned, murmuring to himself with pleasure, and popped it into his mouth, earth and all. He chewed vigorously, thin brows lifting and falling as though with a life of their own, eyes closed in a display of ecstasy.

I waited. One of Hectal's eyes half opened and settled upon me. He produced a smile of sorts, still relishing the delicacy. He swallowed, then turned back to the wall. He picked off another clump, subjected it to the usual examination, then discarded it and searched for another.

His face lit up. 'Aha!'

He broke off a tiny piece and placed it upon the tip of his glistening pink tongue. The tongue vanished inside his mouth, he sampled the titbit with wet sounds and shifting chops, then he nodded enthusiastically. He offered the larger piece to me.

'Ah, no, thank you, Hectal.'

Hectal frowned. He looked closely at the moss, seemingly mystified by my refusal, then beckoned me nearer with his forefinger. I bent forward. Hectal pointed, showing the tightly packed green fur and the reddish tendrils, no thicker than hairs, which stood erect from the green, widening into tiny bulbs at the top. 'Seedheads,' said Hectal, nodding rapidly. 'Seedheads.'

'Quite so. Hectal, I wanted to say – '

He pushed the moss towards me again. Once more I made to decline, but something in his look and manner made me hesitate. His smile had withered and there was a poignant, quizzical quality in his gaze. I reminded myself that this man had aided me, albeit in a roundabout and thoroughly confusing way. I was almost certain he had more to offer. It would not do to disappoint or offend him by trampling on his generosity.

Thus I accepted the moss. Hectal beamed and made circular motions with one hand upon his belly. I opened my mouth and inserted the clump, earth and all. Slowly I began to chew. It was bitter, it was gritty, it was earthy, it was dry. I fought hard to keep myself from gagging.

Hectal nodded delightedly. 'Good?'

'Yes. Good.'

He searched the wall, found another piece for himself and ate it with a muted chuckle of glee. Gradually I masticated my piece enough to attempt to swallow. It went down slowly, tried to come back up somewhat more quickly, then eventually went down again.

Hectal began frantically picking at the wall, casting reject moss here and there until he found more that met his standards of excellence. He offered this to me, several pieces at once. I cupped my hands to accept them. 'I will eat them later, Hectal. Perhaps as a side dish with my supper.'

He cocked his head. He seemed to like that idea. I broached the matter that was on my mind. 'Hectal, you were right. There was nothing there. It was empty.'

Hectal gave a loud whoop of laughter and performed a little jig. He struck his forehead. 'Empty! *Thonk!*'

'And you were right about cooking the baby, and about Condark's troops. Your somethings have proved invaluable to me. You are a clever fellow.'

His mad eyes rested on my face, his smile gently mocking. 'I like the somethings.'

'I too. Are there more?'

'More. Oh, more somethings. Where you can't see.'

'Perhaps I can learn to see, with your help, as I have done already.'

'Mmmh. Are you a fool?'

I hesitated. 'I have not previously considered myself in that light – '

'Then you will not see.'

'Why is it that only a fool can see, Hectal?'

Hectal drew down his eyelid, exposing the moist red flesh and the bloodshot ball of his eye. 'A fool is allowed. He sees, he hears, he knows, because no one cares.'

'You mean you are privy to secrets and perhaps trysts and confidences, because no one considers you intelligent enough to understand them. I can see that that may be so. And I sense that your mind may be a repository of useful knowledge. They have underestimated you, old fellow, as have I. And now you play a game. Is that it?'

Hectal winked and leered. His expression became inward. He

138

bent his knees slightly, tensed and farted. Then he giggled and wafted his hands in the air. 'Whew!'

I waited before speaking again. 'One thing you said to me this morning: "You will not understand her fate." Did you mean Moonblood?'

His expression was suddenly mournful. 'Moonblood. Hectal's sad.'

'Because she's gone? Do you know where? Is she alive?'

'Taken in the night,' he said, and gazed around into the air.

'Hectal, this is important. I think Moonblood may be in danger. Do you know where she has gone?'

'To a woman,' said Hectal. 'There's the where. Hectal sorry. Hectal sad.'

'Which woman? Who?'

He stared fixedly at me and shook his head. 'You cannot understand.'

'I want to understand, Hectal. Help me to.'

He shook his head again and moved off a little way to resume his inspection of the wall.

'You knew about the secret passage,' I said. 'Who else knew? Moonblood?'

He tested some moss with the tip of his tongue. 'Nothing there,' he said in a faraway voice. 'Gone to a woman.'

'Molgane? Is that who you mean? Has Moonblood been taken by the evil Molgane?'

Hectal frowned, as though thoroughly confused. I sensed that I was losing his interest. The game had palled, at least for now. I tried once more. 'What of a missing scroll, Hectal? The one which contains Molgane's Bane.'

He glanced at me sidelong, but without enthusiasm. His eyes were moist. 'You will know.'

'How?'

'It will come to you. There is the blood.'

He chuckled again, but half-heartedly, then gave his full attention to the moss. I watched him for a few moments more, then began to walk back across the quadrangle, passing my guards who observed bemusedly from some yards away. They fell in behind me. I stopped, and turned, wanting to ask Hectal something more. But he had gone, though I could not see where he could have disappeared to so quickly.

Moonblood's chamber had apparently not been touched since I'd been there a couple of hours earlier, which pleased me. There was a guard beside the door, and a good distance along in the shadowed gloom of the corridor I made out the figure of the old sentry posted between the nursery door and that of Blonna's cell, trying hard not to doze.

I was further pleased that my own guards no longer stomped at my shoulders. Presumably Lady Sheerquine had perceived the logic in my argument, and ordered them back to other duties. I had little doubt, though, that every eye in the place had been instructed to observe and report my movements. Wherever I went, or tried to go, I would not be entirely alone.

I entered the room, which was deserted. The bed stood as Marshilane had left it, covers rumpled and drawn back, blood-stained night-robe upon the sheet. The entrance to the secret passage still gaped, the heavy blue drape drawn back. Moonblood's dolls sat as they had sat before. Her clothes and belongings were untouched. The earthenware pitcher stood beside her bedside table.

Taking the pitcher I quickly left Moonblood's room and strode along the corridor to Blonna's cell. At my request the old sentry unlocked the door.

'Blonna, good news.' I entered with deliberate ebullience. 'I am making progress.' I held up the pitcher. 'Have you ever seen this jug before?'

Blonna looked up, strain on her face. Her eyes widened. 'That's the one. That's the one that was taken from the nursery.'

'How can you be sure of this? It's of common enough design; I would guess there are others like it in the castle.'

'Look at its belly, there, sir. It's warped. And there's a tiny chip on the rim, and a hairline crack about an inch long . . .' She reached up for the pitcher. 'Yes, here's the chip, and the crack, here. That's how I know.'

'Excellent!'

'Where did you find it, sir?'

'I will tell you presently.' I left Blonna with a further word of reassurance and returned with the pitcher to Moonblood's bed-chamber. I replaced it where I had found it.

Next I inspected the bed, and the torn, bloody night-robe. The tear was at the shoulder, where a hem had given way as if wrenched with force. The material had not been slashed, nor was there a perforation which a stabbing blade would have made. The dried blood was quite liberally strewn, largely over the middle to lower area of the garment. In the centre of the mattress the blood had collected in a single stain, smearing out towards the edge.

I looked at this for some moments. Its pattern suggested that Moonblood had initially lain still after receiving a wound of some kind, and had then been pulled from the bed. The stain was not particularly copious, as would have been made by a mortal injury, nor was there any sign of blood elsewhere, such as on the floor.

She had not died from her wound, at least not in her room, of that I was virtually sure.

I cast my eyes around the wall. Wainscot, drapes or wardrobe might conceal another hidden passage. I moved to the wall and began to check behind the hangings. I was brought up short by a noise. A muffled scraping, irregular, coming from somewhere close by.

I identified the source immediately. The passage! Somebody or something was in there.

Swiftly I moved to the wooden panel, grabbing a heavy metal candlestick for use as a weapon if need be. I pressed my back to the drape and waited.

The sounds came closer to the entrance. An uneven, stumbling drag of footsteps, the scrape of a body against the confining walls, and a coarse, laboured wheezing.

The panel vibrated suddenly at my back as something thumped against its other side. I tensed. Whoever was there, we were separated by the mere thickness of the wood. I raised the candlestick.

There was another thump, a curse, then a hand appeared, gnarled fingers curling around the edge of the panel. I poised to strike. A head emerged.

'Lord Flarefist!'

Flarefist, his face sweating and begrimed, peered at me in ireful bewilderment. 'You again!' He dragged himself through the opening. 'What are you doing with that candlestick?'

'Preparing to defend myself.' I took his arm and helped him into the chamber. 'What are you doing?'

'Wanted to see the bastard tunnel for myself.' He stood panting and bowed, blinking. 'Cramped in there. And damnably dark. Couldn't see a cursed thing.'

'Didn't you take a lamp?'

'I dropped the damned thing and it went out. Been feeling my way forward blind.' With a shaking hand he brushed at the dust and cobwebs that marked his clothing. 'Filthy in there. Can't think what it was used for.'

'It was almost certainly used most recently to facilitate the abduction or transformation of your son, Redlock,' I said. Another thought had recently struck me, obliging me to rethink my attempts at reconstructing the circumstances of last night. The existence of the passage meant that the intruder would not have had to wait for any great length of time in the armoire in the nursery. Therefore, he or she, or it, could have brought the monstrous brat. Perhaps the creature had slept, or the intruder had left it in the passage between the thick stone walls until the moment came to deposit it in the nursery. At any rate, the risk of the weird-cub's disturbing Blonna was significantly reduced with the discovery of the passage. Thus I had to think once more in terms of abduction and substitution, rather than transformation.

I was not sure whether this was a good or a bad thing. It didn't actually advance me a jot in my investigations. Quite the opposite, in fact.

'You think Moonblood's run off with the baby, don't you?' said Flarefist accusingly.

'I didn't say so. Is that your opinion?'

'Bah! She thinks she's got the magical touch, but it's all in her head. Not by all the devils and demons in the great forest could she have done that.'

'Let's assume you're right, that Moonblood did not create the monster that we found in Redlock's crib. Yet might she have brought it here from elsewhere, and then taken Redlock?'

'What the hell for?'

'That has yet to be ascertained.'

142

'She was in the banqueting hall when Redlock disappeared.'
Flarefist rammed his stick down angrily on the rug. 'You know it,
man. I saw you dancing with her.'

'An accomplice, then?'

His bowed shoulders seemed to tremble with emotion. He
shook his head ferociously. 'What about the blood?'

I glanced back at the bed. 'A good question. Yet we are
assuming the blood is your daughter's. It may not be.'

'It's her blasted bed, dammit! Whose else could it be?'

'I am trying to keep an open mind.' I knew, more certainly than
I had known anything for a good many hours, that I had to find
Molgane's Bane. The Bane *had* to contain some clue, some
reference that would shed light on this miasma of circumstances.
Without it I was lost. I could see no way forward.

I stared at Lord Flarefist. Might he be the thief? Unlikely, but
dare I ask him about the Bane? I considered Sheerquine's words.
What would be the consequences of reminding Flarefist of the
existence of Ravenscrag's age-old curse?

Flarefist returned my stare heatedly, evidently outraged by my
imputations or my presence or both. Then he tipped his troubled
grey head askew. 'What's that kerfuffle?'

I became conscious of noises outside the chamber. A man's
voice was calling, 'My lord! My lord!' There were running
footsteps in the corridor.

I stepped across to the door. A servant came rushing down the
corridor.

'Lord Flarefist is here,' I called.

The man halted, breathless. 'My lord, come quickly. It's the
baby.'

'What? What has happened?' cried Flarefist, lurching from the
chamber.

'You must come, my lord!'

As quickly as we could, hobbled somewhat by Lord Flarefist's
rheumatic gait, we followed the frantic servant. Down, through
the main wing of the castle, to the ground level, then beyond, past
the kitchens and sculleries, and down again into the cellars. Here,
apparently, was where the weird-cub had been kept since its
narrow escape from fire that morning.

We entered a short, dank, torchlit passage with a low arched roof. At its end, where it widened into a small storage area, was a wooden door. In front of this a shocking sight met our eyes.

Stretched upon the dark earth floor was a man, another servant. His clothes were torn, his face and limbs were a bloody, mangled mess. He was moaning loudly, his body contorted in terrible pain. Markin the physician knelt beside him with water and clean linen cloth, trying to staunch the flow of blood.

A pair of soldiers and another servant stood by, gazing with frightened faces from the wooden door to the wounded man and back again. The door, which was closed, shuddered violently, as if something on its other side was trying to break through. A scraping sound and furious snarling, snuffling noises came from the cellar beyond.

'What's going on here? What's happened?' demanded Lord Flarefist.

I knelt beside the wounded servant and invoked a healing rapture. I saw now that he was horribly mutilated. The flesh of his right cheek and temple had been ripped partially away, hanging in bloody strips, the bone exposed. One eye socket was filled with blood and it appeared the eye had been gouged out. There were savage claw-marks down his neck and over his breast and thigh. Chunks of flesh seemed to have been torn from his bones.

Having applied the rapture I straightened, sickened. A soldier was explaining to Lord Flarefist: 'He was taking the thing its feed. He opened the door and stepped in and it flew at him. He managed to get out, and shut the door, but in those few seconds it all but tore him to pieces.'

Flarefist gaped, confounded. 'Flew at him? Tore him to pieces? It's a baby!'

The soldier nodded fearfully at the rattling door. 'No longer, sir.'

I looked at the door. At its base there was a gap of an inch or so between rotting timber and floor. There something moved, a dark, questing, ravening snout, snuffling furiously back and forth. I shuddered.

Flarefist had seen it too. 'What is that?'

The other servant spoke. 'It's grown, my lord. It's changed in hours from a helpless infant to a furied, savage thing. It's as big as a young boar.'

Flarefist stared at him. 'What by all the gods have you been feeding it on?' he demanded absurdly, as if diet could explain the sudden, terrible, unnatural growth.

The servant giggled hysterically. I looked back at the poor, mutilated man on the floor and said, in horror at my own words, 'Try pushing some raw meat under the door. That may quieten it.'

Two more soldiers arrived at a run in the passage. I stared at that evil snout below the door, my ears assaulted by the dreadful sounds that issued from within. And into my mind, unbidden, the words floated darkly: . . . *and Ravenscrag shall give birth not to its saviour, but to its Iniquity. And you will all see its Iniquity rise.*

Chapter Eighteen

. . . And you will all see its Iniquity rise.

The words hung in my mind, lowering and dark, as if written in storm-clouds across the sky. From where had they come? They had not been spoken to me, by Sheerquine or anyone else; nor had I set eyes on them in written form. But I felt certain of their validity. And I knew without question that when – if ever – I came to read Molgane's Bane, I would find those words inscribed there.

I lay upon my bed, my head cradled in my hands upon the pillow. Outside the elongating shadows of early evening crept slowly down from the heights, deepening as they came. The last night of darkmoon was almost upon us.

Tomorrow the new lunar cycle would begin, marked by the reappearance of the radiant slender crescent. But I could not forget or dismiss Hectal's words early that morning: *Tonight is the last of darkmoon, but there will be another before you know it. Shadow-night comes.*

A chucklehead, a halfwit, a congenital lunatic who dined on moss. And an enigma. He knew more than he said, and I was now convinced had a greater insight into what was happening here than anyone else in Ravenscrag. But what did he mean by Shadow-night?

And I thought of the words of the Legend of Ravenscrag: . . .
*four must perish since the blood of the moon was spilled, but that
done, one at last will come* . . .

The blood of the moon . . . Four *had* perished, that much I'd
confirmed. And the one, Redlock, had come – and then . . .

Moonblood. What had happened to her? What was her part in
all this? Could she be involved in Redlock's abduction or
transformation? She had betrayed anxiety over the birth. Had she
known something of what was going to occur?

I almost dozed, I was so weary. But each time, as my eyelids
grew heavy and I slipped towards semi-consciousness, I was
jerked rudely back to wakefulness. The clamour in my mind was
relentless, a maelstrom of questions, doubts, and images of weird
and disturbing menace.

Far below, deep within the ancient castle, in the gloomy cellar
where a servant had almost died, a demonic creature paced.
Following my suggestion chunks of rabbit meat and raw pork had
been pushed under the door. The thing fell upon the flesh with
ravening fury. The door ceased to shudder, the snarls and growls
grew intermittent. Its belly filled, the creature became subdued, at
least for a time.

How had it grown so suddenly, transformed from a tiny helpless
cub to a frenzied monster in just hours? What manner of creature
was it? And, equally important, what was it *becoming*?

I had argued with Lord Flarefist, who wanted the creature
destroyed there and then. Somehow I prevailed, and now the
cellar door, which was not particularly sturdy, was reinforced with
strong boards and further bolstered with heavy sacks of sand and
earth. A space had been left at the base so that raw meat might still
be pushed through to the dire beast.

In the wider area of the passage outside the cellar door, six
nervous guards were stationed. They were well armed and
equipped with strong rope netting and metal mesh. They had
orders to slay the creature should it somehow manage to force its
way through the barricade – an impossibility at present, but if its
present rate of growth continued . . .

I screwed up my eyes, trying to push the thought from my head.
I felt justified in my efforts to keep it alive, but I could not help but
be haunted by notions of its escape. There were moments when I

wondered whether it might have been better to have let Flarefist have his way. But what if the creature, by some sorcerous transformation, was Redlock?

Molgane's Bane. Where was I to find it? I could approach Hectal again, but his game seemed to be to give only cryptic clues, leaving me to solve them myself – or not, as the case might be. And I had no guarantee that Hectal knew of the whereabouts of the missing scroll anyway.

I got up from my bed, fraught and frustrated, and angrily poured myself a cup of wine. Within me I knew an ambivalence. I wanted desperately to be done with this whole business. I was isolated in Ravenscrag, cut off from all outside contact, trapped and endangered. I wanted to be gone from here, never to return. Never again to think of Ravenscrag's Legend or its Bane. Never encounter its people. Escape, and then cast Ravenscrag and everything associated with it from my mind.

But on the other hand – I could not deny it – I was intrigued. Notwithstanding its obvious dangers to myself, this mystery was irresistible. Part of me knew that I could not let myself walk away from it, even if the choice had been mine to make. I would never forgive myself if I took that course. I would be irked for the remainder of my lifetime, never knowing, never having the satisfaction of explaining, or at least coming to some sensible understanding of what had befallen Ravenscrag and its inhabitants.

Ah, but how maddening! Nothing was clear. So much had happened in so short a time, and none of it made sense. Perhaps I was too close, too involved. If I could just attain a little distance I might see something that was presently obscured.

'I am *Zan-Chassin*!' I reminded myself, and with this thought came the recognition that, even if my physical movements were restricted, there was a way in which I might to some extent detach myself from the storm, and perhaps even secure advice.

I returned to the bed and arranged myself cross-legged upon it. I commenced the preparatory steps for entering *Zan-Chassin* trance.

Taking note, one by one, of every object before me I attuned myself to the chamber, to its ambience and physical character. I focused inward upon my body, its muscles, tendons and sinews, its tingling nerves and pulsing organs. The process was second nature and took only moments, yet it demanded a supreme effort of concentration. Ideally the mind is wholly free of encumbrances and distractions when entering trance; one is both mentally and physically refreshed and alert. My mind was far from being unencumbered, and I was tired and my skin was raw and angry from its burns.

But I completed the first preparations and entered trance, dissolving the objective world. No longer anchored, I came from my corporeal form and rested alongside and slightly above myself. I sent forth a summons to my bound spirit ally, my Custodian, Yo.

'I am here, Master.' He announced himself almost upon the instant.

'Yo, I am pleased. I have a task for you. I wish you to take custody of my living body while I journey in the Realms.'

'Very good, Master. Master, may I first ask a question?'

'You may.'

'Have you yet found for me the physical form that I will occupy within your strange world of matter, as you promised?'

I had anticipated the question. The role of the Custodian entity is unique in that, once it has been bound to service, it is provided by its *Zan-Chassin* master with an animal form. By this means the entity comes to familiarize itself with the physical world, of which it has had no previous experience. The Custodian then serves a dual role. It takes temporary protective custody of its master's body when he, or she, journeys into the Realms of Non-Beings; and further, it is capable of providing assistance in the physical world, by dint of its physical form.

'I have chosen your form, Yo,' I replied. 'It is that of a Wide-Faced Bear, a wild species fairly common to my world. Upon my return to Khimmur I will set about the preparations, select a pregnant female bear whose cub you will become, and establish the ritual in order that you may be born into this world.'

'Thank you, Master. But can I not be human like yourself?'

'That is not possible, Yo. The human man or woman is infinitely complex. The human infant would not adapt well to occupation by an unworldly spirit. You must take a simpler form.'

'But why, Master?'

'It is Moban's way. We cannot say why. It is possible that in time, after many rebirths and lifetimes in the simpler life-forms, you may acquire the knowledge and experience to finally be born human. But if it transpires at all, it will be a long, long time hence. In the meantime, consider your privilege. As my servant you have many opportunities denied others of your kind. Not only will you learn of the corporeal world via the animal form which I will provide you with, but you are also privileged to take charge for limited periods of my own physical body. It is an invaluable experience, Yo. Use it well.'

'Of course, Master.'

'And now I would journey, for I must speak with the spirits of the dead. You will take custody of my body while I am gone.'

'I am your servant.'

I pronounced the ritual incantation which would ensure my physical protection in my absence. 'Custodian, enter this form and guard it until my return. Keep it as you would your own. If it thirsts, let it drink, if it requires sustenance, let it feed. If it is endangered protect it and recall its rightful occupant. Ensure that none sever the cord between this body and its rightful occupant. Guard it well, for this is your sacred duty. Fail, and your true name will be broadcast to your enemies. You will be cast out of this world in shame, naked and without ability, for ever.'

'It shall be as you command, Master.'

Yo entered my corporeal form. I hesitated anxiously for a moment. There is always a nagging fear when passing control of one's physical form to an entity and embarking upon a journey within the Realms. One can never be wholly sure of what one will find, either in journeying or upon one's return.

Since my initiation as a *Zan-Chassin* Adept of the First Realm I had journeyed perhaps half a dozen times, and then only briefly, leaving Yo in charge of my body. The demands of a physical body, coupled with Yo's general unfamiliarity with the corporeal world, gave him quite limited capabilities, and I had always returned to find my body more or less as I had left it. None the less, there was always the possibility that, through omission, oversight, or circumstances wholly beyond his control he might fail to heed its welfare, and I took leave with a hollow feeling.

150

I soared high, out of that chamber, over the ramshack, sun-tiled roofs of Ravenscrag castle and town. I sped up, ever up, topping the rocky heights of Pansur, leaving them far behind, rising into the failing blue. High above the world I parted the fabric between realities and passed into First Realm.

The Realms as we conceive them are an extension of the world as it is normally experienced, an incalculably vast, perhaps infinite region of existence which becomes accessible only to a few, and then only after long and arduous training. By such training the *Zan-Chassin* initiate attains a heightened awareness which confers to some extent an ability to perceive this 'other' world. With further development he or she is able to actually leave the physical body and enter this realm and interact with the spirit entities that are its denizens.

First Realm, then, is in *Zan-Chassin* terminology the initial stage of discovery of a formerly unperceived aspect of Moban's great and wondrous creation.

The entities that inhabit the Realms mirror us inasmuch as they have virtually no awareness of us or the corporeal world. Once bound to service, however, they evince a fascination for the physical. This fascination is most pronounced in the case of the spirit which becomes the *Zan-Chassin* adept's Custodian. The Custodian is normally the only bound spirit to actually inhabit the physical world in animal form.*

Deep within the Realms lies a region known as Phor, the Waiting Place of the Dead. Here dwell the spirits of those who have been human. Here they wait while they undergo the mysterious process of re-mergence: over an indeterminate period their essence and their memories, their total life experience, are re-absorbed into Moban's greater essence. It is believed that the souls of the dead follow one of two courses. They are either completely re-merged, in effect ceasing to exist as entities of any kind, or they return at some point in another form, all memories erased, and dwell again in the physical world.

Phor is a remote and secret place, a place of mystery, virtually inaccessible and rarely if ever visited by the souls of living humans.

---

* For a more detailed description of *Zan-Chassin* practice and the nature of the Realms of Non-Being, see *The Firstworld Chronicles I: Dinbig of Khimmur*.

But between it and the physical world has been established a sacred meeting-place. Here a *Zan-Chassin* can journey to call upon and commune with the spirits of the ancestors.

It was to this ethereal meeting-place that I, bodiless, now sped.

Encountering no one, I passed across a shifting blue desert, a vast emptiness, a swirling flux of nothingness that we comprehend as the subtle, unimaginably potent creative energies that underlie existence itself. Physical descriptions are unreliable here. The Realms obey laws not common to corporeality, and one perceives in an altered mode, without organs of sight, hearing, touch or other.

I arrived at the meeting-place, which to my perception was a small floating 'island' of vague solidity, a sense of coalescence within the surrounding formlessness. It was perhaps thirty paces in diameter, its surface seemed to consist of a rippled, powdery grey sandlike substance. Around its perimeter stood a ring of stones, spaced evenly apart with perhaps three paces separating each. At its centre was a small crystal cairn upon which rested a stick and a hand-drum: the Drum of Calling.

I alighted near the centre of the circle, approached the cairn and took up the Drum and stick. I beat three times upon the skin. The resulting effect could not properly be termed a 'sound'; rather it was an unsettling resonance, profound and almost sensual, which briefly cut through the eldritch silence of that place.

I sat down to wait. The sky flowed dark and rapid above and below me, rivers of dimly coloured clouds lapping and whirling, forming into one another, casting shadows that seemed to become living things, strangely familiar yet unidentifiable, which then moved away, merging and dispersing as they went. Presently I became aware that I was no longer alone.

A dim vaporousness gathered before me, a wispy, cloudy 'something' which slowly melded into a recognizable form. The ghost of my father stood before me. Behind him, half-visible in the fluxing dark, floated another whom I recognized as my mother. My father spoke. 'My son, why have you disturbed us?'

'Father, mother, I intended no disturbance. I have come for guidance.'

I was shocked. I had communed with the dead only once before. The spirit who had come then had been anonymous, someone I had never known. To find myself now confronting my deceased and beloved parents was something I was unprepared for. I was thrown into a turmoil of emotion, barely able to articulate my reasons for calling upon them.

'What is the nature of the guidance you seek?'

'I am faced with an insoluble dilemma which has placed both myself and many others in great danger. I am unable to advance in resolving it, and I fear that time is running out.'

'Time is of no meaning here,' my father said. 'We are the dead. We are unconcerned with events within the corporeal world.'

'This I know, but I seek only knowledge of past events, not direct intervention.' I recounted something of what was happening at Ravenscrag. 'I wish knowledge of the dire-witch, Molgane, and of the Bane she cast all those centuries ago.'

My father shook his head with slow, mournful deliberation. 'My son, we are of Khimmur. We have no knowledge of Pansurian affairs.'

'Are there not spirits here, among the dead, who will know something?'

The two conferred silently, then my mother spoke for the first time. 'You may not understand, child, but it is a lot that you ask. To find out that which you want entails locating and disturbing others from their rest, interrupting the process of re-merging.'

'Mother, I would not ask it of you were it not of vital importance.'

'This we know. You are dear to us and we will do what we can. We can provide you with nothing now, nor can we guarantee anything subsequently. You must return here again.'

'When?'

'Within the Realms there is no concurrence with the passage of time as you experience it. I can say only, go now, back to the world of the living. Send your Custodian here. If we have something, or if we fail, he will be told.'

Their forms seemed to glimmer and fade, and then were gone. I remained where I was, for a long time too emotionally dazed to make the effort to take my leave of this place and return to my body.

Chapter Nineteen

Eventually I withdrew my mind from the Realms and returned to my chamber in Castle Ravenscrag. I found myself sitting as I had been when I departed, but in total darkness. It seemed to my experience that I had journeyed for only minutes, but here in the corporeal world hours had passed and the night was well advanced.

'Yo, is there anything to report?'

'No, Master, it has been quiet. But Master, I note that your skin seems not to fit you well. It is tight and sore, and quite uncomfortable.'

'It is not so much a matter of fitting, Yo. My skin was quite badly burned, which has resulted in the effects you describe.'

'Will it always feel like this?'

'No, it will heal in time. Yo, exit my body now so that I may reclaim it, but remain here if you will. I wish to speak to you at some length.'

I returned to my flesh, taking note of the discomforts Yo had described, and cast a small rapture to ease them. Then I proceeded to relate to him, in quite considerable detail, everything that had happened at Ravenscrag in the last twenty-four hours.

'I confess I am mystified by it all, Yo,' I concluded. 'But as you can see I am compelled to investigate further. I would therefore request your help.'

'What can I do, Master?' Yo enquired brightly. As I had hoped, he was pleased and flattered by my request.

'To begin with you can accompany me and take note of what I show you.'

I left my chamber and, with Yo incorporeal and invisible close by, made my way down to the cellar where the monster was held. The castle was quiet, though servants were still at large. Bracketed torches relieved the darkness of the corridors, throwing capering shadows across walls and floors. Through the windows was utter blackness, relieved only by the bright spots of lanterns on the castle walls and the glow of lamp or torchflame through undraped windows. I estimated the hour to be somewhere before midnight.

Outside the cellar a new shift of soldiers stood guard, well back from the barricaded door. They were armed with spears and swords; two held crossbows. In the dancing gloom of the torchlight their faces were grave and tense.

The cellar door could not be seen for the heavy sandbags stacked high in front of it. Over these hung a net and metal mesh. To one side of the passage stood a barrow loaded with raw and bloody meat over which flies buzzed and feasted. On the floor beside the barrow were a long-handled shovel and prong-tipped pole used for pushing the food through the gap beneath the door. The warm air was stuffy and corrupted by a foul, clinging stench.

As I arrived there came a low-pitched, blood-chilling sound from beyond the door, somewhere between a guttural howl and a groan. There was a sudden dull thump against the timbers behind the sandbags. I nodded to the sergeant-of-the-guard. 'Has it made any more disturbance?'

'Not a lot. As long as it's been fed it keeps fairly quiet.'

'How much of this meat has it eaten?'

'This is the second barrowload.'

'The second? *Moban!*' I gaped at the barrow and the haunches and huge cuts of beef and pork stacked upon it. To have devoured such a quantity in so few hours!

I stepped closer to the door and communed with Yo. 'Yo, the creature that I spoke of is in there. I would like you to go in and – '

155

'I'm not going in there!' declared Yo.

'Yo, you will be without a body. It cannot harm you.'

'But it is evil, Master. Can't you feel its emanations? I'm afraid.'

I had not expected this. I turned back to regard the soldiers, who eyed me mistrustfully. They had heard nothing, for my communication with Yo was silent, of the mind. But they knew me for a magician and were clearly far from happy.

'Yo, I ask only that you enter the cellar for a moment. Attune yourself to the life-essence of the creature within, attempt to communicate with it if possible, but do not linger. It is of the flesh and you are not. It cannot touch you.'

'Are you sure, Master?'

'I am.'

Hesitantly Yo left me. He passed through the stone wall and entered the cellar.

Instantly there came a dreadful caterwauling from within, a sound of demented fury. I listened with pounding heart as the thing hurled itself about the cellar, its body crashing against the door and thumping heavily on the floor and wall. A shudder of fear ran down my spine.

Seconds later Yo was back beside me. 'It sensed my presence, Master.'

I allowed myself a sigh of relief. For an awful moment I had imagined that the creature had somehow attacked and inflicted damage upon Yo, even destroyed him, despite his lacking a physical form. 'Extraordinary. Could you identify the creature?'

'No. It is a monster, wholly malign, that is all I can say.'

'Then it is not an entity of the Realms?'

'Many kinds of entity dwell in the Realms, Master, and I have not met them all. But this thing is alien to me, both in its physical form and its psychic expression.'

'And your attempts to communicate made no impression.'

'None at all. It was enraged by my presence but remained oblivious or unheeding of my efforts to communicate.'

'Yo, describe the monster, please.'

'It stands tall and broad, using two legs or four. It is larger than a man, and is not human-like in form. Its torso, arms and legs are immensely strong, wadded with muscle. Its hide is tough, wet and leathery. It has a long, powerful tail and vicious talons, bony prongs and teeth.'

'Thank you, Yo. You have been of great service.'

I went next to Redlock's nursery. A sentry was seated outside the door, younger by four decades or more than the old fellow who had stood guard throughout the day. He unlocked the door at my request. I entered with a torch, showing Yo the room, then had Yo enter the armoire and pass along the secret passage to Moonblood's chamber. I went there myself via the corridor and had him acquaint himself thoroughly with the layout of the chamber, pointing out every detail that I thought could be of any possible relevance.

'Any observations, Yo?' I asked when we were back in my own chamber.

'None that will shed light, I fear. I am as mystified as you, Master.'

I sighed.

After a pause Yo continued, 'Master, why was the stolen pitcher left beside Mistress Moonblood's bed? It would surely have been an inconvenience for whoever stole it to carry it from the nursery all the way along that narrow passage to Moonblood's chamber. Much easier, surely, to have simply left it in the passage. Was it left deliberately, then?'

'A good point, Yo. An excellent one, in fact.' I sat down, enthused, and contemplated his words. Moonblood had been with me – or at least, in the banqueting hall – when Redlock was abducted. But might she have been complicit in the abduction? And whether she was or not, had the culprit deliberately planted the pitcher in her room in order to implicate her?

My impression of Moonblood made me unhappy with the first question. I could not imagine her committing acts that would cause such distress and disastrous consequences. Yet I reminded myself that she had been angry with her father over his banishment of Linvon the Light, and his desire to marry her off to another who did not meet with her approval. And it was obvious that the secret passage was used by the culprit, both in going to the nursery and in returning. And Yo was right, there was no practical need to take the pitcher to Moonblood's room – none that I could see, at least. Could it have been a deliberate ploy to point the finger of complicity at Moonblood?

157

'And the blood, Master,' said Yo, jerking me out of my reverie. 'You say you do not think Moonblood has been murdered, as the blood spilled is insufficient to have brought about her death. You say that her chamber has not been touched in any way. Yet though there are bloodstains, there is no sign of a struggle.'

'I too have been struck by that.'

'Could the chamber have been rearranged to cover the signs of a struggle?'

'It's possible.'

'Might the blood have been Redlock's?'

I would have stared at him had he been there to stare at. As it was I experienced a hollow, sinking feeling in the pit of my gut. I said, after a long pause, 'I had not considered that. But this is the problem, Yo. *Anything* is possible. I am no closer to an explanation now than when I began; I merely find more and more uncertainties rising to taunt me. I make no genuine progress, and I fear that time may be running out.'

'I'm sorry, Master.'

'You have been a help, Yo. Don't doubt it. And now you may aid me further, if you will.' I passed on to him the instructions I had been given in the Realms by the spirits of my dead father and mother. 'Return to me as soon as you are contacted, Yo. Do not delay by a single instant.'

'I am your servant, Master.'

Yo departed. I undressed, extinguished the lamp that was the sole illumination in my room, and climbed into bed. The vast, moonless dark enclosed me. Through the window the stars spread a remote milky glow across the sky, but the world was pitch black and impenetrable.

I found my attention moved to the sounds of the night. An owl hooted. In the distance a dog-fox yapped. At one point, from somewhere far below, I heard a faint, drawn-out, blood-curdling howl, which set my teeth on edge and my spine tingling in fear.

Eventually I slept, but not for long. I had been right, time was running out. Dreadful magic was about to be unleashed.

Chapter Twenty

It was plainly a dream, though I could not recognize it as such at the time. I arrived by horse outside a tall iron-strapped double door set in a wall of unbroken stone which seemed to ascend without limit, its crest hidden in dark, billowing clouds. Upon the door were two great iron rings gripped in the jaws of grotesque, fantastic creatures. A wind howled, raising spumes of dust, driving leaves and skittering branches across my path.

I dismounted and climbed the four stone steps to the door. I grasped one of the heavy iron rings and hammered twice. The sound resounded with a dull, booming resonance, reverberating along ancient hallways as though passing down the byways of time.

Something tugged at the hem of my trouser leg. I looked down to see a raven pulling at the material with its beak. It looked up at me with gleaming eye. I shook my leg, shooing the bird off. It spread its wings and flapped away with a harsh croak. Midflight it changed its form, was no longer a bird but a winged homunculus with leathery skin the colour of dried blood. Its features were set in grim fury; it swooped at me, shrieking harshly.

I ducked: the thing shot by me and passed through the wall. At

159

my feet a greenish pool formed. Its surface rippled, parted. A human hand, blistered, its skin peeled and torn, reached out and grasped my ankle. Within the pool a face seemed to form, a woman, her skin like that of the hand, horribly burned, her lips stretched, teeth bared in an expression of agonized rage.

I drew my sword and slashed at the hand. There was an ear-splitting scream. The severed arm pulled back, pumping blood, and vanished beneath the surface of the pool. The pool diminished and was gone. A hand lay twitching at my feet, the fingers opening and closing spasmodically.

With a scraping and groaning of time-stiffened hinges the great door opened. I stepped through into a wide hallway, long and dusty, part-illuminated by shafts of greenish light whose source was indiscernible. Stone statues representing demonic beings were ranged along the walls. At the centre of the hall, upon the floor, lay an object, too small and far away for me to identify.

I moved towards this thing. A figure appeared before me: Lady Sheerquine, dressed in a long grey robe, her copper hair loose, her head held high. She walked slowly towards me, clasping in her hands a small pillow in a pale blue linen case. She seemed oblivious of my presence, or perhaps, I thought, she chose to deliberately ignore me.

She walked straight by me, and as she passed I was shocked to see the look on her face. For, despite her efforts to maintain her customary self-command, her features betrayed a colossal inner turmoil. She was ghastly pale, her green eyes hollow and dark-ringed. Her jaws were tightly clenched; her shoulders and arms shook, and her cheeks were streaked with tears.

In bemusement I watched her walk away, her spine as ever perfectly erect. She seemed to be approaching the door through which I had entered, then abruptly turned and passed through a small portal that I had not noticed.

I followed. As I was about to peer through the doorway the air was split by a shattering roar.

'*Betrayer!*'

I spun around. Lord Flarefist bore down upon me, his sword raised. He swung. My own sword was drawn and I managed to parry the blow, though the crash of our meeting blades sent a shockwave which numbed my arm from hand to shoulder. I wheeled around to face Flarefist again, but he rushed on, away from me, yelling at the top of his voice, in pursuit of some unseen offender.

I turned again to enter the doorway through which Lady Sheerquine had gone, but I found I had lost my bearings and could no longer find the way.

Confused, I turned back to the object on the floor. Now I could see that it was a baby, but as I approached it altered its form. I realized that it was further away than I had at first thought. It was not in fact a baby but a mound of stinking, decaying flesh, riddled with worms and coated in flies. When I arrived before the mound it dwarfed me.

A voice spoke. In a shadowy alcove away to my left my father stood, beckoning to me. My mother was beside him. I walked towards them, overcome with emotion. As I drew close they stepped silently aside. Deeper in the shadows I saw Moonblood, garbed in soft white raiment bordered in crimson. In her hand she held a scroll of parchment bound in red ribbon.

Moonblood held out the scroll. Her lips moved and her voice sounded softly yet clear. 'This is what you seek.'

I reached out to take the parchment, untied the ribbon and unrolled it. Before me were the words of Molgane's Bane. And I knew I was dreaming, yet I saw them so plainly. I would never forget them. They told me everything I had thought they would. Suddenly everything was clear.

I was alone. The wind howled, a ghastly, malignant sound. Somebody was screaming. There was a deafening roaring noise, and I saw flames leap suddenly up the walls of the hall in which I stood.

I knew I dreamed, but I did not wake. The flames licked and crackled around me, their heat upon my face, burning the rotten meat. I felt the clutch of terror. I ran, blindly. The dreadful howling continued. More screams.

Why did I not wake?

I opened my eyes, but the dream did not end.

I was in my high chamber in Castle Ravenscrag. I no longer dreamed, I was sure of that, and yet . . .

There was a greenish light in my room, of indiscernible source.

161

It was murky, illuminating yet leaving everything shadowed, indistinct and quivering. I was aware of noises: shouts, screams, a ghastly howling, but they were a remote cacophony and as yet carried little meaning to my disoriented senses.

My eyes were on the mirror which hung upon the wall opposite the end of my bed. Its glass had begun to move, with a slow, viscid motion. It was like the surface of a pool of mercurial sludge, stirred by strange currents deep below.

As I watched, the surface lapped, swelled, then broke with a thick sucking sound, and a creature crawled out of the glass. It was vaguely reptilian, with smooth skin which showed a sickening blood-red in the weird light. Its head was blunt and rounded, with a bald, wrinkled pate. Hooded eyes, set close together, blinked slowly. A long yellow tongue slid out from between wide jaws set with rows of tiny teeth.

As I watched, transfixed, the thing crawled effortlessly down the vertical wall, leaving a trail of fluid, and across the floor, then up again to disappear through the open window.

The surface of the mirror re-formed. I got out of bed, quickly, though my limbs were heavy and unresponsive. I put my hand gingerly upon the glass; the surface was cool and ungiving. My haggard reflection stared back at me, undistorted.

I went to the window and looked out, startled for a moment by the leathery beat of wings and a dark, moving form as a raven took off from a gutter close alongside. There was no sign of the beast that had just exited. But I noticed something strange. The entire castle was dimly visible, the blackness of night held at bay by an unnatural, gloomy green light. I had thought it glowed only in my chamber, but now it seemed to imbue the very stones and air of Ravenscrag.

I could see figures running across the parade-ground below, willy-nilly, some coming out of the castle wing, others rushing towards it. They were dim and fuzzy in the eerie light. Some appeared to be fighting. And now I heard more clearly their shouts and screams, and that other sound, the dreadful, unearthly howling that came from deep within the bowels of the castle.

With goose-pimples crawling over my flesh I ran from my chamber. The corridor below was deserted, but illuminated like all else by that ghastly viridescence. I rounded a corner to confront a terrible sight. A Ravenscrag guard, screaming in pain and terror, was under attack by a creature whose like I had never seen. The thing, a savage, flapping monster, clung to his face with ferocious talons, stabbing and pecking with a thick horny beak.

I reached for sword and dagger, only to remember that I had none. Nor was I wearing my belt. In a moment of helplessness I watched the soldier reel back against the wall, blood streaming from his face and head, clawing futilely at his monstrous assailant. Then I saw his bloodstained sword, which lay upon the floor a little way along the passage.

I ran past, grabbed the sword and returned, hacking at the winged beast. My first stroke severed a wing. The creature let out a shrill shriek, and turned with huge glaring eyes to me. Releasing its victim it sprang as if to attack, but with only one wing it flapped clumsily to the ground.

I leapt forward, lunging with the sword, and ended its life. As the blood drained from its body I stared in astonishment, for the creature's form was altering. I found myself gazing at the dismembered corpse of a raven.

Did I still dream?

The soldier's plight prevented me from further consideration of the phenomenon. He was blinded, his head and face horribly gored, his leather jerkin torn and drenched in his blood. I took his arm and helped him along the corridor. A distraught servant came from a doorway ahead of us. I summoned him. 'Take this man to Doctor Markin immediately.'

I strode on without waiting for a reply. I was making for the cellar, dreading what I might find. But on the next level I was brought up short by another unexpected encounter.

From a side passage some yards ahead of me came Lady Sheerquine. She turned into the corridor and walked towards me, but as she approached I had the distinct impression that she had not seen me, though I had made no attempt to conceal myself. She wore a long grey shift, her copper, grey-streaked hair fell freely about her shoulders. In her hands, clutched to her bosom, she held a pale blue pillow. *She was exactly as I had seen her in my dream!*

Lady Sheerquine's movements were stiff and unnatural, as though she was afflicted with a rigor of the limbs. As she came closer I saw her expression, and was shocked. Her teeth were tightly clenched and her lips stretched tautly back in a pained grimace which brought to mind the image of a ewe gripped by lockjaw. The skin of her cheeks was deeply seamed, and her eyes, wide, were fixed straight ahead and glared with an expression of shocking intensity.

Lady Sheerquine moved straight past me, looking neither to right nor left. Her upper torso was inclined slightly backwards; her breath seethed between her clenched teeth. I caught the faint scent of winter-geranium in the air. I had the impression that something impelled her forward against her will, like an invisible hand pushing with a strength she could not counter, though her expression and bearing spoke of her striving to do so. Mesmerized, I followed.

I was cautious, mindful of the dream. I half-expected that Lord Flarefist would materialize out of nowhere and launch himself at me with his sword. Lady Sheerquine mounted the stairs which led to the family apartments. She passed the door to her rooms without faltering in her step, and proceeded on. She walked by Hectal's closed door, and Moonblood's, and eventually was outside the nursery. Here she stopped. The nursery door was part open. The sentry was sprawled upon the floor, unmoving.

Slowly, stiffly, still as if moving in terrible conflict with herself, Sheerquine entered. I moved up quickly to the sentry and felt his pulse. It beat, faintly. His body was locked in spasm, and his face bore an expression of white-eyed horror. I passed my hand before his eyes; he made no movement. He seemed to be held in some kind of catatonic trance.

I left him and went to the nursery door. Sheerquine was within, standing rigid before the crib. Yes, the crib stood there in its original position, charred and blackened and ruined by flame. Sheerquine, clutching the pillow, slowly straightened her arms. She began to raise them. Her back arched, her face turned away from the crib, upwards as if straining against something too terrible to face. Her arms, her whole body, shook.

Suddenly she gave a great cry, which seemed to come from deep within her tortured self, uttered with all the redoubtable inner strength she could summon. 'Nnnnnggghhh-*ggguhhh!*'

The spell was broken. Sheerquine was propelled backwards, arms asplay, with a violent snapping motion. She was thrown across the room like a rag doll. She collided with the wall and sank limply to the floor, her breath leaving her lungs in a long gasping sigh.

I rushed across and knelt beside her. Her face was obscured by her wealth of hair. I brushed it aside and she gave a faint moan. Her eyelids fluttered then opened; the green eyes rolled insensibly and gradually came to focus. She stared at me uncomprehendingly, frowning, then at the room, and back to me again. Her body stiffened, her look turned to one of alarm. With uncharacteristic fervour she gripped my arm. 'What did you see?'

I shook my head. 'Nothing.'

'Nothing? You are sure?'

'Nothing that meant anything. You seemed entranced, motivated against your will. You stood before the crib, there, then fell. That is all.'

Sheerquine stared at me searchingly for long seconds, then released her grip. 'I don't know what happened.'

'Nor I, but it is still happening here in the castle.'

She was regaining her self-control. 'What are you doing here, Master Dinbig?'

'I was on my way to the cellar, to investigate the source of this dreadful noise. I was distracted when I saw you in the corridor.'

Lady Sheerquine climbed to her feet and brushed herself down.

'Do you require assistance?' I asked.

'No, thank you. I am perfectly all right.' She strode straight-backed from the room.

I made to follow, but my attention was caught by something curious. The pillow that Sheerquine had carried lay upon the floor not far from the door. A dark blot seemed to have formed upon it. I stooped beside it, and touched it with a finger. The blot was wet, and warm, and in the green light seemed the colour of blood.

Sheerquine had gone. I hurried down the corridor, gripping the hilt of the sword I had taken from the guard, moving downwards towards the source of that hideous wailing. Through a window I glimpsed the parade-ground. Castle folk were fleeing in panic, in their midst strange creatures similar to the one I had slain upstairs and the thing that had crawled out of my mirror.

I ran on, past the kitchens and sculleries, turned towards the passage that took me down to the cellars. Here another strange sight met my eyes. From the opposite direction came Lord Flarefist; he floated above the ground, his head almost grazing the ceiling, his hands and feet flailing slowly like a man drowning in oil. His old face was ghastly in the green light, eyes bulging and mouth agape in an expression of blanched bewilderment.

'Help me, Bisding!' he croaked as he was propelled past me and into the cellar passage. 'Get me down! Get me down!'

I sensed that I could do nothing. Whatever malign, alien force held sway here at this moment was far more powerful than anything I might conjure. And I had the beginnings of a notion that some perverse purpose lay behind what I was witnessing. Lady Sheerquine had been impelled to act in a particular manner, though its meaning was beyond my comprehension. Now Flarefist seemed obliged to act out another scene.

He was borne along the passage, into the shorter corridor which led to the cellar in which the monster was entombed. Eight guards stood or knelt in consternation before the barricaded door. Four had crossbows aimed, the others wielded swords or spears. A terrific thumping came from behind the laden sacks, and that awful wailing of a vengeful, maddened beast.

With a thin, drawn-out moan Flarefist was pushed forwards, twisting around in the stench-laden air, without volition of his own. Now he was suspended spreadeagled upon the sandbags, looking out so that his tormented eyes stared into the faces of his own men, their weapons aimed at him.

'No! No! No-ooooo!' moaned the old Lord of Ravenscrag. He tossed his head from side to side. His thin body shuddered with the impetus of the blows that penetrated the sacks. I stood breathless, wondering at the strength of a creature that could summon such force.

The sergeant-of-the-guard barked an urgent order. 'Put aside your weapons!'

The crossbows shifted so that their lethal bolts no longer pointed at Flarefist. The soldiers shared fearful glances. Slowly, limply, Lord Flarefist began to sink towards the cellar floor. His legs buckled as his feet touched the earth, and he continued on down, coming to rest at last upon trembling hands and knees. His head was raised towards us, his face etched with shock, confusion and terror.

Then something changed, and I was not sure at first what it was. I feared for a moment that I was now under a magical influence, for my vision seemed to be impaired. Then I realized that the green light was diminishing. At the same time the beast in the cellar became silent. The screams from above, which had been faintly audible, faded then ceased.

The only illumination was that cast by the torches in the wall-sconces. The soldiers glanced around them in fear, like me taking time to accept this reversion to normality.

Lord Flarefist was still upon his hands and knees. As I watched his head tipped forward heavily. His knees and elbows folded and he crumpled onto the floor. From his lips there came one last, anguished sound, in a voice that I hardly recognized as his own:

'*Moooon-bloood!*'

Chapter Twenty-One

I would have said that I did not sleep at all that night, yet at some point I opened my eyes to find myself stretched upon my bed, bright sunlight streaming through my window. I would have said that everything had been a nightmare, a phantasm, but I was soon to find out otherwise.

I lay quietly for a while, going over the events of the night, endeavouring to identify and separate the components of my earlier dream from the subsequent carnage. I recalled how, in the dream, Moonblood had handed me the scroll containing Molgane's Bane, how the words stood out vividly and forcefully. When I read them everything became clear, and at the time I was certain they had engraved themselves indelibly upon my mind.

But now hardly more than scraps remained, and they were elusive and vague.

. . . the blood of the moon shall be shed once more . . . the corruption is complete . . . darkmoon becomes Shadownight . . . then shall my shadow be cast . . . through the power of the woman's sin and the woman's wound . . . Molgane shall be avenged!

These words I recalled, but were they reliable? Were they even relevant, or simply the random, chaotic assemblages of dream?

I rose groggily from my bed, my mind leaden and dense. Standing by the window I was dazzled by the brightness. The morning was near-still, and already the heat was stifling. My skin was hot and sore, though the blisters had not worsened. I mentally invoked another healing rapture. The sun's heat was uncomfortable on my face and arms and I was about to turn away when something caught my attention.

I shaded my eyes with one hand and looked again, out over the courtyards and the parade-ground to the castle ramparts. There was no mistaking what I saw. My blood ran cold.

My first response was one of sheer, disbelieving horror, my first instinct to rush headlong from my room. Reason then took charge. What was done was done and could not be undone; my personal feelings were of no consequence. It only remained to discover the identities of the corpses that swung from the pair of gibbets that had been hastily erected on the castle wall.

I quickly donned a light tunic and went out, downstairs. The corridors were deserted, but here and there I came upon pools or smears of blood, left by those who had been wounded or slain in the previous night's carnage. The bodies had been removed, and I had no idea how many had perished.

Of the corpses of the hideous creatures that had invaded the castle there was no sign, but as I crossed the parade-ground I came upon the mangled, bloody remains of a raven. Then another. And I recalled, with a chill turning of the stomach, how the monster I had slain last night had, in death, been transformed into a raven.

My head a welter of thoughts I paced on towards the gatehouse. The two gibbets came into view from behind a storehouse roof, above me and to my left. Stark against the sky, they were still too far distant for me to identify the corpses.

I turned to follow the line of the wall, walking quickly in its shadow until I reached a wooden stairway which took me up onto the parapet. The gibbets had been erected where the parapet broadened into a platform, close before a tower at an angle of the wall. A winch and pulley was set here, originally for hauling heavy materials up in the event of assault or siege. The gibbets were affixed to the battlements by dint of heavy iron brackets, which had presumably performed this function on previous occasions.

The corpses were suspended out beyond the battlements, high over the stinking moat and dense green scrub below.

The faintest breeze wafted in from the heights. The two corpses rotated lazily, their ropes giving off a barely audible creaking. A little way off three ravens strutted brazenly back and forth, feathers reflecting metallic green and purple in the sun, gleaming round eyes coveting the sight. I eyed them uncomfortably for a moment, then my gaze was drawn back to the two bodies suspended before me.

I stared, moved virtually to tears. Half-consciously I took note of the striking pallor of Irnbold's flesh. He was garbed in a modest, wheat-coloured under-tunic and sandals, lacking all his former ostentation. His spindly limbs seemed excessively thin; his bald head was uncovered, exposing his shame.

Next to him old Elmag looked tiny and almost puppetlike. Her tongue protruded, black, between her gappy teeth, and her face showed livid bruises which, in death, seemed almost indented into the old flesh.

My ears pricked at the soft slap of a footfall behind me. I turned to see Darean Lonsord. He grinned sarcastically, assessing me, hands on hips, a stem of grass between his teeth. I felt a quiver of unease: *did he suspect my liaison with his wife?* But though Lonsord's eyes tested and taunted there was no wrath, no burning rancour, which would surely have been evident had he any inkling of the truth. And I recognized that so great was his arrogance, so pronounced his vanity, as to prevent him from even entertaining the notion of his wife's being seriously attracted to someone other than he. I disliked him the more for it. I turned back.

'Who is responsible for this?' I seethed between my teeth.

'Don't fret, Master Dinbig. They won't be up there for long. In this heat they'll soon start to stink, and we wouldn't want that, would we?'

I faced him, struggling to contain my fury. 'Did you do it?'

'I just carried out my orders.'

'Whose orders?'

'His lordship's.'

'Flarefist? He was taken unconscious to his bed. He was in no condition to order anyone to do anything.'

'He woke in the night and summoned me to him,' said Lonsord, taking pleasure in my anger. ' "Hang them," his lordship ordered. "On the walls where everyone will see." "Who do you mean, my lord?" I asked. "The traitors. The deceivers. They're the ones. They did this tonight. Do not delay, Captain. Do it now." That's what he said.' Lonsord eyed me with sham ingenuousness. 'His lordship was in a state, could barely control himself, even though he hardly had the strength to sit up. I was still unclear as to who he meant, so I asked him again. "Irnbold!" he shouted, shaking his fist and almost falling out of the bed. "Irnbold and the witch! They've betrayed me and they'll swing for it! Hang them! Now! Do it!" '

Lonsord took the grass from between his teeth and smiled unpleasantly. 'So I did, though in Irnbold's case it wasn't really necessary. He'd been good enough to save me the trouble, see.'

'What do you mean?'

'When we got to his rooms to arrest him he was already dead. Impaled himself on a knife. Made quite a mess of his divan. Still, Lord Flarefist's orders were to hang him so as to set an example, so that's what I did. And I thought he'd be good company for the old girl, anyway. She'd have been a bit lonely up there on her own.'

I almost struck him, but somehow controlled myself. I stood impotently, quivering, rooted to the spot.

'Shows he was guilty though, doesn't it?' Lonsord added.

'It shows nothing, Captain Lonsord, except that he was terrified out of his wits. You're a fool if you believe otherwise.'

He pulled a mock pained face. 'Just doing what I was told to do, Master Dinbig.'

'And no doubt it grieved you to do it.'

'Most sorely. But it's over now, isn't it?'

'For these two, certainly; may Moban take their souls. But for Ravenscrag . . . do you really think so?'

He shrugged. 'These two are gone, aren't they?'

'And what if they were not behind what is happening here, and in particular what happened last night?'

'Darkmoon's past, Master Dinbig. That's when their power was strongest. Everyone says so. Whatever the curse is upon Ravenscrag, it's only powerful at darkmoon. That thing in the cellar is quiet now. We've seen the worst.'

But what of Shadownight? I thought.

Despite the warmth of the morning I felt a chill within me, and a tremor of cold fear ran up my spine. But I made no further comment. I pushed past Darean Lonsord and descended from the parapet, taking the steps three at a time. I made straight for Lord Flarefist's rooms. The guard made enquiry within and I was admitted without further delay.

Lord Flarefist was in his bed, propped against pillows. Markin the physician was endeavouring to get him to sip some steaming liquid from a clay dish. A single nurse was the only other person in attendance.

Flarefist looked frail and sick in his night-smock. There was a bloody graze at his temple where it had knocked against the floor last night. He seemed barely aware of his surroundings, though he raised his eyes briefly as I moved to stand beside the bed, then lowered them.

'It's you . . . y' villain,' he slurred. 'Y've a nerve . . . to return here. Have y' brought back the silver?'

I knew then that I was going to get little sense out of him. I corrected him, reaffirming that I was not Linvon the Light. Flarefist looked up again, staring at me fixedly, his scowl of pained indignation yielding slowly to perplexity, and then something else. His eyes brimmed and large, clear teardrops formed and tumbled down the old cheeks. With irritation he pushed aside the bowl that Markin held and tried to reach forward to grasp my hand. But the effort proved too much and he succeeded only in toppling sideways across his pillows.

Together Markin and I helped him sit erect again, and now he did lay a feeble, clawlike hand upon mine. His wet eyes implored and his jaw trembled, and at last a voice came, faint, broken and rasping, like the whisper of dry leaves over stone. 'Find him, Bisding. Please.'

'Who, Lord Flarefist?'

'My son . . . I've waited so long . . . Redlock . . . He's everything . . . Find him . . . Bring him back to me.'

He gave a cough which racked his whole body. When the spasm ceased his eyes closed and his head lolled to the one side as he slipped back into unconsciousness. Markin checked his pulse, then shook his head. 'He is too weak.'

*

172

Leaving Lord Flarefist's room I stood for a moment in thought outside the door. A movement caught my eye. Looking up I spotted Lady Sheerquine passing across the end of the corridor. In fact, I had the distinct impression that she had been about to turn into the passage, but something must have distracted her or caused her to change her mind and alter her course. She gave no indication of having seen me, or at least of wanting to speak with me, and I did not pursue her.

I was making for Ulen Condark's rooms, and then Ravenscrag's gaol, anxious to reassure myself of the welfare of Condark and his family and the others of Ravenscrag's 'guests'. I intended also to go to the cellar to find out the condition of its monstrous occupant. But something nagged at me as I went. A subliminal scratch, a psychic tingle, just below the level of consciousness. A voice spoke inside my head.

Master, I am here.

'Yo! Have you brought news?'

I have been contacted. Someone awaits you at the Meeting-Place of the Dead.

I changed direction and made my way immediately to my rooms. There I settled myself, entered trance, and abandoned my body into Yo's care. I soared out of the corporeal world and sped straight for that hallowed locale, the Meeting-Place of the Dead.

Chapter Twenty-Two

A ghostly figure waited beside the cairn, where lay the stick and Drum of Calling. I suppressed a pang of disappointment, for it was neither my mother nor my father, both of whom I had hoped to speak with again. Instead a stranger stood there, a man, or the shade of a man, seemingly formed out of the flux, part haze, part solid stuff. He held the image of a man of stature, a warrior, noble and prepossessing, garbed in padded leather jerkin over a white blouson, blue cloak, leather boots and hose.

'You are the sorcerer from Khimmur who fights to save Ravenscrag in the domain of the living?'

'I am.'

'Why?'

'I confess, I have been given little choice if I would preserve my own skin – though my skin is imperilled either way. But innocents are threatened, and persons I care for. I will help them if it is in my power to do so.'

The shade appraised me, and I in turn studied him. His features were not well discerned in a physical sense. Being non-corporeal we were not reliant upon accustomed perceptual modes. What I gained, then, was an intuition of the make-up of his psyche, a sense of his being and spirit, and it was an uncomforting experience. I was assailed by a great and intense longing and a profound mournfulness; a sense of tremendous age, of unspeakable weariness, of deepest anguish and dreadful sorrow. I sensed a body borne down upon by the weight of pained existence. Into my thoughts floated an image of Lord Flarefist, on hands and knees upon the dirty floor outside the cellar door upon which a monster pounded.

Age, ruin, disconsolateness, crushing despair, yearning, regret, broken hopes and tormented dreams . . . a sense of all these things came across to me as I stood before this ghost. But also there was a cognizance of a spirit not destroyed, a resoluteness, an intuition of grim and unswayable purpose, a character weakened and yet still ennobled by intense suffering.

And finally, I thought, there was an inkling – the faintest glimmer – of hope renewed.

I mentally withdrew, for the anguish of this shade was oppressively intrusive upon my own spirit.

He seemed satisfied with his appraisal of me. 'Be seated,' he said, and lowered himself cross-legged onto the powdery grey sand beside the crystal cairn. 'We will talk.'

I settled myself before him. The soughing of cosmic winds was the only sound, serving as background to our conversation. The fluxing, swirling essence was broken by occasional flickers of colour or light, and brief streaks or shudders of fiery substance, sometimes close, sometimes distant.

'I am sorry to have disturbed you from your sacred rest. It was my only – '

He shook his head, a bitter smile forming on the bloodless lips. 'There has been no rest. Not for long ages. Not for me. Though it is what I long for, it is denied me even in death. I am not allowed to forget, nor to escape into peaceful re-mergence with the Essence. I have only the torment of limbo, in eternity, unless I can redress the past.'

I perceived his eyes as pale, almost luminous grey as they rested upon me intently, and again I felt myself shrinking from the appalling intensity of suffering that emanated from his soul. He spoke on, sombrely. 'When your revered parents passed word of your quest among the dead, they were surprised that there was one who responded so quickly. They knew nothing of me. But their surprise lasted only as long as it took for me to tell them my tale, and it is this that you are about to hear. So listen, and I will tell you all there is to tell about the woman I loved more than life itself, my cherished, Molgane.'

I started, taken completely unawares. 'You are Lord Draremont?'

He gave a slow nod. 'That is the name and title by which I was known on the last occasion that I walked among the living. In Phor, among the dead, I am known only as the One Who Cannot Pass On. For shades come from the world of the living and are slowly re-merged, some to return eventually to life in other forms, others to be taken entirely into Moban's Essence. But I remain, doomed by my burden to suffer this fate. And let me anticipate another question: yes, a bane was cast upon Ravenscrag, but though it came from Molgane's sweet, agonized lips, it was not she who conceived or uttered it. That I know, and have known since before my death.'

I waited there in silence, considering the ambiguity of his words. He spoke again, and this is the tale he told me.

'When, ages past, I dwelt in the world as Draremont, Lord of Ravenscrag, with my beloved wife Molgane at my side, magic was known to some degree in Pansur. As in other lands, it was utilized by only a very few. The majority of these were women, who seemed to have a greater and more natural affinity with the mysterious art than males.'

I nodded, acknowledging a correspondence with the *Zan-Chassin* Hierarchy, which was essentially matriarchal in character.

'The magic practised in Pansur was not overtly powerful, and was generally beneficent,' continued Lord Draremont. 'Its use and instruction were carefully monitored to guard against malpractice. The body responsible for both the application and the guardianship of what magical power we possessed was called the *Us'temmid Hassut*, which translates roughly from the ancient tongue as the Sharing Sisters of the Hallowed Blood. The title was a reference firstly to their ideology, which held that magic was the province, not of one, but of all, and was to be used for the benefit of all; and secondly to the blood of womanhood, which is first shed

176

by every girl-child as she passes across the threshold from childhood into adulthood. The blood was seen as both the burden and blessing of womanhood, to be shed and renewed with each cycle of the moon, throughout adult life unto old age. Magical power and efficacy is associated both with the lunar cycle in its various phases, and with the corresponding cycle of female fertility.'

Into my mind, with a reeling shock, came the word *Moonblood*. I struggled for a moment as I tried to grasp what I was hearing, the full import of which seemed to elude my comprehension.

'Molgane had displayed an aptitude for magic from an early age, long before I knew her,' said Lord Draremont. 'When she entered womanhood she was therefore initiated into the Sharing Sisters.'

He paused for a moment, staring sightlessly, lost, I believed, in sad remembrance. 'According to ancient lore magic came originally to Pansur out of the mysterious land of Qotolr, known to many as Enchantery. No doubt you are familiar with legends and tales from Enchantery, with accounts of the Enchanter Wars of the First Era, and in particular with the tale of the White Witch Queen, Yshcopthe, who gave up her life that the world might be saved from catastrophe?'*

I nodded, afflicted with a sudden foreboding at the mention of dark Qotolr. 'The tales are well known in Khimmur and other lands.'†

Lord Draremont continued: 'At some point, I believe some years after Molgane's initiation, the Sharing Sisters were approached by a stranger. At the time this was not known by myself or anyone else outside the Sisters. Molgane was by then a prominent adept.

---

* In later years Dinbig would – against his better judgement – enter Enchantery, as would the lovelorn hero, Duke Shadd of Mystoph. Their adventures, embracing a more detailed account of the Enchanter wars, the Story of Yshcopthe's Ruse, and other tales from Enchantery, are recounted in *The Firstworld Chronicles* II: *The Legend of Shadd's Torment* and III: *From Enchantery*.

† Magic is said to have originated in Qotolr. Over millennia – following Yshcopthe's Ruse by which the godlike Enchanters were tricked into yielding up much of their power – its potency slowly dwindled. Lore holds that the nature of magic further changed when it passed beyond Enchantery's strange borders, so that it again lost much of its awful power and became a force which might be harnessed and utilized to some limited extent by lesser races, such as mankind.

177

'The stranger professed himself a white wizard who dwelt somewhere deep in the forest. He called himself Mososguyne, and demonstrated to the Sisters impressive powers, essentially similar to their own, but of a broader scope. He hinted at secrets and knowledge of more powerful magic, and proposed joining with the Sharing Sisters, to pool his talents with theirs. He was by all accounts a charismatic personality, and after some debate and a period of trial, he was granted his wish.'

Dark shadows coursed across Draremont's form, as if to betray the agitation he felt. He resumed in trembling tones. 'It was their downfall. It was not discovered until much later, but Mososguyne had come out of Enchantery where he had spent long years studying foul magics. He is believed to have been a student of one of the surviving Enchanters, who was sent back beyond Enchantery's borders in order to spread his master's influence. Whatever the facts, Mososguyne brought to our land a malign power and a perverse need to gain ascendancy over us, no matter the cost.

'We should, I suppose, be thankful that the magic of Enchanters is not what it was. Even so, Mososguyne brought tragedy and devastation to Ravenscrag, against which we had little defence. His designs were unsuspected for many years, and during that time he gleaned from the Sisters what they knew and took effective steps to corrupt their magic and deprive them of power.

'Despite their experience and wisdom the Sisters fell under his mesmeric spell. He sowed dissent among them and caused them to distrust one another. Their unity dissolved; several succumbed to fatal illness or accident. It happened over a period of time and nobody suspected villainy, but within ten short years the Sharing Sisters of the Hallowed Blood were no more, at least as a unified entity. Their power and place had been usurped and corrupted by this dark wizard.

'Still I knew nothing of all this. Molgane and I were close; we shared secrets, but the esoteric nature of the Sharing Sisters' affairs was sacrosanct, and I rarely sought to encroach in any way upon their privacy. Still, we discussed their growing disunity, which troubled Molgane. But we saw the problem as being one of internal politics, of personalities and sheer ill-fortune, and had no inkling of what was truly afoot.

'So, as I say, the group dissolved, the surviving members going their own ways. Now Mososguyne was free to concentrate his energies on one alone, she who was was closest to political power in the region: my wife, the mother of our two sons and the woman I worshipped and adored, Molgane.'

Lord Draremont paused. His head was bowed in sorrowful introspection. 'In retrospect I consider him to have been mad, perhaps driven that way by the potencies he strove to command, or by his experiences within that unnatural land of Enchantery. I can see no real reason or pattern behind his acts, other than destruction for its own sake. After all, had he wanted political power he could have directed his efforts at kings or princes in nations outside Pansur, who were far wealthier and stronger than I.'

'Perhaps he was testing himself and his powers,' I offered, 'in preparation for greater prizes later on.'

'Perhaps. But he was not very clever. The power he gained in Pansur came through the people he controlled, the Sharing Sisters. But his acts of senseless destruction were ultimately self-defeating.'

'But by then, were not his immediate objectives already achieved? Had he not proved himself to his satisfaction, and that of his master in Enchantery? Was he ready to move on elsewhere?'

The shadows that flickered across Draremont's form became deeper-hued and more pronounced. He shook his head, his ghostly jaw clamped shut, and I sensed his emotion, his grief, so profound even after centuries.

'I will cut a long story short,' he said. 'Molgane was possessed by this vile magician; she had become his slave. She did not know it, of that I am certain, but he controlled her mind, and through her he caused his evil to manifest.

'I had noticed occasional changes in her behaviour. Moods, tantrums, which were not in her character. But I was too busy to pay much heed. Remember, I had witnessed nothing to alert my suspicions. Ah, but reports began to reach me, disturbing reports. A trickle at first, vague and unsubstantiated. Then more, of greater substance. People came to me complaining of Molgane's behaviour – something none would have dared to do without total conviction and the impetus of fear and despair which far out-weighed any anxiety about how I might respond. I could not help but take notice.'

'What was the nature of these complaints?'

'They varied. Cows had produced curdled milk after Molgane had blessed them. Pigs contracted swine fever after she had merely passed by. A child whom she visited suddenly took sick and perished. Then another. She treated a woman for a growth upon her leg; after the treatment the growth rapidly spread and took the woman's life within days. Crops were inexplicably eaten up with mildew and rot, or became infested with mites and beetles . . .'

Lord Draremont turned away, shaking his head. 'I was under terrible pressure. At length I had no choice but to question my wife.

'I spoke to her privately at first. She professed no knowledge of the incidents, and . . . I believed her. You see, while undeniably Molgane caused terrible turmoil and suffering, it was not her doing. She was not the real cause. The real cause was the evil that had possessed her and which directed her actions. She knew nothing of it. She did not even perceive that the effects she created were the opposite of what she had intended.

'Her mind was affected, her reason usurped, there is no doubt. Mososguyne's grip upon her altered her very perception of the world. But this I learned only later, after much research. At the time I saw what was before me: my beloved wife was guilty of monstrous acts, all of which she vehemently and plaintively denied.

'In effect, I was powerless. My advisors and kin – themselves distraught, for they loved her too – made it plain that I had but one recourse. I was forced to invoke an ancient law, prescribing punishment for any person convicted of practising harmful magic. Molgane was tried and found guilty. Her punishment was terrible: she was boiled alive in oil, her agony prolonged so that the evil magic would flee her flesh, leaving no vestige or residue behind, and be forever discouraged from returning. Once dead, she was dismembered in accordance with the law, and her remains buried separately until nothing was left.'

Lord Draremont choked as he spoke these last words. He stood suddenly with a loud sob and strode to the edge of the circle, where he stood between two of the standing stones, staring out into the primordial swirl beyond. I left him undisturbed until he could bring himself to return and sit with me again.

'I apologise. For eons I have lived with this memory, yet never does the pain of it die.'

'No apology is necessary. Your suffering is undeserved; I only regret that it cannot be eased.'

The intensity of his emotion bore upon me, radiating from him in waves, so that again I pulled back.

'Perhaps now it can,' he said, meaningfully. 'I have arrived at the crux of this issue, the Bane that was laid upon my house, Ravenscrag, and its consequences, and the part that you must play.'

Chapter Twenty-Three

'I will not linger over descriptions of Molgane's death, or her earlier pleadings with me when she understood what her fate would be,' continued Lord Draremont. 'No, I must expunge that from this recounting or I will break down. But listen: as she died, in her final agonies she was transformed. Her face, twisted and tortured, came to resemble another, a face I had never before set eyes on. And a voice screamed out, uttering the curse. It came from Molgane's lips, but the voice was not hers. It was a sound alien and terrible, and its tones, seething with hatred and wrath, echo still in my mind, relentlessly taunting and reminding me of what I did.

'The voice said, '*Ravenscrag, you seek to end my reign, but though I perish now I shall not be gone. Beware all things, for you have offended me, and I shall have revenge. Through me, by your own doing, Ravenscrag shall be destroyed. Beware, then, the Legend, for in it I shall ensure your end.*

'*This is my Bane: My spawn will be about you and among you forevermore, but you will not know them, nor will they even know themselves. But they will oversee misfortune, until the child you all await is born. And then shall you know me!*

'Observe the Legend! Waver so much as once from that which is said to be, and your hopes and your longings will fly. There will be Shadownight! You will see that Ravenscrag will give birth not to its saviour but to its Iniquity. And by my power you will all see its Iniquity rise.

'The blood of the moon shall be shed, and then will be death as foretold, and then will be corruption, and the blood shall be shed once more. It will be so, and then is my time, for here will be my instrument. The corruption is complete. Through the power of the woman's sin and the woman's wound, it shall be born. For you are not free of sin; you are not pure, and nor shall you ever be. I will have my way!'

Lord Draremont was silent for a moment. 'Those were the last words that my wife ever uttered, but I say again, they were not hers.'

The phrases resounded in my mind. The foreboding I had felt earlier had intensified. Lord Draremont was studying me intently. I said, 'These words . . . many of them are familiar. I dreamed them, or imagined them, for they have never been spoken to me, nor have I ever read them.'

Lord Draremont gave a slow nod. 'Our efforts were not entirely in vain, then, though I wish we could have impressed more upon you.'

'It was your doing?'

'When we knew that you had been appointed to solve Ravenscrag's mystery we endeavoured to communicate the words of the Bane to you. We tried to contact you in moments when you were receptive, to aid you. But we are the dead; our capacity to interact with or influence the living is very limited.'

'You speak as though you are not alone.'

'I have helpers. Other shades who come from the world of the living, knowing something of Ravenscrag's fate. They are few in number, and their time with me is not long. It is only I who must persist over ages, but they do what they can.'

'My understanding is that there is more to the Bane than you have told me: a reference to one who comes from afar, bringing strange knowledge and shattered gifts. This one may discover the means to lift the Bane, but in doing so he may also perish.'

Lord Draremont spoke thoughtfully. 'There is much yet to tell, but you are correct. It is written thus. I will explain how it came about.

'The Bane was not taken lightly. Fortunately few had been present when it was uttered, for though by rights Molgane's execution should have been conducted in public, I had succeeded in keeping it behind closed doors. A handful of family members and close officials bore witness, though I was afterwards obliged to display my wife's remains and hand them over for public incineration so that the people might be assured she was gone.

'I took immediate steps to ensure that knowledge of what had been uttered was kept secret. Then I established a research programme, intent upon testing the validity of the Bane and searching for means to negate it. To this end I recruited surviving members of the Sharing Sisters, and other persons of wisdom and knowledge from all over Pansur. It was during this time that I first learned of Mososguyne and his terrible influence. He, of course, was not to be found.

'The research was conducted secretly, for I had banned the practice of magic upon pain of death. It became plain that the Bane was interwoven with the Legend and that its effects would not be wholly realized until the conditions of the Legend began to come into being at some future time. But no one doubted that the Bane was valid. We had seen Mososguyne's power, and knew at least something of his origins. Ravenscrag had been visited by an evil, and that evil would return to ensure its eventual downfall. It was depressingly plain that we had no powers to lift the Bane. The only way it might be negated was to somehow prevent the future corruption of the Legend upon which the Bane relied. But how might we achieve that? In what form would that corruption manifest itself? And when?

'A suggestion was made by one of our number to the effect that there might yet be a way to discover more. Iliss, an erstwhile member of the Sharing Sisters, spoke of the giants who lived in the north – '

My ears pricked up. 'There are giants?'

'Small communities lived then in the mountains north of Ravenscrag. They had little contact with men and were rarely seen.'

'And now?'

Lord Draremont lifted his shoulders in a weary shrug. 'I know nothing of now. But the giants are an ancient race whose history predates ours by centuries. They have a love of lore and tradition. Their sagas, poems and songs chronicle the deeds of races, nations and individuals throughout history, and as such constitute a great storehouse of knowledge. Iliss thought that the giants might provide new insight into the Legend of Ravenscrag and perhaps the Bane. It was proposed that I should leave Ravenscrag and journey north to try to solicit their aid, and this I did.

'My journey took several days, and I had no specific destination in mind, for no one knew the precise location of a giant settlement. Nor did I know what to expect. Past times between men and giants had been marked by conflict and bloodshed, and the giants had purposefully removed themselves from the proximity of men. Now, for all I knew, I would be slain out of hand as soon as I was spotted.

'But that did not happen. I asked at every village I came to, and was directed deeper into the wildlands, until I came eventually upon a small community of giants. They received me politely, if warily. I explained my business and was taken to the village head. After much discussion I was permitted to attend a moot that night, in which songs were sung and tales were told around a fire. I have never experienced anything like it. The voices of giants raised in song are like oracular thunder; when they dance the earth shakes. Strong wine was drunk in copious amounts and the songs went on through the night and well into the morning. A song was sung of the Legend of Ravenscrag, and of the Bane, but it told me little that I did not already know. The next day I was taken from the village.

' "Do not return," said the village head. "For one man coming with open hands signifies the imminence of others with swords and arrows, who will hunt us as though we are beasts. Thus tomorrow we will be gone, and you will not find us again."

'They stood watching as I left, and I felt deeply saddened. To think my coming meant that they would now be forced to uproot themselves, leaving their homes to start anew somewhere else. I wondered that they had not simply killed me.

'I had ridden less than a half a mile when my horse shied at a disturbance beside the track. From between the trees stepped a giant, a young male whom I recognized from the night before. "I would talk with you awhile," said he, so we sat beside the trail and he told me a strange tale.

'His name was Eldhorn and he had had a recurring vision, which is the way in which giants collect much of their lore. He told me that he had seen, time and time again, among the many interweaving strands of future time, one which became prominent and which showed a dark visitation upon Ravenscrag which would bring about its end. And when I asked him to describe in detail everything he had seen, Eldhorn closed his eyes and shook his head. "Everything is hazy," he said, "but I see a child who is the blood of the moon in whom resides the potential for both death and life. And another child, a babe, who is awaited and who vanishes. And there is anticipation and confusion, and great terror. And there is another strand in which I perceive one who comes from afar, bringing strange knowledge and shattered gifts. And this stranger may help to end the darkness that lies upon your home, but he will not do it alone, and the price he pays for success may be his own life. But the vision is confused and difficult to grasp. I can tell you nothing more. The vision will be passed on to my descendants, as is our way, in the hope that we can build upon it and understand more."

'And that is it,' said Lord Draremont. 'That was all that I was able to carry back with me to Ravenscrag. And so the Bane, which became known as Molgane's Bane, was written thus, but knowledge of it was kept a secret from all but the immediate line and our closest advisors.

'And my life, though I did not know it, was almost done. For I had lost Molgane, and with her the will to live. I was racked with guilt and remorse, tormented by memories of my dear wife and the unspeakable agony of her death. And now, without the Sharing Sisters, the lives of the people of Ravenscrag became hard, harder than ever before. This too I felt to be my responsibility. I was their lord and protector and I had failed them. I had allowed them – allowed us all – to become the victims of an insidious evil. I longed then for death, for an end to it all, but when death came it was, for me, only a beginning.

'On the night that I died, torn by visions of Molgane, a new vision intruded. I looked suddenly upon a face, terrible to behold, mocking, malevolent, inhuman. And its lips moved and a voice spoke, spewing out the words: *I will have my way!* Whether it was the face of Mososguyne or that of the Enchanter he served I will never know. But it was the last thing I saw in life.'

Lord Draremont sat motionless, tyrannized by his memories, then said, 'Then began my vigilance, when I learned that for me death was no end and that my responsibilities towards Ravenscrag could not be so easily erased. And I have watched, over centuries of your time, waiting, knowing that the day must come when the Legend will be fulfilled, but fulfilled in its grim entirety unless somehow the Bane can be lifted.

'I tried to intervene. When it became evident, from signs and information brought to me by passing shades, that the time was nigh, I did what I could. I defied Moban's laws and had a willing shade return to be born again in the physical world to attempt to prevent the wrongs that would come. But Moban cannot be defied: its laws are immutable. The physical world is no place for any of untimely birth. This shade was born back into Ravenscrag, knowing all there was to know. But his mind did not bear the exertions of corporeality; he was born an imbecile, knowing everything but not knowing how to use it.'

A knowing imbecile! 'Do you mean Hectal?' I asked incredulously.

Lord Draremont nodded. 'That is the name he was given at birth. More recently I tried again, dispatching another to Ravenscrag, hoping that Hectal's condition had been a mere accident. But this one also was lost, swayed and seduced it would seem by the temptations of corporeality. I do not know what became of him.

'And now Shadownight comes. Moonblood, who holds a power we don't understand, has gone, as has the babe, Redlock, who should have been the saviour of my descendants and my ancient and noble House. And you are our only hope.'

Not for the first time I felt that my powers were being overestimated. 'You place too great a faith in me. I am scarcely clearer now than when I arrived. I do not know how to end this mystery.'

'Seek out the giants,' urged Lord Draremont. 'They will know something, I'm sure.'

'I fear there is no time. I do not know where giants reside, and this coming night, I fear, is Shadownight, whatever that may entail. I have only what remains of the single day.'

And I thought, *No matter what I do, if the Legend is right, I have only hours left to live.*

Chapter Twenty-Four

'Yo, has anything happened in my absence?'

'No, Master. There have been no disturbances.'

I repossessed my corporeal self. 'Come.'

I glanced through my window. Thankfully it was still morning; no great time had passed while I had been in the company of Lord Draremont's mournful shade.

I left my chambers and went straight to Moonblood's apartment. The corridors had still not been mopped: the servants cowered in their quarters, too frightened to attend to their duties. The bloody evidence of last night's carnage thus remained on walls and floor.

I passed the place where I had fought to save the soldier. There, on the floor, lay the mutilated corpse of a raven.

My spawn will be about you and among you forevermore, but you will not know them, nor will they even know themselves!

Thoughtful, I moved on.

Moonblood's apartment was as before. I entered unchallenged, for no guard manned the door now. I went straight to the bed and pulled back the cover, stared at the dry bloodstain.

'The woman's wound, Yo. Something, at least, is explained.'

'What do you mean, Master?'

'No foul deed was committed here, Yo. At least, that is, no blood was shed by violence. Moonblood's disappearance remains to be explained, but I will stake my reputation on the premise that she was not physically harmed in this room. And nor, I would wager, is this Redlock's blood.'

'I still don't understand, Master.'

'Moonblood is no longer a child, Yo. And this is the evidence.' I pointed triumphantly at the bloodstained sheet. 'And this.' I lifted Moonblood's night-robe. My heart sank at the sight of the tear in the material. So convinced was I, after hearing Lord Draremont's account, that I now had a non-violent explanation for the bloodstains, that I had allowed the tear to slip my mind. It still spoke of use of force – yet my explanation fitted in every way. I could not dismiss it.

'Master, your words make no sense to me.'

'Ah, Yo, you are not of the physical world. How can you be expected to understand? You've so much to learn. I will explain in detail at a more appropriate moment.'

I turned, taking in the rest of the room. Into my mind came the words of the Bane. *The blood of the moon shall be shed . . . and . . . shall be shed once more. And then is my time, for here will be my instrument.*

I shook my head ruefully. Small comfort if Moonblood had avoided violence. Her initiation into womanhood was yet another element signifying the power and immutability of the Bane. The first shedding had been her birth. Four siblings had since died. And now . . .

Then will be corruption . . . The corruption is complete. Through the power of the woman's sin and the woman's wound, it shall be born.

The woman's sin? Did that refer to Molgane, or to something else that I had yet to understand? I thought back quickly over the preceding days and nights. A vaguest inkling, a seed of suspicion, was beginning to germinate within my mind.

I swept my eyes around the room. The entrance to the secret passage was still open. The pitcher stood where I had replaced it by the bedside table. Upon the dressing-table Moonblood's jewellery and other items of girlish finery lay carelessly strewn. My eyes fell upon a small satinwood casket inlaid with abalone. Its lid was raised, revealing blue velvet upholstery upon which rested an object I recognized. It was the brooch I had noticed Moonblood wearing three evenings ago, when I first arrived, and which I had subsequently remarked upon at the banquet celebrating Redlock's birth.

I picked it up, turning it over in my hand, impressed again by the delicacy of the work. The metal and crystals caught the light, shimmering and sparkling as I turned it. The tiny intricate figures and designs were like nothing I had seen before. But it was not considerations of potential future profit that held my attention now. I was wholly intrigued by this unusual artifact, and as I studied it more closely I realized that I was wrong. This was not the same brooch that I had seen Moonblood wearing. It was its twin. I stared for some moments before I understood that I was holding an opposing section of the brooch. The two pieces would fit together to make one.

I replaced the exquisite object in its casket. So much still remained unanswered! On an impulse I strode from the apartment and along the corridor to the nursery. Inside it was exactly as I had last seen it, except – the pillow that Lady Sheerquine had dropped, and which I had seen grow wet with blood, had gone.

But had it been a dream? The crib stood unoccupied near one corner of the room. I ran my fingers along its charred ribs. A muted sound made me look up; a woman's voice, a cry of distress, and a muffled thumping, issuing from somewhere close by to my left. A brief search and I identified the source of the sound: it came through the stone wall, from the chamber next door.

I went out quickly into the corridor. The door was locked. I banged hard upon it. 'Blonna! What is the matter?'

From within came a pathetic cry. 'Help me! Please!'

I shouldered the door. I had no chance of battering it down. 'Blonna, it is I, Master Dinbig. What's wrong?'

Her voice sounded close on the other side of the door. 'Oh, Master Dinbig! What is happening? I've had no food or water. Last night I heard such screaming and terrible noises. I saw fighting outside in the courtyard, and there was a green light. And now there's nobody about. I'm so frightened.'

'Calm down now, Blonna. It's over. I will find someone immediately to open your door. Just wait.'

I went downstairs, searching the halls and corridors till I came upon a steward scurrying nervously towards the kitchens.

'The key to Blonna's cell, next to the nursery – where will I find it?'

'I'm not sure, sir. You may have to ask her ladyship.'

'Where is she?'

'I think she's in her office.'

'Take me there, please.'

The fellow led me back, down a passage, to a door a little way past the Great Hall.

'Wait,' I said, and knocked.

'Come.'

Lady Sheerquine sat at a desk, a ledger spread before her. She stared expressionlessly as I entered, the merest compressing of her lips her only movement.

'Master Dinbig. What is it?'

'I require the key to Blonna's cell.'

Her gaze was implacable. 'For what reason?'

'The girl is innocent, yet she has been imprisoned there for two days. Today she has not been given food or water. She saw the horrors of last night from her window, and heard the screams. There is no longer a guard upon her door, nor anyone she can speak to. She is scared witless.'

Lady Sheerquine considered just an instant, then swivelled upon her chair to face a row of heavy iron key-rings which hung from numbered hooks set into a board upon the wall. 'This one, I think. Yes.'

She took the key-ring and passed it to me. I handed it to the steward. 'Go at once. Release Blonna. See that she is fed and bathed and taken good care of.'

The man hesitated, looking nervously to Lady Sheerquine. A small frown clouded her brow, but she nodded stiffly. 'Do as he says.'

'Is there something else, Master Dinbig?' enquired Lady Sheerquine when we were alone. 'I have work to do.'

'I wish for the return of my sword and knives. I was lucky to have survived last night. Unarmed, I may not survive another like it.'

Her attention was on the ledger. Her elegant white forefinger,

192

moving across a row of figures, was still for a moment. 'I do not think that will be possible.'

'It must be made possible, if you wish me to complete my commission.'

Lady Sheerquine looked up again, her lips tightly pursed, nostrils flaring. 'I will give the matter due consideration, but, Master Dinbig, please remember your station. You are in no position to make demands or threats. Now, is there anything else?'

I fumed in silence. 'How is Lord Flarefist?'

'No better than can be expected. He is asleep at present.' Her eyes were downcast once more.

'I have discovered more about the Bane.'

A tiny hesitation. 'Indeed? I am pleased to hear it. Perhaps you will now move swiftly to a resolution of Ravenscrag's plight.'

'I doubt that it is within my power to do that. But I am intrigued by what I have found. Tell me, what do you know of Shadownight?'

She paused, but seemed unwilling to meet my eyes. 'Nothing, beyond the fact that it is referred to in the Bane. And that is the truth.'

'And of giants?'

Her hand gave a tiny twitch upon the open page of the ledger. 'Giants?'

'Moonblood claimed to have met a giant. You knew of it.'

'It was a fantasy. There are no giants.'

'Where is your daughter, Lady Sheerquine?'

Lady Sheerquine drew back, raising her head. Her pupils were pinpoints. 'Are you implying that I know? Be assured, I do not.'

'*My spawn will be about you and among you forevermore,*' I quoted, '*but you will not know them, nor will they even know themselves.*'

She stared at me; a muscle high on one cheek had developed a sudden tic. 'So is it written.'

'It has no particular resonance for you?'

She shook her head, eyeing me coldly and, I thought, edgily.

'*The corruption is complete,*' I continued. '*Through the power of the woman's sin and the woman's wound, it shall be born.*'

'You should have been an actor or a cleric, Master Dinbig. I am no

193

expert, but your powers of memorization seem not unimpressive, and you deliver with a certain conviction.'

'I intend to get to the very bottom of this matter, Lady Sheerquine. I need to satisfy myself that I understand the words of the Bane unequivocally. I intend to leave no stone unturned.'

Two tiny spots of colour had appeared high on Lady Sheerquine's pale cheeks. 'There may be nothing to understand.'

'Oh, I believe there is much to understand. And after last night, surely you can have no possible doubt about that?'

'I do not know, Master Dinbig. You will appreciate that this is a time of tremendous stress – for myself and all at Ravenscrag. We all live in fear.'

'Myself not least.'

She nodded, closing her ledger and busying herself with objects upon her desk. 'Yourself not least.'

I felt thwarted. I had been close to something, had again touched an exposed nerve, had penetrated Lady Sheerquine's formidable armour. But within seconds she had regained her composure. She remained rattled, I was certain, but in control.

'My lady, how fare your "guests"? Were any harmed last night?'

'They were not molested in any way. They are understandably nervous, but that is all.'

'I would recommend that you free them. Condark's troops are surely not far away now.'

'They will not be freed, Master Dinbig. Not until their innocence is determined beyond all reasonable doubt.'

'You have murdered Irnbold and Elmag. Will you murder more?'

She fixed me with a gelid stare. 'It was not murder. We believe they were the instigators of this iniquitous business. Their power is now gone.'

'Do you truly believe that?'

'We shall know soon enough. If it proves to be the case, as we hold, then the others will be released.' She placed her hands flat upon the desk, rising. 'As it happens, the order was given by my husband, without my knowledge. Had I been aware of it I would not have permitted the executions.'

She swept up a key from her desktop and moved to the door

with a rustling of cotton and a heady waft of winter-geranium. 'I have other business to attend to, Master Dinbig. As, I have no doubt, have you.'

Passing through the doorway I stopped, directly before her. 'What in your opinion, Lady Sheerquine, is the significance of the Bane's reference to "corruption", and to "my spawn" who "will not even know themselves"?'

Lady Sheerquine's green eyes flickered uncomfortably. Her chin lifted high. Her breasts rose and fell. 'I have puzzled over it, Master Dinbig. As have others. No conclusive interpretation has ever been arrived at.'

I nodded. 'Tonight, I think, we may learn more, though it may be too late to be to our advantage. Indeed, I hold out little hope for our survival. But from what I have now discovered, even in death there may be no escape.'

I stepped through the door.

'Master Dinbig.'

I turned back. Lady Sheerquine stood pressing the iron key to her marble chin, her brow knit in thought. With deliberation she said, 'It is an unusually complicated and dangerous business that you are involved in. I wish for nothing more than your success, for you cannot doubt that I wish to see Ravenscrag freed from this dreadful curse, and my children returned to me unharmed.'

'Quite so.'

'It has struck me, however, that there are numerous strands and facets to this matter. Not all, I am sure, will reward closest scrutiny. My advice to you – considering that the Bane is indisputably active – is to focus your efforts exclusively on the lifting of the Bane, rather than spending precious time on a fruitless search to understand its provenance and precise interpretations, which are in any case obscure and unreliable. Do you understand my meaning?'

'Absolutely.'

'Good. Then that will be all.'

'What do you make of her, Yo?'

'She is an impressive human female, Master.'

'That she is. But she is not being entirely honest with me.'

'I feel that she withholds, Master. There is a conflict, as if she wishes to give, wishes you to succeed, and yet at the same time fears it.'

'My feelings precisely!'

'She has a secret.'

'Indeed so. And it must be a great secret if her fear of confiding it is greater than her fear of the Bane.'

'Do you know what her secret is, Master?'

'Not yet – but I think I may be close. Aha! What is this?'

A shadowy figure moved in the gloom of the corridor ahead, then scuttled across the passageway and was lost from sight. I moved up, warily, close to the wall. Approaching the place where the figure had vanished I saw a recess, which housed an imposing stone statue of a former Ravenscrag lord.

'Who is there?'

There was no reply. I moved closer, again cursing the fact that I was weaponless. I leaned gingerly forward, peering around the statue into the dark at its back. A face appeared, so suddenly that I jumped back in fright. There was a cackle of laughter.

'Hectal!'

Lady Sheerquine's stunted twin came forth, chuckling madly, and performed a little dance in front of me. 'Hectal! Hectal!'

'What are you doing there?'

'Here? There? Hectal everywhere. Hee-hee!'

He stopped dancing and scratched his armpit. I found I was looking at him in a new light. Here was a shade who had returned out of its time in the hope of saving Ravenscrag. For its service it had suffered a lifetime of idiocy, the pain of a twisted body, had been shunned by all – or almost all – and no doubt tormented, and presumably was tolerated only because of family connection. This shade knew nothing of its purpose in life, except perhaps glimmerings, flashes of insight which it could not properly communicate to others.

'Hectal . . .' I began, but Hectal raised his finger to his lips.

'Sssh!' He looked left and right along the corridor, then beckoned with his finger and stepped back behind the statue. There was a heavy grating sound. I squeezed into the space between statue and wall and saw an opening, just large enough for a man to enter. Hectal was nowhere to be seen.

I pushed myself closer to the opening. I could make out a dim orange luminescence within. Hectal's face reappeared, and he beckoned again. 'Come.'

I stopped low and entered, to find myself in another narrow, secret passageway, which branched to left and right and was lit by a torch set in a bracket upon the wall. Hectal braced himself against the stone block which had swung inwards, and pushed, sealing the entrance. He sniggered like a farm-boy in a conspiracy, then reached up for the torch, put a cautionary finger to his lips again, and made off along the secret way.

The passage was as narrow as that which linked Moonblood's chamber with the nursery, and was likewise filthy with an accumulation of dust and cobwebs. It twisted and turned, and climbed sharply by stone steps, so that it became obvious we were ascending to a different floor. At length Hectal paused. He put his ear to what was revealed by the torchlight to be a rough wooden panel. Then, with a grimace of satisfaction, he pushed against the panel, which slid back.

Hectal passed through, and I followed. We were in a bed-chamber, unfamiliar to me. It was untidy, dusty, cluttered with bric-à-brac and motley collections of miscellaneous junk, much of which was damaged. Plainly it had not been swept or cleaned in an age. I looked at the bed and at the furniture, then crossed to a window to try to get my bearings.

'Hectal, is this your chamber?'

Hectal nodded vigorously. 'Hectal's.'

I watched him pensively for a moment. Quite suddenly I had realized that, in our last conversation, in his own cryptic way, Hectal had revealed to me that he knew something of Moonblood's fate. 'Gone to a woman,' he had said. And earlier: 'You will not understand her fate, nor know the blood.'

'Hectal, you were right again. You knew. Your "somethings" . . . You understood. Moonblood, she has gone to a woman.'

The corners of his mouth drooped. 'Moonblood. Ah, Moonblood.'

'Do you know more, Hectal? I think you do. I *know* you do, but maybe you don't know how to tell it. Is that it?'

'More somethings.' He screwed up his face, crinkling his brow and scratching his bald head.

'Moonblood has gone to a woman,' I said. 'But where is the woman?'

'Ah, Moonblood. Hectal tried.'

'Tried what? To help her? To guide her?'

Tears welled suddenly in Hectal's eyes, and coursed freely down his cheeks. 'Moonblood. Moonblood.'

'You love her, don't you, Hectal? She was your friend.'

He nodded. 'We love her.'

'We? Who do you mean, Hectal?'

'Want to help Moonblood. Keep her from woman.'

Yes, I understood. Hectal had known. Through the ravages of his bedevilled mind, he had still somehow held to the knowledge that Moonblood's transition from adolescence to womanhood held powerful implications, both for her and for Ravenscrag. He had wanted to prevent that – or perhaps he had simply wanted her to remain a child.

What would be the effects of her initiation? What did it mean for her, and for Ravenscrag? And in his wish to help Moonblood, had Hectal been involved in her kidnapping?

'Who else, Hectal? Who else loves her and wants to help her?'

Hectal merely stared at me with anguished bemusement.

'I have to find her,' I said. 'Somehow. I think it is vital. And I must do it before Shadownight.'

Hectal started at the word, and this time his eyes were wide with fear. 'Shadownight,' he hissed.

'It's tonight, isn't it?'

He nodded. I wanted to take hold of him and shake him, so certain was I that he had the information I sought. But he had withdrawn into himself. He sat on the edge of his unmade bed, hugging his arms about himself, biting his lip and regarding me mistrustfully. I tried, but could draw no further word from him.

At length, in frustration, and feeling that if I badgered him he would withdraw further, I left.

'I will come back, Hectal. In a little while. Please think about what I've asked you. I want to help Moonblood, and Ravenscrag. I need your help. Together, I think we may be able to find her.'

Chapter Twenty-Five

I left the main wing of the castle. Outside I was dazzled, the bright, hot sun coming as a stark contrast to the cool gloom within. My skin was sore, though mildly improved on the previous day.

I crossed the parade-ground, trying to avoid looking at the bodies of Irnbold and Elmag which still hung from their gibbets. A few workmen and lackeys were now in evidence: the walls and floors indoors were being scrubbed; outside a man with a hand-barrow was taking away the dead ravens, while another shovelled sawdust over the stains they had left.

My bodyguards, Bris and Cloverron, were still quartered in the loft over the stable. I was relieved to find them unharmed, but they were edgy, frightened in fact.

'We saw a lot from the window last night, sir,' said Bris. 'Never seen anything like it. We were afraid those things would come in here, and we had nothing to protect ourselves with bar a couple of pitchforks. What were those monsters?'

'Conjurings, creations of some deranged potent dabbler in dark magic.'

'But they were real?'

'Real enough to have created mayhem, spilled blood and taken lives.'

The two men exchanged nervous glances. 'We'd feel happier if we had our swords.'

'I will see what I can do, though I am not optimistic. The creatures are dwellers of night, however; I don't think you will encounter them during daylight. Now, I want you to take a message to Mistress Cametta. Find out firstly whether she suffered distress or harm last night, and – '

Bris was shaking his head. 'We're confined here. Can't go anywhere. Didn't you see the guards outside?'

I swore. A pair of Ravenscrag soldiers had been slouching on their pikestaffs near the stable door, but I had been too preoccupied to pay them much heed. I left my men and marched straight to the guardhouse. Captain Lonsord lounged at a table with his sergeant-at-arms, taking bread, cheese and ale.

'Captain, I require that my men be given their freedom. I need their services.'

'Can't do that, Master Dinbig,' said Lonsord, his cheeks bulging. 'My orders were to confine them to their quarters, and that's where they'll be until I get orders to the contrary.'

I eyeballed him for a moment, but it was plain I would get no joy. I fought down my anger. Lonsord swigged down a draught of ale, belched, and wiped his mouth on his sleeve.

'I have requested that my own weapons be returned to me. Has Lady Sheerquine passed word to you?'

'I've had nothing to that effect.'

'And my men's weapons?'

'Are under lock and key.'

'But they are defenceless, man! Give them swords and they will be able to aid you if those things come again tonight.'

'Or murder my men and try to escape.' He grinned humourlessly, and said with mock sincerity, 'Sorry, Master Dinbig. I take your point, but the decision really isn't mine to make. Sorry.'

He cocked his head slightly, wrinkling his nose and sniffing. He turned to the sergeant-at-arms. 'Catch a whiff of anything, Obal?'

The sergeant sniffed, frowned. 'No.'

'Ah, must be my imagination. It's early yet, of course. They're still fresh.' Lonsord looked back to me. 'In your experience,

Master Dinbig, how long does it take till a body starts to stink? I'm wondering when to take them down, see. But I reckon it'll be a day at least before they start to get high.'

I could withhold my indignation no longer. 'In certain cases, Lonsord, the stench begins long before a person is dead. No doubt it is your own putrefaction that offends your nostrils, as it offends mine.'

Lonsord rose with a snarl, kicking back his chair. His sword sang from its scabbard.

I stepped back, fearing I had gone too far, opening my arms. 'Would you slay an unarmed man, Captain?'

His face was ashen, eyes blazing. It struck me that the answer to my question was undoubtedly yes, so I added, 'And one who is employed in the service of your liege-lord?'

Lonsord spat a gobbet of bread and cheese onto the floor. 'Take care how you tread, Merchant. Your employment here is of short duration.'

My anger had not yet died. Unwisely I added fuel to the fire. 'I trust your word was good, and that permission was forthcoming from Lady Sheerquine for my goods to be delivered to your home, as your comely wife requested?'

Lonsord's lip curled and the sword shifted in his hand, but I knew now that the moment had passed. Happy as he would be to have skewered me there and then, reason had got the better of him.

'You will find the gowns are most exquisite upon Mistress Cametta. They are not inexpensive, of course, but they are the finest, which I know you are only too happy to purchase for one as beautiful as she. And with such exceptional taste, too.'

For a moment I thought I was mistaken, for Lonsord took a half step forward. But he stood glowering, held back like a mastiff straining on a chain, and came no further.

I backed into the doorway. 'Good morning, Captain. Sergeant.'

I made my way thence to the cellar. A well armed guard of six still stood nervously back from the barricaded door. An occasional low, rumbling growl came from within, and a mephitic stench filled the passage. The stink made me gag as I entered, but the unfortunate guards seemed to have grown inured to it. They reported no further violent activities since last night. They continued to push raw flesh beneath the door every few minutes, to be devoured at a formidable rate.

I returned to Hectal's chamber. There was no answer to my knock. I called softly, then louder. Still no sound, so I tried the handle, but the door had been bolted from the inside. I wondered about going downstairs to the entrance to the secret passage behind the statue, and entering Hectal's chambers via that route. But if he was still in his room, or happened to come in and find that I had taken advantage of this privileged knowledge, he might be greatly offended. Urgency aside, I did not want to risk alienating him, so I discarded the idea.

But why had he shown me this passage? Simply for amusement? No, that was not Hectal's way.

I mused on this as I passed on along the corridor. Marshilane, Moonblood's maid, came from a side passage. She jumped nervously when she saw me, then, realizing who it was, recovered herself.

'Oh, sir, excuse me. I wanted to ask you . . .' Her pudgy cheeks were the colour of oat-paste, and there were dark rings around her eyes. 'Am I allowed to clean up in Mistress Moonblood's room yet?'

'I would prefer not, for the present, Marshilane, if you don't mind.'

'Very good, sir. It's just that I don't like leaving it like it is, with the bed being like that, and – '

'I understand, Marshilane. It must be distressing for you. But it would be a great help to me if it could be left just a little longer.'

She looked at me with wide, frightened eyes. 'What's happening here, sir? Last night . . . it was terrible. Two of the kitchen staff were killed outside in the yard. And there were others.' She dabbed at her eyes with a handkerchief. 'It's horrible, sir. We're all so afraid.'

'I know.' I had no words to offer her comfort. 'Marshilane, have you been into the nursery this morning?'

'No, sir.'

'Have any other of the servants?'

'No. There's hardly anyone about. They're all too frightened.'

'Do you know who put Redlock's crib back in there?'

'I didn't know it was there, sir. I thought it was burned.'

'And something else has been taken away,' I said, recalling the bloodied pillow case that Lady Sheerquine had dropped.

'I'm sorry, sir. I can't help you.'

She went on her way, and I stood gazing out of the window. The two corpses swung in the distance. With revulsion I saw a dark shape clinging to Elmag's shoulder, pecking at her face. Guards patrolled the walls. The parade-ground was clear; a squad of soldiers marched towards the closed gate. A couple of hounds were visible, one sitting in the shade of a wall, and another, liver and white, ambling slowly across a courtyard.

I called to the retreating figure of the maid, striding after her. 'Marshilane. That hound down there: is it Rogue?'

She squinted through the window. 'Looks like him, sir.'

'He seems quite attached to Moonblood.'

'Yes, he's a soppy old thing. Used to be one of his lordship's best hunting-dogs. Too old for it now, though. Moonblood always makes a big fuss of him.'

It was a long shot. I dashed back along the corridor to Moonblood's room, took her torn night-robe from the bed and stuffed it inside my tunic. I cursed again that I had no weapons. The sword I'd taken from the wounded soldier last night had been removed from my chamber, presumably by Radyerd. It seemed unlikely now that Lady Sheerquine was going to grant my wish to have my own weapons returned to me. I patted my belt. At least I had that now.

Downstairs I had a servant direct me to the castle's master-of-hounds, and after some wrangling secured a collar and long leash. I found the old dog in the sun-drenched courtyard, stretched out in the shade of a laburnum bush.

'Rogue.'

An ear twitched, half lifted, then fell again. I repeated his name. This time the ear lifted and an eye half opened. I squatted beside him and ruffled his head. The old dog raised himself and snuffled. Then he caught the familiar scent of the night-robe and began to whine, pushing his nose excitedly against my tunic. I slipped the collar over his head.

'Moonblood, Rogue. Yes, that's right. We're going to find her.'

We went through the castle and out into the gardens at the rear.

I had no clear idea where to commence the search, but the castle itself seemed the wrong place. Literally soaked as it was with Moonblood's scent, I could only expect the old hound to lead me around in circles. And the certainty was growing within me that Moonblood was not going to be found anywhere within the castle precincts, but had gone, or been taken, from Ravenscrag, out into the forest. So I made for the dell where she had recently spent so much of her time, in the hope that there Rogue might pick up a trail or a trace that would lead me further.

In the orchard I took the night-robe from my tunic and showed it to Rogue. He sniffed at it, his whines turning to excited little barks. 'Go, Rogue. Find her. Find Moonblood.'

Nose to ground Rogue started to run back and forth across the grass. Within seconds he had found her trail, and with a triumphal baying set off straight towards the river. I followed, gripping the leash, holding him back.

As I had expected, Rogue led me straight to Moonblood's dell. There, to my disappointment, the trail seemed to end. Rogue snuffled back and forth, whining, pawing sometimes at the ground, but he found no way that led out of the dell – at least, not one that Moonblood had taken. I let the dog have free rein for several minutes, while I sat a little distance from the water's edge, gazing at the cliff and the forested heights beyond. It was then that I thought I saw a ripple of movement, a shift high up in the green that was not the motion of breeze among the leaves.

An animal perhaps. I stared hard until my vision began to blur. Then, just as I looked away, I saw it again. A glimpse of a movement – and this time I was certain: a figure, garbed in green, had slipped away beneath the trees!

It was gone in an instant. I thought back to the afternoon I had lost my wagon on the approach to Ravenscrag. I'd thought I'd seen someone then, standing beneath the trees, watching. I shielded my eyes and cast them back over the spot, but I saw nothing more, though whoever was watching me might still have been there, hidden from view. The cliff forbade climbing up to investigate further, and it would have been fruitless anyway, for my watcher could have been gone before I had ascended even ten feet.

I called Rogue to me and we returned to the castle.

Chapter Twenty-Six

On the way back I found myself pondering on the secret passage that Hectal had just shown me. At the point where I had entered it behind the statue, I recalled, it led off in two directions. One way took us to Hectal's chamber, but where did the other lead?

Was this the way in which Moonblood, and possibly Redlock too, had been spirited from the castle? Was that Hectal's reason for revealing it to me?

To take Moonblood, conscious or otherwise, the short distance from her own chamber to Hectal's without being seen would have been relatively simple. But to get her from there out of the castle in similar circumstances would have presented tremendous problems. A secret way to some unknown destination was surely the answer.

With Rogue still on his leash I strode back through the galleries and passages of old Ravenscrag, until I reached the statue where I had come upon Hectal. I slipped behind, running my fingers over the rough stone, searching cracks and crevices, seeking a handle or catch that would open the hidden door. I found nothing. I put my shoulder to the stone and pushed. Nothing budged. But Rogue was not indifferent to the place. He sniffed eagerly around my feet, whining and pawing at the stone. I grew more certain that I was on the right track.

For minutes I searched and strained in vain, seeking the means to enter that dark byway. At length I could only conclude that the entrance was one way, and could not be opened from outside.

I had to find Hectal!

Frustrated, I stepped back out into the corridor. Darean Lonsord was leaning against the opposite wall, watching me with a look of hostile bemusement. One of his guards stood alongside him.

'Looking for something, Master Dinbig?'

Rogue gave a low growl.

'Yes, as it happens, Captain. I am looking for Ravenscrag's children, in full pursuance of my commission.'

'And you think they may be hiding behind one of the statues, do you?'

I did not want Lonsord to learn about the passage. I said quickly, 'I was simply acting on the wild hope that Rogue here might be able to track down Mistress Moonblood. As we passed along this passage he became interested in something around the base of the statue. I think it was simply a rat.'

'There's been a pestilence of vermin around Ravenscrag lately,' Lonsord said sourly. 'We've eliminated some, but I don't think it'll get any better until we've gotten rid of every last one.'

It seemed politic in the light of things to allow him his little jibe without riposte. With Rogue at my heel I went on my way, conscious of Darean Lonsord's eyes boring into my back.

Upstairs I knocked again at Hectal's door. Again there was no reply. I tried the handle once more, and was surprised this time to find the door unbolted. I opened it a crack, softly calling Hectal's name, then peered inside. The dog, Rogue, pushed in, clearly aroused by the smells of the place. I entered and closed the door behind me.

A cursory glance around the chambers affirmed Hectal's absence. I went to the panel in the wainscot which gave access to the secret passage. Rogue, beside me, went suddenly frenzied, pressing his nuzzle to the base of the wood and whining and scratching like a mad thing.

She had gone this way!

I sought around the edge of the panel. My fingers found something cold and hard protruding from the top of the wainscot. It moved slightly to my touch. I pressed. Something gave with a satisfying click.

The panel had shifted; down one edge a crack had appeared, large enough to insert my fingertips and pull. Slowly the secret entrance opened.

Drawing the door back, I was unable to keep a firm grip on Rogue's leash. As soon as the opening permitted, he pushed through, into the passage. The leash jerked from my hand and he vanished into the dimness behind the wall. I called after him, urgently, though I dared not raise my voice high. It was no use. The scurrying pad of his feet diminished into the darkness.

Swearing, I pulled the panel back. It was pitch black within. I searched Hectal's chamber and found an oil lamp, went cautiously back out into the main corridor and lit it from a bracket, then returned. I eased myself through the opening and into the passage, and set off after the hound.

I could no longer hear Rogue. I made my way through the darkness, down the rough stone steps, onto the level, deep into the building. I calculated that I must have passed the location of the second entrance, behind the statue, though I had not noticed it. The passage went on, descending gradually, leading me deeper beneath the old castle.

Presently I perceived a change in the substance of the walls of the narrow tunnel. Stone blocks gave way intermittently to natural rock, then dark soil, shale and compressed silt. Pale roots formed a tangle in walls and ceiling. Sometimes they twisted down and brushed against my face or shoulder as I pressed forward. In places tarred cedar timbers, ancient and cracked, shored up the walls and roof. I guessed I was now beyond Ravenscrag's outer ramparts, and still the secret way went on. It was stuffy, airless; I had begun to sweat furiously. The flame in my lamp grew weak and I began to fear I might suffocate and die down here. I reassured myself: Rogue had passed this way, for there was no other. Therefore it led somewhere. And it was surely the route by which Moonblood, and perhaps her baby brother, had been taken from the castle.

The gradient of the passage started to rise slowly. I made out the faintest glimmer of grey light before me. Suddenly I was faced with dense vegetation, blocking the way – but it was through this that daylight glimmered. Cautiously I pushed it aside and climbed from the tunnel.

I stood in the cool green shade of the forest, sucking in deep draughts of air. The trees, towering over me, cut out most of the sky. The ground rose sharply ahead of me. Looking back I was able to glimpse Ravenscrag's highest turrets through the green.

I doused my lamp and concealed it beneath a hazel bush. The vaguest path led off into the trees, and for want of an alternative it was this that I now took. It meandered without apparent aim, climbing, dipping, skirting huge boulders and the boles of ancient trees. The vegetation was harsh; I was soon drenched in sweat again. The shade became intense, the canopy blocking the sky, save for occasional bright stabs of sunlight which pierced the foliage and created shifting patterns upon the forest floor. I stopped from time to time to catch my breath and listen. A hush lay over the forest, disturbed only by the soft sough of a warm breeze through the leaves. No birds sang, no beast seemed to stir. Of Rogue there was no sign.

I began to fear that I had taken the wrong path, though at the tunnel entrance there had seemed no alternative. I was deep in the forest now, and quite possibly lost. The track had withered away. Incautiously I had neglected to leave markers of any kind that would help me to find my way back. The chances of finding the path again were not good.

Push on, or try and go back? I hesitated in indecision. 'You are *Zan-Chassin!*' I reminded myself. If needs be I could exit my flesh, rise about the forest canopy and pinpoint my position relative to Ravenscrag. Wiping the sweat from my brow I struck on.

I bent beneath the vine-covered trunk of a great fallen oak. Before me was a small glade where foxgloves and helleborine clustered. A little rill trickled to one side. I stopped, panting, and leaned against a rock.

A sound behind me!

I whirled, ducking instinctively. A dark shape leapt from the fallen oak.

'*Hee-hee!*'

I staggered back. 'Hectal!'

He stood before me, beaming madly, scratching.

'Hectal, I am lost. Is this the way to Moonblood?'

'Moonblood!' hissed Hectal excitedly. 'Moonblood!'

'Can you take me to her?'

He looked troubled.

'I must find her, Hectal. I must.'

Hectal stared beyond me, seeming puzzled, then moved quickly, as if to traverse the glade. As he made to pass in front of me there was a sudden *whoosh* and a muted thud. Hectal staggered sideways as if struck by an unseen blow. He collided with me and slumped limply into my arms. A warm wet flood covered my hands, spilling from his neck which had been split open like a soft fruit. From the wound protruded the stub of a crossbow bolt.

His weight threw me off balance. As I stumbled back a second bolt whizzed past my ear and *zinged* off the rock behind.

I dropped to a crouch, my eyes scouring the forest. A glint of metal between the trees! I dragged Hectal into the shade of the rock and put my fingers to his neck. There was no pulse.

Plainly, both shafts had been meant for me. Sheer chance had saved me, and robbed poor Hectal of his life. Angered, and afraid, I let his body go and rolled into the bushes. Then rising to a half-crouch, I dashed further into cover. No more of the lethal missiles pursued me. I was out of sight of my assailants, and they, having seen me fall, possibly believed me to be lying dead or wounded behind the rock.

The ground rose sharply, rocks and vegetation providing ample cover. I scrambled upwards as silently as I could, my heart pounding. I kept going, seeking the higher ground where I might have an advantage. The bushes broke. On my belly I crawled forward so that I could look down upon the glade. I saw Hectal's corpse sprawled beside the rock. Nothing moved; nothing made a sound.

I cast my eyes around me. A little way below, somewhat off to one side, a Ravenscrag guard crouched on the steep slope beside a tree, crossbow levelled, squinting down at the glade. I could see no one else.

I unclasped my belt, and drew from it the razor-sharp garrotting wire concealed inside. Carefully I moved around until the soldier's back was to me. A distance of ten paces separated us. I half rose to creep forward. As I moved my foot dislodged a stone. The man glanced back, saw me. His mouth opened; he started to rise, bringing the crossbow around.

I had no choice. I threw myself forward, kicking out with all my weight. The kick connected with the man's shoulder. Half erect, he was knocked sideways and smashed into a tree. I fell on my back. The soldier slipped, lost his footing, and with a cry fell flailing down the slope. He came to rest fifteen yards below me, and lay motionless, his head at a grotesque angle, the neck plainly broken.

I cursed. I had wanted his weapons. I could not now risk exposing myself by scrambling down to recover them. I darted back into cover, then called out at the top of my voice. 'Lonsord!'

There was no reply. I called again. This time Darean Lonsord's harsh, cutting voice sounded from somewhere below me on the other side of the glade. 'Aye, Merchant, it is me.'

'You try to murder me! You are exceeding your orders!'

I moved along the slope, keeping to cover.

Lonsord called back. 'You are trying to escape.'

'Not so. I am seeking Moonblood.'

I moved again, not wanting to be pinpointed. 'If you kill me you risk the destruction of Ravenscrag!'

'You tried to escape. I found you, you resisted forcefully. I was obliged to kill you. It is well within the scope of my orders.' Lonsord had also moved. He was slightly higher up, moving around the glade towards my position.

'You have murdered Lady Sheerquine's twin brother. Is that also within the scope of your orders?'

Hesitation, then: 'No, *you* murdered the old halfwit, Merchant. I caught you and tried to save him, but it was too late. Perhaps you also murdered Moonblood. Lady Sheerquine will thank me when I return with your head.'

There was a queer edge in his voice, something I had not heard before. I sensed sheer hatred, and unbridled anger. A shiver ran down my spine. *He knew about Cametta and me!*

Cametta! Was she alive?

I fought down my feelings. I had to get away. I did not know how many men Darean Lonsord had out there; even now they could be closing in on me. I crawled away into the underbrush. Rising to my feet when I judged I'd put a good distance between myself and Darean Lonsord, I made off as quickly as I could into the depths of the forest.

I followed the bed of a small stream, stopped a couple of times, watched and listened. There was no sound of pursuit. I moved on. I was shaking, from exertion, from fear, from sheer helpless fury at Hectal's needless death. I was desperately concerned for Cametta. My limbs burned, and my lungs were scorched from running and climbing.

I stopped to bathe in the stream's cool water. I felt a strange prickling along the back of my neck. The conviction grew upon me that I was being watched. I straightened slowly, peering around.

Twenty feet distant, seated cross-legged upon a twisted oak root, was a young man garbed in green. He looked to be of slightly above average height, with lean but athletic limbs, slim waist and broad chest and shoulders. His skin was pale, with wide-set eyes, a slender nose, wide mouth and even jaw and chin. Fair hair protruded from beneath a green cap set with a panache of partridge feathers. He was exceedingly handsome, and gave an impression of easy self-possession and charmed amusement. He wore a light green shirt, green waistcoat and hose of good cloth, and low boots of soft leather. He carried no visible weapon, save a hunting-knife at his belt.

We watched one another for some moments, he smiling, holding the neck of a leather flask between his fingers. I took a deep breath. 'You are Linvon, called Linvon the Light.'

The young man's smile broadened. 'I know that.'

He held out the leather flask. 'You look tired. Come, share my watered wine and rest yourself for a moment.'

I considered, looking around. I sensed no threat or malice from this youth, yet I was in the presence of the unknown, lost in the depths of the forest, wholly unsure of myself. And there was an unusual aura of the unworldly about him.

Linvon seemed aware of my disquiet. He unplugged the flask and raised it to his lips, swallowing a draught. 'See, it is not poisoned.'

I approached slowly. 'I am pursued. I was ambushed by Ravenscrag soldiers.'

'But you escaped, and they are not close by.'

'They killed Hectal.'

Shock came into the young man's face. He blinked several times and looked down, shaking his head. 'I didn't realize. Hectal . . . He was looking for me. I told him never to come into the forest.'

'He revealed to me the secret way from the castle.'

Linvon nodded. 'I guessed he would.'

'Then you were expecting me to come?'

'I thought it likely.' He watched me with brilliant, alert, and now sorrowful blue eyes, then looked away. 'Oh, Hectal you poor, noble-hearted fool . . .'

I took the flask and drank, relishing the cool liquid in my gullet.

'You are wanted at Castle Ravenscrag for theft, and more.'

Linvon rubbed the side of his nose with a bitter smile. 'Hmph! Old Flarefist still holds to his canard, does he?'

'Canard?'

'I can assure you, sir, I did not steal Flarefist's silver.'

'Then who did?'

'It was never stolen. It was a gift, presented to me by Flarefist himself.'

'A gift? Do you think me so credulous?'

'Perhaps not a gift exactly.' His blue eyes twinkled. 'A bribe, in fact, to persuade me to depart Ravenscrag and, in particular, to see no more of his daughter.'

'I think Flarefist believes otherwise.'

'That does not surprise me. He is quite deranged. But don't doubt that I am telling you the truth. I am no thief. How is Flarefist now, by the way?'

'He is a broken old man – but far from harmless.'

'Quite. I have seen something of what he is capable of. Though he initially welcomed me into his household as an entertainer, it quickly became plain that my life was at risk should I remain.'

'You are fortunate that he allowed you the opportunity to leave.'

'He would not risk murdering me, except as a last resort. Word might somehow have got back to Moonblood, and he knew she

would never have forgiven him. But the offer of relative wealth
. . .' Linvon took from his waistcoat pocket three coloured balls.
He tossed them into the air, passing them swiftly from one hand to
another, bouncing them from his forehead, letting them run along
his arms as if they possessed a life of their own. 'I am a poor
travelling entertainer. I earn my bread where I can, rarely staying
in one place for longer than it takes to earn enough to travel on.
Often my life is hard; truly I am little more than a pauper. Flarefist
perceived quite rightly that a gift of valuables sufficient to greatly
improve my living standard for months to come might well be
acceptable. So he summoned me to his room, stated his terms, and
swept up what items came to hand.'

'Yet you remained.'

'I left Ravenscrag, as was Lord Flarefist's stipulation.'

'But continued to see Moonblood, clandestinely.'

Linvon pushed forward his lower lip, gathering the coloured
balls. He made a fluid motion with his hands; the balls vanished.
'It is true, we continued to see one another, though never within
the castle. We love each other; we cannot be parted, not for all the
silver in the world.'

'And now you have abducted her. Or did she run away to be
with you?'

Linvon settled his blue gaze upon me meaningfully. 'I have
rescued her, sir . . . I am sorry, what is your name?'

'Dinbig.'

'Sir Dinbig. I have rescued her, both from her tyrannical
parents, and from a greater, unknown evil that venges itself upon
her and her house.'

'And the babe, Redlock?'

'I tried, but I was too late. The influence had already taken
effect.'

'Where is Moonblood now?'

'She is safe.'

'I must see her.'

'Why?'

'Despite your efforts, however sincere, I do not think that she is
safe merely because she is beyond Ravenscrag's walls. Nor will she
be until we have understood the nature of the evil that clings to
her, and vanquished it.'

Linvon looked at me gravely. I said, 'You already know that, don't you? You knew I would come. You met me here, and you knew I would be coming for Moonblood.'

He looked away, his expression revealing his anxiety. 'She is not herself.'

'No. She has, I fear, come under the effects of an ancient malignity known by some as Molgane's Bane. What do you know of what is happening at Ravenscrag?'

He shook his head. 'There are many gaps in my understanding. Far too many. Most recently I have learned more, though still I am unsure.'

'Tell me what you know.'

Linvon plugged the stopper back into his flask. 'There is something you should hear, but it should be recounted by another, who has more to tell than I.' He unfolded his legs and slipped with an easy grace from the oak root. 'Come.'

Chapter Twenty-Seven

Linvon moved with surefootedness across the rough forest floor, gliding through dense green vegetation, around outcrops of rock and towering trees, following no visible path. I followed less easily.

We walked for perhaps an hour. Glimpsing the sky I divined from the position of the sun that midday was well past. I felt a shiver of misgiving: Shadownight drew ever closer. I dreaded the setting of the sun.

As we walked I prompted Linvon to tell me everything he had experienced at Ravenscrag, particularly in regard to Redlock's and Moonblood's disappearances. This he did, willingly and, as far as I could gauge, withholding little or nothing.

He explained how he had arrived at Ravenscrag two months earlier; as he believed, by sheer chance. He had travelled there with a man from Dasmere, a small Pansurian town a couple of days' ride away, where he had passed most of the winter. The man was visiting a sick relative, and Linvon, eager for change, had easily negotiated a ride in his cart.

'Why Ravenscrag?' Linvon posed the question half to himself. 'My driver warned me it was a godforsaken place. His advice, and

215

the advice of others, was to travel east into Miragoff, where there were greater opportunities to be had for a vagabond entertainer such as I. Or I could have stayed in Dasmere. I had found good friends there, dallied with comely wenches, and earned a passable living. Yet something about it . . . the very name . . . something I could not explain, convinced me I should come to Ravenscrag. And when I arrived . . .'

His first sight of Ravenscrag had sent a quiver down his spine, he said. 'It was as though I knew it, as though I had been there before . . . and yet, not like that.'

He shook his head, at a loss to explain. This feeling, he went on, was reinforced the longer he stayed there. 'The people I met, the buildings, the streets. It all seemed familiar. Its very history seemed familiar. I was haunted by the feel of the place, by names that I heard mentioned. It felt right that I should be there, and at the same time I was unsettled.'

And then he was invited up to the castle. 'Now I knew that I had entered a mystery beyond my understanding. Still I could not explain it, yet I was no stranger to this place. I knew its ancient walls and its myriad passages, courtyards and hallways. I had been there before, or I had been told of it in great detail. Yet I had no memory of either. Perhaps, I thought, I have lived here in another life.'

I stared at him curiously, a notion forming in my mind as I recalled disconsolate words spoken to me only hours earlier.

'And yet that was not it!' continued Linvon. 'For I knew the people too, though I had never met them before. Flarefist, the pregnant Sheerquine, her lack-witted twin, the old astrologer . . . and Moonblood. Most of all, Moonblood. Ah yes, and the child too, who had yet to be born. I knew of him. Most particularly, I felt something about his imminent birth, and I was disquieted without knowing why.

'Talk, of course, was all of the birth, and of the Legend of Ravenscrag. When I heard of the Legend, again I felt unease, but again, though I searched within myself, I could not discover a reason why.'

I was in no doubt now. Lord Draremont's shade had said, just before we parted: *I tried again, dispatching another to Ravenscrag. But this one also was lost, swayed and seduced it would seem by the temptations of corporeality. I do not know what became of him.*

'It was as though all my life I had been lost, searching for something,' said Linvon. 'And at last I had found it. Without knowing how or why, I had arrived where I was supposed to be. Yet being there did not make me feel comfortable. Rather, I was confused, unnerved in ways I could not articulate.'

I nodded to myself. Linvon. He was the other shade, the kindred spirit of poor, dead Hectal, who had returned to life in an effort to save Ravenscrag. Hence his unworldly aura. He felt promptings, was haunted by strange memories, fears and uncertainties, and he did not know why. *He did not know who he was!*

'And you became enamoured of Moonblood,' I said. 'Or was that also mere dalliance?'

Linvon shook his head emphatically. 'Ah, Moonblood, sweet Moonblood. So fair, such a dream . . . She stirred my blood and stole my heart. Never have I been so captivated. And I found it was so for her too. Initially she was shy – as, I confess it, was I. She was amused by my entertainments. In truth I know but a handful of simple tricks – little more than illusion and prestidigitation – but she believed them true magic. And I divined that within her there was magic. Magic of a very special kind.

'We began to meet at every opportunity. We had much to say to one another. I questioned Moonblood about the Legend of Ravenscrag, and discovered that she was troubled. She was haunted by strange dreams and forebodings, irrational fears, profound misgivings about herself. When I questioned her about the dreams I received another shock, for they corresponded in great part to dreams that I had had.'

'What was the content of these dreams?'

'They centred around what you have already spoken of as the curse, or Bane of Ravenscrag: Molgane's Bane. They involved the birth of a monstrosity, a terrible destruction. In Moonblood's case she often saw herself as being the cause of that destruction. She told me she would awaken in a state of nervous distraction, half believing herself to be an unwitting agent of some terrible malevolence. And she had another recurring nightmare, linked to this one, in which she was pursued by a red-faced wizard garbed in dark robes. He never caught her, but each time she dreamed of him he came closer. She had until now kept these things to herself.

217

She feared, should she attempt to confide in anyone, that she would be ridiculed or dismissed as hysterical. And in her waking hours the dreams did not trouble her, though she often thought about them.'

'So neither of you did anything about it?'

He turned his handsome young face earnestly to me. 'What was there to do, Master Dinbig? We were two young people haunted by things we could not explain. We became closer as a result, and our fears grew, but we still tried to convince ourselves that what we were experiencing was some uncanny kind of trick of our imaginations. We feared we might be mad otherwise. And then I was summoned to see Flarefist. I learned of his and Sheerquine's disapproval of our relationship. Moonblood had been forbidden to see me again; I was told I was no longer welcome at Ravenscrag. When I remonstrated Flarefist became angry. That was when he made his threats plain, and gave me the silver.'

'Tell me about the night of Redlock's birth. What happened, to Redlock and then Moonblood?'

Linvon held up a finger. 'Presently. As I said, there is another who has much to tell.'

We had broken out of the forest gloom and stood at the edge of a sunlit green meadow spotted with myriad wild flowers. A grass track led to a small cottage beside a shaded pool. The cottage looked untenanted, with an air of disuse and neglect. Dirty white walls supported a steep gabled roof of dark, sagging thatch, out of which sprouted a wealth of green grass and weeds. The garden was overgrown, and at the back of the cottage the forest loomed hard. Young saplings and dense thickets of undergrowth grew almost to the walls: initial stages before the cottage became entirely engulfed.

Linvon struck out across the meadow. As we drew closer a figure came from around the side of the cottage and stood beside a tall shrub, watching us. I stared, only half believing what I saw, stumbling as I walked on at Linvon's back.

It was a man who awaited us, but he was no ordinary man. He was of monumental stature, a giant. He stood with mighty hands on hips, dwarfing the shrub at his side. His head reached almost to the windows of the upper floor of the cottage.

He wore loose brown trews which terminated below his colossal knees, and a waistcoat of grey cloth, his great hirsute chest bare beneath. His torso was more massive than a bull's; his arms and legs were as thick as ash boughs, and his huge feet were also bare. At his waist was a wide leather belt from which hung wallets and pouches.

As we passed beneath a broken latticed arch into the old garden of the cottage, Linvon glanced back. He saw the look on my face and gave a wry smile. 'Don't be alarmed. If you are a friend he will do you no harm. He is Gorodur.' He approached the giant. 'Gorodur, this is Master Dinbig.'

I stared up into the ancient craggy face. Big, pale brown eyes regarded me from beneath bushy brows. His huge head was bald on top, ringed by a thicket of coarse brown hair. His brow was wrinkled, his nose fleshy and rather flat, set between ruddy slab cheeks. His mouth was wide, pensive, the lips a deep red. He returned my gaze contemplatively. There was a searching mournfulness in his look, which was vanquished when his lips stretched into a smile and he extended a hand I could have sat in.

'Welcome, Master Dinbig.'

Gorodur's voice was resonant and profound, yet surprisingly gentle. He grasped my hand. His own hand was warm, the skin like toughened hide. He could have crushed mine effortlessly – indeed, had he chosen, he could have squeezed the life out of me with no trouble.

'We will eat and drink and talk,' said Linvon. 'I will bring food out.'

He moved towards the door of the cottage, then stopped, laying a hand on my shoulder and smiling archly. 'It would be cooler to eat indoors, but as you can see Gorodur is too large to enter without bringing the entire place down around our heads! So we will dine in the shade, beside the pond.'

Linvon brought bread, cheeses, meats, fish, fruit, and water, wine and cordials. He laid them out on a cloth spread upon the grass by the water's edge. I found I was hungry, and ate well. Gorodur sat with us, towering above us, but did not dine. 'Our foods are too trifling for him,' explained Linvon. 'He will take something more substantial later on.' He turned to the giant. 'Perhaps you will now tell Dinbig your story, precisely as you first told it to me.'

And so I learned how Gorodur had come to Ravenscrag, how he had marched the long, untracked journey from his home far to the north, beyond Pansur, in the wild and unexplored Interior. There, he told us, was where the few surviving giant communities now dwelt.

What had brought him here, on such a dangerous trek, forsaking the security of his home and the traditional close bonds of kith and kin, not knowing whether he would ever return? The answer, he explained, was the power of a vision.

'Since birth, and even before, I have possessed it,' said Gorodur. 'It was passed down to me by preceding generations, as is our way. It is a vision that originated many generations ago by your reckoning. We of the *Thotán**, as you may know, are collectors of lore and legend. As individuals we have a far greater lifespan than most races, and we know and remember things that others could never recall. We pass down our memories and tales in great detail, building on them, ever seeking to discover, to learn more. Little by little, then, as this vision was contemplated and dreamed and sung over and over, it became clearer and more meaningful. By the time I inherited it it had acquired a power and clarity like no other I knew. It became almost a part of me; I contemplated it day and night.'

The vision was that of a young maiden, Gorodur said. She stood upon the threshold of womanhood, and around her, focused about her, were strange powers and forces which she knew nothing of. 'Other factors were involved, for the vision was strange and complex. There was the birth of a monster; an ancient legend and an ancient curse; complex conditions involving the cycles of moon and sun, the births and deaths of siblings; the precise timing of the birth of another sibling. These things and more were intricately interwoven, presenting themselves as a potential single manifestation which could occur at some unknown future time.

'My task was to study this vision, and others,' said Gorodur. 'To unravel meaning, find clarity, attempt to discover whether what

---

* Earliest documents describe the *Thotán* as a race of colossi who preceded men as inhabitants of Firstworld. Peacefully inclined, they nevertheless became embroiled in numerous wars. Slow to breed, their numbers declined to a critical level, and they withdrew to lands not populated by man.

220

was seen and dreamed could actually come to be. But as I worked this vision became overriding, and the others paled into insignificance. Such intricacies did the vision hold that it seemed most unlikely that it could ever come about, yet I could not stop thinking about it: this ill-starred, innocent maiden who was the blood of the moon, still but a child, cursed without knowing, beset by demons, bringing about her own destruction and that of her entire line. I could not forget a story my grandfather told me when I was very young. The vision had just been passed down to me by my father, and my grandfather called both me and my father to him. "I will tell you now what I told your father when, many years ago, I first passed this vision to him. Listen well, for it is important," he said.

'And he explained how, in his youth, his village had been visited by a nobleman from afar. A man, greatly troubled by events that had taken place at his home. This noble had come seeking advice and help from the *Thotán*, and we had been able to give him little. But my grandfather possessed the vision in its earliest form at that time, and he sensed something of what it might mean.'

'Your grandfather . . .' I interrupted Gorodur excitedly. 'Was his name by any chance Eldhorn?'

Gorodur surveyed me with sombre brown eyes, and I was aware of Linvon, too, watching intently.

'You know of this?' asked the giant.

'I know only of a meeting between Eldhorn and Draremont, Lord of Ravenscrag. Please, I am fascinated by your tale. Carry on.'

'Yes, Eldhorn was my grandfather's name, and Draremont was the tragic noble whose quest brought him to Eldhorn's village. It was long afterwards that Eldhorn told me of this, and he and my father began schooling me in the vision that had become their obsession also. Understand, there is a significant passage of time here. My grandfather was young when Lord Draremont came to his village – less than seventy years of age. When he came to tell me his tale he was approaching his three hundredth year, and his life was almost done.'

Gorodur paused for a few moments, lost in thoughts of past and present. I glanced skywards, my unease mounting as I noted the sun's inexorable descent.

'My grandfather advised me to use all the resources and wisdom and knowledge-seeking abilities at our command, and to *observe*, to build upon the vision. He said we could not know at that time whether it would ever manifest. To manifest in its full destructive capacity would require that all the myriad factors and conditions be met. "You must watch," he said, "be ever alert for any sign that it is coming true."

'And I asked him, "How will I know?"

'He told me: "Turn to the skies. Know how to interpret the portents there, understand the movements of the sun and moon, the planets and stars, for it is through these that the first warning will appear. Consult the ancient charts and instruments, seek the wisdom of ages gathered by generations of *Thotán* star-gazers. Learn the secrets of their art, the methods of calculation and prediction. With luck – or more aptly, with ill-luck – you will one day descry the signs for which you search. When that happens you will know that the vision may be about to come true. And if, as I hope, that day does not come in your lifetime, then pass on all you have learned. Charge one whom you love and trust to maintain the vigil."

'And I said to my grandfather, "But I still do not understand. What is it I am looking for?" And he replied: "Shadownight – one which will fall immediately following three nights of darkmoon, within a month of the coming of the summer solstice. That is what is foretold in the Legend and the Bane. It is a rare conjunction, but should it ever come you will know that there is every likelihood that the other conditions may be met also."

' "And if this occurs," I asked Eldhorn, "what then? What should I do?"

'My grandfather looked at me solemnly, graver than I had ever seen him. "Of that I cannot advise you," he said. "It is not our way to intervene in the affairs of other races. We gather knowledge and lore, we pass it on freely to those with a wish to know, but we do not interfere. Yet you, like me and like your father, may come in this case to feel an inexplicable sense of involvement, of empathy and responsibility belying our usual detachment. I have no explanation for why it should be so, but if it is, and if the signs manifest in your lifetime, I think you will face a profound crisis of conscience. How you respond can be your decision alone. Pray that it is one that you never have to make." '

222

Gorodur fell silent. Insects buzzed and skated across the surface of the still pond. I could not move. Despite the heat of the afternoon sun, a chill had gripped me. Presently, when I found my voice, I said, 'I have heard the term "Shadownight" a number of times in recent days, but its meaning eludes me. Tell me, what is it?'

'It is when a shadow falls across the moon, causing it to vanish,' said Gorodur. 'It is an unusual event in itself; for it to occur in such precise correlation with the other celestial phenomena I have described is to my knowledge unprecedented.'

'And what is its import?'

'As with darkmoon, it can be a time of power for lightless forces. In this instance, coming immediately after the third night of darkmoon – dark eclipsing the light, following so quickly upon dark – I fear it is a dire portent. The power of the Bane will find its greatest focus at Ravenscrag tonight.'

'For how long does this shadow linger?'

The giant shrugged his colossal shoulders. 'Perhaps minutes, perhaps an hour – it is not possible to say. If truly powerful forces are at work, it could be longer. We do not know. But of course, the forces may be unleashed during the shadowtime, but their effects may linger long after.'

'What is its cause?'

'That too is unknown, though there have been many hypotheses. Some claim it is magic, others that there exists in space a second moon, invisible to our eyes, which under certain conditions casts a shadow, or even moves to physically obscure our moon. Probably we will never know the true explanation.'

I shook my head in exasperation. 'Why did not Irnbold foresee this?'

'Irnbold? The astrologer? He cannot really be blamed. No human, however skilled an observer of the skies, has the resources or the knowledge that we have. Indeed, I would not have seen it had I not been searching for it so intently.'

I stared at Gorodur for some time. 'What made you come here, Gorodur? You have forsaken custom and your own kind to come to Ravenscrag. Why?'

He knitted his brow. 'I have no full answer to that. Let us say that I have lived with the vision for so long, have anticipated and come to dread the maiden's fate and the fate of those around her; when I realized its imminence I was, as Eldhorn had predicted, filled with a sense of involvement and responsibility. I could not just sit back and ignore it.'

'But what have you been able to do?'

'Little, I am afraid. I came seeking to discover whether other factors of the Legend and Bane had come into effect. I found that they have. The Bane is active, but I bring nothing that can help to combat it.'

'But you befriended Moonblood, meeting her in the dell,' I said, thinking yes, for a giant those surrounding cliffs would present less of an obstacle to climb. 'Did you tell her all you knew?'

'Not all. It was alarming enough at first for her to be confronted with one such as I. I did not want to terrify her with what I knew, though I wanted desperately to save her. And there was so little time. I felt utterly helpless.'

Linvon spoke now. 'I too was desperate to find a way of saving Moonblood. I had seen the words of the Bane, and though its precise meaning was unclear, I was in little doubt that Moonblood was imperilled.'

'You saw the words of the Bane? Where?'

Linvon reached into his waistcoat and withdrew a stiffened leather tube. He uncapped it and drew out a sheet of yellowed parchment. 'Here.'

I unrolled the parchment and read it. 'So it was you who stole it from Lady Sheerquine.'

'I told you earlier, Master Dinbig, I am no thief. This came into my possession more or less by accident. I found it in Hectal's chambers. *He* took it from his sister, sensing something of its import. He knows – I mean, he *knew* much, did Hectal. He was unable to articulate it, and he could not grasp everything, but on a deeper level he understood. And he loved Moonblood, too. He had befriended me when I first came to Ravenscrag. I felt great affection for him, almost a kinship. Hectal it was who showed me the secret passages, too. As far as I am aware only he and I knew about them – apart from Moonblood, who knew only of the passage between her room and the nursery.'

'Not any more,' I said. I handed him back the scroll. 'Tell me about your plan.'

Linvon gave a humourless laugh. 'We had no plan. Gorodur and I met only days ago. In Moonblood's absence we discussed what we knew, and grew ever more dispirited. We could do little but observe, and hope that something might change. The Bane spoke of corruption, and of wavering from the conditions of the Legend. We did not know whether these things had occurred. And there was the child: despite all the predictions, it might yet not survive birth, or it might be a girl. Anything might happen . . . But it didn't. The child was born, as foretold.'

My mind was working furiously, adding together all I had been told. I was conscious that, if these two were not all they professed to be, I was in grave danger. Yet, if they sought to menace me they had had ample opportunity. No, I sensed no malice – the opposite, in fact – and I found myself believing their tales.

I took a leap into space. 'So you, Linvon, installed yourself in the armoire in Redlock's nursery, intending to abduct the child. To what end?'

Linvon looked at me sharply. 'All I knew was that something evil was focused around both the baby and Moonblood. So I waited there, not knowing what I would do. Truly, I had no clear intention at all.'

'You were clear-headed enough to take the pitcher of water, thus obliging the wet-nurse to go out to fetch more so that you might steal forth and take the child.'

'I took the water, yes, but not for that reason. I was in that cursed cupboard for a long time. It was hot and dusty, and I grew thirsty. Had I left to fetch water for myself I might have missed something. So when the nurse dozed I slipped in and took the pitcher.'

My eyebrows lifted. 'Then tell me, what happened there in the nursery when Blonna went out to fetch more water?'

'There is little to tell, yet it is crucial. The nurse had barely closed the door when a vapour formed, seemingly out of nowhere. It was directly over the crib where Redlock slept, a greenish, amorphous darkening of the air. It descended slowly, enveloping the crib. The child cried out, then was silent. The cloud dispersed.'

'That was all?'

He nodded. 'I wanted to come out, to look into the crib, but I knew the nurse would return at any moment. So I stayed hidden.

Sure enough, within a minute she was back. She put the new pitcher on the table then went to the crib to take the child. She gave a queer shriek and staggered back, clutching her breast. Then she fled from the room. I immediately came from hiding to observe for myself – and there I saw that the babe had been transformed into a hideous thing. What should I do? I hovered in indecision. I heard the sounds of cries and footsteps approaching. I darted back to my hiding-place.'

'So you were there when we came in.'

'I observed you all. Most particularly I saw Moonblood, my sweet Moonblood, so pale and frightened.'

'And then?'

'I waited. Eventually I made my way back along the passage to Moonblood's room. I was afraid for her. The monster of the Bane – Ravenscrag's Iniquity – was born. I did not know what that meant, but it was plainer than ever that Moonblood too was in mortal danger.'

'And did you find Moonblood?'

He shook his head. 'She was not in her room so I stayed hidden in the passage, awaiting her return. She did not come in until very late. She was distressed. Her handmaid, Marshilane, was with her. She too was very upset. Marshilane helped Moonblood to undress, then put her to bed and remained with her, singing to her and stroking her hair until she slept. Only then, when Marshilane had gone, could I come from hiding. I approached the bed and gazed down at my darling as she lay in troubled sleep. I wanted to talk to her, but I thought it would be unwise to awaken her now. So I went back to the secret passage, determined to watch over her until she woke.'

'Why did you take the pitcher of water with you to Moonblood's room?'

Linvon eyed me curiously. 'You seem to lay great store by this water.'

'Please, answer my question.'

'Again, it was simply to quench my thirst. As far as I recall I left it somewhere in Moonblood's room.'

'On the floor by the bedside.' I shook my head. Thirst. So simple, and so obvious, that I had never even thought to consider it, and so had been led along a misleading trail.

'I must have slept, though I did not intend to,' continued Linvon. 'When I awoke again it was early morning. I was struck by a sudden horror that while I slept Moonblood might have suffered the same fate as her brother. I leapt up, peered into the room. Moonblood was out of bed. She was standing naked in the middle of the room, immobile, seemingly in a trance. I went to her immediately, but she was hardly aware of me. There was shock and fear on her face, and she was muttering something incoherent, over and over again. I saw that her legs were spattered with blood. Her night-robe was torn and lay upon the floor; there was blood on her bed.

'I thought she had been attacked, but there was no visible wound. I tried to get her to speak to me, but it was impossible. Something had possessed her. I was frightened. Somehow I had to get her away. I covered her nakedness with a dress then lifted her in my arms. After checking the corridor I carried her the short distance to Hectal's chambers. From there I led her from the castle via the passage. She was able to walk, meekly, not really knowing what was happening. In the forest Gorodur met us. He carried her here.'

'Is she here now?'

Linvon nodded. 'She has been sleeping, in the cottage. Gorodur gave her a sleeping-draught: she was distraught and a touch delirious.'

'Did she tell you anything? I must find out what her experience was.'

Linvon was looking beyond me, up towards the cottage at my back. He stood abruptly, saying, 'Perhaps you should ask her yourself.'

I turned, following the direction of his gaze. Approaching along the overgrown path which led down to the waterside, walking with slow, uncertain steps, was Moonblood.

Chapter Twenty-Eight

Moonblood appeared frail and wan; she walked as though unsure of the ground beneath her feet. She was garbed in the same simple cornflower-blue gown that she had worn at the birthday celebration for her baby brother, Redlock. It was scuffed with grime and slightly torn.

Linvon stepped past me and ran up to her, taking her hand.

I stood as he brought her to us, as did Gorodur, and bowed. 'Mistress Moonblood, it gives me great pleasure to see you.'

Her wide green eyes were glassy, sunk into dark hollows. Her lips were bloodless, her long fair hair uncombed, her expression vague. She stared at me for a moment, then managed a distracted smile. 'Master Dinbig. What has happened to you?'

I raised a hand to my face. 'Ah, I was burned.'

She gazed at me as though trying to fathom something. I said, 'Please sit with us. Take food and drink. I realize that you are tired and perhaps distraught, but there are matters of great urgency to be discussed. If you are willing, I would talk to you now.'

Moonblood nodded and sank slowly to her knees upon the grass. She took some fruit cordial and a little bread and green salad which Linvon offered her. My eyes were drawn by the bright glitter of the unusual brooch still pinned to her gown as its crystal and stone facets reflected the sunlight.

'Can you tell me, what was your experience two nights ago, after Marshilane had put you to bed?' I asked softly.

'I remember little,' replied Moonblood in a voice that was hardly more than a whisper. 'I did not expect to sleep, not after what we had seen. But I suppose I was exhausted. When I did sleep, though, it was as if I had been plunged into a dark, seething abyss. I was beset by the most terrible dreams. I saw . . . horrible things.'

She turned away with a shudder, plainly reluctant to recall the images to mind.

'Please do not think me insensitive,' I said, 'but I must ask you what you remember about waking, or perhaps the moments immediately prior to waking, when you still dreamed. We found your blood, and I know now that it was not the blood of a physical injury, as I first feared. Rather, it was the blood of your newly-realized womanhood, and your shedding of that blood was predicted to occur at precisely this time. This point is most important: what is your recollection of those moments?'

Moonblood blushed furiously, her eyes cast down. Linvon gently squeezed her hand. 'I – The dream – ' she stuttered, then closed her eyes, breathing rapidly. 'In the dream I was pursued by a man in dark flowing robes. He was a wizard or something, of evil bent. I have encountered him in earlier dreams. He hounded me, taunting, mocking, but in those dreams he had never caught me. This time, though I tried to escape him he had a spell on me and I could not run. He caught me and threw me down. I tried – He would not – ' She paused, plainly distressed, and collected herself. 'His face was red and twisted in perverse anger. He called me names, horrible names. "You are corruption; you are mine!" he cried. "At last my time has come!" He . . . ripped my clothes from me, then threw off his own. Then – '

Moonblood gave a distraught sob and hid her face in her hands. Linvon put his arms around her and held her, his face tense.

I waited a few moments, then continued gently, 'I do apologize, Mistress Moonblood. I know this is very difficult for you, but I cannot emphasize the importance of this enough. You are with friends now, good friends. I think you know that. We want to help you, and help your family and home, and your recounting of this grotesque, disturbing dream and its effects upon you may reveal important information that could help us to do that.'

She nodded, slowly withdrawing her hands from her face. 'I'm sorry, I'm being very childish.'

'Not at all. You are very brave.'

Taking another deep breath, she went on, gazing not at me or either of the other two, but away towards the surface of the pond, her eyes unfocused. 'It was so real, horribly real. I could feel his breath upon me, smell his sweat, feel the force of his hands brutally pinning me down. His horrible red face was just above mine, leering and filled with hate, his eyes burning with lust. He tried to take me – in the way a man takes a woman – violating me. I fought him but he was too strong; and I pleaded, but he only laughed. Then as he prepared to . . . force himself into me, there was . . .' She bit her lip, tears forming in her eyes again. She looked at me with an anguished expression. 'There was . . . *blood* . . . Everywhere . . . It came . . . I can't explain it, it came out of me . . . The wizard fell back, covered in my blood, crying out as though scalded or injured. I thought he would kill me then, but he backed away. "You are still mine!" he snarled, but he hurriedly gathered up his robes and left me then.'

'And then you woke, or was there more?'

'I am not sure where the dream ended. Certainly everything changed. I was in my bed, in my room. It was light. I felt at first relieved to have woken, and then I felt . . . on my legs, on the bed . . . a warm wetness. I threw back the covers. There was blood. I thought I had somehow been injured. I leapt from my bed, tearing off my night-robe which was also bloody. I was so frightened. I made to call for Marshilane, but my voice got trapped in my throat. It was as though I was still dreaming. I thought I heard laughter, insane laughter; my tormentor taunting me still, shouting, "You are mine! I will have my way!" But I couldn't see him. After that it is hazy. I recall glimpses of a dark tunnel, Linvon leading me by my hand, and then being carried through the forest in Gorodur's strong arms.' She turned to me beseechingly. 'I'm so frightened, Master Dinbig. For weeks I've had dreams, premonitions. I see Ravenscrag beset by monsters, my family and friends being slain, and somehow it is I who am making it happen. And

230

now . . . now it is all coming true. What is happening to me? What does it mean? Am I evil?'

'No, you are not evil, Moonblood. Far from it. You are the victim of a bane placed upon Ravenscrag and its descendants ages ago. It has lain dormant for centuries, unknown to most. Now, for reasons we are not entirely certain of, it has become active.'

'But the dreams . . . only a sick or wicked person could dream such unnatural things.'

'Not so. There is evil at work, and it is that which has made you dream these dreams.'

She was hardly listening. 'The blood . . . it was real, yet I had suffered no injury. What do you mean when you say the "blood of my womanhood", and that its shedding had been predicted?'

'Were you never given warning of this, by your mother or Marshilane, or your governess?'

The poor girl shook her head, baffled and tormented.

I cleared my throat, choosing my words carefully. I found myself in the delicate position of having to explain a difficult subject, the intimacies of which I truly knew little about. And even as I struggled ineptly to enlighten Moonblood, I grew uneasy. For her this transition, this rite of passage into womanhood, signified so much more than for any other.

'But this does not explain what has happened,' protested Moonblood when I had done. 'Nor does it explain the Bane.'

'In some ways it does,' I replied, and I told her of the Sharing Sisters of the Hallowed Blood, and of the corruption and usurpation of their benign power by the dark wizard Mososguyne. 'The blood which was shed with each cycle of the moon had become a sacred symbol of their strength and devotion, of their good magic, of their fertility harmonized with the fertility of the earth. It was a blessing, then; but through fear or jealousy of their power it was debased, turned into its very opposite, subverted by evil Mososguyne, who himself was the instrument of another more powerful malevolence. The Sharing Sisters were used and destroyed; the blessing became a curse. Mososguyne was in part defeated, but his curse remained. Through the mouth of your illustrious ancestor, Molgane, he uttered a bane, vowing that he would return at some future time to oversee Ravenscrag's destruction.'

'I know of Molgane,' said Moonblood. 'She was a dark witch. She was boiled in oil, as have been all witches since.'

She shuddered. I shook my head. 'Molgane was one of the Sharing Sisters. She suffered unspeakable agonies for crimes of which she was essentially innocent. She was the victim of another's dark designs, as are you.'

'Is it Mososguyne who assails me in my dreams?'

'It is.'

'Then he has returned, to use me to destroy Ravenscrag.'

'That is his intention.'

Moonblood swallowed. 'I feel him, inside me. I feel that he has the power to control me, that I am his, as he claimed.'

'His method is to undermine you, cause you to fear yourself, even hate yourself. You grow weak, and he feeds upon that weakness; he grows strong.'

'It is all so strange . . . The other evening, when I spoke to you, do you remember I said I thought I had seen something?'

'I do. You seemed, for a moment, quite alarmed.'

'Because just for a second I looked at your face and it changed. It resembled his, out of my dreams. I was frightened. Then I saw that it was nothing. I had imagined it. Yet now, your face is all scarred and burned, as if . . .'

I said nothing, shaken for a moment to my core. Moonblood turned with fearful eyes to Linvon, then Gorodur, and said in a low, quavering voice, 'There is nothing we can do. We have no power to prevent him.'

I intervened. 'Your two friends here took you from Ravenscrag in the hope that by removing you from the source of the evil they might save you, and save Ravenscrag also – '

'But they are wrong, aren't they? For I *am* that source.'

'No! You are not! Do not think that way for an instant. The Bane does state – by my understanding – that you may be the instrument, and that through you Mososguyne may achieve his ends. But it is also written that within you lies the potential, not only for death, but for life. I believe it is possible that the Bane may be lifted.'

Gorodur made to speak, but I raised my hand to bid him keep silence. I did not want him informing Moonblood that the slim hope of her salvation incorporated the likelihood of my own death. Nor did I wish to think about it myself.

'How might it be lifted?' enquired Moonblood, a first, diffident glimmer of hope in her eyes.

'I do not have a full answer to that. The words of the Bane are cryptic and not easily interpreted. But I am encouraged by your dream. In it you did not succumb to Mososguyne, though he exerted his greatest effort to take you. You fought him off, and you did it through the very symbol of your innate power: the blood of your new womanhood.'

'But he was not beaten.'

'No, he was not. But he did not gain control of you, at least not wholly. He was thwarted by a strength that came from within you and which you did not even know you possessed.'

Linvon's blue eyes were upon me, bright and questioning. Gorodur licked his lips pensively. Moonblood shook her head in distress. 'But it was only a dream! I have no power. I am just a young girl.'

'But a child no longer! You have passed across the threshold into womanhood. Though you do not realize it, you have attained your power. That is why Mososguyne is so desperate to control you: he fears your growing strength, as he feared it ages ago when he destroyed the Sharing Sisters. He has waited all this time, to seize your power at the moment it was conferred upon you, and he failed. Already, then, you have achieved one victory over him.'

Moonblood put her hands to her temples, weeping. 'I want none of this. I am frightened.'

I calmed my voice. 'Mistress Moonblood, whether you wish it or not, I believe there is Destiny upon you. I believe you embody the lost power of the Sharing Sisters. Your very name implies it, as do the words of the Bane. But that power, as I have explained, has its potential now in two forms, the good and the corrupt. You have a trial before you. You must confront evil. If you subdue it, it is my belief that the heritage that was stolen from the Sharing Sisters may be restored.'

No one asked what it would mean if she lost. We could all envisage something of the horror of such an outcome.

'But why me? I am all alone. I cannot do anything.'

'You are not alone. I am here, as are Linvon and Gorodur. We will do everything we can to aid you.'

She breathed deeply, her pale face streaked with tears. 'What must I do?'

'Return with me now to Ravenscrag.'

She gaped at me, horrified. I said, 'Mososguyne will gain his greatest power this evening, when the moon vanishes from the sky. He knows how to find you regardless of where you are. If you are absent from Ravenscrag then his task there will be made easier, for he can bring about its destruction himself without fear of your power.'

'My power! My power!' cried Moonblood. 'You keep talking of it, but I feel no power. There is no evidence. I cannot fight him!'

'There is magic within you,' I said. 'I have sensed it, as has Linvon. I believe you have too – you have hinted as much to me. And I repeat, it is because Mososguyne recognizes and fears it that he must control you. He has caused a monster to be born. It resides now in a cellar beneath the castle. That monster is the embodiment of Ravenscrag's iniquity, all the wrongs of ages committed by former scions of Ravenscrag. That monster grows by the minute. If I am correct, then tonight, when the Shadow obscures the moon, it will reach the summit of its strength and be turned loose upon Ravenscrag. Then it will come for you.'

I let the words sink in, aware that I was terrifying her more than I had a right to do. Yet what else could I say? I was convinced that the only hope Ravenscrag had was for its daughter to return to do battle with the evil that held it. It was Moonblood's only hope, too – or her nemesis.

She would face evil in two forms. In the flesh, the monster that howled and thrashed in the cellar; those creatures that crawled from mirrors; the flapping, taloned spawn that had been ravens. And in the spirit, the ages-old, grasping power of a mad wizard who had learned his craven art in a land whose very name struck fear into the hearts and minds of decent folk – dark Qotolr: Enchantery. Could Mososguyne make Moonblood his, as he claimed? Would she, too, become a monster, a raging demoness, wreaking mayhem and death in the name of that which we sought to extinguish?

I realized now how afraid I was, how uncertain of success. I banished the thoughts from my mind.

Moonblood turned her big, reddened eyes to me, strands of tear-dampened hair half concealing her face. 'But I don't know what I will do. How will I confront this thing?'

'I have access to magic which will aid you.' I spoke far more confidently than I felt. My magic was of negligible power compared to that which we were to challenge. It would be like throwing pebbles at an advancing wave.

I gazed unhappily at the frail, exhausted, bewildered girl before me, and wondered at myself. Was I condemning her to a terrible death, or a living hell?

'I have the rudiments of a plan,' I said. 'If your decision is to return with me I will explain it as we go.'

Moonblood was silent. At length she gave a slow nod. 'I will come.'

I expelled a long breath of air and glanced anxiously upwards through the trees. 'We should make haste. The sun is beginning to set and there is little time.'

I wanted to confront that dire creature before Shadownight came, for I knew that when the Shadow came to hide the new moon, then would Mososguyne's power be strongest. I added, 'And we must move cautiously. The woods harbour men who would do us harm.'

'I will come, too,' said Linvon.

'And I,' said Gorodur.

I looked sadly at the giant. 'You may come, but your bulk will prevent you entering the castle by the tunnel. Should you attempt to enter by any other means you will strike terror into any who see you. You will surely come under attack from Ravenscrag guards. Neither will you be able to comfortably enter the low passages or the cellar where we must go.'

Gorodur gave a disconsolate grunt. 'Aye, I know it. And nor can I accompany you through the forest. My size will slow you down as I struggle through the trees, and I cannot travel as silently as you. Nevertheless I will follow, and I will wait beyond the castle walls.' He turned to Moonblood, and I saw that he was blinking away huge tears. 'You understand that I cannot be with you. Be assured, I will do whatever is in my power to give you aid.'

Moonblood reached up and took his hand. 'I know it, and I

understand. Dear Gorodur, you are such a good, true friend. I know you would do all you could for me.'

She stood on her tiptoes and the giant bent low so that she was able to plant a kiss upon his great leathery cheek. He straightened, putting his fingers to the place her lips had touched. Moonblood turned, hiding her face, and began to walk back towards the cottage.

I followed her. Linvon remained behind for a moment, speaking in low tones to the giant, then ran up after us. As he passed me I reached out and took his arm, drawing him close. 'I would ask you a personal question. I hope you will forgive, and understand my reasons for asking.'

'What is it?'

'During the time you have passed with Moonblood, have you made love to her?'

He looked at me sharply, his cheeks reddening slightly, then glanced away. 'No, she is a virgin. Why? Does it matter?'

I shrugged. 'I do not know. But I am pleased that that was your answer none the less.'

Chapter Twenty-Nine

In the west the sky was a blood-red stain. The sun had almost gone, sinking into banks of dark purple cloud that had accumulated above the heights. The gloom of the forest had become intense.

We crouched in trees, Moonblood and I. Yards away was the hidden entrance to the tunnel that would take us back into Ravenscrag castle. Stationed outside was a Ravenscrag guard.

'I will speak to him,' Moonblood had said. 'He will obey me.'

'No!' I had drawn her back. I was nervous, almost certain that other guards would be in the woods nearby. I was concerned as to their orders. Almost definitely they would not hesitate to kill me, and probably Linvon too.

And Moonblood?

I wondered. Was it possible that her life was also in danger – even from her own kin? I reasoned that Darean Lonsord might be acting to some extent on his own initiative, but to keep Moonblood quiet he might well resort to extreme methods. But his orders to dispose of me had surely come directly from Lady Sheerquine. Would she sanction the murder of her own daughter? On the surface the notion seemed preposterous, yet nothing at this mad time was impossible, and I had a growing suspicion that Lady Sheerquine held a dark secret which she would stop at nothing to keep hidden, and which, if I was right, would indicate that she was capable of virtually anything.

I was taking no chances. Even if I was wrong it remained vital that Moonblood be smuggled into the castle in secret. If she announced herself she would at the very least be taken into 'protective custody'. Vital minutes, even hours, would be lost – and we did not have that much time.

So we waited. Somewhere out of sight Linvon crept silently, edging up behind the guard. I twisted the garrotting wire in my hands, scanning the glade, ready to move.

Behind the guard a shadow rose out of the bushes: Linvon, his hand raised to strike. He brought the hilt of his hunting-knife down hard on the back of the man's neck. The man fell, partially stunned, emitting a cry. Linvon bent and struck again; the man lay silent.

From the undergrowth, off to the left, came a call: 'Jamis?'

Linvon was no longer to be seen. The voice came again. 'Jamis? You all right?'

Silence, then a shrill, short whistle. A signal. There were at least two men hidden in the woods.

I listened tensely. A twig snapped in the bushes. Then another. I peered hard. There! A shadow, too dense, and a glint of metal. I made out the form of a man crouching, crossbow in hand, edging forward.

He was scarcely a dozen paces away. I left my hiding place, stealing around the edge of the glade to come up behind him. As I came closer he moved, half rising, bringing the bow-stock to his cheek. He was aiming across the glade. I glanced across.

Linvon!

Linvon was in full view, crouched at the base of a tree. He was peering across the other way, wholly unaware of the danger.

I leapt forward with a shout, intended to startle the bowman. He spun towards me. I thrust out an arm, knocking the weapon aside. The trigger clicked and snapped, the bolt shot off somewhere high. But the man brought the crossbow around hard, slamming it into the side of my head. The pain half-blinded me. The soldier kicked out, his foot smashing into my groin.

I fell, in excruciating pain. I glimpsed my assailant drawing his sword, looming over me, poised to strike. A dark shape flew across my vision. There was a thud, a groan.

I struggled to my knees. The soldier lay dead upon the ground, blood seeping from his belly into the earth. Linvon stood over him clutching a sword. He was grey-faced, staring at the blade.

I rose, grabbed him by the shoulder and pulled him down into cover. Linvon stared at me haggardly. 'I have never killed a man before.'

'The other one?' I queried.

'He is unconscious. I hit him hard, but his pulse still beats. This is his sword.'

'There is at least one other soldier hereabouts.'

I moved to the dead man and stripped him of his sword and dagger, then peered again into the bushes. From somewhere to my right came a muffled scream.

Moonblood!

Linvon heard it too. He was on his feet, sprinting towards the place where we had left her. I struggled after him, still in severe pain.

We had covered scarcely five paces when the bushes parted. A soldier broke free, clutching Moonblood. One hand held her fast to him, the other held a dagger to her throat.

'Drop your weapons or she will die!' He was edging towards the tunnel entrance. I recognized him as the plump, piggy-eyed guard who had brutalized old Elmag. I had no doubt that he meant what he said. I dropped the sword, as, after a moment's hesitation, did Linvon.

'Move back, away from the weapons,' ordered pig-eyes. He was close now to the hidden entrance. 'I am taking Lady Moonblood back. If you try to follow us I will kill her.'

His cheeks were flushed and there was a wildness in his eyes. He was nervous and unsure of himself. I judged him capable of anything.

'Please, hold a minute. Let us talk. You do not know what you are doing,' I said.

Pig-eyes gave a snort. 'I know exactly what I am doing. I have rescued Lady Moonblood from her captors. I will be well-rewarded.'

It was possible that he genuinely believed us to be her kidnappers. No doubt that was the story told in Ravenscrag. I thought quickly as he yanked at the bushes that concealed the entrance.

Suddenly, in the undergrowth behind him, something moved. There was a low growl. A shape sped from the gloom and leapt at the soldier, sinking strong teeth into his thigh.

He gave a cry of pain, spinning around, releasing Moonblood. 'Rogue!' Moonblood cried.

Pig-eyes raised his dagger to strike the old hound. Moonblood threw herself at him, knocking his arm aside. He lashed out at her, but off-balance his blow went wide. Both Linvon and I dived for our fallen weapons.

We ran at the soldier. I was faster. I plunged my sword into his gut. He wheeled, screaming, groping at the wound with a look of horrified disbelief. Linvon's blade hacked savagely into his neck and he fell dead without another sound.

'Rogue, oh, Rogue! Good boy! Good boy!' Moonblood threw her arms around the old dog, who snuffled happily and licked her face with a long pink tongue.

I searched the bushes, found the lantern I had left there earlier when I came from the tunnel. I relieved the dead soldier of a tinderbox, then took Moonblood's arm. 'There is no time to lose.'

As we entered the tunnel Moonblood halted suddenly. She stood stock still, an anguished, intense look upon her face. She turned to Linvon. 'You cannot come!'

Linvon gaped at her in surprise. 'What?'

She took his hands, wide-eyed, shaking her head. 'I have just seen your death. You must not come with us.'

'I will not leave you! How can you say that?'

She gripped him harder. 'You must! My love, you must!'

He turned to me disbelievingly. I observed Moonblood. She had changed since we had set out from the derelict cottage. As we had made our way through the forest I had observed with growing concern how distracted she was. She walked as if in a trance, dragging her feet and frequently stumbling. Her eyes were downcast, hardly looking where she was going. When I spoke to her her replies came in monosyllables, if at all; mostly she seemed not even to hear me.

She looked so thin, plainly weakened by her recent ordeals. I sensed that within her the demonic presence of Mososguyne, though not yet her master, none the less sapped her strength. Equally, she was tense and fraught at the knowledge of what she was to face.

Unbeknownst to her I had cast a calming rapture upon her then. I was reluctant to expend my psychic energies, knowing that I too would need all the strength I could muster in the forthcoming confrontation. But it was obvious that Moonblood would be destroyed by her enemy within an instant if her condition remained unchanged.

Almost immediately I saw the effects. Moonblood lifted her head; she straightened her shoulders and spine. Her gait became more purposeful, and she looked straight ahead, lips pursed in concentration. Her expression, though still clouded, was no longer as anxious, and her deep green eyes had brightened.

Now, standing at the entrance to the secret tunnel, I could not doubt her conviction. Even were she wrong, it could be disastrous now to invalidate this newfound belief in herself. I touched Linvon's arm. 'It must be as she says.'

'But I cannot leave you! What are you saying? You need me!'

Moonblood gazed at him sorrowfully. 'My love, I have seen what will happen if you enter the castle now. You will be killed; Dinbig and I will be captured and prevented from doing what we must do.'

'But how? How can you know this?'

She shook her head. 'I do not know. I know only that this is how it will be.'

'And if I stay behind, what then?'

'That has not been revealed to me. I know only that if you accompany us we will fail, and you, at least, will not survive.'

Linvon turned away angrily, clenching his fists in frustration. He looked back at Moonblood once, pleadingly. There were tears in her eyes, but she shook her head. 'Remain here, sweet heart. Guard the entrance, and wait for Gorodur. That is how you may best help me.'

Linvon took her suddenly in his arms and embraced her fiercely. I moved away a few paces, busied myself striking flame to tinder and lighting the lantern as the two young lovers said their painful goodbyes. Moments later Moonblood and I continued on alone, with the faithful old hound, Rogue, leading the way back into Ravenscrag.

We advanced with caution, for it was quite possible that Darean Lonsord had stationed guards along the passage. But we encountered no one, and with Rogue preceding us arrived safely at Hectal's chamber without incident. I carefully eased open the secret door and peered into the room. It was unoccupied.

I stepped in, quickly crossed the twilit bedchamber into the main room and pressed my ear to the door. I heard nothing in the corridor outside.

Grasping the iron handle, I slowly, with infinite care, turned it and drew the door open a crack. Eye to the gap I saw, hardly more than a pace away, a sentry. His back was to me. He leaned on his halberd, apparently half asleep.

I closed the door again and shut my eyes for a moment, thinking. It was too risky to attempt to leave. I took the bolt and slid it soundlessly across into its housing. I motioned to Moonblood to return to the bedchamber.

'We must maintain silence as far as possible, and hope that nobody tries to enter. For now we will remain here. The door is bolted, so if anyone comes we will be forewarned and can escape down the passage.'

'But why do we wait?' queried Moonblood. 'Surely it is best to go now and confront the creature.'

In the lamplight I saw both resoluteness and fear in her eyes. I smiled grimly. 'I must enter trance, to try to recoup some of the energy I have lost over recent days. I would advise you to meditate also, to gather your strength.'

Suddenly her fear dominated; she began to tremble. I stepped forward and put my arms around her, drew her slight body to me. 'Be strong!' I whispered into her ear. 'Centre yourself, search within, find your inner strength. This is your test. I know you can meet it. This is your Destiny!'

'And if I cannot?' Her voice was small.

'Do not even think that way. All of you – every fibre and atom of your being – must be focused upon this task. Envision success, and allow your inner self to guide you along the right path.'

I released her, but held her shoulders with my hands. She looked at me with wide-eyed, imploring sweetness. 'Help me,' she whispered.

I smiled. 'Remember at the banquet, I told you I was forbidden to teach you *Zan-Chassin* magic?'

She nodded, so vulnerable.

'I'm going to break the rules. I will teach you now the techniques to enter trance. I sense that you have already touched upon your own magic – and it is a different magic to mine. But what I will show you may help you to look within yourself and draw upon the strength that lies there. But you must never tell. Do you promise?'

She nodded again.

'Good.' My attention was caught again by the brooch on her breast. 'This is most unusual – I found another, a matching piece I think, in your room. Does it have any particular significance?'

'It was a present from dear Gorodur. He made it for me, and brought it with him all the way from his home. When he came to give it to me he found that it had broken. He said that on his way to Ravenscrag he had slipped and fallen heavily down a steep slope. That was when it must have happened. I felt so sad for him. I had never seen anything like it. There are three pieces, not two. The third is very small. I have it in a drawer. I attached a new pin and grip on each of the two main pieces, so that I might still wear them. When all three pieces are put together they form a crescent moon set within a heart. These tiny rubies represent teardrops of blood.'

'Fascinating. It is a most beautiful artifact. One wonders that such huge fingers could craft such a delicately wrought piece.'

'Gorodur is very clever. I am lucky to have such friends.'

She glanced at Rogue who lay at her feet near the end of Hectal's bed. I said, 'Rogue can perhaps help us again. If you can have him guard the door he will provide one further deterrent to anyone trying to enter.'

As Moonblood took Rogue through I went to the window. Outside the sky was turning from turquoise to deepest indigo. Low in the west were streaks of crimson and purple fire. Cold, bright stars shone far away. I felt a tremor of fearful anticipation as I saw, high above the silhouetted heights to the southeast, the pale, slender crescent of the new moon.

Moonblood came and stood at my shoulder.

'We do not have long,' she whispered.

I took her hand. 'Come, we must use every moment.'

Chapter Thirty

I came from trance.

'Yo, are you still here?'

'Yes, Master.'

'Good. Remain with me.'

I crossed to the window. The woods and heights were invisible in the impenetrable black of night. The waxing crescent hung in a fragile crystalline radiance in the dark void, brighter and somewhat higher than before. I noted with some relief that no Shadow had yet begun to obscure it.

I went to Hectal's bed where Moonblood lay. Her eyes were open. She sat up, blinking in the lamplight. I smiled. 'How do you feel?'

She gave me a candid look. 'Afraid.'

'Good.'

'Good?'

'If you were without fear in this endeavour then I would know that all was lost.' I took up the lamp. 'Come, we can delay no more.'

I eased back the wall-panel and stepped into the secret passage. My intention was to descend to the doorway behind the statue.

The corridor there was closer to the cellar than Hectal's apartment, and that part of the castle was generally less frequented, especially at night.

As she entered behind me Moonblood paused and looked once around the chamber. 'Poor Hectal,' she whispered in a voice soft and filled with sorrow. 'Nobody even tried to understand him.'

We descended to ground level and I proceeded more carefully, searching for the hidden door. The night was hot, and the passage airless and stuffy. My heart thumped and my singed hair clung to my forehead in damp tails.

I found the door without great difficulty – a stone block, indented into the wall and somewhat less begrimed than its neighbours. A loose brick in the floor, pressed hard with my heel, caused the block to shift a fraction, enabling me to grip its edge with my fingers and drag it open. Handing the lamp to Moonblood and motioning her to remain in the passage, I bent and passed through.

Crouched behind the statue I was able to peer cautiously to left and right along the corridor. It was dimly lit by distant flambeaux set upon the walls, and appeared unoccupied. I beckoned to Moonblood, taking the lamp and reducing its flame to a minimum. I took her hand and we stepped out into the corridor.

Thus we made our way through Ravenscrag, darting, hiding, skulking like criminals, towards the cellar where the monster awaited us. Once or twice we spotted servants, but were able to duck unseen into shadows until they had passed. More difficult to avoid were the sentries. Twice we were forced to make long detours. Finally, as we neared the passage which led down to the cellars, we came upon a solitary guard. There was no way around him.

I was mindful of my magical strength, knowing that all my *Zan-Chassin* powers would be tested to – and beyond – their limits down below. Yet if the sentry attempted to obstruct us I would have little choice. With Moonblood beside me I stepped from the shadows into his full view. We walked straight along the corridor, as if to pass him by.

'Halt!'

We kept on. He stepped out into our path, gripping his halberd, his face tense in the flickering torchlight. Moonblood stopped and fixed him with a challenging glare. 'Guard, do you speak to me?'

He quailed slightly. 'Lady Moonblood, I have orders to stop this man.'

'Master Dinbig is with me. I vouch for him.'

'Yes, Lady, but – '

He might have let us pass, but it was plain he would have informed a superior immediately. I had no choice; I invoked a Passing Stupor. The guard's eyes glassed over. His muscles relaxed and his expression became vacant.

'Come.' I urged Moonblood on along the passage. 'He will recover within five minutes. He may remember nothing, but if he does he will surely sound the alarm.'

We passed a window. I glanced out, and a sudden cold fear clutched my innards. High in the night sky was the sight I had prayed not to see: the lower horn of the new moon's bright crescent had been truncated, as though the glowing tip had been swallowed by some monstrous dark maw. The moon hung awkwardly now, without balance or symmetry. Something unseen, as black as the surrounding night, was advancing inexorably to devour the entire crescent.

Moonblood seemed not to have noticed, and I did not tell her. We descended the stairs that led to the cellars. The air was stifling. A foul stench assailed our nostrils like a hammer-blow. Moonblood glanced back over her shoulder as, faintly, the sound of a scream, cut short, came to us from somewhere back in the castle.

'What was that?'

'I don't know,' I replied, though I suspected that Mososguyne's spawn had returned to renew their assault upon Ravenscrag's occupants.

As though to prove me right there came more distant shouts, and another frantic scream. Only now did I notice the change in the air. A sickly illumination part-lit the passages, the same lurid, seeping greenness that had seemed to come out of the very stones and earth of the castle the previous night.

From somewhere ahead of us came a terrifying sound – a low, inhuman wail, which set my teeth on edge and sent tremors along my spine.

Moonblood came involuntarily to a halt. She was shivering, despite the dreadful warmth. One hand covered her nose and mouth as she struggled against the assault of that unspeakable odour which hung like a vapour in the stifling air. I propelled her on, my hand at the small of her back, fearful lest she falter now. My throat was dry, yet sweat streamed from my pores. I glanced at Moonblood; her face, too, gleamed damp in the dim torchlight, long strands of hair stuck fast to her skin.

I found I was having to apply more and more pressure to keep her moving forward. Unconsciously she was willing herself away from this place and the confrontation that awaited her. That loathsome voice from the cellar issued forth again, a moaning, spine-tingling monotone, imbued with hate-filled menace. Moonblood pressed back against my hand. I prayed that she would not let me down now. I looked again at her pale young face; she was wide-eyed with terror. Suddenly my own terror swelled. *What was I doing? Was I insane – pushing this poor girl-child to a certain death?*

I forced down my fear, instilling a semblance of calm upon my mind. I knew – within myself I *knew* that there was no other way. Something demonic had been unleashed upon Ravenscrag. Unopposed, it would destroy us anyway.

I had no time to think further. A movement caught my eye. Out of a narrow fissure in the wall beside Moonblood came a squirming, reptilian thing, similar to that which had last night crawled from my mirror. I leapt at it, drawing the sword I had taken from the soldier in the woods, and slashed hard. The blow took the creature's head from its neck. Its body withered before my eyes; I found myself staring at the decapitated corpse of a huge black rat.

I grabbed Moonblood's arm. We turned the corner into the hot, reeking passage at the end of which the prison-cellar lay. As we did so the wail rose to become a frenzied shriek, shocking, mocking, filled with dreadful, malevolent lust.

Did the creature sense our presence? Or did it sense its power growing as the Shadow crept forth to engulf the moon?

Moonblood halted with a strangled gasp.

'Be strong?' I urged. 'Look within! Find your power!'

There was evil here. The very air, close and suffocating, held a tension as though something were striving to manifest. The barricaded door loomed in front of us. To the side was the meat barrow, laden with raw, bloody flesh. Swarms of flies buzzed and crawled. The stench was appalling.

There was a subtle whisper of shifting air behind us. I wheeled. A flapping, hopping thing was bearing down upon Moonblood's undefended back, horny beak open, cruel talons extended. I threw myself forward, lunging with the sword. The blade pierced its breast, puncturing a lung. The creature lurched and fell with a harsh croak, its body transforming even as it twitched in its death throes.

I pushed Moonblood on. Six terrified soldiers stared wide-eyed as we halted in the wider area in front of the cellar door. None moved to challenge us; they seemed scarcely able to move. 'Defend the passage!' I yelled. 'We are attacked!'

None obeyed. Did they have orders to arrest me? It did not appear so. I yelled at the sergeant-of-the-guard. 'It is like last night. We are under assault. You must defend this passage at all costs!'

He was plainly confused, but the weird light and the memory of the previous night left him and his men in no doubt of the danger. He barked an order and three men ran to guard the corridor. I stared for a moment at the barricade of sandbags and nets.

Be ready, Yo!

I turned again to the sergeant. 'Sergeant, have two of your men remove the barricade. We are going in.'

He gaped at me incredulously, then at Moonblood.

'There is no other way! Ravenscrag may be saved if we enter this cellar. Hesitate, and its doom will be upon your head.' As I spoke I mentally invoked the rapture I had prepared for this moment, spurring the sergeant's mind with thoughts of doom and responsibility. 'Clear the door, sergeant. *Now!*'

There were cries from the men in the passage. I glanced their way, to see another blood-hued lizard-thing advancing upon them. The three guards, swords drawn, were retreating before it, plainly terrified.

I leapt between them and hacked at the thing. It reared before me, hissing, lunging with snapping jaws. I jumped back, then charged. The creature drew back. My blade ripped across its soft belly, which opened, spilling ichor and guts. The thing fell, and withered.

'See, these creatures are not invincible! Now, do your job, defend this passage!'

The three, shamed as much as heartened by my display, moved back to their places. The howling within the cellar rose in pitch. There was a muffled thump against the door. I turned back to the sergeant. 'The barricade!'

He signalled. 'You two, do as he says.'

I communicated silently to Yo. *Go, Yo. Enter there and keep that creature distracted until we can enter too. It cannot harm you, but you must keep it away from the door.*

I am your servant, Master.

Yo was gone. The two guards dragged aside the netting and began heaving at the sandbags.

'Quickly, now!'

At this moment there came a frightful din from within the cellar as the monster responded to Yo's entrance. The men fell back, stricken with fear.

'The creature cannot escape. It is my magic that distracts it now. Be about your task. Make haste!'

The men obeyed reluctantly. I glanced at Moonblood, who stood stock still beside me. I could not judge her state of mind. She seemed transfixed, whether with terror or some other, less identifiable emotion I could not tell. I forced myself to concentrate, fighting down my own rising fear. The last of the sandbags was dragged away.

'The timbers!' I ordered. 'Pull them free!'

Using jemmies the two guards began to lever frantically at the boards that were nailed across the door. There were shouts from the passage behind us. Suddenly there was a resounding crash. The door shuddered violently and almost gave. One of its central timbers splintered. The insensate caterwauling within rose in a maddened crescendo.

So close!

The two soldiers leapt back with terrified shrieks. The door shuddered again. Something dark and monstrously clawed scraped along the gap at its base. The men fled, gibbering. I looked back. Their panic infected the other three, who also took to their heels. Only the sergeant remained, hesitant, but then the door shook again and he too made off as fast as his legs would carry him.

We were alone.

I swore, and leapt at the door, taking up a jemmy and prising furiously at the last remaining timbers of the barricade.

Yo, draw the creature away from the door. We are about to enter!

Flies buzzed, settling on my face, crawling into my mouth. I wrenched hard. The door no longer shuddered, and with relief I heard those blood-curdling sounds move away, deeper into the cellar.

The last plank came away with a groan. I gripped my sword, and reached out to take Moonblood's hand. 'Be strong!' I screamed. 'Find your power!'

Without waiting for her response I kicked at the door. It flew open. I released her hand. Mad with fear, I rushed in.

The sight that met my eyes was enough to freeze my blood.

The cellar was a long, rectangular chamber with an arched roof of damp, ancient brick. It had been used for storing ale, and the remains of a couple of barrels could be seen, smashed to pieces and flung across the floor. In the weird viridescence I could see that the floor was also strewn with discarded offal and shattered bones. Flies were even thicker in the air here than outside, and the floor seemed to writhe with a sea of maggots. The stench here was overpowering, far worse, though I would not have believed it possible, than in the passage.

But what truly commanded the attention, striking sheer horror into my heart, was the sight of that maddened creature at the far end of the room. Its back was to me, and it leapt and scrabbled furiously at a spot within the ceiling close to one corner. Though the ceiling was more than ten feet high, the beast reached it with little effort. Bricks and mortar were clawed and pounded till they fell away as it vented its mindless fury.

The last time I had seen this thing it was the size of a baby. Two days ago I had held it in my arms! Now it was huge; its broad, leathery back was mottled grey and black, ridged with thick muscle and gleaming with an unwholesome oily sheen. A column of tough, bony plates ran the length of the spine. A long, powerful, thrashing tail bristled with savage, hooked barbs. Arms and legs spoke of colossal strength, and the hands and feet were each armed with three murderous curved claws.

In its frenzy to get at Yo the monster seemed unaware of my entrance, which was as I had hoped. Taking advantage I gathered all the power at my command, concentrating it into a single rapture of calming.

It was a desperate ploy, but I had thought it through and could envisage no other course. I had no power to enter direct combat with this monster – my one hope was to distract it – lull it – for a brief space, giving Moonblood time to respond. Her potential – for death or life, darkness or light – would be realized now, or never. The fate of all of us would be decided in this moment.

And it was only now, as I cast the rapture, that I realized that Moonblood had not come with me into the cellar.

She stood outside in the passage, rooted to the spot, staring sightlessly, transfixed as she had been moments before.

'Moonblood!' I screamed, for the creature had wheeled to face me.

She showed no sign of having heard. It was as if she were held in some unnatural stasis. The thing lowered itself onto all fours. Hooded, malevolent yellow eyes, their pupils reflecting deep red, settled upon me. The heavy brow, a mass of deep folds of skin above which sprouted long red hairs, seemed to knit in concentration. The lips drew back, revealing bright pink gums and twin rows of vicious yellow fangs. Two sharp, ribbed, curling horns protruded from the sides of the wide skull, their tips pointing forwards.

As far as I could tell the rapture had had little or no effect. Though the monster's frenzy had abated, the manner in which it eyed me and, now, began to advance towards me made it plain that it was in no way becalmed. Rather, it moved with slow, deliberate calculation. I sensed its cunning, and had the horrible impression that it was taking pleasure in witnessing my helpless terror.

I screamed again. 'Moonblood! Find your power!'

She seemed to snap back to an awareness of herself, but she merely raised her fingers to her mouth, shaking her head as she stared in terror at the scene before her. In her eyes was utter, dreadful hopelessness, and she spoke, faintly. 'I have no power.'

'You must!' I was backing slowly towards the door. 'It is yours! Find it! Reclaim what is rightfully yours.'

The monster moved suddenly to the side, barring my retreat. It raised its head a little, its nostrils dilating, then licked its lips with a distended purple tongue.

'*Please!*' I cried, for I realized I was about to die.

Then it sprang.

Its movement took it beyond me. One long arm was extended, reaching out for Moonblood as it smashed heavily into the frame of the open door with a force that shook the room. Leaping back, I slipped and fell to the maggot-coated ground. I heard Moonblood scream.

Now the monster's frenzy was renewed. Too large to pass through the door, it tore and pounded, wrenching away frame and surrounding brickwork. Its terrible voice lashed and roared deafeningly, a sound of sheer rabid fury. Its body blocked my view outside the cellar, so I did not know what had become of Moonblood.

I was sitting up, scrambling to my feet. A piece of brick, hurled randomly back, struck me hard on the forehead, and almost simultaneously a section of woodwork slammed into my chest. I fell back again, dazed and severely winded.

Desperately I rolled over onto my knees. The room slewed; warm blood ran into my eye. But I could see that the doorway had gone, leaving a large, ragged, dust-fogged gap in the wall. The creature pushed through into the passage. Beyond it I saw Moonblood, pressed up against the far wall.

Advancing upon Moonblood, the monster's voice dropped to a loathsome purr of quiet menace. I heard shouts, screams, then another sound, a deep, furious bellow. Two of the guards suddenly appeared, running back towards us along the passage. I could not believe it. Why had they come back?

Then a shadow loomed behind them, filling the corridor. At the same moment the guards saw the creature that waited for them at the cellar door. Before they could react the monster, momentarily distracted from Moonblood, was upon them. In a spray of blood and savaged flesh they were torn to pieces in instants.

I crawled towards the ruined door, in such pain that I could barely breathe. The creature cast aside the guards' mangled corpses and turned back to Moonblood again. She had sunk into the corner, cowering in terror, helpless and small. The thing reared above her, seeming to relish its easy victory. In desperation I called out to her, but she seemed not to hear.

The monster's head turned and it cast me a glance, hatefully intelligent, but contemptuous, which shook me to the core of my being. Then it lowered itself and pressed its massive head up to her so that its wet snout nuzzled her fragile form. Moonblood stared wide-eyed in terror, pushing her head back against the wall, her lips stretched into a soundless scream.

The monster opened wide its murderous jaws.

Then I heard again that furious bellow from the passage. It was louder and closer this time. I saw that the passage was blocked, and now I saw what it was that had sent those two soldiers running back to their deaths.

From the mouth of the passage a huge hand reached out. It fastened hard upon the monster's upper limb and dragged it aside.

The creature wheeled with a roar, then craned its neck to snap at Moonblood. But its jaws closed just short of its prey. Thwarted, it tore with claws and fangs at the hand that pulled it towards the passage. And Moonblood half rose, crying out, '*Gorodur!*'

Gorodur clung on, even as his flesh was ripped to shreds. He was on his knees, too bulky to stand in the narrow confines of the corridor. His head was thrust vulnerably forward. His upper arm and breast were bloody, and I saw the stubs of two crossbow bolts sticking from the flesh. He was striving to edge further into the wider area where there was more space to move. But now his monstrous opponent realized the giant's disadvantage and fought savagely to prevent Gorodur from leaving the passage.

Gorodur's other hand had come forward to grasp the monster's throat and squeeze. His face was white with concentration and pain. Razor teeth and talons ripped into his hands and arms. The barbed tail swung around, lashing his shoulder and flank again and again. Blood poured from his injuries, but still he did not let go.

Measure for measure the two were arguably of similar strength. But Gorodur lacked weapons or armour, as well as the space to move. His adversary was not confined, and its terrible barbs, teeth and claws were doing appalling damage to the giant. It had brought its rear legs beneath it to kick and rip at its opponent's chest, while its taloned hands tore at the flesh of his face.

Still Gorodur maintained his grip, horribly bloodied and torn, remorselessly squeezing his assailant's windpipe. Slowly the monster's threshing grew less. It hissed and gurgled, but it was weaker as it failed to draw air into its trapped lungs. With his colossal strength Gorodur forced it down until he was kneeling over it. Blood poured from his wounds, but he continued to bear down with all his power to throttle the life from the thing.

And then came Moonblood's voice: 'No! Gorodur! You mustn't kill it!'

The giant looked up in surprise, as did I. Moonblood was on her feet, one hand reaching out, sobbing. '*It is my brother!*'

Instantly Gorodur eased back, lessening his grip upon the monster's throat.

Moonblood cried, 'Hold it there, just for a moment more. Please. Let me find my strength.'

Her eyes were turned beseechingly upwards, her hands extended. 'Help me!' she implored. '*Help me!*'

In that moment, with the pressure upon its windpipe eased for a vital instant, the creature rediscovered its strength. It slashed savagely. The dreadful claws tore into the giants neck, ripping away hair and flesh and opening the great artery there.

Gorodur's blood gushed out in a great fountain, drenching his assailant. Moonblood screamed. With his dying strength Gorodur threw himself forward, pushing himself upon his killer and using his weight to pin the creature to the floor.

The monster struggled, roaring in triumph, squirming and thrusting itself out from beneath its now unresisting foe. Its covetous eyes were upon the young maiden as it worked itself free. From its mouth came now a most hideous sound, made all the more dreadful by the fact that it was a word, distorted and corrupted, yet recognizable as human speech.

'*Mine,*' it said, blood and spittle oozing from its jaws. '*Mine.*' And it advanced, its yellow eyes aglow with lust and loathing.

'Oh no!' Moonblood stood helpless and distraught, throwing her head from side to side, her arms still extended. 'Oh, no, no, no! Oh, help me! *Molgane, help me!*'

Almost instantly, as she mouthed those last words, something changed. Around Moonblood appeared, faint and barely visible at first, an aura of silverish light. The expression of anguished terror upon her face faded. She grew still, and looked suddenly almost tranquil, but resolute, filled with a new strength. The silver light around her pulsed more brightly, piercing and beginning to dispel the dreadful green glow.

The monster tilted its great head curiously. Then it issued a terrible snarl, and sprang. In the same heartbeat I saw something else. Beside Moonblood a ghostly figure had formed, the image of a woman, garbed in a pale robe and bathed in the same crystalline lucence. She stood, as did Moonblood, with her hands raised, extended towards the creature.

And behind this figure were others now, forming within the very stone of the walls – a host, a phantom assembly, all of them women.

The Sharing Sisters of the Hallowed Blood! It had to be. And she at their fore, who stood stalwartly beside the frail figure of Moonblood, was surely the ghost of Lord Draremont's dead wife, Molgane.

From the fingertips of Moonblood and Molgane the silver lucence seemed to extend. The air was filled with a new sound: female voices, chanting in unison. The beast, even as it hurled itself upon Moonblood, was held in the air. It slashed and swiped, its claws passing within a finger's breadth of Moonblood's face, gnashing its murderous teeth. Moonblood took a step forward; the creature was borne back. It fell snarling, backing up against the far wall.

The light now was bright within the passage; no trace remained of the murky green. The creature cringed, snapping and making half-hearted lunges, but seemingly afraid to attack. Moonblood, with Molgane, moved towards it.

'Back. Your time has passed. You have been born and defeated. Back now whence you came.'

The creature retreated. The glow that surrounded the two women extended to form around the creature too. Then it parted, so that the creature was isolated within a sheath of radiant silvery luminosity. It raged and struggled, but plainly it was bound and confined.

I threw myself aside as it was pushed back through the smashed door into the cellar. Even as I watched I could see that the monster was diminishing in size. Moonblood stood alone now in the door, hands still directed at her cowed adversary. A dark mist, a foul vapour, poured from the monster's flesh. It came out of the silver membrane to form a cloud which attempted to coalesce into another form, as if with a volition of its own. It grew reddish in hue, concentrating into a single large irregularly shaped mass.

As I stared, rude features formed. I thought I myself to be gazing at a face, and for one shocking moment I thought it was the distorted image of my own, reddened and scorched as it was by the fire in which Lord Flarefist had almost sacrificed the monstrous infant. Then the features grew more solid. They formed into a writhing, twisted image, a living mask, contorted into an expression of the most venomous hatred. Incandescent eyes glowed yellow, fixed upon Moonblood's frail figure, seeming to contain a power of their own. I was reminded forcefully of Lord Draremont's account of the terrible vision he had beheld on the night of his death; and of Moonblood's own distraught recollection of the wizard who had haunted her dreams. I had no doubt, then, that I gazed upon the embodiment of evil, the face of Mososguyne.

The figure of Molgane had vanished, as had those of the Sharing Sisters at her back. Moonblood was alone. The ruddied lips on the apparition drew back into a mocking, loathing snarl. Once more the room resonated with that dreadful sound as a single word was formed: '*Mine!*'

The thing lunged forward. Moonblood stood firm, resolute and unfearing.

'Begone!' she cried, and the image drew suddenly back. The dreadful face now held a different expression. The lips stretched, the eyes bulged, a glistening red tongue extruded, writhing as though in pain. The image was failing, returning to vapour, growing thin and dispersing into the foetid air, until finally nothing remained to be seen.

Now the silvery glow also faded. The passage was lit by the torches on the walls, no vestige of unnatural light lingering.

Moonblood turned, tears streaming down her cheeks. She rushed forward and threw herself upon the fallen body of the giant, Gorodur, her body racked with sobs. She kissed his face, his lacerated hands, his hair. 'Gorodur, oh, Gorodur. Faithful friend, dear, good friend. I am sorry. Forgive me. Forgive me.'

Beyond, in the passage, I saw a figure standing. Linvon the Light, dressed in blood-drenched green, a bloodied sword in his hand. He came forward, squeezing carefully by Gorodur's prone form, and leaned upon the wall beside me, panting hard. His eyes shone with tears as he stared at Moonblood and the lifeless, heroic Gorodur.

'It is over,' he said.

I nodded, clutching my ribcage. 'Aye. And I am alive and Gorodur has died.'

He swallowed. 'That is how it was written.'

'Not quite.'

'You are wrong, Master Dinbig. I believed it might be you who was referred to in the Bane, from the moment I witnessed your accident on the road to Ravenscrag. But Gorodur had doubts.'

I stared at him hard, recalling my accident and the glimpse of a figure in green standing beneath the trees. 'You are not making yourself very clear.'

Linvon lowered his voice. 'It was the vision of the *Thotán* that a stranger would come from afar, bearing strange knowledge and shattered gifts, and that in lifting the Bane he would pay with his life. And that is what has happened.'

It hit me then, with force. 'Gorodur?'

Linvon nodded. 'He brought knowledge, did he not? And the shattered brooch.'

'And he knew?'

'Not at first. But when he came to give the brooch to Moonblood, and discovered it in pieces, then it struck him. And then you came, and you brought shattered gifts, and he began to wonder again.'

'But wait . . . No, the Bane refers to gifts, in the plural. Gorodur brought only the one.'

Linvon shook his head with a grave, sorrowful smile. His voice now was barely more than a whisper. 'No, Master Dinbig, he brought another, and one that I did not understand until just a few minutes ago. He brought his love.'

'His love?'

'For Moonblood. Gorodur was enamoured of her, just as I am. He had lived with her vision for a lifetime – the equivalent of three lifetimes for you or I. She became the one thing, the one person, he lived for.' Linvon closed his eyes, squeezing back tears. 'In other circumstances we would have been rivals, Gorodur and I.

But he knew that Moonblood could never be his. He was *Thotán*, she was human. It simply could not be, and he accepted it. Yet he came anyway, knowing this, and he stayed and fought for her, even knowing that he might die. He brought her another shattered gift, his broken heart, though he never spoke of this to her.' Linvon turned his face to me. 'That is love in its truest, purest form, is it not?'

I gazed down at the great, bloodied form before me, and nodded, too overcome to speak.

Linvon put his hand upon my shoulder. 'Master Dinbig, you too are like noble Gorodur. You proved yourself a true friend to Moonblood. You stood with her, believing that you would almost certainly perish. For that you have my undying gratitude.'

I turned away uncomfortably. 'My circumstances were different; I was given no choice.'

'I do not think it is so simple.'

Moonblood raised her head and turned her tear-streaked face to us, stretching out a hand. Linvon went to her and took her in his arms. Together they wept over the body of their loyal friend.

No one but I heard the faint sound, like a feeble, animal cry, that came from the depths of the cellar. I turned, guardedly, drawing my sword, and stepped to the doorway. It was black in there; I took a torch from the wall.

I advanced gingerly towards the corner where the monstrous creature had been overcome. In the dancing shadows I thought I saw something move.

I crept closer. The torchlight revealed a small mound of mottled grey-black skin, which writhed before my eyes, turning to a dark, sickly vapour which dissipated into the air.

And beneath this vanishing skin I found the source of the sound I had heard. A tiny babe lay there, naked, kicking its fragile limbs, its head crowned with a growth of flame-red hair.

Chapter Thirty-One

I made my way up nervously, painfully, through the castle to the family apartments, carrying my precious charge wrapped in a shirt taken from a dead soldier. Though all seemed quiet now I could not rid myself of the fear that some new horror would crawl from a dark crack in the wall, or leap from around a corner and attack me.

The slaughter of Shadownight had truly been terrible; between the cellar and Lord Flarefist's bedchamber I came upon eleven bodies of Ravenscrag soldiers and staff, as well as the mutilated corpses of rats and ravens. Moban alone knew how many other bodies littered the castle precincts.

From Linvon I had learned that he and Gorodur had been forced to fight the guards as well as the weird creatures that the Bane's magic had spawned. Meeting at the entrance to the tunnel where Moonblood and I had left Linvon, they had gone on through the forest to Moonblood's dell. There they waited tensely. They saw the tip of the moon blunted by the Shadow. Then, with the first glow of the green luminescence around the castle, and the accompanying sounds of struggle, they had put all caution aside and rushed into the castle in the hope of aiding us. But the troops, seeing Gorodur, had assumed him to be an ally of the monsters which had materialized in their midst, and had fired upon him without hesitation. By the time Gorodur had reached the cellar passage, there to confront the monster that threatened Moonblood, he was already badly wounded and suffering serious loss of blood.

Passing a ground floor window I glanced out at the night sky. The crescent moon was whole again, surrounded by the brilliance of its pure silvery radiance. But there was something unusual which made me pause and watch. A small, fiery body, deep red, was visible a little way below the moon. It flickered and flared erratically, darting in a wild, patternless course like some living, flaming creature in its death throes. Even as I watched the unnatural thing faded, then burned up in a shower of bright particles, and vanished. I walked on, carrying the sleeping babe to its father.

'Lord Flarefist, I have brought you back your son.'

The old man lay gaunt upon his pillows, ghastly grey and unmoving. His eyes were closed, the lids trembling as though he were beset by troubled dreams. His fleshless chest rose and fell weakly, the breaths shallow, rapid and laboured. Markin, the physician, sat patiently at his side, potions and powders set out on a tabletop at his elbow.

I spoke more loudly. 'Lord Flarefist.'

Flarefist's eyes slowly opened and found their focus, settling blearily upon me.

'Your son, Lord Flarefist. He has returned. Look.'

He stared blankly at the tiny babe, then at me again. 'What?'

'It is Redlock, Lord Flarefist.'

'Who?'

'Redlock, your son and heir.'

He was completely befuddled. His lungs wheezed, a muscle on his cheek twitched. A dribble of saliva spilled from the corner of his pallid lips and stained his nightshirt. His jaw began to make movements, and eventually he said, in a dry, whispery rasp, 'Who are you?'

'Dinbig. Ronbas Dinbig, from Khimmur. You commissioned me to find your son – and your daughter too. Moonblood is also safe.'

'What?'

I felt a light pressure on my arm. Markin solicitously drew me aside, shaking his head gravely. 'He is incapable of grasping anything.'

'His son . . . he means so much to him. I thought that seeing him and knowing he has returned might give him strength, spur him to recovery.'

'He is beyond that. I do not expect him to live through the day.'

'Has he been aware of what has happened tonight?'

'No.'

'Were you? Did the creatures come here?'

'There was a greenish light, and apparently the guards encountered and fought off some dreadful thing outside the door. I heard the commotion but saw nothing. What of you? I should examine you.'

'I am cut and bruised, nothing more.'

I left, handing Redlock into Markin's care. The physician had already dispatched a servant to summon Blonna, that the child might be given suck. Stiffly, for I was in some considerable pain from the blows I had received in the cellar, I went on through the castle, seeking out Lady Sheerquine.

I came upon her at length in the Great Hall. She stood alone at one end beside the cavernous fireplace, sunk in a reverie. She looked up as I approached to stand before her. Her expression was strained and severe, her pupils pinpoints.

'Master Dinbig.'

'Your children are safe, Lady Sheerquine. Both of them. You must be overjoyed.'

'Quite so. You have performed admirably. For returning my children to me you have my intense gratitude.'

'I imagine you rushed to be with them the moment you learned that they had returned unharmed.'

She drew up her shoulders. The torchlight flickered upon her face. 'Save your sarcasm, Master Dinbig. This has been a terrible night; I have had many things to attend to. Parental devotion must at times take second place to duties of station.'

'A terrible night indeed. We are fortunate, all of us, to have survived. But Ravenscrag has overcome its Bane, and has done so despite my being constantly hampered and discouraged, and in

262

the end almost killed in the pursuance of my commission. Tell me, why did you order my death?'

Her chin went up. 'My orders were that you should be taken into custody and brought back to the castle. I was told you were trying to escape.'

'Captain Lonsord seems to have placed a different interpretation on them.'

'He is at times a little over-zealous, as you know.'

'He – or one of his men – killed your brother, Hectal. It was, I think, a tragic misshot. The shaft was meant for me.'

Lady Sheerquine glanced away. 'Captain Lonsord told me that you murdered Hectal as he tried to prevent your escape. He says he tried to arrest you but you made off, killing one of his men in the process. He also stated that you had kidnapped Moonblood.'

'Did Lonsord truly say those things, Lady Sheerquine? If he did, then plainly you do not believe him, or you would have called the guard and had me arrested now. My feeling is that Captain Lonsord had been given certain information, pertaining to his wife and myself, which ensured that he pursued me with murderous intent.'

She looked back at me icily. I said, 'Would it interest you to know what really happened?'

'Whatever happened in the forest is irrelevant now, Master Dinbig. I have said I am grateful for what you have done. Ravenscrag is saved, my children are alive and well. Therefore you are now free to leave. Your wagons and goods will be released from impoundage forthwith. All restrictions on your men will be lifted. I am sure you will want to leave at the earliest opportunity.'

'Indeed, I will be gone as soon as I may. But there are a few things I would like to clear up to my own satisfaction. I am intrigued, by the Legend, the Bane, and the extraordinary and dreadful events that have overtaken us all. Those ancient writings gave us so much in cryptic form. I believe I have successfully deciphered most of it, but one or two things remain unexplained.'

'I have said before, both the Legend and – particularly – the Bane, are obscure and defiant of rational explanation. I do not think that I, or anyone else here, can help you any further.'

'On the contrary, Lady Sheerquine. I think you personally may be able to help shed some considerable light on those aspects which continue to elude me.'

Sheerquine took a sudden step to the side, turning her body so that she no longer faced me. I said, paraphrasing the words of the Bane, '*Through the power of the woman's sin and the woman's wound corruption shall be born*. I have wondered a great deal about those two elements: the sin and the wound. What was meant by them? By roundabout means I came to understand the latter to be the "wound" borne by all women, the periodic letting of blood which concurs with the cycle of the moon. In Moonblood's case, of course, it held a very special significance. But what of the sin, I wondered. Is this a reference to all women, or, again, might it refer to one in particular? What would be your opinion, Lady Sheerquine?'

'I have told you, I have made no interpretation of the words.' Her voice had become a little shrill.

'I asked you recently why you chose that name for your daughter. Was it in order to set events in motion, to bring about the realization of the Legend?'

'Events were already in motion, Master Dinbig. Ravenscrag was in decline; Flarefist was the father-to-be. We – and our advisors – saw a possible correspondence.'

'Moonblood was your firstborn, wasn't she? After her you lost four children, one after the other, at birth. That must have been almost too painful for you to bear. Yet perhaps you, and Flarefist, took some heart, some hope, even in your grief, for did not the Legend of Ravenscrag state that four must perish since the blood of the moon was spilled?'

Lady Sheerquine nodded stiffly but said nothing. One white hand had gone to her chest where it fiddled with the hem of her robe.

'As I understand it, three of your children died at childbirth, Lady Sheerquine. But tell me about the fourth, little Misha, the baby girl who survived.'

Lady Sheerquine gave a queer throttled sound. She moved abruptly away, as if propelled. 'What do you mean? What is there to tell? Misha lived . . . for a few days. But she was not strong. Her nurse found her dead in her crib. Why do you torture me with such memories?'

'I appreciate that it must be painful for you to recall. But you see, last night I was beset by a strange dream. In it, among other things, I came upon you. You seemed to be in a trance, and were bearing a pillow to some unknown destination. Then, when I awoke, I met you in the corridor. You were dressed precisely as you had been in my dream; you held a pillow, and you seemed to be in a trance. Certainly you were unaware of me. Almost against your will you proceeded to the nursery, where you paused over the ruined crib, holding the pillow *as if to smother a child!*'

'No!' She wheeled upon me like a cornered animal, the skin of her face stretched tight across her skull.

'I saw you, Lady Sheerquine. Remember, I was there.'

She was shaking. She reached out suddenly with one hand and stumbled forward, grasping the mantelshelf for support.

'Was that what happened, Lady Sheerquine? The first three died of natural causes, but the little girl, Misha, was a robust and healthy child. She showed every sign of living to enjoy a long and happy life. But if the fourth child lived, then the Legend would not come true; Ravenscrag's decline would continue, and its saviour would not come – at least not yet. So Misha, too, had to die. And is that why I, despite everything, had to be discouraged from discovering the truth? And when I got too close, did you decide to have me murdered, knowing that your complicity would never be suspected?'

Sheerquine hung her head, breathing hard, still clutching the shelf. 'You have an extraordinary imagination, Master Dinbig. But no one would believe you.'

'On the contrary, I think Moonblood would believe me. As would Lord Ulen Condark. Others would at least be deeply suspicious.'

Her look now was wild. 'Will you tell them?'

I shrugged. 'It is true that I lack firm evidence. And I do not wish to establish a witch-hunt. We have already seen what effect that can have. But one thing surprises me: were you truly so anxious that the Legend come true that you were prepared to risk so much, even knowing that in doing so you might be activating the Bane?'

Her lip curled. 'I knew nothing of the Bane at that time. It was kept secret, so that it might not cause concern or create an insidious influence. Only after Misha's death did Sardus bring it forth and show it to me.'

'It must have come as quite a shock.'

Lady Sheerquine glowered at me. I recited, in a quiet voice, the words of the Bane: '*My spawn will be about you and among you forevermore, but you will not know them, nor will they even know themselves*. Plainly it is not only the ravens that are referred to.'

Her look hardened with intense animosity, then her spirit seemed to flee her. Her head tipped forward. I continued, 'You would have died, had I not brought Moonblood back. All of you – and she could have been transformed, like Redlock, into something monstrous and evil. Evil born out of the evil you committed in order to fulfil your own ambitions.'

'It was for Ravenscrag!' she began, but then her shoulders shuddered. Something small and silvery dropped to the floor by her feet. I looked and saw a patch of glistening wet as she lifted a hand to her eyes.

'Recall Or-Hurun of Dyarchim,' I said quietly, 'who says everything without uttering a word. Such is the nature of dark secrets; they may never be uttered, yet they have the power to make themselves known.'

She half glanced my way but made no comment. I went on, 'As I have said, I feel there is nothing to be gained by making public your crimes. There is probably no punishment greater than that which you will inflict upon yourself. But I do require your assurance on one or two points.'

'What are they?'

'First, that you immediately set free your prisoners, or "guests", as you term them. Second, that on behalf of your husband, Lord Flarefist, you relinquish all power in favour of your son, Redlock, and permit a deputy to be installed to govern in his stead until he is of an age.'

'Impossible! That will allow Condark to gain Ravenscrag!'

'If Lord Condark wants Ravenscrag he, or his brothers and sons, could take it now by force. But I believe Lord Condark may be willing to acknowledge Redlock's birthright. Flarefist is dying and someone must stand in his place. It would be preferable if that person was somebody acceptable both to Ravenscrag and Condark, that you might work towards a rapprochement between both houses. It will require careful negotiation of terms. I would suggest a meeting be called forthwith.'

She nodded, a broken woman, all the colossal reserve of her person shattered in mere instants. She was a pathetic sight, but I felt little sympathy.

'Next, the bodies of Irnbold and Elmag must be cut down immediately and given a proper burial. Captain Lonsord's orders in regard to me, whatever they may be, must be rescinded. Is that understood?'

She nodded again, weakly.

'Now I will leave you. I will return later to discuss my proposals with you and Lord Condark.'

I turned and strode across the hall, then hesitated. 'One other thing. I recall that mention was made by yourself and Lord Flarefist of concessions and rewards for my services.'

'We are not wealthy, Master Dinbig, but I will see to it that you do not leave Ravenscrag . . . without proper payment.'

Chapter Thirty-Two

I went straightway to the loft where Bris and Cloverron were barracked.

'Restrictions have been lifted. You are free to move as you will. Get your weapons and follow me. Remain several paces behind so that it looks as though I am unaccompanied, but do not lose track of me for an instant.'

I left the castle and made my way down through the darkened streets to the home of Cametta and Darean Lonsord.

From a doorway in a deserted side-street two figures stepped out in front of me. They had chosen their place well: I was easily visible beneath a lantern hung outside an inn. They stood beyond the light, their faces in shadow.

They spoke no words. I heard a light scuff behind me. Instinctively I dropped to the ground, drawing a dagger and spinning. A third man was upon me, but my motion threw him for an instant. I stabbed up hard into his thigh, and rolled away as he yelled out in pain. I caught a glimpse of a fourth figure coming at me, the lamplight glinting on his dagger blade.

Then there were shouts and the clash of blades as Bris and

Cloverron threw themselves into the affray. Two of my assailants, caught unawares, were cut down instantly. A third put up a bold fight, then tried to flee and was taken in the back by Cloverron's sword. The fourth, he whom I had wounded, tried to crawl away unseen. Bris grabbed him and would have ended his life, but I called out, 'I want him alive, Bris!'

Bris took away the man's dagger and sword. I put my knife to his throat.

'Who sent you?'

For a moment he remained defiant. I pressed the blade more firmly. 'Tell me and you may live. Was it Lonsord, or Sheerquine?'

He hesitated a moment longer, then hissed, 'Lady Sheerquine.'

'As I thought.' I removed the blade. 'Go to her now, then, and tell her precisely what has happened here. Tell her this: I am returning to the castle in due course.'

He looked at me, blinking. 'Is that all?'

'It is more than enough. With the knowledge I have, Sheerquine will be in no doubt of my meaning. Now go!'

He made off, limping, into the dark. I sent Cloverron on into the town with specific orders, and continued on my way accompanied by Bris. Outside Cametta's house Bris concealed himself in nearby shrubbery while I knocked upon the front door.

After a brief wait a window opened upstairs and a servant nervously poked out his head. I requested an urgent audience with Cametta.

'Madam Cametta is seeing no one, sir.'

'I must see her. It is most important.'

'Her orders were definite. She will see no one. Besides, it is the middle of the night.'

'I am aware of that, but – '

The man retracted his head. I cursed, but seconds later he was back at the window. 'One moment, sir.'

After a short pause the front door was opened by the same servant. I noted the sword that hung from his belt, though he carried it awkwardly and with little conviction.

'Have you been under assault here?' I asked, entering.

'No, sir. But strange and terrible things have been happening at the castle. We have all armed ourselves, just in case.' He closed the door hurriedly behind me. 'Madam Cametta will see you in the reception room.'

As I crossed the entrance hall I saw Cametta descending by the stairs. I stopped short in shock. Her face was swollen, a mass of cuts and livid contusions. One arm was in a sling and she leaned heavily on a stick.

'Cametta!'

She said nothing, but hobbled with difficulty down the stairs and straight by me, into the reception room. I followed, and when we were alone said, 'Did your husband do this?'

Cametta nodded.

So, Sheerquine *had* told Darean Lonsord about Cametta and me. 'Is he here now?'

'No. He has not returned tonight.' She spoke with obvious difficulty, barely able to move her swollen jaw and smashed, bloodied lips.

I felt my anger rising. I moved towards her, wanting to take her in my arms. She flinched and jerked back. 'Don't touch me!'

I was shocked by the venom in her tone. 'I am sorry. You must be in terrible pain.'

She stared at me for a moment through eyes barely visible between brutally swollen, purple and blue lids. 'Pain? What would you know about pain?'

'My love, – '

'*Don't!*' It emerged as a tortured shout. She winced, obviously jarred by the effort. She lowered her tone, her breath seething between broken teeth. 'Don't insult me.'

'Insult? Cametta, I don't understand. What is the matter? Have I offended you?'

'Offended?' She hobbled away to the side of the room. 'Look at me, Dinbig. Take a good look at me now. Do you find me attractive still, all bruised and hurt and broken? Is that thing between your legs still aroused by the sight of me? Because that's all it ever was, isn't it? I loved you, but you – you knew nothing more than the need to satisfy your lust.'

'Cametta, why do you say this? It is not true. My feelings for you have not changed.'

'Bastard!'

'There is some mistake, Cametta.'

'Stop your squirming, Dinbig! Darean told me.'

'Told you what?'

'That you tried to leave Ravenscrag two mornings ago. You tried to run away, leaving us, leaving *me*.'

She was fighting back tears, too proud to let me see her break down and cry. 'Deny it, I dare you!'

I said nothing. Her voice rose. 'You can't deny it. You see, I didn't believe him at first, so I sent a servant to make enquiries.'

'Cametta, I wasn't leaving. I wanted to get help. I felt unable to handle what was happening here alone.'

'I don't believe you! You were leaving me, without a word! Even knowing what might happen here.'

'I did not believe you to be in any way endangered,' I said, but I made no further effort to exonerate myself. 'Cametta, what about Darean? I am concerned, for you.'

She scoffed. 'Save your concern.'

'He tried to murder me in the woods.'

'He told me you were dead.'

'Where is he now?'

'At the castle, I imagine. He will not murder me, if that is what you're thinking. No, he has said that he will throw me out into the street in shame and disgrace, penniless and friendless, and in such a condition that no man will ever look favourably upon me again.'

'I will not allow that to happen.'

'You? What can you do?'

'I can prevent him.'

'I don't want your help. I don't want anything from you. I despise you, Dinbig, for what you have done. Now leave me – and don't come back. I never want to see you again.'

'Cametta, let me explain. I – '

'*Get out!*' Furiously she grabbed a metal figurine from a shelf beside her and hurled it at me. I was caught unawares. The ornament struck me painfully on the nose. I reeled back in blinding pain, clutching my nose, blood pouring down my face.

'Get out! Get out!'

Two armed servants appeared at the door. There was nothing to be gained by further remonstration. I turned and left.

Outside, as Bris came from hiding to join me, I stood with my head back, staunching the flow of nasal blood with a handkerchief. Presently we were able to make steps back towards the castle.

We had gone barely more than twenty paces when the sound of marching feet broke the silence of the night. Out of the dark loomed a squad of six guards led by Darean Lonsord. He halted in front of me, his men fanning out around him with swords drawn. He glared at me, hot-eyed. 'Well, Merchant, it is a pity that you are going to resist arrest and I am going to have to kill you here.'

'I think not,' I said. Bris beside me stiffened, his hand on the hilt of his sword. I spoke loudly. 'Captain Lonsord, I am arresting you for the murder of Master Hectal, the attempted murder of myself, the unlawful killing of Irnbold and Elmag, complicity to prevent the safe return of Lady Moonblood and her baby brother, Redlock, the brutal assault of your wife, and other crimes yet to be specified.'

He laughed, without humour. 'You are a bigger fool than I took you for.'

'No, Captain, I think you have miscalculated. Listen.'

From beyond Lonsord and his guards came the sound of running feet. A moment later figures became visible. Cloverron could be seen running towards us with the rest of my men.

'We outnumber you by more than two to one, Captain. I suggest you order your men to lay down their arms.'

The Ravenscrag guards shifted edgily as Cloverron and the others surrounded them. Lonsord looked back at me, his teeth bared. A knife appeared suddenly in his hand, and in a quick, deft movement he flicked it hard at me.

I was prepared. I dodged to the side and the weapon flew harmlessly past. Lonsord lunged at me with his sword, but Bris stepped in, knocking the blade aside and in the same movement ramming his elbow into Lonsord's face. Lonsord staggered back. Cloverron stepped in from behind and stuck him hard on the back of the head with the pommel of his dagger. Lonsord's knees buckled and he fell senseless to the ground. The remaining Ravenscrag guards gave up without a fight.

We stripped them of their weapons and had them truss Lonsord's wrists with his belt and carry him back with us to the castle.

The first grey fingers of dawn showed tentatively in the east as we arrived at the gatehouse. There were soldiers on horseback ranged outside. My heart dropped, but as we drew closer I saw that they were not Ravenscrag's men. They bore the colours and arms of House Condark.

The gate was barred. The horsemen waited without impatience outside. Their leader was a portly fellow in breastplate and helm, seated upon a white gelding. He eyed us suspiciously as we drew close.

'What have we here?'

I stepped up to him. 'I am Ronbas Dinbig, of Khimmur. May I ask whom I have the honour of addressing?'

'I am Lord Harwen Condark, brother of Lord Ulen who is unlawfully incarcerated with his family inside this rotting remnant of a castle.'

'I believe your brother and his family are now free, or on the point of being freed, as are those others who were likewise wrongfully imprisoned. Certainly that was my recommendation, and I was given to understand that it would be followed through.'

Lord Harwen raised his eyebrows. 'And what might your role be in this matter?'

I endeavoured to explain in as few words as possible, then asked, 'How strong is your force?'

'I have seventy-five mounted troops stationed a quarter of a mile down the road. A further two hundred foot troops led by my nephew, Jesmond, will be here within a day and a half.'

'I think they will not now be required. Have you sought entrance?'

'Aye. The gatekeeper seemed confused and has gone off to seek advice. If Lord Flarefist is incommoded, as you say, who now commands the garrison here?'

'Lady Sheerquine. Her manner is somewhat erratic, but I do not expect she will resist you now.'

'And who is your prisoner?'

'He is the captain of Ravenscrag's guard, a pitiless villain and murderer. There remains much to be explained, but I would request that you take him into custody and hold him securely until he can be tried for his crimes.'

As I spoke there came the sound of the heavy bar on the other side of the gate being lifted. The gate was drawn open with a creaking of hinges. Beyond, standing beside the gatehouse entrance, was Moonblood. She looked shaken; her gown was rumpled and still covered in blood. Linvon the Light stood with her, clasping her hand.

Lord Harwen gazed upon them in perplexity. I approached Moonblood. 'I had expected your mother.'

She turned her deep, sorrowful green eyes to me. 'My mother is dead.'

'Dead? But . . . How?'

'She was found just minutes ago at the base of one of the towers. She had apparently fallen from a great height. It is strange – in her hand she clutched a tiny garment, a baby's smock. I have seen that smock only once before. My little sister, Misha, was wearing it on the day she died.'

Moonblood's voice faded and she bowed her head. I closed my eyes, praying to Moban that Ravenscrag's Bane had now claimed its last victim.

Chapter Thirty-Three

Early the next morning, after a semblance of order had been
restored under the auspices of House Condark, and the castle had
settled back into a kind of shocked routine, a meeting was
convened. We assembled in the dusty reception chamber in
Ravenscrag's private apartments where only three days earlier I
had met with Lord Flarefist and Lady Sheerquine and been
assigned my new commission to locate and return their missing
son.

Present around the long table with its three silver candlesticks
were myself, Moonblood, Lord Ulen Condark and his son, Ilden,
and brother, Lord Harwen, plus Linvon the Light – who sat with
Moonblood, clasping her hand – and Markin, the castle's
physician.

Talk was of matters grave and important. Ravenscrag's future
hung here in the balance. Old Flarefist still somehow clung to life,
but Markin reported that he had slipped into coma and grew
weaker by the hour. Decisions were made, therefore, without
reference to the old man's authority, on the plain if unspoken
understanding that he would not survive to effect their outcome.

But the main decision, as to how Ravenscrag would be

administered until young Redlock came of age, remained unresolved. That in itself was actually a positive result, for it underlined Lord Ulen's earlier sentiments to me, that he had no particular ambition to procure Ravenscrag for himself. Rather, his aim was to work to establish a firm rapprochement between the two houses and secure a future for the rightful heir and his kin.

So the talks progressed in a spirit of amity, constructively and with a genuine desire to bury past differences. Moonblood, her eyes red and darkly circled, said little. I felt she had hardly taken in the scale of responsibility that had fallen so suddenly upon her shoulders. And I could not help but be struck by the sheer irony of the situation as I sat there and listened to those men deciding the fate of that young girl. Plainly, none of them understood what had happened here. It was true that they were not party to what Moonblood had done. They did not know what she had become, nor could they know the truth behind the mysteries that had occurred. But it was equally true that their minds would not allow them to see. To them it was inconceivable that Ravenscrag might be governed, even temporarily, by a female, be she the daughter of its rightful lord or any other. Nobody questioned it.

Everything changes and all remains the same.

I suspected, as it happened, that Moonblood would have wanted nothing of it anyway. There was a change, a knowingness in her, which I sensed even through her sorrow. She had found her power, her true heritage and her independence, and nothing that good and powerful men could do could alter that. It was for the future to reveal the real consequences of her struggle.

Tentative mention was made of marriage between the two houses. Moonblood spoke up then, declaring politely but firmly that she would not entertain such an idea. Young Ilden blushed to his roots, but his father, Lord Ulen, nodded sagely and glanced, not unkindly, at Linvon the Light, and made no further reference to the matter.

At length the meeting was adjourned. Moonblood was plainly exhausted and preoccupied, and could not be expected to give her fullest attention to such weighty matters just now, no matter their import.

Lord Ulen stood, then, saying, 'I am optimistic. We have yet to arrive at a full settlement that is acceptable to all, but I feel we have paved the way that will take us to that desired condition. With your permission, Lady Moonblood, I would like to remain here at Ravenscrag for a while longer, with a small retinue and guard, to oversee administration and continue to work with you towards an amicable resolution. There is no question as to your brother's birthright. My aim is purely to establish the means whereby Redlock's – and your own – future security may be assured, and a close relationship be cemented between Ravenscrag and House Condark.'

Moonblood nodded graciously. 'Of course, my lord. You are a welcome guest here – and be assured, the key to the door to your apartments will remain in your possession at all times.'

Lord Ulen laughed. 'I am relieved to hear it!'

Outside the chamber, as he left with his brother and son, I drew him aside. Earlier I had drafted a signed statement detailing the crimes of Darean Lonsord. 'His future is a matter of concern to me, Lord Condark. I fear for Ravenscrag if he is set free.'

'Lonsord's reputation as a thug and bully has long been known to us,' replied Condark sombrely. 'In the past we could but remain silent, for it was not for us to involve ourselves in Ravenscrag's internal affairs. Now it is different. Your statement has been supplemented by others from a number of Lonsord's own men. They, realizing themselves seriously implicated, did not hesitate to provide damning evidence against him. Add to these certain unfortunates who have been found in Ravenscrag's dungeon, many in a most dreadful condition, who have also attested to Lonsord's predilection for cruelty and torture. His fate is sealed. Tomorrow morning he will be taken into the forest and, beyond sight of the castle, executed and buried in an unmarked grave.'

Perhaps surprisingly, I felt nothing. 'Is Lady Moonblood aware of this?'

'She is. She has seen and heard the evidence against him, and knows him for what he is. She accepts, albeit without pleasure, that it must be this way.'

I nodded and made to leave. Lord Ulen said, 'Master Dinbig, I have not yet extended to you my personal gratitude and that of my family and house for what you have done. Without you I fear we might not have been here today to tell our story.' He extended his hand and shook mine firmly. 'Know that you are a welcome guest in my house at any time, and if there is anything you wish from me, now or in the future, do not hesitate to ask.'

The reception chamber door opened and Moonblood came out, Linvon at her side. As Lord Ulen went his way I joined them. We walked through Ravenscrag's ancient ways, and came eventually into the sunlit courtyard where – it seemed an age ago – I had first been received by the Lord of Ravenscrag. I recalled with a pang of sadness how I had sat here with Flarefist, Irnbold and Lord Ulen. I recalled the excitement and anticipation as Redlock's birth drew near. I recalled the arrival from the shadows of Moonblood, and I looked at her now and realized suddenly what a profound transformation had taken place. Just days ago Moonblood had been a child, hardly touched by the concerns of the world. Now she was another person, and her universe was an unimaginably different place.

Old Rogue lay stretched upon a step nearby. Seeing his mistress he climbed to his feet and ambled across to greet her, swinging his tail from side to side. Moonblood stroked him distractedly, gazing out beyond the castle walls to the rugged green heights.

I cleared my throat. 'You are greatly burdened at this time, and it is not for me to add to your concerns, but I wonder if I might ask a small favour of you.'

She turned her big green eyes to me with a wan, dimpled smile. 'You may ask anything of me, at any time, Dinbig. Surely you know that? What is it that you wish?'

'I feel concern for Madam Cametta. From what I understand she has suffered greatly at her husband's hands. Now, with his imminent . . . demise, it appears she stands to lose everything. Really she is an innocent victim of circumstances that are entirely beyond her control.'

Moonblood's look was knowing – or so I perceived – and I shifted my eyes away uncomfortably. 'I am aware of Cametta's misfortune, Dinbig. I will do all I can to ensure that she does not lose her home, or anything else. And I believe she ought to be due at least a modest allowance from the castle treasury, in recognition of her husband's years of service to my parents.'

I nodded gratefully. Moonblood's gaze still rested upon me. 'Is it true that you are leaving us today, Dinbig?'

'Aye, it is.'

'I will be sad to see you go. We will miss you. Will you not stay a while longer? We would be so happy if you would.'

'You are very kind, and I wish it were possible. But I have lingered too long and am expected elsewhere.'

'But you will return to visit us, often, won't you?'

'Of course.'

She stepped forward and kissed me upon the cheek, then threw her arms around my neck and hugged me. 'Thank you, dear Dinbig, for all you have done.'

'I did little, Lady Moonblood. Truly. At the most, I simply helped clear the path that enabled you to discover your true heritage. And I have learned and, I feel, gained immensely from that experience. Really it is I who should be thanking you.'

Linvon stepped forward and clasped my hand, then embraced me. 'You must promise us that at the least you will return as guest of honour at our wedding.'

'Your wedding? My, this is news indeed! Congratulations!' I warmly embraced them both again. 'When is the happy day to be?'

'Not yet,' said Moonblood, tears brimming in her eyes. 'There is so much else to be done. But when all is settled here we will formally announce our betrothal, and you will be among the first to know.'

I stared at them, and suddenly the joy I felt for them was clouded with deep misgiving. *Young Linvon*, I thought, *you know nothing of your true origin.*

What was his future, here among us? Now that the Bane had been lifted and Ravenscrag's troubles were over, his original purpose was done. Could he still remain, or did other, immutable laws apply? Was he to be struck down suddenly, by illness or accident, recalled to the Realm of the Dead from which he had come?

I masked my fears, but when we parted I made my way quickly, for the last time, to the high turret chambers that had been my home these past three days. There I entered trance. While Yo took custody of my corporeal form I sped anxiously to that hallowed and mysterious locale, the Meeting-Place of the Dead.

Beside the crystal cairn where rested the stick and Drum of Calling, I perceived a ghostly figure seated cross-legged upon the ground.

'Lord Draremont!'

The shade of Ravenscrag's erstwhile lord rose to greet me. 'I waited, hoping that you would come here. I was prepared to remain here until you did, or until I might find some means of contacting you. I wish to thank you for all you have done. The Bane is lifted from Ravenscrag; our foe is defeated. My home and my descendants can at last know peace.'

'Aye, the work is done, though the cost was high.'

'Perhaps not as high as you conceive. Hectal is back among us, relieved of his earthly suffering. His shade may pass on now in its proper course. Lady Sheerquine has been borne to us, as have Irnbold and Elmag. They too are cleansed and liberated from their sins and sufferings and the dreadful burdens that existence in the corporeal world so often lays upon us. Soon Lord Flarefist will come, too. They will experience peace at last.'

'And what of Linvon the Light, who returned to end Ravenscrag's suffering and now seeks to remain there as the husband of Moonblood? He knows nothing, or almost nothing, of his real nature. What will be his fate?'

'You need not fear for Linvon. He returned of his own will to the flesh. Happily he survived without the sad consequences that often occur. There is no inherent condition to prevent him living out his full span.'

'I am relieved to hear it. I could not bear to see that young girl suffer any more.'

'Nor I.'

'And you, Lord Draremont, what is your future now?'

'Future? None.' He smiled. 'I too, at last, can know peace. Ravenscrag is saved, I am no longer chained. I go at last into eternity where my beloved Molgane awaits me.'

He moved aside and I saw at the edge of the ring of stones the phantom form of a beautiful young woman. It was the same woman who had materialized to stand with Moonblood outside the cellar deep beneath Castle Ravenscrag.

'My thanks to you, Master Dinbig,' said Lord Draremont. 'And my blessing and the blessing of my house and my folk be upon you. Fare well, go safely, in the knowledge of what you have made possible.'

So saying, he moved away across the grey powdery earth to

where his love awaited him. She opened her arms as he approached and the two ghostly forms embraced and, as I watched, began to merge into one. They rose together above the stones, a single entity now, and as it went it faded until there was nothing left to be seen.

Epilogue

The wagons, laden with spirits, pottery, cloth and other local goods, rumbled slowly out of the market-place along Ravenscrag's dusty main street towards the town gate. I rode on my mare at their fore, glancing about me from time to time, scanning the faces that watched us pass. I looked beyond, to the cluttered houses rising behind the main street, and higher, to the house where Cametta lived.

Her door was closed, as were the shutters on the windows. Any hopes I had entertained that I might catch a final glimpse of her – that she might perhaps have reconsidered, be making her way down here even now – were lost.

The old castle walls loomed above us. Upon the ramparts stood two figures: a pale, fair-haired maiden in a sleeveless blue frock upon which, even at this distance, the sunlight glittered on the stones of a most unusual brooch; and beside her a handsome, slender youth clad in green. Together they raised their arms and waved as we moved on along the way.

A mile or so beyond the town we came to the place where we had lost the wagon. Its wreck still lay upturned in the shallow river bed below. The road had yet to be repaired but there was sufficient space for us to pass. The boy, Moles, bandaged and bruised, sat beside the driver of the second wagon.

'Do you wish to take the reins?' I asked.

He smiled, lifting a splinted arm, and shook his head. 'Another time.'

I nodded, then swung my horse around to gaze back through the heat-addled air at Ravenscrag town huddled in the distance between the soaring crags, its rooftops shimmering pink, grey and blue in the sunshine. The mouldering hulk of the castle, its ancient walls, towers and turrets, rose at its back. There were no dark specks circling now in the skies over Ravenscrag. The Bane was lifted; the ravens had gone.

I felt no jubilation.

I sat still for a moment, immersed in my thoughts, then turned back to join my wagons. We moved on, past the fated spot. The forest closed in, blocking the sun. Ravenscrag passed from sight.

Unlike the ravens, I believed that one day I would return.

APPENDIX
The Zan-Chassin

Out of the shamanistic beliefs and practices indigenous to the regions of Southern Lur was born in the nation known as Khimmur a formalized, stratified system of applied ritualized sorcery, called Zan-Chassin. 'Powerful Way', 'Path, or Ladder, of Knowledge', 'Mysterious Ascent' are all approximate translations of the term. The Zan-Chassin cosmology held that the universe was created by the Great Moving Spirit, Moban. Moban, having created all, moved on (in certain mystical circles Firstworld is still referred to as the Abandoned Realm). Creation was left to do as it would without interference or aid.

Numerous modes, or realms, of being were conceived to exist within the Creation, not all of which were readily perceived by or accessible to men. In the normal state man realized two domains, the corporeal and the domain of mind or intellect. The power of the Zan-Chassin adepts lay in their ability to transcend these and enter various supra-physical domains, termed the Realms, there to interact with the spirit-entities active within them. Emphasis was also laid upon contact with the spirits of ancestors who had passed beyond the physical world to dwell in the realms beyond, and who could be summoned to an ethereal meeting place to provide advice and guidance to their descendants in the physical world.

Where Zan-Chassin practice differed from that of the shamans of many other nations was in its systematic and quasi-scientific approach. Understanding the nature of the Realms became paramount, resulting in the introduction of a set procedure whereby the aspiring adept, through precise training and instruction, might learn in stages both the sorcerous art and something of the nature of the realm of existence he or she was to enter, thus mitigating somewhat the inherent dangers. Previously the non-corporeal world had been conceived of as a single realm of existence. Men had gone willy-nilly from their bodies to encounter with little forewarning whatever lay beyond. The risks were considerable. Many perished or were lost or driven insane by their experiences.

The Zan-Chassin way revealed the Realms to be of varying natures, with myriad and diverse difficulties and obstacles being met within each. Just as normal humans might realize different 'shades' of existence, depending upon the development of intellect, organs of sense, etc., so could Zan-Chassin masters come to know and experience the differing natures of the Realms. Adepts were taught to subdue spirit-entities within each level of experience before progressing to the next, thus providing themselves with allies or helpers at each stage of their non-corporeal wanderings. The dangers, though still very real, were thus partially diminished. Aspirants progressed from one realm to the next only when adjudged ready and sufficiently equipped by their more advanced mentors.

None the less, over time many of even the most advanced and experienced Zan-Chassin masters failed to survive their journeys beyond the corporeal.

Within Khimmurian society Zan-Chassin proficiency was a key to power and influence. Practitioners generally enjoyed privileged social positions, and indeed the national constitution, such as it was, was structured so that Khimmur could be ruled only by one accomplished in the sorcerous art. A few Zan-Chassin chose the anchoretic life and lived beyond society, but they were in the minority.

To some extent the Zan-Chassin were feared by normal folk, who were much prone to superstition. Their magic was not understood, their ways were somewhat strange and wonderful. The Zan-Chassin made little effort to remedy this, it being expedient in certain circumstances.

Women enjoyed honoured status within the Zan-Chassin Hierarchy. The female revealed a natural affinity with the concepts of non-corporeality and spirit-communication which few men were able to emulate. They were equally highly proficient in the exploration and 'mapping' of the furthermost discovered territories of Moban's great and mysterious Creation. Thus the Hierarchy remained matriarchal in character, withstanding efforts to reduce the feminine influence.